THE TIME STORE

Andrew Clark & Dee Matthews

THE TIME STORE

CLOCK FACE

CLOCK FACE PUBLISHING
78 Loynells Road, Birmingham B45 9NR
Published by Clock Face 2014

First Published in Great Britain
In 2014 by CLOCK FACE

A CIP catalogue record for this book
is available from the British Library.

ISBN: 978-0-9930744-0-0

Typeset in 10.5 / 13 Palatino by CLOCK FACE.

Printed and bound by CPI Group (UK) Ltd, Croydon, CR0 4YY
Cover Design by Bespokebookcovers.com

For Hassie, Cally and Lauren.

Acknowledgements.

To Elisabeth Glenister and Freda Matthews, thank you for your help in reading, listening and pointing out the errors of our ways.

Another big thank you goes to Joan, Helen, Gareth, Lydia, Carol, Laura and all at WU. Good luck with your own books guys.

Andrew and Dee would like to thank all their friends and colleagues at AML and Grosvenor for their patience and support.

"Sometimes we go to extraordinary lengths
to get the simplest things."

Sarah Bradbeer.

CHAPTER I

Flamsteed Way
Friday, July 30th ~ 1751

"Sod off, Jase - you chopped his hand off. Pick it up yourself." Sarah gave her brother a look of contempt and strode a few paces away from the figure on the ground.

Jason nudged the hand away from the body with his foot. "I couldn't get the bloody bracelet off his wrist," he said, exasperated. He picked up and shook the severed hand, but the bracelet refused to fall off.

"Who is he anyway?" asked Dan.

"God knows. Haven't got a clue."

"Well I think it was a tad impetuous. Don't you?" said Sarah, calming down from her initial disgusted response to Jason's request. "Idiot."

"Well, we didn't plan on stumbling over a corpse. What was I supposed to do? We all heard the voices - we all thought someone was coming." Jason still had the axe in his hand. A workman's tool – maybe if it hadn't been there...

Dan was looking at the body with a combination of

curiosity and distaste. "He's already dead – why did you even need to cut it off anyway?" he asked, trying to emulate his sister's withering look, but not quite succeeding.

Sarah thought this question was valid; quite reasonable given the circumstances. After all, they'd only come down here to look at The Time Store – their house and business – in its early days, just after construction. The building process was pretty much complete, just some internal finishing work to do. They were interested and intrigued about their family's history and once they'd had the idea it seemed amazing they'd never thought of it before.

Sarah, twiddling with the ribbons of her bonnet, leant against the black wrought-iron railings. She looked across at the row of large four-storey terraced houses, all elegantly constructed from Bath stone. Theirs was the middle one of five.

Each house had a total of fifteen sash windows, all with small glass panes. The three windows on the ground floor were arched – even the doors had glazed arches above them to match. The first floor windows were large and imposing, with a brick-built semi-circular embellishment on top of each one. The remaining eight on the top two floors were smaller and plainer, but in no way detracted from the grandeur of the construction.

There was another row of houses, exactly the same, behind where she was leaning. In a few weeks, or months, all these houses would be occupied.

Sarah knew that behind the door to The Time Store, there was a vestibule leading to a second, ornately glazed inner door – made to the Bradbeers' personal design. She wondered if it was there yet. There were six, unworn, stone steps leading down from each solid wooden entrance door, and the houses were set behind railings – everything so familiar to her, and yet, because of the newness of it all, so strange.

Number Five, Flamsteed Way, Greenwich, London. Her home.

In later years their ancestors would acquire one of the adjoining houses. The trees at the end of the road were much smaller now, she realised, and the railings she was leaning against were not the ones she was used to. It was a summer's evening and they'd come on this trip to have dinner with James Bradley, the astronomer at The Royal Observatory.

Although it was getting dark when they'd finished, it still felt fairly early. Sarah had wanted to go straight home; the walk down the hill to see the house had been an afterthought suggested by Dan. He'd figured that at this time in the evening they wouldn't bump into any workmen who might be there completing the final stages.

So now they'd encountered a dead body instead. He was quite a stout chap, dressed plainly, in the typical clothes of the day. It didn't look as though his death had been a violent one. There was no blood – well hardly – not even after Jason's involvement, so Sarah presumed he'd been dead for a few hours at least.

She had no idea who he was – a builder maybe – she almost certainly didn't recognise him as being anyone from the Bradbeer family. However, he had a Bradbeer bracelet on his wrist. They'd been trying to remove it, but it had a lock over the clasp, unusual in itself. It was possible that they'd have found a way to undo the lock, but then they'd heard voices – thought someone was approaching – they didn't want to get caught bending over a dead body – that could lead to all kinds of repercussions.

Sarah had thought the best option would have been to disappear back home immediately, but Jason wanted the bracelet, to examine it. He'd picked up and used the axe which had been lying on the ground next to a hammer and a few planks of wood. Health & Safety would have a field day on this site, Sarah thought.

So Jason had hacked off the dead guy's left hand – and a good part of his forearm too. As it was, the voices had grown quieter again – no-one was entering Flamsteed Way. But the deed was done, and Jason was left holding a hand.

Sarah sighed. Jason and Dan were still squabbling.

"We could have gone away and come back later," Dan was saying.

"Yeah, but what if someone else had found the body, and moved it? Then we wouldn't have been able to get a good look at the bracelet."

"How do you know it's one of ours? It's not as though he's got a ring on as well, is it?" Dan was smug.

"Try it – what do you think?"

Dan touched the platinum links, which instantly glowed with a familiar iridescence. "Fair point, but I still think it's a bit brutal. And right on our own doorstep."

"Okay, okay. It's done now. And I still can't get the sodding bracelet off him - his arm's too fat. Anyway, let's just get back, and get out of these clothes. We've seen the house – very nice, and very new. Now come on. You ready, Sarah?" Jason discarded the axe, and straightened his waistcoat.

Dan shrugged. Sarah walked back to where her

brothers were standing.

Two seconds and two hundred and fifty-eight years later, three people and a hand arrived back in the centre of the Round Room.

"Shit – what's Dad going to say when he finds out?" said Dan.

CHAPTER 2

St. Michael's Hostel
October 2009

He could barely sense his tired fingers slowly slipping out of her warm gentle hand, the tips feeling the ridge of every fold within her tender palm. Desperately he willed for his hand to take hers, to hold and to clench it tightly, but to no avail.

Cold droplets of water now pounded incessantly onto the side of his head. He could feel the biting night air on his face and taste the raindrops as they landed upon his lips and instantly found their way into his open mouth.

Gradually he felt his senses returning and he could hear what he thought was heavy breathing. This turned into a mix of grunting and somewhat vulgar garbled swear words; where it came from, how far away, he couldn't tell. He could feel something pulling repeatedly at his jacket, but what? It felt like he was a child again, being put through his paces at his yellow belt judo grading all those years ago. No, it wasn't something grabbing at his jacket, it was someone. The grip wasn't firm. He could feel it relaxing, then jerking, then relaxing once more before taking the strain again.

Each pull was accompanied by a warm, tingling sensation in his legs which sent a numb itchy feeling to his feet; but worse, with each pull his fingers slipped more and more out of her hand. He could now make out a smoother, cooler surface – a delicate patterned finish almost as fragile as his own fingertips. His index finger rested there as once again the grip on his jacket slackened, and the sensation in his legs disappeared.

Sounds could be heard crying out amidst the grunting, it was a young voice, a man's... no, it was voices, perhaps three. He'd heard the accent before, Midlands possibly but he'd need to hear more to be sure. The men sounded as though in pain, almost screaming at one another between the incoherent words. The voices drifted in and out of the myriad sounds created by the falling rain. There were several to be picked out, he could hear the noise as more and more drops filled a nearby puddle, maybe a roadside puddle growing in size as each minute drop pattered into it. Then there was the sound of the rainfall as it danced off the trees before drizzling to the ground, with its force now spent. The loudest of the sounds he could sense was made by the downpour as it rattled on to the Turtle-Wax finish of the car roof, almost beading directly on impact.

His thought process immediately focused on 'car', why had his mind used that word? He needed to open his eyes to get a visual impression of what he could feel, of what he could hear. But he couldn't, they wouldn't open. He could feel his eyeballs rolling within their sockets - first left and then right, a grunt would come, or perhaps a word and he could feel his eyes trying to look upwards towards whoever had caused the sound. In the background of all the confusion he could vaguely hear what seemed to be the urgent calling of a woman shouting out what may have been a name. Was it his name he pondered, albeit briefly, was it a name at all? Was it actually a voice or could it be some deceptive noise the heavy rain was making as it relentlessly bombarded some distant, once vibrant but now crumbling building?

Suddenly, at last, two words were making sense, two words he was able to understand. "Come on!" Confusion hit him again. Was it a man's voice or could the words be those of a woman? Again the words echoed through his mind but this time with the pull of his jacket, followed quickly by the numbness and itching to his feet. He could feel the cold bead of water across his face, passing his lips and finding a resting place on his tongue. Bitter, acrid in taste. He could feel his index finger slipping away from the smoother surface and once again finding the warmth of her palm. Whose palm? His mind was desperately trying to project a name in place of an image.

He knows her, he knows her well... Very well. He loves her, he loves her with all his heart, his mind, his body and his life. He could almost say her name but his mouth wouldn't engage. He could sense a ring... it's her ring... it's her hand, and he gave the ring to her. White dress! My God, my wife!

"CATHERINE...!"

The scream reverberated around the small but private room of the hostel. He bolted upright from his tormented sleep. The sweat that had trickled from his cold, clammy face was soaked into the pillowcase where his head had lain and he could still taste the drop that had found its way onto his tongue whilst he suffered his psychological anguish.

"John! Are you alright?" asked Winnie, her knuckles whitening as her mottled hands still clenched tightly onto the lapels of his second-hand nightshirt. "John?"

"Catherine...?" He was almost pleading, refusing to open his eyes because he could see her face so clearly with them tightly closed. In his heart he had already accepted the voice wasn't that of his beloved wife, it was Winnie, kind and helpful Winnie.

John knew that Winnie kept an open ear out for him on stormy nights, but oh God! What was he putting her through? She'd seen him distressed a few times before, but what had she seen this time? How bad must his nightmare have appeared to her? He could feel her hold on him relaxing to the point of release. He realised that he was shivering from the cold of his rapidly drying sweat and shaking from the trauma that the nightmare had put him through again... these were after-effects he recognised all too well, along with the phantom pain in both legs. He needed to get a grip, but he'd felt a terrible comfort from his awful dream... where Catherine felt so real to him.

He finally opened his eyes. He couldn't prevent the tears.

"Bad one this time, love?" Winnie touched his trembling hand. "Come on, let's get a cup of tea."

John had apologised, Winnie had said not to worry, and now they were sitting at a table in the canteen of the hostel. John wished his tea was half whisky, but the hostel rules would never have allowed that, and therefore neither would Winnie.

"I just don't think I can bear it any longer," he heard himself saying.

Winnie took a sip of her regulation hostel lukewarm tea, and winced. "Were you dreaming about the crash again? You were calling out Catherine's name."

John looked up at Winnie. "Yes. It's always the same – we're trapped – I'm grasping her hand, twisting at her ring. I know I'm losing her. She's unconscious... but I'll stay with her." He stopped.

His voice had been getting louder. The canteen was starting to fill up and people were looking. He suddenly felt ashamed of his behaviour and appearance. Although why, he couldn't explain – he'd been using the hostel for a couple of years now.

"Go on," urged Winnie. "I know your Catherine died in the crash, but do you feel able to tell me more this time?"

And so John quietly and steadily told Winnie about his beautiful Catherine, mother to his two precious daughters. How they'd been returning from a rare weekend away, just the two of them. A lovely romantic, fun, happy, sunny weekend that had reminded him of when he first fell in love with her. It had been perfect. And then, when they were driving back, on the way to Catherine's sister's house to collect the girls, the weather had changed quickly and dramatically. Dark clouds appeared, followed by strong winds and torrential rain. They'd been taking it in turns to drive, Catherine was already driving when the rain came. He'd asked several times if she wanted him to take another turn at the wheel, but she said she was okay for a while longer.

And then, a momentary loss of control on the water-laden road. And the crash. She must have died pretty soon after impact, that's what they'd said afterwards. There was nothing anyone could have done. Her side of the car was completely mangled, the engine and tree had seen to that. They had to use cutting tools on the roof to get her out.

But he'd tried to do something, hadn't he? He'd reached across for her hand, trying to hold it, to comfort her, as she was fading. However, John had nearly died too. It could've easily been as bad for him as it was for her. He was seriously injured, just ready to follow her into death.

And then someone had rescued him. Pulled him out of the car. Pulled him away from her. Rescued him as he was clutching at her hand. Saved him. How lucky, everyone had said, how lucky that a cyclist had been passing in that awful rain when he did… another few minutes later and it could have all been so different. Yes, thank God. Such a tragic accident. But how much more tragic if the girls had lost both parents?

So John had lain in hospital, and then at home, for weeks, months, recovering. He'd suffered multiple fractures and a crushing to the legs. Thankfully the cyclist had flagged down a passing motorist and together they had managed to free John. He was fortunate that his legs hadn't been crushed for too long as the build-up of toxins in the blood could have made matters worse, far worse. He'd had medication and physiotherapy until he could move pretty much normally again, although he still suffered from chronic paraesthesia in his feet.

The girls, his and Catherine's daughters, would come to see him, every day at first, then less often, opting for the safe haven of Catherine's sister's home, their young minds confused at the loss of their mother, and the complete change in character of their father.

Eventually, towards the end of the following summer, Claire, the girls' aunt, had gently but firmly tried to insist that Alice and Emma should return to live with their father.

Oh yes, their wonderful father, John had thought, their father who loves them so much he actually resigned from work a couple of months ago because he thought he could look after them. Their fantastic father and his blossoming love for cheap brand whisky, easily chosen in preference to the care of them; and easily chosen in preference to the bereavement counselling he'd been offered, and sorely needed.

Winnie picked up her cup of cold tea and then put it down again. John felt sorry for her. After all, she was only a volunteer working just a few hours a week at the hostel, and although she was a good friend she was not his personal counsellor. But today he had felt, unusually for him, able to open up more to her.

"So what did happen to the girls, John?" Winnie asked.

"Claire moved overseas with them when her husband got promoted with his company. I haven't seen them since."

"I'm so sorry, John. So sorry your wife died."

"So am I," said John.

But oh God, there'd been many times he wished he'd died along with her.

Half an hour later, wrapped up warmly against the

elements, Winnie Holroyd left the hostel. She walked with short but quick steps, as briskly as was possible for a fairly active seventy-year old woman. Winnie was on a mysterious mission. She had an important appointment booked for ten o'clock. It was already after eight and she needed to go home to get changed first.

Before leaving the hostel, she'd quickly, so not as efficiently as usual, helped the others clear up the breakfast things. She'd rushed out, not wanting to be late. John had still been sitting at the table, apparently deep in thought. She was glad he'd confided in her more fully at last. He still needed to open up a bit more though, as she was very much aware that he'd glossed over the details about not seeing his daughters. Any other morning, she probably would have tackled him on this, but because of her pre-arranged meeting, she'd had to postpone her natural caring curiosity.

Winnie didn't live too far from the hostel, only about half a mile or so. This distance was usually covered at a far more leisurely pace, maybe stopping to look in the occasional shop window, or have a quick chat with one or two people she knew, although they were becoming fewer as Winnie was becoming older. She was quite out of breath, but she kept up her new-found rushed pace. She was meeting a young lady called Sarah Bradbeer – they'd already had a short chat on the telephone and then met in a local coffee shop a couple of weeks ago, but today was a proper meeting, at Sarah's work. Winnie had even received an official appointment card in the post. Actually... there was the coffee shop now, Winnie observed, not stopping.

It had all come about quite strangely. Winnie had been idly flicking through the Camden Tribune when she spotted an unusual paragraph in the classified section.

LOST. *Life experience? Memory? Event? Recapture the gift of time with our help. See history as reality or as the future. Tel: 020 8858 4141.*

On reading this Winnie had felt that she came close enough to what they seemed to be suggesting. What mattered most was the emotion she was feeling. She knew exactly what moment in time she'd like to talk about. Maybe by talking it through she could get clear in her head what had happened, and how she had felt all those years ago, and perhaps have some resolution.

Once past the shops Winnie turned down a side road, cut through an alleyway and soon arrived home. She unlocked the front door of her small, neatly kept two bedroomed house and went into the front room. She had no time this morning for sitting down with her customary cup of tea after work. She walked over to the sideboard and picked up the appointment card that Sarah had sent. She'd placed it there when it had arrived six days ago and had been looking at it ever since, trying to fathom out exactly what she'd let herself in for. It seemed fitting that she'd propped up the card between a pair of silver framed photographs of the two men who'd seen her through her younger years; and who meant so much to her. She picked up the one to the left, the one of her late husband, Les, and smiled. And then the other, this one of the music legend, Elvis Presley. Both long gone but certainly not forgotten, especially by Winnie.

She'd first really started liking Elvis, and his music, way back in 1957, a few months before her eighteenth birthday when her friend Irene had lent her a record. That was also around the time she first met Les, who'd told her he was an Elvis fan too. She often recalled with much fondness their first cinema date at the local Odeon, both excited at the thought of watching Elvis in *Jailhouse Rock*.

Over the years of their courtship, engagement and marriage, they'd enjoyed listening to Elvis records and going to the pictures to see a good many of his films. Sometimes though, Les hadn't wanted to go to the cinema, so Winnie had gone with Irene. For years Winnie, Irene, and Les had eagerly been anticipating news of Elvis coming to perform in England, or even Europe. And for years they'd been disappointed. So when she made her New Year's resolutions at the beginning of 1976, Winnie had decided to be adventurous. She told Les that she was planning a trip to America in October of that year, so that they could see Elvis in concert in Chicago. Les had appeared shocked – how would they afford it? But Winnie had been putting a little bit by in the Post Office for many years and she was sure they'd have enough, especially with that bit she'd had from grandma's will. It was settled, and Winnie was counting down the days.

That summer though, Les had increasingly been complaining of feeling unwell, so much so that he announced that he was too ill to make the trip. Winnie was distraught, concerned for Les, but reluctant to abandon the trip of a lifetime. After some thought however, Winnie had the ideal solution – Irene could go with her. And so the two friends had tremendous fun in the ensuing weeks waiting for passports, shopping for outfits, and trying them on whilst dancing around Irene's living room to *Hound Dog* and *Heartbreak Hotel*.

All was going to plan until a couple of weeks before the holiday. This was when Les took a turn for the worse. He needed Winnie. He could not possibly manage without her, even for a short time, let alone a whole holiday. He begged her not to go. The holiday was cancelled. Irene told Winnie she was too scared to go alone. Winnie knew her friend too well however, Irene wasn't going as she didn't want to have Winnie's dream without her. Either way all that money was wasted. Les did seem really ill, but Winnie in her upset had begrudged staying at home. She could not stop herself thinking that he was over-exaggerating his pain and suffering, because he didn't want her to go.

But these doubts were soon to become irrelevant as Les passed away a couple of months later, just before Christmas, leaving her mourning for her husband, and feeling guilty she'd ever doubted him. The following summer she found herself mourning the death of Elvis. Now she would never have the chance to see him.

She replaced the photographs on the sideboard, put the appointment card in her handbag and then hurried upstairs to get ready. She'd already set out her change of clothes on her bed, so she took off her casual hostel clothes and put on these fresh ones. It was a new situation for her and she'd not really known what to wear, but she'd chosen a smart day dress and low heeled court style shoes.

Sarah had asked her to bring along some personal possessions, maybe items of clothing which reminded her of the specific time Winnie wanted to talk about. So of course Winnie had raided her wardrobe in the spare room where she still kept those clothes from her shopping trips with Irene, along with the tickets for the two shows that she kept in her keepsake box. She walked through to collect the clothes, which she'd already folded up and packed in a small travel bag. She placed the tickets, still in their original envelope, in her handbag next to the appointment card. She was somewhat concerned about bringing them out from their safe shoebox haven – she'd had them all these years and didn't want to lose them now. But she was so excited; Winnie was doing something for herself for the first time in ages.

It would probably take a good hour to reach the address sent to her by Sarah. The Time Store, Greenwich. Well she'd never heard of it before, so wanted to give herself extra time to find it. She put on her coat, checked in her handbag for her Oyster card, double checked she'd got the appointment card and the envelope containing the tickets then finally picked up her bag of clothes. She went downstairs, paused in the hallway, checked herself in the mirror, took a deep breath, opened the front door and then locking it behind her, set off for the tube station.

As John cleared away the mugs that he and Winnie had used he noticed a press cutting framed on the wall, it was an article about a converted ice-cream van that was, at the time, being used as a mobile soup kitchen. In the picture, Winnie could be seen leaning on the bonnet alongside Pete Smith, who still volunteered every so often, and Irene. She'd died last year from emphysema. "I told her those cigarettes wouldn't do her any good," he remembered Winnie saying shortly after she'd been to Irene's funeral. He waited for a few seconds to see if Irene's surname would come to him, but it didn't.

The picture reminded John of when he and Winnie first met. It was on a bitterly cold winter's night a few years back when John was a destitute, desolate cardboard city dweller, living on begged scraps and goodwill hand-outs from anyone who cared to show pity. The soup van was at its regular Monday night stop near Kings Cross railway station when he happened to find it. He'd been told by one of his 'friends' that a van had started pulling up around there between ten and half-past. If he planned it right he could fit in both the one at the back of the Adelphi and this new one without having to rush from one to the other.

It was on his third or perhaps fourth visit to the van that he ended up in conversation with Winnie. He remembered arriving late as there was a frost on the ground and he couldn't walk as fast as he would have liked. Winnie was handing out missing person pictures, usually of runaway kids, to the people who still remained. The van had finished serving and the last few were drifting away having had their broth and bread roll. Thankfully there were still some leftover sandwiches which had been donated at close of business by a local shop, and Winnie had managed to squeeze a drop of tea from the urn for him.

It was during their little chat that Winnie had explained to John that this was her last night on the van as it was becoming too cold for her, but if he was ever in Camden he should pop into St. Michael's hostel as that would be where she'd be 'doing her bit' as she'd put it. They'd chatted about a few other things, mainly the anguish felt by the parents of lost children; Winnie had also touched on the recent deaths of five prostitutes in Ipswich. "Even they're somebody's children," she'd said, and John had felt a little ashamed that he knew nothing about it at all.

In the three years since that night at the soup kitchen John's living conditions had improved greatly. He'd gone from living rough to using a combination of night and day shelters depending on the season, then progressed to an emergency hostel before getting a chance to stay at St.

Michael's... all had been achieved with Winnie's help and encouragement.

Moving away from the picture John made his way back to his room nodding the occasional 'hello' to the residents he recognised on the way. His room was one of six private ones just off the men's bunk area. He stopped off at the notice board which had the names of the fifty male residents who'd stayed last night. He scanned down the list to see if any of the names were familiar to him – there were a few – but other than the five in the private rooms they all melded into one.

Alcohol, along with drugs and offensive weapons, was not permitted on the premises and anyone found in possession would be politely turned away until they'd disposed of it, usually by hiding their bottles under one of the nearby shrubs. Nonetheless there was certainly a lingering stale odour permeating the air, especially from the coats hanging on the pegs at the ends of the bunks.

During the fifteen years since the car accident John had battled with an alcohol problem in one form or another. Mainly as an excuse to help him cope with the loss of his home, his two beautiful daughters, his amazing wife Catherine... but most of all the recurring nightmare of the crash, especially his feelings of guilt. He felt guilty that it hadn't been him who was driving. If only he'd insisted on taking over at the wheel, or saying 'yes' when Catherine had asked if she should drive first, then she'd be the one alive today, not him. The alcohol helped him temporarily forget this guilt, and so he drank.

He'd been fortunate to get one of the small private rooms available. These were normally awarded on a point scoring basis, becoming free only after another resident had left, having been found permanent accommodation by either a local council or a housing association. This was a lengthy process as it involved having to apply for and be granted state benefits and a bank account. John had jumped the room queue for two reasons; firstly his traumatic nightmares were disturbing everyone else and causing friction in the middle of the night, although this only happened when it rained particularly heavily, and secondly by a recommendation made by Father Elston. Hearsay had it that John had seen Father Elston and Mrs. Wilson, one of the church cleaners, in an amorous embrace – whether he had or not was for the gossips and rumour mongers to debate.

"Johnny."

"Morning, Patrick," he replied, cringing at the use of the name Johnny. It was Paddy Kelly – beggar, recovering alcoholic and professional liar. Paddy, a gaunt man with teeth like a row of fragmented gravestones, at one time or another in his youth must have worked on every motorway construction site in England as well as laying the tarmac on copious suburban London driveways.

He considered Paddy to be a friend, and with the exception of Winnie, possibly his best friend, and probably the only one out on the street he could trust. He hated being called Johnny though, and in response always called him Patrick. They'd become good pals over a bottle of Irish whiskey, which bottle neither can remember as there'd been many more since.

"You going down the tube station, Johnny?" asked Paddy in his thick Irish accent. He was well wrapped up in several layers of ill-fitting clothes, and clutching a handwritten cardboard sign and a folded blanket.

"Yeah, give me a minute or two... I'll see you outside," waved John, turning towards his room.

He opened the door to his clean and very tiny accommodation. It was no bigger in size than a box room in a standard three-bed semi, it allowed for a lockable chest of drawers and a skinny wardrobe – any other storage had to be under the bed. To save on maintenance and decorating costs residents weren't allowed to hammer or screw anything into the walls. But John had a fading school photograph of Alice and Emma aged twelve and nine taped to the wall along with a stunning picture of Catherine taken at a restaurant one year when they were on holiday in Carcassonne. Following an argument with an old landlord these were the only pictures of his family that he now possessed.

Between losing his home fourteen years ago and finding himself on the street John had bounced from lodgings to lodgings. He usually ended up back on the homeless pile following the aftermath of a nightmare, be it the screaming that accompanied the waking up, or the drink binge that came after.

At one point, maybe ten or eleven years ago he was renting a room off a couple, Brian and Anita Cooper, in Brixton. He'd been receiving regular communication every couple of months from Claire and the girls over in Dubai, usually with a photograph of Alice and Emma at some posh private school. This was the last address that Claire had for him. John had been thrown out by Brian, who'd accused him of stealing from the house... John vehemently denied this... and although Anita could see the truth in John's eyes she'd suffered too many bruises from Brian and knew when to keep her mouth shut.

For over a year or so John would keep returning to the house hoping to collect any letters as he was desperate to forward his latest address to Claire and couldn't for the life of him remember hers. Brian would just hurl abuse and threaten him, John would leave empty-handed and seek comfort from a park bench and a bottle. The photographs on the wall were the ones in his shirt pocket on the day Brian threw him out.

John got changed, ready for a day out on the streets, begging for small change. Not that he had many clothes to choose from, most were shabby-looking and a bit frayed but beggars can't be choosers. On a good day he could scrounge not only enough for his hostel fees and alcohol, but he could also afford food. On a bad day however, both the hostel and any decent food would have to wait. On the days he chose not to work the streets, he didn't really care if he had a drink or not.

John unlocked the padlock on the metal bar which secured his chest of drawers, removed the bar and pulled open the top drawer. It didn't contain much; there were a couple of folded newspaper cuttings, yellowing with time from oxidation, both of which reported the accident. There were a few coins scattered about, mainly cents, both American and European, and a plastic bottle. John took the bottle, slipped it into his pocket and then replaced the bar and padlock. He reached behind the wardrobe, pulled out two cardboard begging signs and a carrier bag which contained a small chequered picnic blanket and an old flat cap. Then he left his room.

John walked through the bunk area which was now virtually deserted. The few stragglers who remained were also preparing for another day of being shifted from one street corner to another. He acknowledged one of them with a slight incline of the head, and then walked down the corridor to the main entrance.

"Morning, Mr. Brewer." It was young Ben, helping out on the front reception desk as part of his Duke of Edinburgh silver award. "Paddy said he didn't have all feckin' day and he's gone to the station. Said something about seeing you later at the end of the world."

Paddy had been referring to a pub in Camden, The World's End. "Okay, Ben. Thanks," smiled John. "Nearly finished your stint, haven't you?"

"Yes. Not long now. Although I might just hang about for a while, probably until the end of next term." Ben had to do a minimum of six months volunteering as part of the DoE program.

"Good, good," replied John.

John pulled out a pair of gloves, from which he'd cut off both thumb and forefinger, and put them on. He reached into his bag and placed the cap upon his head. He was glad the rain had stopped, although looking through the window, he thought it may be only a temporary respite. John turned up the collar of his coat and with a long sigh reached out for the brass door handle, pulled it downwards and the door towards him.

CHAPTER 3

Prime Meridian

The opaque glass panels on the upper half of the heavy wooden inner door had numerous ornate patterns etched around the outer edges. On first glance they appeared to be a mix of little arrows, various circles and numbers, some of which were Roman. The arrows were actually clock hands and the circles were clock faces with the odd cog thrown in here and there. Anyone who cared to look more closely would have seen the letters making up the word 'Bradbeer' entwined within the shapes.

Winnie, oblivious to any shape or pattern at all, closed the door behind her and took one small step inside. She gazed around to take in her surroundings; of course she'd been in many a store before but not one as fine as this. It wasn't stacked wall to wall with clocks as she might have at first expected, but just a few, the likes of which she'd never seen before. Winnie smiled to herself, having noticed that the floor was made of solid wood – she did like a nice bit of polished oak. There was a straight gold line embedded into the floor, starting from the wall at the opposite end of the store and running along the floor under her right foot and then stopping just behind her at the door through which she had just entered. Surely that can't be real gold she thought.

Winnie ventured further inside the store hoping that this would attract the attention of someone, but no-one could be seen as yet. Clutching both of her bags she stopped in front of what she assumed was a clock – well it had dials, numbers, hands, months and some fancy writing on, so it must be a clock, she concluded. Winnie was fixated by it, initially by the smallest of cogs which could be seen slowly moving at the side. Then her gaze moved back to the clock face. The outer circumference was probably made of brass, she figured. Each of the twelve Roman numerals had its corresponding month either above it, below it, or by the side depending on which number it was.

Winnie looked at the III and then to the right she read March. "That's nice," she said quietly.

"Yes it is, isn't it?" replied a man's voice. It came from behind, slightly to her left.

Winnie wasn't at all startled; she was quite pleased that someone had noticed her at last. "Unusual." She didn't turn towards the man but instead just kept staring at the timepiece, hoping that she'd actually get to know some more about it.

"It's such a wonderful clock – modern, with such intricate craftsmanship. Not only telling us the time, but also the month and day." The man indicated towards the upper half between the centre of the clock and the XII, as he moved to Winnie's side. There in a circle were the days of the week and a small hand indicating towards Monday, today. "The lower part tells us when the sun will rise and set. If you follow the small hand to October, and then the first week, you'll see that the sun rose at 6.04am and will set at 5.30pm. Of course some allowances will need to be made for the months that have daylight saving, and also which degree of longitude the clock is used at."

"Not that we've seen the sun rise much at all this past week," came Winnie's reply. At which they both smiled.

"No, I suppose not," he replied. "You can also see the clockmaker's name across the centre, and where it was made."

"C.E. Beacham the third. Sisters... Oregon," read Winnie, having to make sure that she wasn't about to mistakenly say 'Oregano'. She was more familiar with cookbooks than atlases.

"Yes. But to be truthful all I've told you about is what we can clearly see. I'm no expert on clocks, unfortunately." He paused, slowly came round in front of Winnie and held out a business card. "My speciality is more that of bracelets – my father is the time expert. Hello. I'm Jason Bradbeer."

Winnie was pleased that was where Jason's knowledge stopped, as all his talk of allowances and longitude had lost her. "Hello, I'm Winnie." She accepted Jason's card from his outstretched hand and didn't pay it any attention as she placed it into her coat pocket.

She'd expected him, from the sound of his voice, to be smart and very well-presented – suit, tie, clean-shaven and with short neat hair. However, Jason's appearance was in complete contrast to the image her mind had conjured up

– black jeans, open-necked shirt, dark straggly hair and a short beard to match. Winnie thought he'd look more at home in a *Three Musketeers* film rather than a posh clock shop.

"Mrs. Holroyd?" asked Jason.

"Yes. But please call me Winnie. I much prefer Winnie."

"Well, I'm sure you're not here to look at clocks all day. Would you like to follow me, Sarah is expecting you." He strode off ahead of her, Winnie followed, almost breaking out into a trot to keep up.

Jason led her past a large packing crate, a roll of bubble wrap and another four clocks, each sitting on either a glass or marble plinth, each a delicate and stunning work of elaborate craftsmanship.

Winnie noticed there was an empty plinth at the end of the store, empty except for a card, she paused briefly to read it. "Made by the legendary Abraham-Louis Breguet, watchmaker to Louis the sixteenth, Marie Antoinette, Napoleon, and the sultan of the Ottoman Empire."

Jason had noticed Winnie hesitate. "That's for a clock we're expecting to arrive any time soon. If you could, this way please, Mrs. Holroyd." He gestured towards the rear of the store, forgetting her previous request to be called Winnie.

The large abstract canvasses along the wall didn't appeal to Winnie – far too much colour for her liking, and so her eyes were once again drawn to the straight gold line running the length of the store. She was tempted to ask what purpose it had, but thought better of it. In the far left corner there was an archway, possibly where a door had once been – Jason led her through it. Winnie wondered if the gold-coloured line would still be running along the oak floor at the other side of the arch. It was.

The line ran directly under the central support column of a large, decorative wrought iron spiral staircase before continuing under yet another wall. They ascended the staircase side by side, Winnie running her right hand along the smooth wooden handrail as she took each tread slowly to the next floor of The Time Store.

As she stood at the top of the stairs Winnie noticed that the first floor opened out into a more familiar type of shop. In contrast to the ground floor this was far better lit, much brighter and it was certainly like a typical store, although somewhat upmarket. There were no abstract paintings on the walls here, instead there were photos – large canvas prints of celebrities, past and present, flaunting what she would describe as fancy watches. Amongst the faces Winnie recognised one as Charlie Chaplin. There were glass display cabinets around the sides of the room with others arranged in the centre, although from the top of the stairs she couldn't see into them. Along the left side was a small reception area where Winnie could see another man talking to a middle aged couple who she assumed were customers, wealthy customers by the look of their clothes. The man talking to the couple appeared to be slightly younger than Jason, perhaps in his late twenties and, from where Winnie was standing, he was maybe a tad smaller.

They'd only taken a few steps into the room, when Jason stopped. "Excuse me a moment please, Mrs. Holroyd. Just need to have a quick word with my brother." Jason, indicating for her to remain where she was, headed over to the reception area. He approached the customers, smiling and enthusiastically offering out his hand to greet them.

Winnie couldn't hear what was being said between the four of them, but there were plenty of smiles, introductions and hand gestures. Whilst waiting, she decided to look into one of the glass cabinets. She chuckled to herself with some amusement at the sparse display. There were only four wristwatches on show, each resting on a light grey velvet pad. It would have been quite easy to put at least twenty or so in there without cluttering.

One of them, the second from the left, she almost certainly recognised. She was sure that her late husband Les had one, or at least one very similar, back in the seventies. The one on the far right was a kids' *STAR WARS* watch, she could tell this as it had the words clearly on the front along with a couple of robot characters whose names she possibly once knew. The watch between these had a calculator on the front and, although Winnie had seen these in newspapers and magazines in the past, she was always of the opinion that people should be able to do basic maths without the need for modern-day gadgets.

"Sorry about that, Mrs. Holroyd. I'd forgotten to mention something to Dan earlier." Jason moved to the opposite side of the cabinet, adopting a more historian approach, as opposed to that of a salesman. "I can see the beginning of the digital era has caught your eye. Let me briefly explain."

"That would be nice," she responded.

He pointed to the first watch on Winnie's left. "Electronic digital wristwatches first came on the market over forty years ago, but the first purely digital wristwatch actually appeared decades before. This here is the Cortebert Digital Wristwatch from the twenties. Many believe it to be the first digital wristwatch ever sold. No batteries though -

you still had to wind it like any other watch back then." Jason paused before moving to the next watch in case his audience of one wanted to ask any questions. She didn't.

"Fascinating," said Winnie. She wanted to know about the second watch, the one she now considered to be Les's.

"The next is the very first electronic digital wristwatch to go on sale in early 1972 – April I think. It's the Hamilton Pulsar P1 – priced at just over two thousand dollars back then. It used an LED display behind a synthetic ruby crystal, all encased in eighteen-carat gold."

Jason then realised that Winnie had lost interest. Whilst he assumed it was because of the technical information, it wasn't that at all, it was because she'd decided that it couldn't have been her husband's watch… at least not at that price. He very quickly skimmed over the 1976 Hamilton Pulsar Calculator watch and the Texas-Instruments Star Wars Watch from 1977 which had revolutionised the digital wristwatch industry, and once again invited Winnie to follow him.

They walked through a doorway just a few feet to the left of the staircase they had climbed. They entered a room about three times the size of the Watch Room; this one was not like either of the other two in any way. As they walked through the room they passed collections of compasses, sextants, globes, barometers, astrological clocks, sundials, clepsydrae, even a gnomon or two thrown in for good measure.

Thankfully for Winnie each section had an information sign hanging above, similar to the aisles in her local supermarket. There must have been pieces from all ages, civilizations, cultures and continents. Pieces made from various woods, precious metals and stone... some ornate and delicate and some which could best be described as work in progress. Some ticked, some tocked, some turned back and forth and some just kept turning. Water could be seen trickling from one point to another in one of the clepsydrae, this sounded quite soothing. The globes were of various styles and sizes, some mirrored the world of today and some depicted the past, having islands, countries and even continents missing. Winnie wondered if there was a globe which split in two and contained half-empty bottles of spirits and liqueurs like Dorothy's, her next door neighbour.

"Are you moving?" asked Winnie, pointing at another packing crate and roll of bubble wrap.

"Ah. No," replied Jason. "We're loaning a few pieces to a museum exhibition."

"Oh, are you? Perhaps I'll visit it - which one?"

"Well, when it finally gets to London it will be the British Museum. But I'm afraid it won't be for a few years yet. The exhibition has Paris, New York and Tokyo to visit first."

"I'll keep a look out for it."

From The Globe Room, as Winnie was now describing it to herself, they stopped at another door. This was a biometric fingerprint controlled door which Jason opened by placing his right thumb onto a pad above the handle. Mounted over the door Winnie spotted a small video camera and for extra security the door carried the obligatory PRIVATE notice on it.

Once through, Jason secured the door behind them. "Could I take your coat for you, Winnie?" he asked.

"Thank you." She put down her bags, removed her

coat and handed it to him before once again picking up the bags.

He placed the coat on a hanger and hung it in a small cupboard to his left. "Let's hope Sarah has the kettle on for you, warm you up a little. It's a bit nippy out there this morning, don't you think?"

Winnie just nodded, and wondered if now was a good time to ask about the straight line in the floor downstairs, but instead decided on, "A cup of tea would be nice, thank you."

Jason walked off at a much slower pace, one which Winnie found easier. Turning a corner they descended two flights of stairs which brought them to a small basement room with four more doors, three of which also had the fingerprint controlled door handles. Jason opted for the only one without and opened it inwards.

It was a fairly big room with a large table in the middle. Sarah was standing at a small kitchen area at one side, waiting for a kettle to boil. "Morning, Winnie. I hope Jason has been looking after you. Tea?"

"Yes please."

Sarah smiled, pouring out the now boiled water from the kettle into a stainless steel teapot. "We did have a nice china one until my clumsy brother Dan dropped it earlier." She rolled her eyes towards a mop and bucket propped up by the sink.

"I've given Winnie a bit of a tour," said Jason.

"Good. I've done a coffee for you to take to the office, Jase." That was Sarah's way of asking him to politely, but quickly leave.

"Thanks, sis," said Jason, picking up the cup and

moving towards the door.

"Help yourself to tea, Winnie. Oh and please do sit down." Sarah pulled a chair out from under the table next to where Winnie was standing, gestured for her to sit, and then placed the teapot onto the table next to the already laid cups.

"Thank you." Winnie smiled, sat down and pulled one of the cups towards her, raised herself slightly out of the chair, poured herself a cup of tea and added the milk. She then poured a cup for Sarah.

"See you later, Winnie." Jason said to her with a smile as he was leaving for the office. "Sarah, let me have the final details when you have them and I'll finish the bracelet whilst you two are getting ready."

"Okay. Will do," replied Sarah, as she sat in the chair opposite Winnie. She reached over for her tea, and added both milk and sugar. She began slowly stirring the tea in a clockwise direction, catching the rim of the cup as she stirred.

Winnie recognised the ring on Sarah's right hand – it was the same one she had been wearing in the coffee shop. She'd remarked on it then. Sarah had held it out for her to see more closely. It was made from platinum and bore an unusual raised motif of an hourglass.

Before they had met in the coffee shop Sarah had taken Winnie's call when she'd responded to the classified ad. Sarah had asked a standard list of initial questions such as; name, age, residential area and contact number. Then she'd moved on to discussing where they should meet, saying she enjoyed meeting people in a relaxed, friendly environment, so tried to choose coffee shops. Winnie had changed her mind several times before settling on the recently opened Camden Coffee House. Sarah had then wanted to know about possible health related issues such as glasses, hearing aids, missing limbs etc. After that Winnie had been surprised that Sarah had asked if she had any visible tattoos, and if so what they were. Then finally she'd asked, "Keeping it very brief, why have you called?" Sarah had told her jokingly that occasionally when asking this question she'd have to reiterate the word 'brief'.

During this initial call if Sarah had an immediate feeling that The Time Store couldn't help, for one reason or another, then she'd spin a few white lies from which the caller would usually back away, making some excuse to hang up. Of the ones which she felt were 'possibles' she'd invariably arrange to meet them for a much longer face to face chat. Then if she felt they could be helped, she'd review with Jason and Dan, over Friday lunch. Usually the three of them would bring several 'possibles' each, from which they'd discuss and decide on whom, if anyone, to help. Occasionally they'd be able to help all of them, if what they referred to as true time allowed, but more often than not they whittled it down to two or three a week each. These would then be sent an appointment card inviting them along to the Time Store.

Suddenly Sarah stopped stirring, removed the spoon and pushed the cup to one side. She began to twist her unusual ring around her finger, and then she looked up at Winnie and smiled, with an impish, almost childlike glint in her eyes.

"First, let's go over your reasons for coming to The Time Store," Sarah said, still smiling broadly. "So, you had a plan some time ago to visit America to see Elvis in concert. This trip had to be cancelled, and you were for various reasons unable to rearrange."

"Yes, that's right," Winnie responded.

"You experienced some strong emotions at that time, because several things happened in quick succession, all of which you felt were beyond your control. As in – husband ill, no trip – husband dies, still no trip – Elvis dies, definitely no trip."

"Yes," agreed Winnie. "A bit blunt when you put it like that, but yes."

"Okay, so although you were unable to attend the concert, which was, after all, the main reason for your trip, the show still went on ahead without you."

"Er…" Winnie was perplexed. Where was this strange conversation heading?

"Of course it did. We know that," continued Sarah. "And that's why we can go and see it!"

Although her mouth opened, Winnie didn't speak… but she felt her body lurch with anticipation.

"We can go and see it now. Today." Sarah smiled. "We're going on a trip. This is The Time Store – and I'm taking you on a time trip! Back to Chicago, 1976, to see Elvis Presley… The King of Rock and Roll."

"What?" Had Winnie's ears just deceived her? Had she really just heard Sarah, a rational, adult human being just announce that they were going to time travel? How had she put it? On a time trip. Winnie was having difficulty in accepting what she'd just heard.

"Yes, I know it's hard to believe, but that's what we're going to be doing." Sarah spoke reassuringly. "I see you've brought some things, did you bring the tickets?"

"Yes," replied Winnie, still recoiling from Sarah's

revelation. She reached down for her handbag almost as if on auto-pilot, and pulled out a buff manila envelope, which had Winnie's name and address typed on the front. In the top right corner were two 31 cent stamps both showing an image of an aeroplane and two hemispheres of the globe on the background of the American flag. Both stamps were postmarked *Chicago.IL. August 23rd 1976*.

"Do you mind?" Sarah asked Winnie, indicating that she wished to remove the contents.

"Go ahead," replied Winnie, trying to appear calm.

Sarah opened the end of the envelope and using her thumb and index finger pulled out the four unused tickets. There were two for Thursday October 14th and two for Friday the 15th… each ticket had cost Winnie ten dollars. "If you could have gone to one of the shows which would you have chosen?" asked Sarah.

"That's easy. The Thursday," replied Winnie without any hesitation at all. "He sang *Love Me Tender* on the Thursday."

"That's sorted then, Thursday it is." Sarah picked up the two Thursday tickets and then stood up. "You finish your tea, Winnie. I'll give Jason the final details for our trip. I'll only be a few minutes, so when we get back we can get changed."

"Thank you." Winnie was feeling a strange mix of excitement, confusion, and panic.

She was still having a conflicting battle with herself and reality about what was happening, or going to happen. She didn't know whether to run and scream for the hills, to play along with what could be a very elaborate and costly charade, or to prepare herself to travel back in time. But no matter. Winnie definitely felt that she could trust Sarah and so was happy to humour her, at least for the time being.

She wanted to ask Sarah lots of questions on her return, but wasn't too sure how to phrase them, or whether to ask any at all. Winnie decided that for now, the best thing she could do was to relax. Sarah was a nice girl after all, and if she turned out to be as batty as a piece of mouldy old fruitcake... then so be it. Winnie kept calm, and poured herself another cup of tea.

Before she had the chance to finish it Sarah returned. "Right – if you're ready, I'll take you to our Costume Room. We need to look the part for 1976." Sarah picked up the bag of clothes which Winnie had brought, took her by the arm and together they went to get changed.

The door to the Costume Room was one of the three with fingerprint locks that Winnie had seen earlier. Sarah scanned her right thumb on the pad and opened the door. Winnie was stunned by what she saw. The room was overflowing with double height clothes rails bulging with a vast array of outfits. All styles and eras were catered for, each costume protected by a transparent polythene cover. There was a distinct strong, pungent, sickly-sweet mothball odour lingering in the room and Winnie could see several neutralising air fresheners strategically placed around.

"I know you've brought your own clothes, but we may find some extra accessories in here for you, and you can perhaps give me a few tips on what to wear." The rails were marked up in a similar way to the sections in the Globe Room. Sarah went over to the 20th Century area, and then to the 1970's rail.

With a little bit of Winnie's input Sarah chose some bell-bottomed purple trousers and a floaty top, not too dissimilar to her current style of dress, but with an obvious seventies slant. From her bag Winnie retrieved her A-line green and blue bold patterned dress, then chose some beads from the accessories. Sarah pointed Winnie in the direction of a changing cubicle and she entered the one opposite.

The women were still admiring, yet having a good laugh at their attire when there was a knock at the door. "Come in," called Sarah. "We're nearly done."

"Wow... look at you two groovy chicks. Think you'll be needing this though." Jason was holding a small, saucer sized tray on top of which sat a bracelet.

"Let Winnie have a look," prompted Sarah, who was still putting on her left boot.

Jason held out the tray. Winnie picked up and examined the bracelet, only then noticing that Jason was wearing a ring – very similar to Sarah's, she thought. She'd not seen much platinum but recognised it almost instantly by its greyish white colour. The bracelet's design was very similar to that of a plain linked watch, about 2cm wide and about 4mm thick with a slightly chunkier disc where a watch face itself would usually be. There were some numbers engraved on one side of the disc along with what appeared to be a series of Roman numerals. It read:

"Okay. Just need to check a few things and then we can get off. Pretty isn't it?" commented Sarah.

"Yes, it's lovely." Winnie held out the bracelet.

Sarah took this from her and slipped it on over her left hand. Winnie couldn't help but notice that once on Sarah's wrist the bracelet started to radiate a very mellow, lily white aura, almost ethereal.

"I've sorted the money," Jason informed Sarah, handing her a bag. "$3,000, all pre '76 bills."

"Are the tickets in here and is that going to be enough money?" she asked, taking the bag and patting the side.

"Yes they are, and it should easily be enough cash for you. I've put some water and a camera in the bag as well. It's an Instamatic, should be easy for you both to use."

"That's good. What about film, batteries...?" Sarah put the shoulder bag over her head and an arm through the strap.

"Batteries? You're having a laugh aren't you? It's a wind on one." Jason laughed. "It takes a 126 cartridge, there's a twenty shot colour one in it. Oh, and two flash cubes."

"Sounds just like my old Kodak," interrupted Winnie. "Did you say you've got dollars?" she then asked inquisitively.

"Of course. They don't take pounds over in Chicago, you know. I'm even bringing some extra for souvenirs and dinner." Sarah dipped into her bag, pulled out the small camera and offered it to Winnie. "You might as well look after this."

"We'll have time for dinner as well?" Winnie hoped so. It had been a few hours since she'd eaten, and that had only been a slice of toast before she'd gone to the hostel.

"Am I going to need my passport? I haven't brought it."

"Knowing my sister, she's booked the best table downtown, probably in The Loop or something, and no, Winnie you won't need that."

"I've heard of that. Think I read about The Loop in an encyclopaedia." Winnie recalled Irene borrowing some books from the library for research purposes; this had entailed looking at as many pictures of the Chicago area as they could get their hands on.

"Right, let's get going then," Sarah said firmly, not wanting to delay matters any longer. "You taking the walk with us, Jason?"

"No... I need to get ready for Dan's trip to July '66 this afternoon. We've got another football fan wanting to see the glory days. And then I'm in Stratford with Will."

"Okay. And don't forget to sort out that sodding hand!"

"Yes sis, I'm on it," replied Jason.

"We can't have it in the freezer forever," she hissed under her breath. "Come on then, let's go shall we, Winnie?"

"Yes." Winnie beamed from ear to ear, a grin far bigger than any Cheshire cat could ever make. "I believe it now, Sarah. We're really going to be travelling back in time to see Elvis." Winnie was finally going to be having her big adventure, and she followed her guide eagerly and willingly.

Sarah stood in front of another of the three doors with a biometric lock. It was slightly wider than the other two and had an intricate design crest carved into the wood. Sarah placed her right hand upon the carving. "Tempus...

Tempus... TEMPUS," she called, the third in a raised voice.

The crest immediately lit up with an incandescent light. In the middle Winnie could see a crescent moon which was itself in the centre of a clock face, but one with no hands, just numerals. There was an outer circle divided into twelve. Within each segment there were carved words and then a final circle divided into four, each quarter having a word inscribed.

"These are the months, and these the seasons." Sarah pointed out. "Ver, aestas, autumnus, hiems."

Winnie was amazed at the level of detail in the carving. "And these?" She pointed at an array of circles. "Planets?"

"No, but you're close. These are moons – Callisto, Hyperion, Rhea, Oberon, Nereid, Ophelia and Sinope." Sarah called them out in turn and as she did so each of the moons brightly shone a different colour of the spectrum. "CHRONOS."

As the door opened it disturbed a dormant motion sensor which in turn woke a sleeping light. The two women walked into what Winnie assumed was a corridor or passageway and the door closed behind them. The passageway was arched, it was about three metres wide and a similar height. The walls were constructed of limestone, smooth to the touch and the floor was covered with rectangular terracotta and ochre coloured tiles. Winnie once again noticed that the gold coloured line had returned, running centrally along the floor into the distance before them.

"We have a short walk ahead of us now, but no need to rush. How are you feeling?"

"Excited, worried, scared. I've got butterflies,"

replied Winnie. "I really didn't know what to expect when I set off this morning."

"What did you think was going to happen?" Sarah enjoyed asking this question, it often gave some strange answers.

"Well, at first I thought it was going to be some sort of photo-shoot type thing. I then went onto being hypnotised and having some memories put into my mind."

Sarah laughed. "And now you're about to travel in time. What do you think about that?"

Winnie didn't reply immediately. They kept walking along the passageway and she focused on the never-ending line as it stretched out before them. Every so often they'd pass another motion sensor which again would give life to a filament in the distance.

"You don't act or look like a fruitcake... and just because I've never met God it doesn't mean that he doesn't exist or that I shouldn't believe in him." Winnie tried to explain her rational thoughts on it all. "Only thing is... do I now have to start believing in fairies?"

Both ladies laughed out loud. Sarah put her arm around Winnie and gently hugged her. "Fruitcake... "

"Sarah, can I ask you about this line? Is it the same one that's in your shop? How far does it go?"

"The line runs along 0° longitude, the Prime Meridian, which goes from the North Pole to the South Pole of course... but only our little bit is golden," explained Sarah. "The store stands directly on the Meridian and we're currently walking under Greenwich Park."

They didn't speak for a minute or two, the only sound that could be heard was their own footsteps which echoed off the three-hundred year old walls. Winnie was deep in thought about the wonder of it all – who, what, why, where, when – question after question filled her head.

Sarah was still inwardly laughing at being almost called a fruitcake, after a while she broke the silence. "Okay, Winnie. We're nearly there. I need to go through some basic things we can and can't do. Unfortunately there are a few rules. Our main concern is that we can't alter or change things. Rule number one – we must preserve true time."

"True time?"

"True time is what's supposed to happen. We're not allowed to stop people dying or to kill Hitler – those sorts of things. We're also not allowed to offer advice to people we meet, or to discuss the future... so no telling anyone that Elvis is going to die in 1977."

"I won't, don't worry. What would happen if you stopped someone from dying then? I don't mean anyone famous – just perhaps a relative or a friend."

Sarah took a breath. "That would alter true time. If we stopped Joe Bloggs from jumping into a river to save his dog and drowning, then the following week he may have driven to work and killed a pedestrian who could have been the grandparent of a future surgeon who in turn could save thousands of lives. It's like a domino effect. The smallest touch can start thousands of dominoes toppling over. "

"So what *can* we do?" asked Winnie.

"That's easy – enjoy yourself."

"I was just about to come looking for the pair of you, thought you might have got lost." A tall man stood up from a brown leather winged armchair and approached the two women. "Mrs Holroyd, let me introduce myself. I'm

David Bradbeer, Sarah's father."

"Hello," replied Winnie, shaking his outstretched hand.

David was dressed smartly – wearing a pair of very well pressed, belted, navy pinstriped trousers, a loose fitting light blue monogrammed shirt tucked in at the waist, and a blue and red paisley patterned cravat. His hair was black with patches of defining grey, and his face was adorned with a trimmed moustache and beard which gave him an almost naval look.

"What have you got planned for the day, Sarah?" asked her father.

"Well, hopefully we'll lunch at the Hancock Tower. I know there's a restaurant on the 95th floor now, and from what I can gather there's one there in '76. If not then we'll try The Bergoff."

"Sounds nice."

"Then we're going to take in a few shops, including Peacock's of course, followed by an evening's entertainment with The King himself."

"Looks like you're in for a busy day then, Mrs Holroyd. Don't you be letting Sarah drag you around too many shops, she has a weakness for handbags."

"Dad!" scowled Sarah.

"These feet might be getting on a bit, but when it comes to shopping they'll keep going all day," said Winnie.

"I'm sure they would," David laughed. "Shall we?" He guided them into a large circular room.

The limestone walls of the passageway had now become a wall of marble on which Winnie could see a frieze. Various people, planets and hourglasses were carved around the entire circumference of the room. The ceiling was a high dome painted with a night sky and Winnie could make out celestial constellations amongst what looked like a giant dot-to-dot of stars. It was supported by four arches which met at the sculpted, round central keystone. She looked from the centre of the ceiling to the centre of the red granite floor. A familiar carving was engraved into the entire floor area; it was a larger version of the carving which appeared on the door Sarah had taken her through, only this time the moon wasn't in the centre of the clock face. Still running through the centre of the room, the floor carving and the clock face, as though purposely splitting them all in two, was the golden line – the Prime Meridian. Winnie followed it to the adjacent side of the room where once again it disappeared under the wall making its way to the South Pole.

"Okay... you two ready?" asked David. "Where's your arrival point?"

"Hopefully in the basement of the John Hancock Tower, that's if Jason has got the co-ordinates right."

Sarah linked arms with Winnie and led her to the centre of the room, stood her on one side of the meridian and took her own place on the other. Sarah then turned the signet ring on her right hand so that the engraved motif was palm side. She could feel Winnie's grasp on her arm, becoming tighter and tighter. Sarah then placed the palm of her right hand onto the bracelet.

Seconds later David watched as the two women disappeared. No noise, no lights.

CHAPTER 4

Love Me Tender

"Within a heartbeat we were there... I mean, we could hear American accents, and there were these big cars, and I mean big cars everywhere. It was just like in Starsky and Hutch. Well, we went over to the lift. Well, no... the elevator! Of course we had to wait for someone to let us in." Winnie paused, and moved herself closer.

"Oh, he was very charming, looked just like J.R., but without the hat, and he even asked us where in England we came from. Don't think he'd heard of Camden before though – asked if it was anywhere near London. And do you know how long it took the lift to get to the top? Go on. Guess." Winnie waited very briefly for a reply.

"I'll tell you. Seconds. It went up hundreds of floors so fast you would never have believed it. Oh, and the view from the top! I mean, it was so clear. And I tell you now – that is never a lake. It was bigger than the sea at Brighton, and that's big. I mean, you couldn't see the other side... at all!" She paused for breath.

"We walked all the way around the top. Buildings everywhere – some even had swimming pools on the roofs. Yes, that's right... pools, just like we see in the movies. There was a big tower... bigger than the one we were in. Shears Tower... or something like that. Then we had lunch, next to the window. It was wonderful. We were looking down on the street with all the fancy shops. We saw an old water tower – looked just like a castle from up there. Have you ever had clam chowder? No, me neither. I mean, if it had said clam soup on the menu I'd have thought, yuk..." Winnie made a grating sound at the back of her throat "...and had something different. But it was really nice, surprised me, and you know how fussy I am with food. Then I had some chicken pasta, which *really* was nice." Winnie only briefly touched on the pasta dish.

"Have you ever heard of an eggplant? It was on the menu. Sarah had it..." Winnie stopped. "What do you mean, Sarah who? Don't give me that, I told you about her last week, remember. Anyway it looked just like aubergine to me. Egg!! I'd have been sending that back if it was brought to me."

Winnie reached for her bag and took out a bottle of water, drank a little and then poured the rest over some nearby wilting flowers, replaced the lid, then laid the bottle by her bag. "Then we went for a walk down the High Street, talk about posh... What was that? Oh! Twelve dollars for the two of us, including our drinks of course. Anyway these shops were more than posh... these were very posh. Reminded me of going into C&A or Lewis's... No, not as posh as Harrod's."

"Good afternoon, Winnie."

"Oh! Hello, Sheila. How are you keeping? You

going to clean your Alan?" replied Winnie, as Sheila Cowling, a hefty woman carrying a scrubbing brush scuttled past.

"Yes... Blooming pigeons. Shit everywhere!"

Winnie continued in a much quieter voice, at least until she knew Sheila was well out of earshot. "I had to promise Sarah that I wouldn't tell anyone about the trip... But I'm sure she wouldn't mind me telling you. Anyway, Sarah bought a handbag, not my taste, but she liked it. And I got these new shoes."

Winnie pointed down to the blue, low heeled court shoes she was wearing. "I'm bedding them in. I don't think I'll wear them much though... too tight. I told her I was a size five. Sarah told me their sizes are different from ours, so I'm not too sure what I've ended up with. Then we went to this jeweller's shop at this big hotel so she could buy a fancy watch. I'd seen one just like it in one of the cabinets at Sarah's shop. Gold with a calculator on the front... Oh gosh! Silly me, nearly forgot to tell you about the doors. Yes, doors to the shop. I took a picture, so when I get the film back I'll let you see them. They were very nice, with beautiful brass peacocks on them, you wait till I show you the picture and you'll see what I mean."

"Then we went to the stadium – Chicago Stadium, by cab of course." There was so much excitement in Winnie's voice; she just couldn't wait to talk about it. "It was heaving out there, as busy as the Boxing Day sales, if not busier. We stood in the queue... Do you know they call it the line? So anyway, there we were, I was so excited."

Tears began to well up in her eyes as she relived the memory. "These two girls from Milwaukee... apparently that's where someone called The Fonz lives... they were asking us all about our trip, of course we couldn't tell them how we got there. One asked if we'd had our tickets long... Mmm!!! That was a mistake, well I didn't think, did I...? It just came out. You should have seen Sarah's face when I said thirty-three years!" Winnie laughed between crying and wiping a tear from her cheek with a piece of kitchen roll, which she'd fished out from deep within her coat pocket.

"There was this very big..." She stopped. "Well, yes I know that everything there was very big. Anyway there was this huge red sign with the word 'stadium' on it hanging all the way down the front of the building, with lots of American flags flying everywhere. I took a picture of that as well. I do hope they come out okay. You know me, I've never been any good at taking photographs. Oh, then the queue... the line... started moving. I had to hold Sarah's arm tightly, thought I was going to get pushed over. Everyone was so excited, so happy."

"We went inside... and I have never, ever been in a building with so many people in before. I thought there must have been over fifty-thousand in there, but Sarah told me the crowd was just under twenty. Think she must have – what do they call it - goggled it? On the internet. Anyway we sat down quite early - very good view as well. It was so enjoyable just watching the stadium fill with people. Oh, and the noise level... do you know how loud it sounded in there? Wish I'd taken some earplugs with me."

"Then the show started. Now I like a bit of church music, as you know. But this was... now hang on. What did the girl next to me say?" Winnie dug deep. "Oh that's right, she called them a god-awful gospel group! Then there was a comedian who told stories about pot, marriage, and something about teenagers doing stupid things. He'd have plenty to talk about with the kids of today. Then there was these three men singing some soul songs, reminded me a little of Otis Redding, but not as good."

"Well, did I need the loo? I was bursting at the seams. Good job Sarah needed it as much as me. I'd have never have found our seats again in that place. Oh… I bought an Elvis mirror during the break. Here, let me show you." Winnie opened her handbag and pulled out a small round pocket mirror, with a picture of a young Elvis on the back. "What do you think? I know it's a bit tacky but I like it." She then put the mirror back in her handbag.

Winnie started crying again, trying to compose herself, struggling to get her words out between the sobs and sniffs. "You should have heard the squeals when they turned all the big lights off and played the moon music." She rubbed some tears from the side of her face. "You'd know it if you heard it."

She stopped, smiled with her mouth firmly closed, inhaled a deep breath through her nose and started again. "Sarah was screaming as loud as me. Think she's a bit of a fan deep down. Anyway, guess what he opened with, go on guess… " Winnie waited for an answer, possibly a bit longer than she'd have normally waited, but this was because she was now struggling to get any words out at all. She fought hard to talk, she wanted more than anything to tell the only person she could, about her day. "Okay, I'll tell you. *See See Rider*. It was more than I could have ever have hoped for…" The tears took over; Winnie, for now, couldn't continue.

She stood up and walked slowly away, still brushing the tears as they fell down her cheeks. There was a small wooden bench a few feet from where she'd been talking. Winnie sat down and closed her eyes tightly. She could feel the autumn wind as it wrestled with the leaves on the nearby trees, knowing that it would only be a matter of time before the wind would win the battle and the leaves would fall.

The sounds of birds chirping happily away could be heard, only to be drowned out as a passing number 29, with standing room only, growled its way past. The music from a car radio could be detected faintly in the distance, becoming louder and louder as it got closer... but then fading away as the car changed direction. After about five minutes Winnie opened her eyes, stood up, and then walked back to finish her conversation.

"He was wearing his white Inca suit, with lots of gold glittering on it, and a really big belt. He looked just like a king, especially with a collar so high... What songs did he sing? Okay, have some patience will you... " Smiles now replaced tears. *"Jailhouse Rock, Teddy Bear, Shook Up, Hound Dog, Fever...* oh and *Love Me Tender..."* Winnie rattled off nearly the complete list of songs which she'd seen Elvis perform – if she missed any there'd always be another day to tell.

"When it had all finished, we just sat and watched everyone leave. It must have only taken fifteen minutes or so for the place to empty. Once Sarah was sure nobody could see us, she turned her ring around again. We stood up, linked arms... and then she touched the bracelet with the ring. I'm telling you – it was magic – we were back in the circle room with her father. Sarah told me that in true time we'd only been gone two hours. We'd spent all day in Chicago and it only lasted two hours. Never in a million years!"

"Anyway, listen, I need some advice." The excitement in Winnie's voice was replaced by concern. "I think that John could really do with meeting these people. I *know* they'd be able to help him. What do you think?"

Winnie smiled – she'd guessed the answer without needing to hear it. "Alright, that's settled then. I need to get going now." She removed the wilting flowers and replaced them with some fresh ones. "I'll see you next week."

Winnie stood up, blew a kiss. Then walked slowly away from Irene's grave.

CHAPTER 5

Sobering Thoughts

It was early evening, daylight was drawing to an end and civil dusk was taking over; the first of the sodium vapour streetlamps was flickering into life, preparing to light up the local pavements and roads. Sound asleep, propped up against one such lamppost, leaning slightly to the right, slouched John. The neck of his empty glass bottle slipped from his grimy hand and crashed the short distance to the floor, the last remaining drops of its malted amber liquid spilt out in front of him.

Whilst John was sleeping, numerous people had walked by. Some chose to walk faster when passing, some chose to look into the window of a shuttered clothes store, some swerved, giving John a wide berth, whilst fixing their stare anywhere but on him. Others opted to throw a coin or two down at him, possibly in pity, probably to ease their own conscience in compensation for walking past and not really caring. One person discussed with a friend whether they should call the emergency services, but in the end thought 'sod it' and walked on. They could hardly be blamed – perhaps it was the sight of John sprawled out there in a potent cocktail of his own urine and vomit which pushed back the Good Samaritan within these people.

With his nightmare still crystal clear in his thoughts, John had spent the early part of the day outside a local burger bar, scrounging small change from passing shoppers, students and affluent tourists. On one occasion someone with a high and mighty attitude had brought out a burger and coffee for him, explaining that they'd be concerned about their money getting spent on alcohol, not meals. John didn't mind as it eased his own moral dilemma about which would come first, booze or food. Although not feeling his best, he'd fared well today. By the weight in his pockets he must have made a good £30 or so by lunchtime. His cardboard signs helped. Today's was:

SPARE SOME CHANGE.
HELP A BUM TO BUY AN
ASTON MARTIN.

It was usually the American tourists who'd give money – maybe from some form of cultural tipping obligation after taking John's photograph, probably for upload to a social media site.

It was whilst on his way to meet Paddy for a much needed afternoon drink or two that he detoured into a nearby Lo-Cost Liquor store to offload some of the copper weight. He left with £25 in notes, a handful of shrapnel and, not being able to help himself, a litre bottle of whisky. He never made his afternoon rendezvous with Patrick. Once the top had been twisted off the bottle, his troubles were eased and that was John as good as wasted for the rest of the day.

Maybe another twenty minutes had elapsed before a crouching policewoman, who'd been sensible enough to put on a pair of latex gloves, gently shook John, eventually rousing him from his slumber. "Are you okay, sir? Can you hear me?" asked the officer.

"Is he awake, Karen?" It was her male colleague returning from depositing the empty whisky bottle into a nearby bin.

"Yes. He's coming round. Give me a hand to get him sitting upright." Karen and her colleague pulled John away from the kerbside gutter and rested him against the shutter of a clothes shop.

A small crowd had gathered, drawn to the flashing blue lights of the Met patrol car; those without time to stop couldn't help but rubberneck as they walked by. From amongst them a young man approached Karen, offering a bottle of mineral water. "Here, take this... He may want some."

"Thank you," she smiled, accepting the water.

John was gradually coming to his senses. He closed his eyes in self-disgust, if *he* thought the stench was abhorrent then what did these poor people think? He could see the remains of what looked like a regurgitated doner kebab down the front of his coat – he couldn't recall eating one though. He took the water and slowly sipped at it.

"How are you feeling?" asked Karen. "Are you feeling alright?" She waited patiently for a reply, but none came. Karen turned to her colleague. "Request ambulance support, better get him checked out."

"Echo-Kilo-one-four-one requesting paramedic support, male, caucasian…"

"I'm okay, I'm fine," John called out loudly. "Just a little groggy still… but I'm fine," he insisted.

"Can you stand up?" Karen asked. "Here, let me help you up."

With Karen's help, and with the support of the shutter, John managed to raise himself to his feet. "There, I'm fine."

He took his hand away from the shutter and thankfully he remained upright. He cringed his face in a sudden feeling of embarrassment – he could feel the clammy wetness of his trousers around his crotch. He didn't need a more sobering thought.

"I think these are yours." The policeman handed John the coins which had been thrown down at him whilst he was sleeping. "Do you have a bed for the night? We may have a warm cell for you if you want – perhaps get a shower as well, back at the nick."

"Thank you…" John accepted the money. "I have a room, not far away, at St. Michael's hostel."

"Right then. Let's give you a ride, get you there before it starts raining."

Both officers helped John into the back of the police car, having first placed a protective sheet on the seat, and rolled the windows down. During the short, uneventful journey to St. Michael's, John remained totally silent. If either officer had turned, they'd have seen a very frightened man. This was possibly John's second car journey since the accident – the last one he could recall involved a black funeral car.

"I think this one's yours," said Karen, approaching St. Michael's reception.

It was Pete Smith running the desk that evening. "Bloody hell. Look at the state of you," he said, as he looked John up and down.

John was quiet. Pete guessed that he'd been out drinking steadily all day. Thankfully he appeared to be over the worst of it though. Any other hostel may have turned him away at this point, but the staff here were more than familiar with John's occasional lapses and issues.

"Come on, mate. Let's get you to your room. You look done in." As Pete moved to guide John lightly by the arm, he recoiled inwardly from the stench, and changed tack. "Mate, how about a shower before bed? Let's get you in there and I'll sort your clothes out."

John, in a daze, allowed himself to be led to the showers, where, with Pete's understanding assistance, he removed his awful clothes, and stood under the warm calming spray.

Pete was well aware of John's bad dreams; he was pretty sure that the nightmares happened during periods of torrential rain. If the forecast was anything to go by, there would be more heavy rain tonight. By the way he looked though, there was a good chance he would sleep through the night without even hearing the rain, thought Pete, as he returned carrying John's towel and nightwear.

Soon afterwards, in his nightshirt and shabby dressing gown, John shambled towards his room. Pete had asked him if he wanted any dinner, but John had declined, feeling his stomach churn in rebellion at the thought of any type of food. He sat down heavily on the edge of his bed, exhausted, embarrassed and mortified. Could he get any lower than this?

He could hear distant clattering and chattering from the canteen and although he couldn't face food, he wished he could be part of the general camaraderie... far better that than lying alone in personal shame and dejection. But he didn't move; he was too lethargic. He flopped down carelessly on the bed, his head resting on the pillow, expecting immediate sleep. However, after what felt like fifteen minutes of fidgeting and pillow fluffs, John was still awake. Not anywhere near wide awake, but conscious enough for jumbled thought. He figured it would be a good idea to remove his dressing gown and get under the covers, that would help. He struggled to push himself back up to a sitting position, and then tentatively stood up.

Dropping his dressing gown on the floor next to his chest of drawers, he noticed a folded newspaper on the top. He couldn't remember putting it there, but that didn't worry him, it was a common occurrence to find evidence of his various actions without actually having any recall. He picked up the newspaper – it was folded open to show the classified section – now that was definitely odd. He didn't think he was the sort of person to sift through pages of small ads. One listing was circled boldly in red ink.

LOST. *Life experience? Memory? Event? Recapture the gift of time with our help. See history as reality or as the future. Tel: 020 8858 4141.*

Hang on a minute – this was not your normal run of the mill 'sofa for sale' ad. He certainly had an unwanted moment in time that he already unwillingly revisited quite often. But he didn't view that as a gift, so why would he choose to go there again? John tossed the paper to the floor and got under the covers, turned his pillow over to the cold side and laid his head down. Pity he couldn't revisit his chosen moment in time and change it absolutely and completely... then he wouldn't be lying here alone in this half-dazed state. His life would be totally different; he would still have Catherine and the girls. He slept fitfully that night. He heard the rain – really heavy – the same as the night before, but unusually for John, he had no dreams.

The following morning, at breakfast, he sat down at his favourite table with a mug of tea. He still couldn't face any food. The mood in the hostel canteen seemed subdued. They'd probably got wind of his escapade the day before and had decided to give him a wide berth. He kept his head down, finished his tea, and left the canteen to make his way back to his room to consider his plans for the day.

He noticed Ben arriving for his morning shift, and raised his hand in greeting. He hoped Ben's youthful optimism wouldn't cause him to be overly judgemental. But Ben rushed over to him and grasped him by the arm.

"Oh God, John. You must feel really bad... I'm so sorry." Ben's face was creased with concern.

John shrugged his shoulders and formed his face into an apologetic look as if to say 'shit happens'.

"Have the police been yet?" Ben questioned.

"Only last night when they dropped me off."

"Were you with him then? I didn't realise."

"With who?" asked John.

Ben looked confused. "Were you with Paddy when he was killed?"

John allowed the words to replay in his head, and then sink in. "What...? Are you saying Paddy's dead?"

Ben had turned ashen and looked unsteady on his feet. "But I thought you knew..."

John felt nauseous. "What the fuck? When did this happen?" he demanded.

"I'm not sure, he was stabbed... early evening... but he wasn't found until late last night. Pete called me first thing this morning... told me what he knew. I'll find out more at the handover."

"Oh God... I need to sit down."

John ran the short distance to his room and sank down on his bed. He felt as though he was going to be sick. Paddy gone... how the fuck could this have happened? They were meant to be hanging around together yesterday, meant to be drinking together. John should have met Paddy at the pub... but he hadn't. After just a few minutes he was already beginning to blame himself for not being there. He couldn't help feeling a sense of looming dread, after all he'd neglected his best friend... if there could be such a thing in his world. If only he could rewind to yesterday morning and done less dawdling around dwelling on the past, he would have left the hostel with Paddy, then it would have been totally different.

Hold on... what did it say in that paper last night? Something about recapturing time. What the hell did that mean anyway? He snatched up the paper from where it still lay on the floor; who on earth had left it there? Bloody hell, maybe it was Paddy. Somebody had made a particular effort to ensure the advert was seen. There was a number to call. Maybe he should just ring it – what harm could it do to talk to someone? He not only had his nightmares to talk about... there was now Paddy's death.

Clutching the paper, he left his room and went to Ben on reception. "Ben. I need to use the phone."

Ben, still in shock from the news about Paddy, and startled by John's purposeful manner, handed over the phone without uttering a word and moved a respectful distance away. John dialled the number from the paper, and waited impatiently for the few seconds it took for it to be answered.

"Good morning," said a male voice. "Can I help you?"

"Your advert..." said John. "I think I need to talk to someone."

"Okay. Well, my name is Dan and I'm going to take some details and ask you a few questions to see if we can help."

John gave his name and age, and then found himself hesitating before reluctantly giving the hostel address and telephone number. Following these initial details, there were some strange questions about glasses, migraines and tattoos, none of which he had.

"But I do have terrible nightmares," he said. "And I think that's partly what I need to talk about."

"Yes, okay. I think you may benefit from a more detailed chat with me – face to face," said Dan. "One moment, I'll just get my diary – see if we can make an appointment for you."

John noisily drummed his fingers on the reception desk as he waited for Dan to return. "Any news about

Paddy?" he mouthed to Ben, covering the phone with his hand.

"No... Nothing new yet," Ben responded, and John nodded in acknowledgement.

"Would Friday morning suit you?" asked Dan on his return to the conversation.

"I think so," said John, having formed the impression that Dan was some sort of freelance counsellor – that was until he'd suggested that they should meet in the pub.

"Do you know The World's End?" asked Dan.

John nearly dropped the phone; he suddenly went lightheaded and for a brief moment thought he was going to pass out. "What are you on about? Have you been talking to Paddy? I can't be doing with any of this supernatural shit. So if that's what this is all about I'm not interested."

"No, no. It's not that at all," Dan reassured him. "I like to meet in pubs – find it more relaxing. That's the first one I thought of that I know is in your area. If my sister had taken the call she'd have suggested a cafe."

"Would you mind too much if we met in a cafe?" asked John. "I'm not very good in pubs."

CHAPTER 6

Planning Time

Just along from Camden High Street, down a small side road nestled between a newsagent and a drycleaners, stood the Cafe Rasa, a small but very popular coffee shop specialising in New World coffees and Far Eastern teas. John arrived there ten minutes before the pre-arranged meeting time, and waited apprehensively outside for Dan to arrive as agreed. It was a chilly October Friday morning, but John was a hardened outdoor type, and although his attire didn't appear to be ideal for the approaching winter months, it was fine for him.

He spotted Dan as soon as he rounded the corner into the side street, easily identifiable, partly from the description he'd been given – 'tall, black leather bomber jacket, dark gelled-up hair, you can't miss me' – but mainly from Dan's demeanour and bearing.

Dan walked confidently up to John and shook him warmly by the hand. "John? Good morning, I'm Dan

Bradbeer. Shall we go inside?" He pushed open the entrance door to allow John to enter first.

John was thinking Dan reminded him of someone, and then realised with mild shock it was himself in his younger pre-crash days. He hadn't said a word to Dan as yet, but immediately felt comfortable about the meeting. He'd done a lot of thinking over the past three days. He hadn't had any more drink – Paddy's death had scared him. It was about time he tried to get his life back on track. He was ready to talk.

He found his voice. "Would you like tea or coffee, Dan?" They decided on a cappuccino each, both with chocolate sprinkles. John insisted on paying.

Dan scanned the small but cosy café, looking for a table which would offer some privacy from any accidental eavesdroppers. He pointed over to a small table hiding in an alcove – well away from the other customers. "Shall we sit there?"

"I'm not really sure why I'm here..." faltered John, taking his seat at the table. "But I think I'm doing the right thing."

"Well, let's start with your phone call the other day. You mentioned someone called Paddy. In fact you became quite agitated at one point."

"Yes," said John. "Sorry about that, it was when you mentioned the World's End pub – that's where I should have met him the day before I spoke to you. But I didn't make it..." John reached down and took a sip of his coffee to compose himself. "The next morning I found out he'd died – stabbed."

"So you thought I was a psychic and could contact the dead?" Dan smiled ruefully.

"Yeah, something like that," said John. "It freaked me out – I was still a bit hung-over." John tried to make light of his drunken binge.

"Was Paddy a good friend?"

"Yes – and I let him down – that's what made me ring the number." John leant back in his chair. "I even thought briefly that it was Paddy who left the newspaper in my room – but when I had time to think about it properly I realised it couldn't have been him."

"So you're saying someone left a newspaper? At your hostel? And you saw the advert? Was it just a random paper?" Dan questioned.

"No, it wasn't random. The ad... it was circled in red... someone obviously wanted me to see it," replied John, wondering again who it could have been. "But I haven't got a clue who."

Dan looked thoughtful and for a brief moment considered terminating the meeting there and then. The rules of The Time Store were quite simple: tell no-one. But this was borderline, and whoever had left the paper had only planted a seed. For now Dan stayed neutral on the matter, and allowed the meeting to continue. "So now you know I'm not a psychic – what are you thinking will happen from this conversation?"

"I thought you were a counsellor until you suggested meeting at the pub." John smiled hesitantly. "But later that night I started thinking you were some sort of hypnotist who could take me back somehow – to make my peace with what happened. You don't look much like a hypnotist though, not that I've met many."

Dan shook his head. "No... I'm certainly not one of those. Can you imagine the fun if I were any good at it?" He grinned briefly. "Joking aside though – you also mentioned that you have terrible nightmares. But I got the impression these had been happening way before your friend died?"

"Yes, way before." John took a deep breath, and poured out his life story from crash to cafe. "My wife Catherine was killed in a car crash. She was driving, I was the passenger. It happened in torrential rain, almost fifteen years ago. There was nothing anyone could have done to save her – that's what they told me at the time. But I think I could've done something perhaps, before I blacked out. I don't know. Whenever I have the dreams I reach the point where if I opened my eyes in that car I could just see it all... but then I wake. I think that's why I get the nightmares – it just goes over and over in my head – was there anything I could have done to save her? I just wish I could go back there to find out."

"And if you could?" asked Dan. "What would you do? I mean... if you could go back, that is?"

"Not gone away for the weekend. If I could turn back the hands of time and do things differently, I'd... we'd... have done anything but gone away that weekend." John stared down at his barely touched coffee cup. "I so much wish I could just see them all. Kiss them... hug them... be with them."

"Them? Was there anyone else in the car?" questioned Dan.

"No, no..." John looked back up at Dan. "The girls were at their auntie's. It was just Catherine. Just Catherine and me."

John continued to tell Dan about his family and how much he missed his daughters. How much they made him laugh, smile... and at times cry, but mainly with tears of joy.

How well they were doing at school, how much they enjoyed Brownies and being with their friends. He smiled as he recalled family picnics on the banks of the River Severn. Then he told Dan about building sandcastles at Weston beach, and having the girls run to the sea to fetch buckets of water to fill the moat, only for them to watch the sand and the mid-afternoon sun take it as quick as the girls could carry it. John had been a very proud husband and father, and as he recalled his distant memories over the small cafe table, Dan couldn't help but feel for him. John went on to tell Dan about how he lost his daughters, he talked of his plight living amongst the homeless, the ups and downs of his binge drinking problem, just another one of the countless unwanted souls existing on the streets.

After listening to John for nearly an hour Dan knew he had to help this man. Most of the people who Dan encountered wanted help to experience other eras – past and future, or to enhance their lives one way or another, perhaps with money or skills. John just wanted his life back, a simple family life – pretty much in the same way Dan wanted his own mother back.

John felt as though revealing his life had lifted a weight from his heart. He'd not told anyone some of the details he'd confided to Dan – not even Winnie or Paddy. And yet he still didn't know why he was here.

"I'm not used to talking in so much detail about myself these days. But it feels as though it's the right time to be doing it." John inspected his cup of cold coffee. "I really need to find a way to move on now – that's why I rang your number – I'll try anything. Talking about it has made me realise I need help – mainly with analysing the crash. God, it would be so much simpler if I could see it for real, don't you think?" He looked up at Dan, for encouragement, and answers.

Dan was looking directly at him, keeping a very straight face. He didn't say a word... merely raised an eyebrow. John felt his stomach lurch – not with the usual dread that he was accustomed to, but with a childish excitement. A rush of realisation hit him.

He knew what Dan was here for. "Dan?"

"Yes?" said Dan.

"Are you a time traveller?"

Dan tried to hide his shock. A few people had guessed before, but never so soon. "What makes you ask that?" he said, playing for time. "Have you met many time travellers before?"

John felt as though he'd been given a new lease of life.

"I didn't read Tom's Midnight Garden over and over for nothing you know, and God knows how many episodes of The Time Tunnel I watched when I was ..." John paused and remained silent for a few moments, mulling over what he'd just said, trying to mentally put it into context.

"So what would you do, given the chance?" asked Dan, breaking the silence.

"Well. First I need to go back to a few days ago – the morning of Paddy's death – so we can leave the hostel together – then he'll be alive!"

"Mate, I'm sorry," interrupted Dan.

"I know you can travel in time." John ploughed on. "Once we've sorted Paddy, I need to go back further. To save Catherine!"

Dan felt awful. The anticipation was transparent on John's face; lighting and lifting him up, making him look so alive and so much younger and healthier. But he knew he had to dowse him down. "Do you think you could you do that? I mean wouldn't that be changing time?"

"Why not? What would be the point in going back if you can't change anything?"

"Would you want anyone to be able to go back in time and stop... erm... Kennedy from getting assassinated, for example? What would have happened in the world if he'd have lived? I'm not saying it would have been any better or any worse for you and me. But for thousands, perhaps millions it would have been."

"So what you're saying is... that even if you could really send me back in time, I wouldn't be allowed to make any changes?"

"You can change one thing," replied Dan, smiling. "You can change how you feel – I mean, supposing you could actually go back – to the accident that is. Then you might see that you were helpless to do anything, and perhaps your torment would stop."

John slumped in his chair. "I understand that, and yes, that would be good. But not being able to save Catherine, that can't be right..."

Dan nodded. "Yes. It is." He stood up. "Another drink?" Not waiting for an answer, he just turned and walked towards the counter.

John was shaking his head, for a brief moment unable to speak. Bloody hell, he'd been potentially given the gift of time nicely wrapped up like a Christmas present – he was expecting the latest gadget, but all he'd got was a pack of hankies and a poxy Christmas jumper. But John's boyhood fascination with time travel had been re-awakened, and as Dan returned, John looked at him with a scaled down version of his initial hope.

"Listen, I didn't realise the time. I have to go – I have a meeting to attend. Here's a coffee." Dan placed the drink down on the table.

"What will happen now?"

"I'll discuss your needs with my family today, at the meeting. If we think we can help you then we'll be in touch."

"When?" demanded John, standing so as to be able to look Dan straight in the face.

"You'll either receive an invitation to our offices, or, and no pun intended, a Dear John letter within the next few days," answered Dan.

"How soon is the appointment likely to be?" John pressed.

"Oh... we like to do those pretty quickly. So it'll be next week, probably Wednesday or Thursday." Dan then shook John warmly by the hand and left the Cafe Rasa.

After Dan had left for his meeting John remained in the cafe. Sitting alone clutching his coffee cup, the doubts set in.

When he'd been talking to Dan, he was absolutely convinced that Dan was somehow a seasoned time traveller who could help him return to the moment of the crash. Dan had let a few things slip, and had dropped a couple of hints without completely admitting it. So why hadn't Dan just revealed his time travelling abilities the minute John had guessed? Was this a massive wind-up? No, it couldn't be... however far-fetched and science-fiction-like it might sound,

John was sure it was all true and possible. So therefore – and here John was surprised at his logical train of thought – therefore, there must be another reason for Dan not enthusiastically patting him on the back, shaking him by the hand and saying, 'Yes, mate. You worked that one out quick enough. Let's catapult ourselves back to 1994 right now and sort it out.'

Shit, so if he had no doubts about Dan – and God knows he probably should have – that meant that Dan was having doubts about him. John was overwhelmed with a sudden burning panic. He needed air. He stood up quickly, almost knocking over his still warm cup. Ignoring his light-headedness he stumbled towards the door of the cafe, and out into the fresh October air.

He careered his way back towards the hostel, breathing deeply, trying to calm himself down. A few streets later, he had his body back under some sort of control, but his mind was still racing. He couldn't face the sameness of the hostel right now, and as he passed the church grounds he decided to go in. He sat down on one of the new teak memorial benches by the moss-encrusted gravestones.

Dan had mentioned that he had a meeting with his family at which they would discuss whether they could help him. Help him? How many others were they planning on helping? How would they decide? They must choose him... He was fairly sure Dan would fight his corner... but what about the rest of his family?

And there was another thing – John had been a tad over-enthusiastic about altering a great massive chunk of time. Dan had very heavily implied that this was not allowed. "Please, Dan. Don't let that put you off," he implored under his breath.

Oh God, maybe they were discussing him right this minute and rejecting him. 'Ooh far too risky,' one of them would be saying. Also there was the issue of the newspaper and the circled ad. Dan had questioned him somewhat fiercely about this – as if it wasn't allowed – another factor towards him not being accepted – although that was hardly his fault. How was he to know every person who time-travelled was supposed to keep it secret. He needed to find out soon who was responsible for that bloody advert – so he could either thank them... or curse them.

He looked across at the old weatherworn gravestones, and realised with a sickening agony that he'd not been to Catherine's grave for years... and years; too embroiled in his own sad and sorry life to pay any basic respect. He was sure his girls, Alice and Emma, were having a good life, but how had he lost touch so easily? At the first hurdle of the lost address and the doorstep abuse from Brian Cooper, he'd not made any further attempts to locate them for several years. When he did finally resume his paltry efforts to make another search, the Coopers had moved on.

"I'm sorry... I'm sorry. So sorry, Catherine. I'll find them... I'll get them back for you." John put his head in his hands and silently sobbed fifteen years' worth of tears.

After a while, he looked up. The afternoon sun had moved behind the gnarled yew trees, and it was becoming colder. He saw Father Elston standing outside the church doors. John stood up from the bench and walked towards him with a new found purposefulness. If Dan could somehow let him see Catherine, he could settle things in his head, and then begin his quest to find the girls.

"Afternoon, John," said Father Elston. "I've been standing here for some time. I hope I did right by leaving you alone."

"I think so... yes," responded a much calmer John. "I had some stuff I needed to sort out in my head."

"And is it sorted now?" asked Father Elston, shivering slightly in his cassock.

"Hopefully," replied John. "Hopefully... Although I need someone to agree to help me first."

CHAPTER 7

Items on the Agenda

Jason looked at his watch once again, and then stared at the door with an impatient look before releasing a loud sigh. Sarah agitatedly straightened the pile of papers sitting on the table in front of her, reached for a small glass of iced water, took one sip and then replaced it on the table.

"Where the hell is he?"

"Dunno," replied Sarah, trying not to sound frustrated. "I know he had an appointment over in Camden, but I thought he'd be back in time."

Most Fridays were the same for the Bradbeer clan. At around one o'clock they'd meet up and discuss each of the clients they'd met up with over the past few days – the following week's potential time travellers. It was nearing twenty past before Dan finally turned up clutching two clear A4 folders similar to the ones in front of Sarah.

"Sorry, guys." Dan pulled out a chair and sat down. "Some fucking idiot had left a bag on the tube at Goodge Street… It shut the Northern Line down for nearly an hour. They stopped my train between Euston and Warren Street."

"Okay. No problem, you're here now." Jason's frustration eased as he understood his younger brother's tardiness was outside his control. "Let's do clients first and then discuss where we are with the exhibition items. How many have you both got?"

"Three in total, I've not managed to prepare notes for the third as I only met him this morning."

"Same here, three," replied Sarah.

"Good. I've also got three, plus one from Dad to look at as well. Shall I start?"

There was no answer to that question from either Sarah or Dan, both just accepted that he would start. Jason opened up the first of his four folders, took out three sheets of paper and passed one to each of his siblings.

"Okay. This is Rob Gifford, from West Heath, Birmingham." They all turned their page over to look at a small photograph of a gaunt looking man. "Rob is forty-three and married to Tina. He's recently been diagnosed with terminal brain cancer, although from what I'm told he's suffered from some symptoms for quite a while." Jason scanned his notes looking for the details. "These are... weakness, difficulty walking, seizures and headaches."

"Did the doctors not pick it up in time for anything to be done?" asked Dan.

"Apparently not. Anyway, Rob's wife is expecting their first child early in May, but if the consultant's prognosis is right Rob only has, at best, another three or four months to live. So I'm suggesting that we take him on the usual two trips..."

"Birth and first day at school?" interrupted Sarah.

"Yes, that's it. But I'd want you two to take a trip

first – make sure that there are no complications. We can't have this poor guy going into the future to watch his wife lose their child in labour."

Both Sarah and Dan nodded in agreement. "Is there anything in it for us?" enquired Dan.

"Not really. We've already been as far forward as 2075 in Birmingham and all the important timepieces in the area are still intact up until then." Jason put his paper back into the folder. "Right... What do you think?"

Jason was asking Dan and Sarah for their approval to accept Rob Gifford as a client and take him into the future.

"Risk?" asked Sarah.

"Very minimal on trip one, as I'm sure Rob wouldn't want to jeopardise seeing his child attend school. On trip two it'll be more distant, there'll be lots of people around, so again I don't see a risk, especially as no-one will be expecting to see him."

"Okay. Put a scarf round his face and I'm happy," said Sarah, handing Jason her copy of Rob's details.

"Me too," replied Dan.

"Good. Then we'll go for next Wednesday, mid-morning. Rob has told me that he can come to London anytime for a consultation. Can you check everything out before then, please?" Jason directed this towards Sarah.

"Yes. I'll sort out the details and let you know what's happening. My turn?" Sarah handed to her brothers a sheet each from her top folder.

"Go for it," smiled Dan, accepting his sheet.

"Next we have Richard Upton from Coventry. I'm not too sure about this one to be truthful. Personally I'm on the fence, as it's a bit close to the bone with true time. Let's see what you two think." Sarah reached down and took another sip of her iced water. "Richard appears to have lost his lottery ticket, a winning lottery ticket."

"Hold on, Sarah. You know the rules. I didn't think the word lottery was allowed at these meetings."

"I know, Jase. However, I think – well I hope – this one is somewhat different. Richard plays and has played the same five lines for at least three years. He's been able to show me some old tickets all with the same selections including what would have been a winning line for the first August draw this year."

Dan had a feeling that this one would be over pretty quickly and reached into his top folder for his first potential client's details, one of which he handed to his brother. The other he placed down in front of Sarah.

"Thanks," said Jason, accepting his sheet.

"Are you two listening to a word I'm saying?" demanded Sarah. "This guy, Richard Upton, was mugged at knifepoint for his wallet and phone. He has eighteen stitches down his right arm where he was slashed."

"Sarah. That's a matter for the police, not us. We can't be going back in time to catch every petty criminal, can we? What do you think this is – *Crime Traveller*?"

"No. I know that. But all Richard wants to find out is where he put the ticket he bought - is it in his wallet or his jacket? He's turned his house upside down several times looking for it."

"What about the shop's cameras?" asked Dan.

"Not working..." Sarah replied.

"Okay. We need to move on," interrupted Jason.

"I'm not happy with this one, Sarah. You should've known better than to even get involved with a lottery ticket... I'm saying no to this one. Dan?"

Dan knew that Jason wasn't in any mood to have tit-for-tat discussions, as his unavoidable lateness had probably wound him up too much. "Shall we park this one, come back to it later? Maybe the two of us could go back and see where he put the ticket – at least that way we don't run any risk. Have a think. My turn next." Dan didn't give Jason the opportunity to reply.

Sarah smiled a thank you towards Dan for his input and especially for not dismissing her client completely. However, Dan would've normally had the same opinion as Jason about this, but he knew he needed Sarah's support if he was ever going to get their approval for John Brewer's journey back.

"My first is one which will interest you, Jase." He directed his opening towards his brother, who was looking at the photograph of a young woman in her mid-twenties on the back of Dan's sheet. "This is Leigh Hancock. She's from Pyecombe, just outside Brighton. Leigh is studying history, especially 1066, Battle of Hastings, Harold et cetera."

Jason's ears pricked up on hearing the date 1066, as it was by far his most favourite year in pre-medieval English history. Any opportunity to go back to East Sussex and the time of the Norman Conquest appealed to him.

"Leigh has this theory from research that the battle didn't actually take place on Senlac Hill at all, but Caldbec Hill."

"What? You're saying that she thinks Harold stood his ground and didn't actually advance at all?" asked Jason.

"Come on, Jase. You've been back there. You'll already know if she's right or not."

"Yes. But my God. Do you know how many history books would need re-writing?"

"So is she right?" asked Sarah.

"Well, let's put it this way, she could be. I'd just be worried about an army of metal detecting morons descending on Malfose Ditch if we take her back in time."

"Well, does that mean you don't approve then?" questioned Dan.

"I didn't say that... but I'd like to talk to her first, before I decide," answered Jason.

"How does she think we're going to help her?" Sarah chipped in.

"Oh... genealogy, heraldry, that sort of thing. I did drop a travel hint in our meet, but she didn't pick up on it. I think she's keen to research as much as she can from any source... even us," laughed Dan.

"Well, I'm in if you two are, and I'd like to do the trip with you."

"I'm sure you would, Sarah. I'm sure you would," Jason replied to his sister, still smiling from Dan's comment. "Arrange for her to come here. We'll take her to the Battle of Fulford or perhaps Stamford Bridge first, let her see what we can do."

"Okay. I'll arrange this for next Wednesday as well." With that Dan placed his sheet with Leigh's details back in his folder. "Sandwiches... coffee?"

"Yes, good idea. I'll put the kettle on." Sarah stood up and walked over to the small kitchen area of the room, filled the kettle and began to make the drinks. Dan opened the fridge and took out a carrier bag with some baguettes that Sarah had bought earlier from a local deli.

"I think you could be right about the lottery ticket, Dan. Perhaps we could go and take a look at what happened," Jason commented, whilst his brother and sister were preparing their lunch. Sarah smiled inwardly.

"We could do it this afternoon if you want, get it out of the way," suggested Dan, sitting back down.

"Let's see how quickly we get through these first. Right, mine again," replied Jason.

Over the course of the next hour or so the three of them discussed six more potential time travel clients. The second of Jason's involved taking Sean Watts, a toilet cleaner from East Grinstead, back to the time of the Roman Empire. Rob wanted to go back to Rome, 80 A.D. to experience a day at the Flavian Amphitheatre in its opening glory. This trip was passed by the trio, with several minor conditions. Jason's third was for steam train enthusiast Deb Beijer from The Netherlands to be allowed to take a trip to see Stephenson's Blucher locomotive haul coal for the first time back in July 1814, followed by a journey from London to Edinburgh on The Flying Scotsman. Again the three of them passed these time trips for Deb with no cause for concern.

The second of Sarah's potential clients was Wendy Bell, an administrator at the American Embassy in London. She had discussed with Sarah, over coffee and a slice of carrot cake, her fascination with the women's suffrage movement in the early 20th century. Wendy wanted more than anything to witness the brave actions of Emily Davison at the 1913 Epsom Derby. This was rejected, as Emily died whilst allegedly attempting to throw a 'Votes for Women' sash on the King's horse. However, the team decided that they could take her back to perhaps meet Emmeline Pankhurst, another significant person in the suffrage movement, should she wish.

Sarah's next probable time traveller was Ian Jacques, a vet from Braintree, Essex. Ian was, as Dan would quite often put it, 'another dinosaur chaser'. Ian wanted to be able to go back to the dawn of time when prehistoric monsters ruled the earth and see them in all their majestic splendour. These trips were always passed by the trio and the client would always be taken back by David.

Sarah wasn't happy with Dan's second one, although she didn't disapprove of it with as much vigour as she intended, as Dan had helped her out earlier. He, on the other hand, would have preferred it more if she had rejected this one and left her support for his last one, John's. However, Jason fully supported this trip for Geoff Pears to go back to the American Wild West and take part on a cattle drive. Geoff wanted to ride the Chisholm Trail between San Antonio, Texas and Abilene, Kansas. Dan was a better horse rider than Jason and the time trip would mean that he and Geoff would be spending two months in 1870 riding the trail. They pencilled this in for Thursday morning at 9.15 followed quickly by Dan taking a trip to the year 2751 for two months age rejuvenation at the Harrogate Tec-Spa.

"Right, what's your last one about then, Dan?" asked Sarah.

"Can we leave that one until after Dad's if you don't mind? Please..." Dan stood up. "Back in a mo... excuse me, nature calls."

"Okay, another drink?" Sarah didn't receive any answers but she still went to the kettle, filled it and began to make the three of them another drink.

"You're still not keen on the long trips are you?"

"No, Jase. No, I'm not." She turned and looked at her brother. "You know what happened with me and that idiot who wanted to sail the Titanic last year. I was stuck on that bloody boat..."

"I know, I know," interrupted Jason. "Five days, I know. But that's hardly a long trip is it? You've done longer, you even did the Land's End to John O'Groats walk with Tracey Doyle last week, and that took over thirty days."

"Yeah whatever, Jase! That's in this bloody country and every step was planned to the last detail. You... no, we... are going to let our kid brother go back and play at being a cowboy with real guns. Look what happened at Gallipoli for Christ's sake."

"Sarah! That was completely different – that was war. This is the west – cowboys, horses and cattle," replied Jason, reacting to Sarah's snap at him.

Sarah placed both hands firmly on the table and leaned in towards where Jason was still sitting. "Hello! They don't call it the Wild West for nothing you know!" She straightened and went across to the now boiled kettle, just as Dan came back.

"Have I missed anything?" Dan could sense that in the few brief moments he'd been gone, the atmosphere in the room had altered.

"Not really. Our sister was expressing her concern about us placing you in possible danger for a long period of time," Jason informed him with an almost condescending tone which was more aimed towards Sarah.

"Oh, come on. It's gonna be awesome. Horses, guns, cowboys..."

"Boys," tutted Sarah. "*Brokeback Mountain* springs to mind here."

"Brokeback what?" asked Dan.

"Nothing... nothing, just a film. Perhaps you should watch it before you go," she replied sarcastically.

The three of them then returned to the matter in hand.

"Okay. Let's discuss Dad's." Jason handed out information sheets. "This is a really lovely couple from Swansea, Albert and Sylvia Smith. They're about to celebrate their platinum wedding anniversary."

"Wow. Seventy years together, amazing," said Sarah.

"Yes, and Dad wants to take them back to the day they first met, January 17th 1939. They were married that November just before Albert was conscripted into the Royal Navy. This was shortly after his twentieth birthday," continued Jason.

"Where did they meet?" Sarah was getting quite sentimental.

"They met on The Mumbles Pier... shared a dodgem car. A ride which was to last a lifetime. Dad wants them to be able to watch their first meeting again, then share a fish and chip supper on the pier."

"How does he know them?" asked Dan.

"Albert saved our granddad from drowning during their basic training. Without him, none of us would be here," replied Jason. There was no need for any deliberating and it was sorted that David and Sarah would make the journey to Swansea next Thursday afternoon and fetch them back here.

"Right, Dan. Let's have the last one then," prompted Sarah.

"Okay. Apologies for not having prepped, but I've only just returned from meeting him." Dan took a sip of his coffee. "John Brewer is a homeless street beggar and an alcoholic." He paused. "Actually that's not quite right as he's accommodated in a church hostel in Camden, but he's still a beggar and a fairly regular drinker... John's not always been down on his luck though, not always been one of society's dregs, and certainly not always suffered from a booze problem." Dan stood up; he wanted the higher ground to pitch John's case to the others.

"Pretty much exactly fifteen years ago he was a loving family man, good job, nice home – two lovely daughters and a beautiful wife – Catherine, with whom he was going away for a romantic weekend. This weekend marks the fifteenth anniversary of the horrific car accident which took the life of his wife and became the catalyst for the downward spiral leading to where he is today."

"Dan. We can't..."

"Let me finish please, Jase. Hear me out." Dan reached down for another drink, but this time took some of Sarah's water before continuing. "In the aftermath of the accident John couldn't care for his daughters and they went to live with their aunt. He couldn't bear work, driving... well anything. Unfortunately he shunned professional help and found solace in a bottle. Over the following years he lost his job, his home, his girls – John Brewer effectively lost his life."

"This is all sad, Dan. But we can't bring people back from the dead – you of all people should know that."

"Yes. I'm well aware of that," he replied to his sister. "But that's not what this is about. There's been many a time that John has wanted to pull himself up, build his life anew – make a fresh start, but there's a problem." Dan was lying, not a blatant out and out lie – just a small evasion of the facts, as Dan hadn't discussed with John whether he'd tried to rebuild his life or not.

"Which is…?"

"Nightmares. John Brewer quite often has terrible nightmares. He relives the crash through the torment of unstoppable dreams. Whenever it rains heavily – on those nights, he once again lives through his own personal tragedy, his own personal hell. Since the crash and losing his soul mate, this man has gone through a series of setbacks to be where he is now, where we are now. His wife, gone... His children, gone... His home and job, gone... and more recently his best friend Patrick, gone – murdered, perhaps killed for the few small coins he carried – or just because he was homeless and an easy target."

Dan was aiming his pitch at their heartstrings. He was now in full flow of his sales spiel, as that's what it had become... he had to sell John's story to the two people closest to him – they were not only his brother and sister, but also his best friends.

"Alright, Dan. We get the picture. But what are you suggesting, what can we do for him?" Jason had accepted that John needed help, but he wasn't too sure if it could, or would, come from The Time Store.

"John believes, and I agree with him, if he could just witness the crash, see it for himself, see that he was helpless to have done anything to save Catherine. Then, and only then, his nightmares might stop."

"So you're asking if we'd allow him to go back in time so he can see his wife die all over again?" quizzed Sarah, straightening her folders as if to ready them for leaving. "I think not. There's too much uncertainty."

"I have to agree with Sarah on this one. The risk of altering true time is too high. We can't take a chance on him attempting to stop the crash, or trying to dive in and save her," added Jason.

"Come on, guys. True time my arse." Dan spoke louder. "You both know it's a load of bollocks and we all change true time the moment we go back and with every little action we make. The second any of us interact with someone in the past... buy anything, eat anything or whatever... then we change true time."

"DANIEL!" A shout came from the direction of the now open door. All three had failed to notice their father enter the room. "What's all this about? What's going on here? Can't the three of you have these meetings without one of you getting all high and mighty about something?" David pulled up a chair and sat at the table with his children. "Arguing over true time isn't going to move anything forward. You won't get anywhere, not anywhere at all."

The three siblings remained silent whilst their father was talking, as if they were three small children being told off for using colouring pens on their bedroom wallpaper.

"How many have you been through?"

"Nine. This one of Dan's was the last," Jason replied.

"Right. Let's get something sorted before we move on shall we? That jaunt of yours, the other night – that should've been the top of your agenda, not all this." David slammed his hand down on one of the files. "Why did you bring a severed hand back from the seventeen-hundreds?"

"I couldn't get the bracelet off," said Jason.

"We thought we heard someone coming," said Dan.

"So he took an axe," glared Sarah.

"Right," sighed David. "The man in question – the owner of this hand – was definitely dead? Before the arm chopping incident? Before your decision to deprive him of it?"

"Yes, of course. Sarah checked for a pulse." Jason looked indignant. "And he looked dead."

"And have we any idea who this poor unfortunate man was?"

"No clue at all," said Sarah. "But the house looked nice back then."

"Yeah, very new," said Dan.

"We've examined the bracelet now," added Sarah. "There are marks on it, but we can't decipher them, so still no clue."

"What did you do with the hand?"

"And part of the arm..." pointed out Dan.

"Well, once I'd managed to get the bracelet off, I mounted it and put it on display in the Globe Room," said Jason.

"No need to be flippant, Jason," said David. "Have you incinerated it?"

"It's in the freezer compartment." Jason glanced across to the fridge in the corner.

"Good. Can you arrange to get it fingerprinted? And get a DNA sample while you're at it," suggested David.

"Didn't think of that," acknowledged Jason. "But yes, that's a good idea."

"Fine," said David, trying to bring the discussion to an end. "We're agreed then – more investigation is needed. Who was the man? And why did he have one of our bracelets?"

"I'll do it," said Jason.

"Good, but it's not desperately urgent – probably some drunken workman back then who nicked our bracelet. Probably not important in the grand scheme of things."

"The family hadn't moved in at that point in time – so there were no possessions in the house." Jason clarified what he knew for sure. "It would have probably been easier to get answers if they had."

"Okay, at least you're looking for answers. Keep on the case, Jason. But only when you have a spare moment. Probably a good job you brought the bracelet back."

"Yeah – that's why I chopped his hand off – to get the fucking bracelet back!"

"Don't swear," said David. "But yes, I take your point. No further discussion now. Okay – let's move on to this client you were just discussing – who is it? What's it about?"

Dan started to once again tell the story of John Brewer, but this time keeping very much to the facts, including the addition of the newspaper article. "So that's about it. John could perhaps put his life back together if he can put an end to the nightmares." Dan wound up the recap.

"Your brother and sister are right to question you on the risk, Daniel. So would I. Have you given that any thought?"

"Yes. Yes I have... lots. I've been stuck on the underground for an hour mulling it over and over. I know there's an element of unpredictability with everything we do. We put ourselves and our clients at risk when we take them on their adventures – and yes, Sarah, I know the west was wild. But Dad... this is what we do... this is what our lives are about. We travel in time." Dan paused, took a deep breath, thought not only about what he was going to say... but also more importantly whether he should say it at all. He decided to go for it.

"This man – John Brewer – wants to find his girls, his daughters. He wants to move on from where he is. We're not only helping him – we're also helping his daughters find a father – find their lost parent. Time travel is a gift. The four of us in this room have the ability to topple governments, we could prevent Hitler from being born, we could save countless lives from plane crashes and disasters... Christ we could be anyone or anything we want to be, we could be richer than Bill Gates, more powerful than Red China..." Dan hesitated and looked down at the table. "But we aren't, are we? We aren't powerful at all... we don't control time. Time controls us. If we could do anything... then Mum would still be here. Wouldn't she?"

"That's not fair, Dan," protested Sarah. "You can't bring Mum into this."

"Alright, enough. I agree with Dan," said Jason sharply, and although none of his children saw it, this comment prompted a smile from David.

"You do?"

"Yes. I completely agree with you that we are in a position to offer assistance to this man. Providing that you can put an infallible plan in place, one where John can't – in any circumstances – prevent his wife from dying, and then I'll agree to it," Jason replied. "Now if there's nothing else, can we adjourn this until Dan has his plan? Sarah, will you send out all the invites please?"

"Yes, Jase. What about Mr Brewer's?"

"Get that one ready. Let's see if Dan's proposal is any good, before we send it. Right – where are we with the items we're lending to the museum exhibition?"

The Time Store had been contacted by the British Museum who was keen to put together a World of Timepieces exhibition to coincide with the 2012 London Olympics. The Bradbeers saw this as an opportunity to free up some much needed space, especially in the Globe Room, and although they weren't too happy with the exhibition leaving the country for a couple of years, they were pleased to be doing their bit for 2012.

"Everything's to plan. Simon Ward from the museum and the man from the insurers are both due in for final acceptance and collection next Friday," relayed David. "So, all okay there."

CHAPTER 8

Clepsydra

On that Friday after his meeting with Dan and his interlude at the churchyard, John eventually returned to the hostel in time for the evening meal. He polished off a plate of fish and chips and a large portion of apple pie, and as most of the other permanent residents were beginning to leave the canteen, he was approached by Pete, who sat down opposite him. "Just to let you know that Paddy's funeral is set for next Friday... eleven in the morning... I thought you'd probably want to be there."

"Yes of course," answered John. "Although it won't be much of a send-off for him I don't suppose."

"You might be surprised," said Pete. "It's not going to be extravagant, but Paddy had a lot of mates... and word's got around, so hopefully a good many of them will turn up for it."

"Well, I'll definitely be there. I've got nothing else on." John attempted a weak joke.

Pete smiled. "You're cheery today."

"Maybe," John agreed. "But I think it's more like I'm trying to mask my stress levels." He was fishing for evidence, and was examining Pete's face for any revealing signs that he was the one who'd strategically left the newspaper. "I'm waiting for something to arrive in the post."

"Tell me more..." said Pete guilelessly.

"Nah, not yet... I'll maybe tell you about it in a few days." Having briefly brought up the subject John swerved rapidly away, convinced Pete had nothing to do with it.

John spent the remaining hours of that Friday evening chatting to a few of the hostel regulars, partly to pass the time without too much over-thinking about whether Dan would reply in his favour, and partly to try to ascertain whether any of them had left the newspaper. He was unsuccessful on both counts.

At about 9pm he retired to his room and settled into bed. He was exhausted, more mentally than physically, and he fell easily into a deep sleep.

On the Saturday, John went out onto the streets to beg. He worked hard all day, chatting to tourists, shoppers and students. He moved location a few times to take advantage of where he thought there would be more people. He posed for photographs and gave a potted history of London to an old American couple on their first visit to the capital. At lunchtime he treated himself to a chicken sandwich and coffee, but otherwise didn't spend any of his takings, and at about half past four he made his way back to the hostel, stopping off at his favourite Lo-Cost Liquor to change up his coins to notes.

"Usual, mate?" said Mick the shop manager, reaching for a bottle of whisky.

"Urm… Not today, thanks," replied John. "I'd really like one, but I've got other plans for this money."

Mick counted out three twenty pound notes, one ten and a five. Raising his eyebrows, he handed the notes to John, along with a few spare coins. "Blimey, if you get any better at this you'll be able to do it for a living," Mick commented, as a stunned but satisfied John left the shop.

A day outside without the numbing effect of alcohol had given John an unusual feeling of exhilaration. He felt as though he'd actually achieved something. Feeling successful was something he'd not experienced for a good while, and although he reasoned he had not particularly accomplished anything significant, it gave him a taste of what he hoped was to come. He figured his future could depend on whether or not he was allowed to go back in time to make his peace with the whole crash scene. However, if this didn't happen, he had to stay positive to find the girls. He was determined now. He hadn't had a drink for four days, out of choice not poverty, and he planned to continue in this way. He had a purpose, and when he found the girls, he didn't want them to be ashamed of him.

He returned to the hostel in time for a delicious meal of cottage pie, broccoli and sweetcorn, followed by ice-cream for dessert. He half-watched the National Lottery's game show on the recently installed television, and then, for the second night in a row, went to bed early, and slept peacefully.

On Sunday, he woke early, showered and shaved before breakfast, and then decided to go to church. He was not religious, never had been, but he felt the need to be around people who possibly did believe. Plus he quite fancied singing a few hymns.

Father Elston noticed him amongst the congregation and nodded in acknowledgement, pleased that John had turned up to a service for the first time in years.

Following a selection of rousing hymns and a very interesting sermon about moving on and being positive, John made his way out of church feeling buoyant; almost religious.

Father Elston was standing near the doors. "Morning, John," he said. "Would you mind waiting a minute? I need to have a quick word."

For the next few minutes the parish priest continued to shake hands and converse with his departing parishioners, then he turned back to speak to John.

"I'm so pleased to see you here. How are you keeping?" he asked.

"Good, I'm good, thanks," replied John, not wanting to go into any detail.

"We have Patrick Kelly's funeral this Friday... I trust you'll be attending?"

Seeing John nodding in agreement, he continued. "I wanted to ask you something. The funeral director enquired about Patrick having any family, and carrying the coffin... You're the only one I could think of – I know he was a very good friend of yours. Do you mind if I put your name forward? Only if you're up to it, you understand."

John hesitated, confused.

Father Elston felt the need to clarify what he was asking. "Will you be a pallbearer?"

John was taken aback – shocked, but honoured.

"Yes of course," he replied. "Of course I will."

He dropped some loose change into the donation box as he departed, remembering guiltily a time in his past where he'd swiped coins from the collection plate during a service. It was about time he started giving something back, monetary and otherwise... he'd been take, take, take for far too long.

He spent the afternoon walking and thinking... and returned to the hostel in time for a roast beef dinner, complete with Yorkshires and horseradish. John was appreciating his food far more since he'd stopped his alcohol intake. He had a bigger appetite and everything seemed to have much more flavour.

Yet again, he retired to his room early... third night in succession.

On Monday morning, John rose early. Already dressed, but still in his threadbare slippers, he padded down to the canteen. He was the first one in, so he made himself a coffee, and sat down at his favourite table. He noticed Winnie arriving for her morning shift. She hung up her coat, rearranged a few plates and put a couple of slices of bread in the toaster. She busied herself putting out some cereals, milk and bowls on the small table next to the counter and then retrieved the now toasted bread and put it on a plate.

Winnie approached John, looking distraught. "I'm sorry about Paddy," she said, handing him the toast. "I heard last week, but I haven't seen you since. How are you coping?"

"Well... not too bad now," replied John, taking the plate from Winnie. "Although obviously it was a shock. Father Elston has asked me to carry the coffin at the funeral.

Will you be there?"

"Yes of course." Winnie seemed distracted. "Better go and do some work, eh?" She hurried back to the kitchen area as a few more people came into the canteen.

John was, in fact, glad of her conscientiousness, he was ravenous and just wanted to be left alone to eat. Plus he didn't want any further analysis of the sweat-ridden nightmare that she'd witnessed last week. He spread the toast with butter and apricot jam from the pots on his table, and took a couple of large bites, followed by a few swigs of coffee.

He heard someone calling his name, and looked round to see Ben approaching from the doorway. "Something's arrived for you, John," announced Ben, looking intrigued.

Mail, even for the regular hostel dwellers, was a somewhat infrequent occurrence, and the envelope was not of the usual white or brown basic business type, so John was aware that Ben's curiosity was piqued even further. John guessed, from Ben's quizzical expression, that he was not the small-ad culprit. The envelope was cream-coloured and made of thick vellum paper. John knew immediately where it had come from; his thudding heart told him in no uncertain terms.

"Thanks, Ben," he replied, as nonchalantly as he could manage, placing the envelope down on the table. He had no intention of opening it in front of Ben, who, finally realising he was not to be enlightened, skulked back to reception.

John snatched the envelope back off the table. No postmark... but there was a stamp... looked like someone had decided to deliver it by hand. His heart thumped fiercely, and he felt the cold sweat of anticipation. The contents could determine his future... and his past. The other hostel goers were oblivious to his apprehension as he slit open the envelope with his knife, and removed the contents. A card. Not a letter... and on the card, a simple typed message:

THE TIME STORE
No.5 Flamsteed Way, Greenwich
LONDON SE10 9LZ.
Tel: 020 8858 4141

Your appointment with Daniel Bradbeer
has been set for:

10:00 a.m. Wednesday 14th October 2009.

"Oh. My. God," John spluttered.

Two days' time, two days to prepare himself. He replaced the card in the envelope. As he did so, John had a very clear impression in his mind's eye of the preceding three days since his meeting with Dan, strikingly juxtaposed with the forthcoming two days which would culminate in his visit to The Time Store; two distinct phases of time cleaved apart by one simple appointment card.

He gulped the last of his coffee, and although still hungry, his stomach was too jittery to have any further food intake, so he left the remaining toast on the plate. He stood up, and as he did so, glanced across at Winnie, who was standing quite still, not her usual bustling self at all. She was watching him, with the merest hint of a smile upon her face.

"Bloody hell," uttered John under his breath as realisation dawned on him.

He went over to her on his way out of the canteen. "Oh by the way, Winnie – thanks for last week."

Winnie looked a tad uneasy. "Last week?"

"Yes, you know... thanks for your help last week. When I had that bad nightmare."

"Oh, oh... yes... no problem..." Winnie blustered.

"See you on Friday," said John as he made his way out of the canteen clutching the envelope.

Ben was mopping the floor of the bunk room as John walked past. "Anything interesting?" queried Ben, failing to disguise his curiosity.

"Nah, not really," bluffed John. "Just got somewhere to go on Wednesday morning. Actually, I'll be busy, with the funeral as well. I'm going out now – to see if I can buy some new clothes from the second-hand shop."

He started walking towards his room, but then paused, and turned back to Ben. "I've been thinking recently about trying to track down my daughters – haven't seen them in years – would you be able to do some research on your computer? I wouldn't know where to start."

"Yes, yes, I'd be happy to," said Ben, pleased to have a bit of potential detective work to distract him from his studies.

"Good, shall we discuss it at the weekend? As soon

as the funeral is out of the way?" Seeing Ben nod in agreement, John continued. "But in the meantime, would you do me another favour, ready for Wednesday morning? I have to get to Greenwich – would you be able to print out a map for me?"

"No probs," said Ben.

John returned to his room, and placed the envelope, still containing the card, on his bedside table whilst he put on his shoes and overcoat. Leaving forty pounds in his drawer to put towards his hostel fees John put the remainder of his earnings from two days ago into his pocket. He picked up the envelope once more, removing the card to re-read the details. "The Time Store..." Idly he turned over the card in his hand.

On the back... he hadn't noticed before... were some hand-written words. *You were right / Dan.*

"Fucking hell," said John, aloud. "I'm gonna be a time traveller." He quickly looked around to ensure nobody had heard him, but then realised he was in his own room.

With a feeling of exhilaration, John set out from St. Michael's hostel. It was as if a black cloud had lifted, not only from his mind, but from the buildings, trees, roads and people. It all seemed so bright and fresh and clean. The world was great.

He walked to the high street where he took time browsing in three charity shops in search of some new attire. He found the ideal pair of trousers and a black tie in the third shop, but had no luck with anything else, and eventually decided to splash out on a twin pack of brand new shirts from the nearby Sainsbury's. He also bought another more colourful tie, thinking that if all these clothes weren't appropriate for time travel, they would definitely come in useful the following week, when he would need to look smart to begin the search for Emma and Alice.

He treated himself to a caramel macchiato latte and a cream cake in a small coffee shop. As he sat enjoying this rare luxury he assessed his finances. After his spree, he had some loose change, a few pound coins and a ten pound note. He would need to hang on to that tenner – he owed Dan a bloody good drink.

Winnie had gone by the time John returned to the hostel, but he smiled a secret smile as he cherished the thought of what she had done for him.

Another early night, and then Tuesday was spent preparing for his trip. With Ben's help, together with the map of Greenwich, John planned his route. Satisfied that he'd accomplished all his tasks, he enjoyed a pasta meal in the canteen and spent the last night in his room before his journey.

On the morning of his appointment with Daniel Bradbeer, John set out from the hostel with an almost boyish skip in his step, his hands deep in the pockets of his second-hand, premium quality overcoat, his right hand clenching tightly at the card he'd received from The Time Store.

John was still overcome with gratitude and relief every time he thought about the invitation card. Dan had come good for him. Today was the day he would see Catherine again. He knew it was also the day he would see her die. He was not sure if he could bear it, but he knew he had to do it. He had to go back, to observe the accident in all its gruesome, devastating detail – to prove her death was unavoidable.

His emotions had been in turmoil over the last few

days – worrying about Dan accepting him, then *seriously* worrying when he found out Dan *had* accepted him. It was only because he'd given himself so much to do over the last few days, that he'd been able to keep himself relatively calm. In addition to that it was Paddy's funeral the day after tomorrow – a macabre coincidence what with it being the fifteenth anniversary of the crash.

However, John had it all planned. Today – get the tube to The Time Store in Greenwich. Nip back to 1994. He wavered a bit. Watch Catherine... Be brave. Rid himself of nightmares. Next – attend his best mate's funeral. Finally, and most importantly, search for his lost girls.

The Docklands Light Railway deposited John at his station. He emerged into bright daylight, and with the aid of the street map Ben had printed out for him, began the uneventful but scenic twenty minute walk to The Time Store. He was not sure what to expect – he hadn't really thought about it until now – and consequently when he turned into Flamsteed Way, he was impressed. He looked upwards and took in the splendour of the four-storey Georgian building, which resembled a residential dwelling far more than a retail establishment. Climbing the stone steps he saw the main door was invitingly wedged open. Venturing into the vestibule he noticed the elaborate detail etched within the glazing on the inner door; John knew he was at the right place.

Dan was waiting in the first room, shuffling his feet over to the left of the gold line, then over to the right, and then back to the left again.

John immediately relaxed when he saw Dan and moved quickly to shake his hand. "Dan, thank you so much," he said.

"Hey, no problem," replied Dan, showing no sign of the family battle from last week. "Come on, let's get kitted out – I'll show you around the store on the way through."

John showed only a mild interest in the clocks displayed on the plinths in the main downstairs room of The Time Store, dismissing them as far too expensive and ostentatious for his current tastes. He was oblivious to the gold line that had so fascinated Winnie, and when Dan pointed out their latest acquisition, a Breguet carriage clock, John managed a mere 'ooh'.

However, as they passed through the archway at the back of the room John's interest was stirred when he saw the large spiral staircase. As they ascended, he recollected that the last time he'd walked up any type of spiral staircase was the stone one at York Minster, with Catherine... all those years ago.

They entered the upstairs sales room, and John's eyes goggled with amazement, as he realised that The Time Store contained a considerable number of very expensive timepieces, available for the discerning customer to purchase.

"This is the Watch Room, where our clients can make their choice in relaxed surroundings," commented Dan, smiling indulgently, and allowing John to take a few minutes perusing some of the displays.

"Wow. I used to have one of those," said John, pointing at a Mickey Mouse watch.

"Yes. But was it a 1933 Ingersoll?" laughed Dan.

"Probably not," acknowledged John.

"Oh – let me introduce you to Sarah, my sister," Dan said, as he saw her approaching from the other side of the large room.

"Pleased to meet you, John," said Sarah as she shook his hand. "I hope your experience at The Time Store is all you want it to be."

"Thank you," replied John. "I hope so too."

"Has Dan showed you the Globe Room?" asked Sarah.

"I'm taking him there now," interrupted Dan, before John had a chance to reply.

When Dan opened the door to the Globe Room John was astounded. This was impossibly unbelievable. The history of world time assembled above a shop in Greenwich – who would have thought? My God, they've got this thing well-sussed John realised. He stood mesmerised in front of a working clepsydra, watching the water drain down, showing the progress of time. An ancient invention born out of necessity – and how had it managed to make its way here, along with all the other time related devices?

"I've got a soft spot for these clepsydrae," enthused Dan. "It's where the expression running out of time comes from. To all intents and purposes it's how the measurement of the passing of time started."

John was fascinated. Of course, he had heard of water clocks... and had a vague recollection of them being called clepsydrae, but had never seen one in action, actually working. Not one from the past, and in such immaculate condition.

"So how long ago would something like this have been made? Invented?"

"Oh... It was around the third century BC," Dan answered, offhandedly.

John summoned a distant memory. "There were simpler types of water clock centuries before this, weren't there?"

"Yeah, but this is an advancement. A guy called Ctesibius... he updated the basic bowl with water draining out type affair, like that one over there. He found a way to obtain a uniform inflow of water, and this meant he could measure short intervals of time a lot more accurately. Easy, once some genius had thought of it, eh?" Dan winked. "Nice guy."

John raised an eyebrow.

"Did you know another name for the clepsydra is water thief? Fascinating."

"Yes... water thief," mused John, as he read an information card about the clepsydra, which mentioned Ctesibius and his inventions.

"Have you read the bit about him using water to sound a whistle, and make a model owl move?" Dan's voice was becoming more animated – he obviously relished his subject.

"Yes," replied John. "It was the first cuckoo clock apparently."

"That was so funny – people's faces were a picture," blurted Dan.

"You've got a major collection here," ventured John.

"Thanks – it belongs to the family," replied Dan as he picked up one of the smaller timepieces on display.

"You must have had a hell of a time fetching it all."

"Yes, we've had some hilarious experiences, some close shaves, but we've still got more to acquire," Dan replied. He was finding out that John was far more astute than he had originally given him credit.

"Wow," whispered John.

"Have a look around if you want," said Dan, as he placed the small timepiece back, altering its position by a mere millimetre. "Mind the crates though – rough edges, splinters and what have you."

"What are they for?" John felt he'd been lured into asking.

"Oh. We're loaning some pieces to a museum exhibition – it's going to be touring the world," boasted Dan, happy that he could tell somebody.

Surrounded by this vast historical collection of time, and knowing why he was here, John suddenly felt overwhelmed. Here he was, waiting to travel back in time a trifling fifteen years, for something very, very important to him and his personal mental well-being. But compared to all this inventive and insightful creativity, he was a mere blip, a tiny drip of water from one of those clepsydrae, a little tick or tock of a minuscule second on an ornate pendulum clock.

He hesitated.

"John...?"

"Maybe I'll have a proper look when I come back," said an overawed John.

He said a silent thank you to all those creators and inventors from the past – and from the future – who had somehow played a part in his present.

"You ready then?" asked Dan.

John nodded.

Dan ushered John out of the Globe Room, and stopped at a door marked PRIVATE. John watched, incredulous, as Dan put his thumb onto the biometric pad, thus enabling the door to be opened; John had never seen such a complex device before.

"We need to go down to the basement now," explained Dan, closing the door behind them, before leading John around the corner to the stairs. Once down the two flights of stairs John saw four additional doors, three with similar fingerprint locks on.

John was curious. "What's behind the door without the lock on?"

"Ah, that's just our kitchen and rest room – we sometimes stop off there for a coffee – but as we're going straight to the pub, I thought we'd give it a miss. You okay with that?" Seeing John nodding, Dan continued. "I think we'll check in on Jason first, and then we'll get changed."

As they entered the office, Jason stood up from where he was huddled over a laptop. "Hi, you must be John... I'm Jason... has Dan mentioned to you we'll be using exact co-ordinates for your arrival in 1994? I'm just working on them now."

"No," said John, slightly out of his depth but still curious.

"Remember what we were talking about the other day, Jase?" asked Dan. "You thought we should arrive somewhere near that pub just down the road from where the accident took place."

"Yes, I've planned for you to arrive thirty-five minutes before the accident." Jason glanced at his diary log entry to confirm the time. "I've looked on the internet at the surrounding area of the pub. It's called The Raven... there's a small building in its garden. Looks like a tool shed, or storage shed or something. I think that's a suitable place for you both to arrive – you don't want to appear from nowhere in the middle of the car park"

"What happens if it wasn't there in 1994?" enquired John.

"Then you'll arrive far enough away from the pub windows not to be seen at that time of night," he answered.

"Okay. Yes that's fine," remarked Dan. "Then it's a short walk down the road to the bus stop."

"I'll bring the bracelet to you in the Costume Room," said Jason.

"Okay," replied Dan, beckoning to John to follow him out of the office. He then approached another locked door, which again he had to open with his thumb. "This is our Costume Room," he explained. "We just need to make a few small checks and changes before our journey."

Yet again, John had cause to be surprised and intrigued as he scanned the vast array of assorted clothes, costumes and accessories from various centuries. He almost wished he could go further back, to a time before he was born... to the Industrial Revolution perhaps, and wear one of the large top-hats he could see; almost thinking he was Brunel himself. Possibly once today was over, he could have a word with Dan.

"Right," began Dan. "It's going to be hammering it down back in '94, so we should wear suitable coats. I think there are some over here which would be good."

He walked over to a rail of outdoor pursuit clothing – ski wear, climbing clothes, sailing jackets and hiking coats all hung in one long line. "Try this one on – but go into the changing room, in the corner – there's a mirror in there."

John, unquestioningly, ventured into the changing

room, which was a fairly large, well-lit cubicle with a full-length mirror. He took off his overcoat, removed his remaining money and slipped it into his trouser pocket. He then put on the coat from the Costume Room, a navy blue Berghaus waterproof. Admiring himself in the mirror, John had to admit he looked far better now than he had done a few weeks ago. He twisted and turned for a few more moments, checking himself from all angles and testing out the many coat pockets.

"Are you ready yet?" called Dan. "Jason's here with the bracelet."

"Get John to check his pockets for coins," prompted Jason, handing Dan a platinum bracelet.

John emerged from the changing cubicle. "This coat is great, can I keep it? What bracelet?"

"Have a look in your pockets, John," instructed Dan. "We don't want you taking any coins back with a future date on, do we?"

John, impressed that The Time Store seemed to have covered all eventualities, fished in his pockets and examined his coins. Two of them were dated 1998.

"Leave them with Jason, he'll give you them back when we return," indicated Dan.

"You'd better get a move on now," said Jason. "We have other clients arriving soon."

"Okay," replied Dan. "See you soon, Jase. Here you go, John – you can have a look at the travel bracelet."

"Thanks," said John, noticing that it had a radiating glow which diminished as he accepted it. Once John had scrutinised the bracelet, Dan took it back from him and clasped it around his left wrist. John once again noticed the bracelet's incandescent glow.

"Ready then?" asked Dan. Giving a slight incline of the head, he gestured that they should leave the Costume Room.

Dan approached the final biometrically locked door. This was slightly wider than the others, and considerably more ornate, noticed John, so therefore he deduced that something important must be behind it.

He watched, agog, as Dan performed the Tempus ritual, expecting to see – well – he was not actually sure what he'd been expecting – but certainly not something that resembled a passage on the London Underground.

He followed Dan into what could almost be described as a tunnel, and although suitably impressed by the central meridian line and the movement-sensitive lighting system, he had to conclude that the tunnel itself was quite drab.

"Could we just stop a moment please?" asked John, grabbing Dan by his arm. "Only... I've not had the chance to thank you, all of you, for what you're doing for me. I appreciate it, more than anyone could imagine."

"John. There's really no need, you're welcome," replied Dan, who chose not to tell him about the anguish, trouble and relentless questioning that he'd had to endure when coming up with a plan, which thankfully, had finally been approved by his family on Saturday evening.

Neither man said a word for quite a while as they advanced along the passageway; the sensors triggering the lights one by one, fleetingly illuminating each small section as they progressed, and then effecting darkness behind them once more.

After a few more minutes John could see what, from a distance, looked like a chair against the left wall of the passage.

"That's odd," said Dan, staring at the empty armchair. "I was expecting Dad to be here, I wonder where he is." Immediately beyond the armchair the tunnel opened out into the elaborately decorated Round Room. It looked to John as though it had been there for a few centuries.

"Is this where we time travel?" asked John, as good as knowing the answer. He felt his stomach lurch. How would they actually do it – what would he feel physically?

"Yes, this is the place where it all happens," replied Dan casually. "My father isn't here yet, but we'll go anyway." He led John to the centre of the Round Room.

"Brilliant, absolutely amazing... I honestly can't believe this place," John was far from lost for words, as he surveyed the Round Room in all its splendour.

"It is rather good isn't it? I love the ceiling. It constantly changes... not that you can tell," mentioned Dan, pointing upwards.

"Wow," replied John, looking up at the celestial ceiling.

"Okay, stand on that side of the meridian." Dan pointed down to where John should stand. "And crouch."

Both John and Dan crouched down into a squatting position, one on either side of the Prime Meridian. Dan linked his left arm with John's right, turned his signet ring inwards and then... paused. He could see a distant light in the passageway, triggered by the sensors.

"What's that?" asked John, also noticing the light.

"Oh, probably Dad. Don't worry, he'll be waiting

for us when we get back." Dan replied. "Are you ready?"

"Yes," replied John, closing his eyes.

They disappeared.

CHAPTER 9

Screaming Wheels

John opened his eyes. He'd half-expected them still to be in the Round Room, but they weren't. Wherever they were, it certainly wasn't where he'd been crouching just seconds earlier. It was near total darkness with just a few chinks of light creeping through the gaps in the walls. Neither man moved nor neither made a sound. If Jason's co-ordinates were right they should be in a small potting shed on an allotment to the rear of the pub. There was one thing for sure though, this shed certainly had a very obnoxious ammonia tinged smell.

There was an unfamiliar scurrying noise, followed by lots of rustling. John's breathing pattern abruptly changed. "What's that?"

"Shhh!! Probably the rain," hushed Dan. He was also crouching down, his left arm still linked with John's. He took his right hand from the bracelet and placed it on the floor, fingers outstretched to steady himself, but not for long. Dan lifted his hand – something was on his fingertips.

He slowly brushed his thumb across the ends of his four fingers, whatever was on them was moist and yet flaky. He lifted his hand to his nose and sniffed. Still not too sure exactly what it was, he tentatively offered his tongue to his finger... and then quickly withdrew before spitting, and spitting more.

"What is it?" asked John, whispering.

"Shit!"

"Shit?" John's voice was a little louder. "Are you sure?"

"Yes. Shit... and sawdust. Here – smell." Dan held out his hand to John, who less than politely refused. "Come on," he urged. "Let's get out of here."

Dan was the first to attempt standing, but all he could manage was a very low stoop before he made contact with the shed roof. More noises ensued, erratic scratching, scurrying, flapping... as one sound was made another followed, each in turn becoming louder, becoming wilder. Something moving very quickly brushed past John's leg sending up a dust cloud which caused both men to wince and close their eyes and mouths almost in unison. Wherever they were, whatever they were inside, John was starting to feel a sense of urgent panic, coupled with the need to get out; he knew they were not alone. He tried to stand, but his head met the roof with a thud.

"Let's crawl," suggested Dan, no longer bothering to whisper.

"Crawl... where?" John asked, but got no reply.

Dan started to shuffle himself along on his haunches, careful not to touch the floor again with his hands. He could see a vertical sliver of pale light coming through a crack in the wall and made his way over to it. The light was coming through the slight gap where the door and wall met. Dan blindly felt along the edge, searching out a handle to open the door.

"Ow...! Fuck!" There was a silence, followed by a hasty sucking sound, progressing to, "Shit..." and intense spluttering, supplemented by rasping spitting noises.

"What's happened? What's wrong?" asked John, now close behind Dan.

"Caught my finger on a nail," he replied. Dan's immediate reaction once his finger had met the nail was to take it straight to his mouth to soothe it, briefly forgetting about the faeces he'd just placed it in.

After a further, this time hazard-free minute of feeling around in the dark, Dan deduced that the door opened outwards and that it was fastened by a simple hook and eye latch.

"I need a pencil or something."

"Why...?"

"To flick open the latch."

"Sod the latch." John's boot hit the door, which in turn flew open. Both men stumbled out into the cold, wet night air, followed by lots of sawdust, straw, feathers and several startled chickens which made their escape into the wilds of the Worcestershire countryside.

"Close the door," said Dan, whilst quickly unfolding the telescopic pocket umbrella he'd brought along. It gave scant protection against the rain, but offered nothing at all when it came to the accompanying icy cold wind. "Let's make for that little shelter."

The chicken coop stood at the edge of The Raven's

private garden. On a good day the landlord would get perhaps a dozen or so eggs from his brood, but the best he'd get tomorrow would be several – scrambled! Visible from the coop at the far side of the car park, was a small brightly lit shelter. Dan set off for that, with John following at his heels.

The pub car park was, in the main, level and fairly well maintained, but the never-ending rain had created several large puddles and one mini-lake. However, following their foul encounter, rather than avoiding these watery obstacles, Dan justifiably chose to walk... or wade straight through and head directly towards the shelter. He wasn't too sure, in the wake of their ruckus with the chickens, how either of them looked. He wanted, in addition to the benefit of protection from the steadily falling rain, somewhere to check themselves out, somewhere that was much brighter than the cloud covered fading daylight.

"It seems busier than I expected," remarked John loudly, trying to converse over the sounds of the wind and rain whilst also removing some small breast feathers from Dan's clothing.

"I know," shouted Dan in reply. "Do you think that bike belongs to the guy who saved you?" Dan was referring to the solitary bike leaning up against the wall of the customer bike shelter. The shelter was seldom used this time of the year, although during the summer weekends it would often be overflowing with resting cycles taking a hard earned break from their journey up and down the nearby canal towpath.

"Yeah, possibly. Nathan Cross. It stands a good chance. I know he's the first on the crash scene." John had felt a cold shiver run down his body when he mentioned

Nathan's name, and for the first time since linking arms with Dan, he realised that he was, incredibly, back in time.

John didn't have much in the way of coop debris to remove, once he'd swilled his boots in a shallow puddle to wash off the residual sawdust, all that remained were a few lingering feathers which Dan plucked from his hair.

Once back to relative normality, this time trying to avoid the ever-expanding car park puddles, the two men left the shelter and hastily made their way over to one of the pub entrances. Dan had decided that the pocket umbrella offered between little and zero protection from the weather and in conclusion was more hassle than it was worth, so he'd ditched it in an almost overflowing litter-bin attached to the outside of the shelter.

They entered the pub by the bar entrance where several people had congregated. Snippets of conversation hinted that they were deciding on the best course of action they should take to get out to their cars.

"Try to avoid that big puddle... just to the left," suggested Dan as they walked past the group. "Seems to be a lot busier than we expected in here tonight."

"Okay. Thanks," replied one of the men. "It's darts night... they're playing The Pig and Stone."

"Ah... Where's the gents?"

"Straight through – on the left just after the fruit machine." The man held out his left hand to confirm that he knew what he was talking about, and although he didn't point in any specific direction it was clear to Dan and John that he definitely knew his left from his right.

John pulled open the bar room door; the first thing to hit them full in the face was the cigarette smoke and accompanying bitter smell. Of course, thought John, the smoking ban isn't in place yet. The room was very busy with roughly thirty to forty people in there. Some, if not most, were obviously there for the local darts league and sat around in their team cliques, and others were there more out of social habit.

"I'll get some drinks in, we've got time for a quick one." John, hoping that a pint would relax him, walked towards the bar. "Lager?"

"Please," replied Dan as he headed into the gents toilet to freshen up.

Whilst waiting to be served, John surveyed his immediate surroundings. There were two men at the board throwing arrows in turn for their respective teams. A larger-than-life woman, with a somewhat gruff sounding voice, was calling out their individual scores. He didn't care one way or the other about them... or their friends, family and fellow team members watching them throw. John's attention was drawn to a young man over in the corner, in his late teens, sitting with a couple of his own friends and currently lifting up a pint of Strongbow cider. The young man was Nathan Cross, and John was well aware that in around thirty minutes Nathan would be saving his life. He wasn't too sure whether he felt like thanking him or punching him.

"Yes sir. What can I get you?"

"Oh... um. Two pints of..." John quickly glanced over at the beer pumps lined up along the bar. "Carling please," he replied to the waiting barman. John reached into his trouser pocket and pulled out a folded £10 note. Leaning against the bar, one foot resting on the well-worn brass foot rail, he slowly unfolded the note as he watched the two beers being poured. Looking at the clock behind the bar he saw there were twenty-five minutes between now and the accident. That gave them fifteen to relax and enjoy a pint, that's if relaxing was at all possible, and ten to get to where he'd see Catherine once again. John smiled.

"That'll be £3.40 please," announced the bartender, placing the drinks in front of John.

"Here let me get these." Dan had returned and offered out to the barman his own £10 note. "I insist!" He smiled at John. "You put your money away... it's my shout."

John didn't argue; still clutching his note he picked up one of the pints and placed it down in front of Dan. "Cheers!" He raised his glass and took a long slow drink. "That's better," he declared, replacing his half-empty glass down on the bar. "I wouldn't have minded paying," he said, turning to Dan.

"Yes I know." Dan touched John's £10 note with his finger. "But you had the wrong Charlie," Dan whispered. "Yours is Darwin. We don't use him until November 2000. Mine was Dickens." Dan then lifted his pint, and so as not to be outdone, drank about the same from his glass as John had.

"Shall we go into the lounge? Probably be a bit quieter in there," suggested Dan, pointing to a sign above a door near to a cigarette machine.

Before the barman had time to offer Dan his change, the two men made their way through to the adjoining lounge. Had they been in earlier, the room would have been moderately full of people enjoying the pub's much fancied Sunday carvery. As it was, there were just two lone couples sitting a few yards apart. They sat down at a small table a few feet away from the door leading to the men's toilet.

John took the seat which gave him a direct view of a clock above the door.

"Right." Dan leaned in closer to John. "This is what we'll do – the plan."

Do? John was confused. *What we'll do*? He placed his near-empty glass down on one of the cardboard beer mats on the table. *We...? Plan...? What fucking plan is this?*

"There's a bus shelter almost directly across the road from the one the car nearly hits. We should be able to see everything from there."

"Across the road? Are you sure we'll be able to see Catherine?" questioned John. *Across the road? We won't see a bloody thing.* "That's not really close enough given the weather..." *It'll be pitch black out there, I'm not gonna see a fucking thing.* "Can't we be closer than that, close enough to see Catherine?" *Like next to the frigging car.*

"Hopefully, we should be able to see everything, but remember we can't risk anyone seeing us… seeing you. Especially Catherine or yourself."

Hopefully? Fucking hopefully... What the hell? Cath dies. Does it matter if she can see me? I want her to fucking see me, to know I'm there for her. Isn't that why we're here? Isn't that why we've travelled back in time? "Yes, Dan. But Catherine dies – almost straight away – according to what they told me, and... and I... lose consciousness." *So neither of us will see a fucking thing... Dimwit!* John looked up at the clock – it was ten minutes before they were supposed to leave. *I'll go now. No… too early, he'll follow. Fucking hell, I never expected this.*

"Yes," replied Dan. He could sense that John was becoming stressed and fidgety, and noticed him looking up at the clock. "We also have to make sure Nathan doesn't see us... He'd expect us to come and help. You know we have to avoid that. Don't you?"

"Yes. I realise that. But we have two minutes before Nathan arrives." *Longer if I stop him leaving. I could take his bike, that'll slow the fucker down.*

"Sorry, John. I can't risk him seeing us. It was bad enough being in the bar with you staring at him. Imagine him freaking out if he then saw you in the car?" Dan knew he had to reason with John, get him to understand. "That's why I suggested we came in the lounge, because the longer we spent in there, the more chance he'd have of noticing you and remembering your face at the car. Think of the consequences."

Consequences. I've lived with consequences for the past fifteen years. What the hell does he know about consequences? All I want to do is say goodbye, bollocks to anything else.

Dan picked up his glass and drank nearly all that remained of his drink, save for a last mouthful. "At best, and I mean at best, we could run across the road. Have twenty seconds at the car window, and then run back. Any longer and we could blow everything."

"What?" *What the hell does he mean by that?*

"If we alter things, change anything, then we, the family, have to do a clean-up. Put things back to how they should be – and that would mean our paths would never have crossed."

John thought about this, considered what was on offer, and what he could lose. He picked up his glass and finished his drink. "I understand," he said. *I understand, but that doesn't mean to say I have to agree.*

"Good." Dan felt a slight sense of relief. The last thing he wanted was John getting in the way of his own rescue; he'd never live that one down with Jason and Sarah. "Shall we make a move?"

"We've still got a few minutes," replied John, glancing furtively at the clock. "You finish your drink. I'm just going to the toilet before we leave, that's gone straight through me." John pointed to his empty glass as he stood up. *Thanks all the same Dan... But I think it's time to do this alone.*

Thankfully for John the toilet window was left slightly ajar, probably to allow for extra ventilation, and drops of rainwater were pooling on the shoddily-glossed windowsill. He struggled to push the old wooden window fully open – years of wet weather and summer humidity had long since warped the framework. Perhaps it wasn't left ajar at all, perhaps it just wouldn't close. John could feel the rain coming through now as he'd opened up a route for it.

Placing his left foot in the urinal bowl and using both the hand dryer and windowsill for handholds he made an attempt to hoik himself up and out of the window, but he failed. He tried again, this time wildly flailing with his right boot to get some grip on the tiled wall, again in vain. John quickly assessed the situation – he needed something that would offer him some purchase for his right foot. He looked for a bin, there wasn't one. He looked for a chair, there wasn't one of those either. He briefly thought of going back into the lounge for one, but quickly dismissed that idea.

Time was running out, he should have been out on the road by now and he started to panic. He made another attempt to pull himself up, but again no success. A door opened.

"Bloody hell, mate. What the hell are you doing?" It

was one of the men John had seen playing darts earlier, he'd come in from the bar to the sight of John trying to climb out of the window.

"I need to get out. I'm on a date... blind date... and she's such a minger, you should see the state of her teeth. Give us a hand can you?"

The man laughed. "I've been there before, some right dogs out there. She in the lounge?" He turned his head and nodded towards the exit door to the lounge. "I'll check her out when I leave... come on." He cupped his hands together to form a stirrup. John used this much needed help and was out through the window in seconds.

"Cheers, mate," shouted John from the car park, as he pushed the window back to its previous position.

"You're welcome." The man finished his business, zipped up and quickly ran his hands under the tap. He chose to shake off the excess water and rub his hands down the front of his blue denim shirt in preference to using the hand dryer. Instead of leaving the toilets through the bar door he'd used to enter, he exited to the lounge, eager to get a look at the lady in question.

He walked virtually straight into a tall, beautiful blonde lady, attractive enough to grace any of the world's catwalks or glamour magazines. She was facing the door of the toilet, her gaze shifting alternately between her wrist watch and the door.

"Wow!" commented the darts player under his breath, as he tried to avoid openly gawping at her amazing figure. "No way!" He walked to the end of the lounge and took the through door back into the bar, turning as he did for one last look.

The woman turned around and walked over to the table where an impatient Dan was sitting. "Excuse me. Is that the right time?" She pointed to the clock on the wall just above the toilet door. "My watch has stopped."

John made his way quickly across the puddle-filled car park towards the bike shelter; the rain was noisily bouncing from the surface with angry venom. Out of the corner of his eye he could see a group of people hurrying towards a waiting taxi, their coats raised over their heads for protection. Time was running out, the fiasco of getting through the window had cost him dearly. He hadn't got the time to worry about the biting cold wind, or the water which had already found its way into his right boot. John needed to make a decision – and make it quickly.

The solitary cycle was still leaning against the shelter wall, so he knew Nathan was still in the pub. He entered the small plastic corrugated shelter – the rain was thrashing so heavily at the roof it sounded like a thousand snare drums had been beaten to a harsh cacophony. *Shit!* The bike was locked – the decision had become easier now. John kicked at the back wheel of the mountain bike, kicked hard and then kicked again. Then he ran. He made for the road as quick as he could, as quick as his tired legs could carry him. At best he had three, perhaps four minutes to get to where the car would eventually come to rest.

He crossed the narrow country road and headed for the T-junction as the rain continued to fall relentlessly. There was a fast-flowing stream of water building up along the roadside as the local drainage struggled to cope with the downpour. The trees offered a little protection and gave some respite from the bitter wind. John turned his head back towards the pub – he could just about make out a bright yellow figure crossing the car park. He assumed that it was Nathan, clad in his waterproofs and heading for his cycle. John stumbled, his foot caught a slightly raised tree root, but he managed to keep his feet as he lunged forwards. The headlights of a truck flashed across the junction ahead… he had no recollection of a truck, the only vehicle he could remember on the road that night was a caravan being towed.

"Wonder if they've been anywhere nice for the weekend?" John recalled Catherine saying. He'd not answered, but he remembered thinking about the Easter week when the four of them took Claire's caravan down to Cornwall.

John suddenly found himself singing as he was running – he didn't want to sing and even after he stopped the words repeated over and over in his mind. He tried to shake them from his head, but the more he tried, the more the bass line thumped away – and then the words returned.

He reached the junction and turned left. Thankfully, alongside the main road there was a footpath which led towards the small concrete bus shelter.

"Turn it up... He formed a mental impression of Catherine's left hand on the controls of the radio, adjusting the volume as he sang along.

My Sharona by The Knack – John loved this song – it had been the first single he'd ever bought for Catherine, something he'd tell whoever he was with when he heard it play. The rain was falling onto the windscreen as fast as the wipers could beat it away.

He stood sheltered against the wall of the bus stop, he was soaked through, he could feel the wet cold rain upon his skin. He pushed his fringe back, the water dripping from it was annoying him. John could see the spot where the car was going to come to rest. He reached his arm out towards the huge horse chestnut tree which would prevent the car from rolling down the embankment, but would also take the life of his wife. He knew it had to be soon, very soon.

Then he could see it. Distant headlights came into view. His mind was flitting between the now, crouching under the boughs of the tree, back supported against the side of the shelter. The repetitive lyrics nagged at him, and then, his mind was back to the passenger seat of the car, the song and his wife. The persistent music beat still thumped in chorus with his heart. He could feel the car drift as a sharp gust of wind forced Catherine's grip tighter on the leather-bound steering wheel. The same gust blasted through the trees, branches swayed, shaking the last leaves not yet taken by autumn, and releasing the rainwater hiding within.

John could see the car veer off slightly to the right into the centre of the road before it regained its rightful course. The music continued to play in his mind, but his singing had now stopped. John watched as the car came closer, as he came closer, as Catherine came closer.

From within the car his singing had stopped, he'd turned down the radio to allow Catherine to concentrate on driving. Then he felt it, heard it. The front nearside wheel had hit something. Catherine struggled to hold the steering wheel, but she couldn't.

John could now see the spray coming from the wheels of the car as it displaced the surface water, then he heard it. It was as though a crow scarer had gone off in some nearby field... BOOM... But it obviously wasn't that at all, it was the sound of the tyre bursting as the car wheel hit the deep water-filled pothole in the road.

Catherine was unable to scream, her throat tightened as the shock started to take its hold, wild panic set in as her hands tried to regain control of the wheel. John frantically reached over and made a grab – attempting to help her. "Brake... Brake!" he shouted. But she was; if Catherine could have put her right foot through the floor, that's where the brake would have been. John pulled hard at the handbrake, and the tyres screeched out against the night wind. The car spun.

"Brake... Brake!" John shouted at the approaching car. Seconds later it was spinning. Round... round. A wall of water surged up around the car as the screeching tyres sent it spraying high off the road. Round... round.

"Would you like me to drive first?" Catherine asked, smiling at John as he placed their bags on the back seat. Muted screams filled the car from both of them – they'd completely lost control.

"No, I'm fine. You can do the middle bit after dinner." Round... round.

John was playing back the same two lines that haunted his every nightmare... If only he'd have said 'yes'. Accepting the inevitable, he braced himself.

The car impacted the tree – the tree held firm. The music stopped, the car stopped. It had crumpled with ease as it hit the tree, boughs and branches shuddered alarmingly, but the car barely scraped at the bark on the trunk. White steam billowed out from under the bonnet and the wiper blades ground to a halt upon the fragmented screen. The driver's headlight, along with the right wing, had shattered to smithereens. The sudden impact on the right side had rammed the car's powertrain towards Catherine and she stood no chance – no chance at all.

John was rooted to the spot. He knew what was happening, he knew exactly what he should have expected... but shock had gripped him. He could feel himself as helpless as the John trapped within the car. He looked at his right hand, at his fingertips, feeling phantom senses of touching Catherine's palm... as though he was sitting back in the car, as though he was sitting right next to her now... not all those years ago.

It was pointless trying her door, the driver's door – the tree had taken care of that. He moved closer, wiped away the water beads from his side window, and then from his face. He could see his own hand barely touching his wife's, straining to reach, to hold tightly. He looked at his own closed eyes, feeling himself straining to open them. As he stood there, John yet again felt the agony of extreme pins and needles, as he watched the horror of the car's instrument panel crushing against his legs.

He was aware of a car pulling up about a hundred yards away on the opposite side of the road. Two people were running towards his car, both shouting... John could tell that one of them was Nathan. Oh God, had they seen him? How much time had he really bought himself? In less than a minute they'd be there, pulling him from the wreckage. If they did, if they managed to get him out too soon, then he'd have to endure the same repetitive torment forever. He couldn't face that, not now, not now he'd seen Catherine die.

John reached for the passenger door handle and pulled open the door. He looked straight at Catherine.

Blood was trickling down from an open wound above her right eyebrow, where her forehead had struck the side window. The inertia seat belt had fired into action restraining her from hitting the screen, but it had failed to save her from the abdominal crushing of the steering column which had been forced towards her by the momentum of the engine block. He wanted to hold her, to cradle her... he didn't have time. He stretched over as far as he could; he had to kneel on his own left leg to reach over to Catherine. John gently kissed her soft, tender lips and he could feel her warmth upon his own. "Sleep well. I love you to the end of the stars... and back."

He pulled himself away – pressed the latch on the inner door handle and got out of the car, back into the rain. He took one last look at Catherine and then closed the door behind, locking it. John was at peace now, knowing that he was leaving his barely conscious injured self a little extra time with his wife.

"Oh... thank God. There you are!" John was confronted in the pub car park by Dan, looking equally as rain-soaked. "Where the hell have you been? I've been looking everywhere for you." Dan was relieved to have finally found John. He'd desperately searched the bars, toilets and foyers, even the chicken coop got a cursory check. "Look at the state of you!"

John had made his getaway from the crash scene just in the nick of time by rolling down the muddy embankment. Another second later, then Nathan and the motorist would have seen him. He had heard the two men shouting out to one another over the noise of the wind and rain as they attempted, and failed, to prise open the car door.

By the time John had hobbled back to The Raven, the rain had rinsed most of the mud from his face and hair, but left more than a few tell-tale signs on his clothes.

"I've seen it... I've seen her." With both hands clenched, John grabbed the shoulders of Dan's jacket; the energy in his voice was so intense. Dan had never seen such raw emotion in his entire life. John wept.

"I saw Catherine..." Releasing his grip, John sat on the small wall separating the car park from the roadside. "I saw her. She was there... in front of me." He swallowed. "You should have seen her. How beautiful she looked, how beautiful she looked..."

The urgent sound of distant sirens grew louder. Dan knew that Nathan Cross had played his part. John broke down, it was all too much for him, the adrenalin had finally given way and the moment was catching up with him.

"Come on. Tell me what happened." Dan placed a comforting arm around John's shoulder, and gave it a firm, reassuring squeeze. "You can tell me."

"I really didn't know what I wanted..." he sobbed. "I didn't know whether I just wanted to watch – to see what happened – to understand what happened to us both, to Cath."

John held Dan's forearm. Tears flooded down his cheeks, but soon merged with the unremitting torrent of rain on his face. "I didn't know whether I wanted to save her, but I couldn't help thinking what you told me in the cafe, about time... about how I couldn't change it, and how it could make things worse... But I don't know how it could be any worse... It couldn't, could it?"

Dan was lost for words. He just didn't know what to say, what he ought to say. How much he hated his job right now, how much he wanted to stop this couple from ever going away that weekend... it was in his power to change it all, but he mustn't. True time should be maintained at all costs, he knew that, he was born and raised with that, but for the second time in his life he wished he could turn round and say, "Fuck true time!"

"I wanted to die with her." John fought hard to hold back total breakdown, he needed to get it all out, he needed to tell everything. "I wanted to go to sleep with her, to rest with her forever... and ever. Just to be with her." His voice trailed off into an almost silent murmur.

After a short pause, John composed himself and released his grip on Dan's arm. Although he was still very tearful, the passion within his voice seemed to subside. "But..." he paused, then smiled. "I kissed her goodbye. I got the chance to say goodbye... and I'll be next to her until they pull me out."

Dan didn't prompt any more from John, he'd heard enough to know that he hadn't saved his wife and that true time hadn't been altered. Hopefully, Dan thought, what had happened would be enough to enable John to rise from the life he had, and become the man he should be.

"Come on." Dan stood up and helped John to his feet. "It's done now." He turned his signet ring around once again so the motif was palm side, and linked his left arm with John's right. He then checked that they were well out of sight, away from anyone leaving the pub. Dan placed his right hand over his bracelet. "Shall we go home?"

CHAPTER 10

Lost Time

"Daniel.... DAN? Are you alright?" called out a startled David, as he walked into the Round Room, wearing dark green waders and carrying a fishing pole. "I didn't expect to see you in here."

"Yes... Yes. I'm okay, Dad," he replied, lightheaded, dazed and confused. Dan then crumpled to the granite floor, falling like a tranquilised wildebeest targeted on the savannah.

David dropped the pole, rushed over and knelt by his son. "Dan, Dan... Open your eyes." He tapped his shoulders for a response; none. David gave his son a gentle shake. "Can you hear me?" No response came.

David leapt to his feet. "I'm going to get help," he called. He darted to the entrance. On the wall, just next to his winged armchair was a bright red button. With clenched fist David struck the button with all his might, raising the alarm.

Returning, he tilted Dan's head back and opened his mouth, ensuring that his airway wasn't blocked by his tongue, then David placed his cheek gently above Dan's mouth and nose... "Thank God." He could almost sense the adrenalin fading from within as he felt Dan's weak breath upon his cheek.

He quickly, but gently, ran his hands around Dan's head, checking for any fluid loss before patting over his limbs and torso for signs of bleeding or breaks. When satisfied that his son wasn't injured, David turned him over and placed him in the first-aid recovery position. Seconds later Jason came running into the room, stunned to see his brother on the floor before him.

"What's happened? Is he okay?" he panted.

"He's breathing... I think he's just fainted, passed out. Give him a few minutes... he should come round."

"Where's he been?" Jason asked.

"I don't know, I was hoping you could tell me. He must have just returned when I walked in – then collapsed. Can you smell that?" David sniffed the air around Dan. "Something's burnt – he's been near a fire."

Jason could also smell the burnt odour around his brother, and acknowledged his father. "Yes... it certainly smells that way. I'll check the diary log, check what bracelets have been made for today. I know I've only done two – I was working on a third when you raised the alarm."

"Who were they for?"

"One's for the Rob Gifford trip, and one's for taking Leigh Hancock to Stamford Bridge – they're finished. Dan didn't ask me to do any for him, not for today – he may have done one for himself though."

"What's the third?"

"That's for my trip back here, 1751."

"Here? 1751?" asked David. "What's that about?"

"The hand." Jason paused. "The one in the freezer." He paused again, waiting for his dad to comment. "You know? The one I chopped off."

"How could I forget?"

"Dad... Jase," Dan was stirring. "Dad?" He raised himself slightly from the floor. "What's happened?" he mumbled, before his strength gave way and he sank back to the ground.

"Dad! Give me a hand. Let's get him into your chair," said Jason. The two elder Bradbeers slowly helped Dan to his feet and then taking due care, guided him to David's brown leather chair, where they slumped him, not so gently, down in the seat.

"Have you noticed his coat? It's soaking – wet through – but not his left arm." David pointed out.

"His link arm," replied Jason, touching the fabric of his brother's coat. "Wonder why that is?"

"Dan. It's me, Dad. Jason's here. Can you hear me?" David once again gave Dan a gentle shake.

Dan didn't reply, but responded with a slight nod.

"Oh God – quick! Out of my way, give him some air the two of you," instructed Sarah, as she arrived carrying a first-aid kit, blanket and a bottle of water. She knelt before her brother, opened up the water bottle and moistened his lips with a few drops.

"How many fingers am I holding up, Dan? How many fingers?" she demanded, waving her left hand in front of his face.

"Four," he replied groggily.

"Good. That's right," she turned to her father. "We need to get him to bed, let him rest."

"Keep him here then," said Jason. "I'll go and make a bracelet with his apartment co-ords on and take him home."

"No, Jase. We don't want to put him out of true time – we've got enough problems with him as it is," said Sarah. "Why don't you two get him out of these wet clothes?"

Whilst Sarah scouted around for any additional clues as to what could have happened, Jason and David eased Dan's wet, cold clothes from him. Wearing just his boxers, a travel bracelet and his signet ring, they covered him with a thick woollen blanket, but Dan still shivered. "What's happened to me?"

"You fainted. You've been on a trip somewhere... arrived back and fainted," replied his father.

"Trip... where to?"

"Well, we were kind of hoping that you could tell us that. What can you remember?" asked David.

"Dad, leave him be. He's drained. Maybe after he's had a rest," insisted Sarah.

"Yes, you're right, Sarah. You're right," replied David, as though he'd been told off.

"He's still freezing," said Sarah. "Let's get him back to his apartment. He needs rest now."

"Come on, Dan," said Jason, as he helped him up to his feet. David wrapped the blanket around Dan.

"I'll bring his clothes and follow along behind you," said Sarah. "I don't want either of you two firing twenty questions at him, not until he's rested."

By the time David and Jason had put Dan to bed and returned to the rest room, Sarah had Dan's clothing laid out flat on the table.

"Did you notice his left arm, the hairs?" Jason was saying.

"No," replied David. "What about them?"

"There weren't any. Seems whatever kept his coat sleeve dry managed to take his hairs at the same time."

"Singed...? Burnt...?"

"Possibly, would account for the faint burnt odour don't you think?"

"Found anything?" David asked Sarah.

"Not a great deal. His clothes are clean. Wet, but clean... except for the left sleeves on his coat, jersey and shirt – they're all bone dry," replied Sarah, picking up the shirt and running her hands over the fabric. "And his boots, other than being wet inside and out are as clean as the day they were bought. Not even a scuff mark on the soles. Did Dan say anything to you at all?"

"No. Nothing," replied Jason.

"What about the bracelet he was wearing? Any clue on that?" asked Sarah.

David reached into his pocket and took out the platinum bracelet he'd removed from Dan's wrist. He looked at the disc to check for any engraved details. "Looks fine to me, a set of co-ordinates and a time." He then rubbed the disc through his fingers before handing it over to Sarah. Like her father she also examined the bracelet, much in the same way, and then passed it to Jason.

"Funny! I've not seen that before," remarked Jason, taking out his mobile phone and selecting an app.

"What's that?" asked both Sarah and David almost simultaneously.

"The co-ordinates are for here. Look." Jason showed them his phone together with the bracelet – both indicated the same location.

"Here?" Sarah was puzzled.

"Are we sure that he actually went anywhere?" said Jason, holding the bracelet up to the light and tilting it to and fro in his fingers.

"No, it's just an assumption. From his wet clothes and from him fainting. He was already in the Round Room when I entered," replied David.

"I need to take this next door. I'll need a better light than this, and a magnifying glass or something." Jason left the rest room, with his father and sister not far behind, and went into the adjoining office.

Laid out on the desk, next to his laptop, was an assortment of gravers, most contained within a carousel, a couple of palm-held engraving tools and a small, opened tub of tallow. In the centre resting on a thick, round, sand-filled leather pad was the platinum bracelet Jason had been working on when David had called for help.

Moving the pad to one side, Jason placed Dan's bracelet on the desk and turned on the small portable spotlight. From within the top right hand drawer of the desk he pulled out a collapsible framed magnifier which he stood between bracelet and light.

After what seemed like several minutes of staring at the bracelet, which involved tilting light angle, adjusting the magnifier power, getting both closer and further away from the lens – lifting, tilting and rotating the bracelet in every conceivable position, then cleaning it, followed by polishing it – Jason finally had to declare, "Other than the Round Room co-ords there's nothing, not a sausage. I don't get it!"

"Right. Our travel clients will be arriving shortly, plus we have Mr Chandler's appointment to view the Rolex. Jason, you finish off here. Sarah, have another look at Daniel's clothes – see if they can offer up any clues. Other than that we'll have to wait for him, see what he can recall – if anything," instructed David. "What appointments does he have for the rest of the week?"

"He's supposed to be heading for the Wild West tomorrow morning for a couple of months, on a cattle drive," answered Jason.

"Right, you can either rearrange it, perhaps for a couple of weeks' time – or one of you two do it," said David, almost cracking a smile.

"We'll rearrange," both Jason and Sarah replied, at the same time.

"Good, that's sorted. I'll greet our visitors."

For the Bradbeers the remainder of the Wednesday was mainly business as usual. The first to arrive at the Time Store for his short jump into the future was Rob Gifford, who'd travelled hassle-free via rail from Birmingham to Euston Station, yet commented that the taxi journey from Euston to Greenwich took just as long as the train ride. Waffler extraordinaire Rob, if presented with the chance, would have taken at least another hour to give an intense mile by mile summary of the entire journey. Usually The Time Store would have used travel bracelets, and offered to collect clients who weren't in the best of health. However, Rob had insisted that whilst he could get anywhere under his own steam – then he would; something for which David respected him.

First, Jason accompanied Rob to the Birmingham Women's Hospital where they admired the soon-to-be opened new Queen Elizabeth Hospital with its modern twenty-first century architecture. Jason then introduced Rob to senior midwife, and erstwhile time traveller, Trixie Cooke. Like a good many of The Time Store's previous clients, Trixie couldn't wait for the opportunity to repay them in kind for her journey a few years earlier to meet Charlotte Bronte. Neither Trixie nor Jason could permit Rob to be at the actual delivery when Tina would give birth, but Trixie had slotted her into a delivery suite with a student viewing window for Rob to enjoy the moment. Other than that, they also had to be mindful of the doting future grandparents wandering aimlessly around the maternity unit.

From there, it was a blink-of-an-eye journey back to the Round Room, quick bracelet change and then off to September 2014 for young four and a half year old Millie Gifford's first day at school. Rob wept.

Next up was David's potential Rolex purchaser, entrepreneur and playboy, Paul Chandler. Paul was attending The Time Store with the very much younger glamour model, Louise Taylor, to view a rare 1970's Rolex Datejust 1601, in 18k gold. In, of course, a mint, unused condition; well it had to be, David had only bought it yesterday from a jeweller's shop in Hatton Garden, before popping along to the F.A. Cup final between Chelsea and Leeds United.

It was through the sale of 'rare' and 'exclusive' timepieces that the Bradbeer family were able to sustain their whole existence and way of life, not only to maintain and upkeep the grand Georgian house and collection, but also to fund their own individual lifestyles which, although not extravagant, were certainly well above the breadline. In addition, it allowed them to give free life experiences to random strangers, assuming that they met the criteria.

Paul was delighted that his visit to The Time Store was not wasted, the condition of the watch far exceeded his very high expectations – David secured the sale.

Sarah's day was more hectic than usual, Dan had unwittingly seen to that. There were no clues at all to be gained from his clothes – only sympathy for his lack of dress sense. She'd visited two coffee shops to meet potential clients, one in Wembley, and then the other in Greenford; this second appointment she was doing on behalf of the recovering Dan.

The final visitor booked in for the Wednesday was Leigh Hancock, initially Dan's client. Jason had telephoned her a few days earlier to discuss the theories she had regarding King Harold and The Battle of Hastings. It was quite an intense conversation, leaving Jason's ears feeling verbally battered and bruised, yet he relished and enjoyed the call.

It had, at first, been Jason's plan to take Leigh to experience the Battle of Fulford and the defeat of Morcar of Northumbria and his ally Edwin of Mercia. However, Leigh had argued a good case that The Battle of Stamford Bridge a week later was much more of a pivotal conflict in the historical events of 1066. This was the battle which saw the defeat of the combined forces of Viking invader King Hardrada of Norway and Tostig Godwinson at the hand of his brother King Harold, and so Jason agreed wholeheartedly.

On her arrival at The Time Store and the brief discussion she had with Sarah regarding her thoughts on the possibilities of time travel, Leigh almost stormed out of the building ranting and raving about how her time was being wasted by a bunch of complete prats. How humble she became when she found herself standing on the north bank of the River Ouse, watching as hundreds of Hardrada's and Tostig's ships sailed toward the City of York.

It was whilst watching this mighty fleet sail down the river that Jason explained to Leigh that her theories on Hastings may have some credence, but it would be far better if history was left alone. Leigh pondered, but didn't necessarily agree, arguing that truth always wins the day. Unfortunately Jason couldn't concur, so that was where Leigh's time travel adventure ended. As with a few previous time travelling clients Leigh was greedy. She wanted more, she wanted everything – threatened Jason with the press, the police and with the might of academia – Jason looked out across the last of the passing ships, turned to Leigh and said. "Who would you tell if I left you here... alone?"

Jason disappeared.

"You did what?" Dan laughed as he listened to his brother recount his earlier trip with such detail. "Would've loved to have seen her face when you vanished."

"You do know that you can't leave her there? No matter how much she may deserve it."

"I know... I know, Sarah. I'll let her stew for a few

more minutes then go back and get her."

"Get who?" asked David as he entered the rest room, just catching the end of the conversation.

"Oh… nothing, Dad," replied Jason.

"Very well then." David turned to his younger son, who was sitting at the table. "So how are you feeling? Sleep well?"

"Yes, slept well. Very well, thanks."

"Good. That's good. So tell us then, what do you remember."

"Just collapsing. Seeing you and collapsing." With his right palm Dan brushed his left, hairless forearm. "I remember feeling a heat, an intense heat, just before seeing you. That's all."

"What about from last night? Talk us through everything you can remember from about six last night to when you arrived back in the Round Room this morning," said Jason.

"Nothing much. Went over to New York to see a gig, but…"

"But what?" interrupted David. "When did you travel back to?"

"I didn't, I went forward – August, 2011 – to watch Dave Matthews. I only saw one show – the other two were cancelled. A hurricane – it shut down most of New York apparently." Dan looked gutted. "So had a night in – few beers and a curry. Was in bed for ten."

"This morning, then. Tell us about this morning, what do you remember?" prompted Jason.

"Nothing exciting, breakfast – muesli, coffee. Got dressed, then… then…" Dan paused to recollect. "Then… I just don't know. Saw Dad I suppose, honestly I don't know."

Initially, Sarah was only mildly concerned over Dan's mysterious materialisation onto the floor of the Round Room. She dismissed Dan's inability to remember anything as just another unhappy consequence of what looked like one of his escapades. However, the following morning, when Dan still couldn't recall a thing, she *did* begin to worry – this increased over the next few days when Dan still hadn't remembered the slightest fact.

But soon after, frustrated by his lack of interest in his clients and his continual search for answers, she had a pop at him; the mystery could have occurred any day, any year, any time... and worse, anywhere. Dan had to admit Sarah was right, there were no boundaries for his search.

Jason was more worried than Sarah, at least for the first few days. He felt he needed to spend some time with his brother deliberating the various options and possibilities of what had happened. He postponed his planned trip back to the Flamsteed Way of 1751, suspecting that his findings could potentially result in a considerable amount of extra investigations. However, he was conscious of the current workload they were all under, especially with Dad having to be in true time Paris for the opening of the World of Timepieces exhibition. Dan would have to start pulling his weight again and so, unfortunately after these initial concerns, and adopting a 'life goes on' attitude, Jason left Dan to wallow on his own.

As for David, his conclusion on the incident of Wednesday October 14th 2009 was simple. "All of us are here, and we're all safe. I can only be thankful that we'll all sleep in our beds tonight – who knows, perhaps one day the mystery will be solved."

CHAPTER 11

Shilling

With his father over in Paris for the opening of the World of Timepieces exhibition and Dan not really being much use for anything, Jason finally turned his thoughts once again to the severed hand in the freezer box. It had been just over two weeks since the Flamsteed Way incident, and it was now time to get some answers. Sarah wasn't much help – suddenly becoming too 'busy'. He had his suspicions about what she was doing though. To Jason constant texting and whispered phone calls, along with the extra make-up and lingering fragrances, definitely equalled – dating.

Late that afternoon, using the travel bracelet he'd made a several days earlier Jason ventured back to London, July 1751. His point of arrival was Greenwich Park, just behind the Vicarage. From there he took a leisurely stroll to Flamsteed Way, via a pint in The Feathers of course.

There was a hive of activity around the construction site. Several drays, with sawn timber and sacks of white chalky powder, were being unloaded. The dray horses waited patiently whilst being tended by scrawny looking boys in scally caps. Workmen wandered around the site, carrying, sweeping, stacking and painting. Shouts, clunks and the occasional bangs could be heard from within the houses. Jason looked down at the flat stone road surface, at the spot where, in a few hours, Sarah, Dan and he would stumble across the corpse – the owner of the severed limb now wrapped up in last week's Sunday Times and stashed away in the rest room freezer compartment.

Jason took one of the sacks from the dray closest to No.5. It was far heavier than he'd expected. Passing an axe he clearly recognised, he walked towards the front door.

"Top floor… and be quick about it. We haven't got all day," barked a rather pompous weather-beaten man, who looked as though he chewed nails for a hobby.

"Gaffer," acknowledged Jason, dipping his head, as he panted his way by.

Once through the door it all looked so strange, no spiral staircase, no wooden floor, no meridian line, but then he remembered that his grandfather had once told him that the house had been chosen because of where the meridian would be in years to come. Discarding the limestone powder in preference for some lighter riven lath, Jason made his way upstairs to the third floor.

The rooms were more familiar now, same walls, same doors and same stairs. For the next hour or so Jason kept out of sight, hiding inside the built-in cupboard in the master bedroom, waiting for the last of the workmen to wind down for the day and head off home. Once all was quiet he headed back down the stairs.

The second floor, right hand window, gave Jason an excellent view of Flamsteed Way. Nothing could come or go without him seeing. He knew that it had been near enough eight o'clock when they'd originally left James Bradley at the observatory, and upon Dan's suggestion they'd made their way straight down the hill, so it must have been about ten past eight when they'd arrived here. He'd been watching for well over an hour, it was now seven-thirty – and still nothing.

There'd been no rings, visible marks, scars or tattoos on the limb which could offer up any viable clues as to its owner's identity. Jason, following his father's suggestions, had taken some DNA swabs along with some fingerprints, but as yet hadn't done anything with these. With Sarah's help he'd finally managed to remove the bracelet from the limb, although this was more down to the fluid loss and paraffin jelly than working out how to open the lock which covered the clasp.

That's if it was a lock. Once detached from the wrist Jason was able to examine it more closely. There was no keyhole as such – nothing to press, squeeze, twist or poke – just a somewhat smaller disc where the Bradbeers would have expected a clasp. His conclusion? Once this bracelet was on – the wearer had no intention of taking it off.

Jason had tried to make sense of the coin-like markings milled around the edge of the travel disc, but soon gave up when his efforts failed. There were no clues on the surface of the disc, not even a scratch. They'd surmised that the bracelet was from the future though, it had to be. *'Surely if it was from the past there'd be a record of it in the diary log?'* Dan had said during one of his recent moments of helpfulness. The modern laser welding on the links and disc supported this theory.

It was just after eight when Jason noticed movement outside. Three men had suddenly appeared in the street below – time travelled. Two of the men, shaven-headed, both wearing sunglasses and long black trench coats, were standing tall, supporting the third. They released their hold – the third man, the corpse, slumped to the ground. Jason eased the window open a little so he could hear what was being said.

"We can't leave him here," growled one of the men, who'd now crouched over the figure on the ground. By his accent, South African.

"Yes we can. I've got his ring. Just get the bracelet off him. By the time anyone finds him – he'll be dead."

"Oh, shit! He's not dead!" Jason was shocked. He could've – they could've – sworn he was dead. He hadn't moved – he wasn't breathing – they'd checked. Sarah had checked – she wasn't one for making mistakes – not like this. There was no blood – well not much – when the axe fell – he had to be dead.

"It's not coming off."

"Turn it tighter."

What? Turn what tighter? The bracelet? Jason was panicking. He couldn't see what was going on. The man, the one crouching, was blocking his view.

"It's as tight as it'll go – we'll have to cut it off."

"No – it won't work again if it's damaged."

"I meant the hand – we'll have to cut the fucking hand off. Pass me that axe."

"Shh, voices. Someone's coming." Both men looked towards the park.

Jason could also hear the distant voices. It had to be us, he thought. Coming down from the observatory – this was never meant to happen – they were the ones who should have chopped off the hand – took the bracelet – not me. The voices drew closer, he could make one out quite clearly – Dan's.

Jason watched as the two men vanished, seconds later he watched as Sarah, Dan and himself walked into Flamsteed Way. He could see that Dan was the first to approach the figure on the ground – but he stopped about two or three feet away.

Then me – I was next. Sarah's pushed by – she's holding his left wrist – checking for a pulse – nothing – she's shaking her head. I've seen the bracelet – we need it – they agree – it won't come off – there's something covering the clasp – I'm showing it to Dan – I can't get it off.

Voices – we've all turned – we've all heard them – I take the axe. Fuck – he's still alive, and I'm down there like a deranged madman hacking at the poor guy's friggin' arm. The voices – the people – they've changed direction – they're not coming.

Sarah's walking away – across the street – she's disgusted – I've picked up the hand – Dan's arguing with me. I drop the axe – offer him the hand – he touches the bracelet – it glows – we disappear.

Jason ran down the stairs, the front door was locked. He ran to the basement, to what would soon be the kitchen, opened up a window and climbed through. He darted up the stone steps, pushed through the gate in the railings and he was out on Flamsteed Way.

Who was he? Who was this man before him? Jason knelt beside him and pulled back the man's coat, there was a tourniquet on his upper left arm. He realised immediately that was what one of the South Africans had been tightening – and that explained why Sarah hadn't felt a pulse. He picked up the axe, to throw it away – as far away as possible – if only it hadn't been there.

"Leave him to die." There was someone behind him. He recognised the accent. They'd returned.

"No. That wouldn't be right, would it?" said Jason, slowly standing up and turning around. "I can't just leave him to die."

The two South Africans, who, unlike Jason, hadn't dressed for the period, stood before him. From his earlier vantage point they'd appeared somewhat taller than they actually were. One of them moved away and stood within the shadow which had been cast by the building as it suppressed the moonlight.

The other one walked forward. "Trust me, you can," he said, removing his shades to reveal his dark inset eyes.

"Why did you bring him here?" asked Jason.

"We didn't. It was his bracelet," said the South African, shaking his head. "It brought us here."

"From where? The future?"

"From one future."

"But whose? When?"

"I can't tell you that. You should know – there are many futures if true time isn't maintained."

"Or if the past is altered."

"It hasn't been... You've done what was needed – chopped off his hand." The South African pointed to the axe Jason was holding. "Great minds run in the same gutters."

"Gutters?"

"Never mind. You've got his bracelet now – may as well destroy it. So let's all leave here – and let him die."

Jason allowed the axe to fall from his hand. Destroy

the bracelet? He recalled what he'd heard earlier, they hadn't wanted it destroyed, far from it. It won't work again if it's damaged – surely that's what one of them had said?

He quickly assessed the situation. The guy, whoever he was, was pretty much dead anyway. He might even be dead now. Jason decided there was nothing he could do for him. Even if he could get him back to the Round Room – he'd then have to get him to a hospital – how was he going to explain the hacked off limb at the triage reception desk?

"Do you need it? The bracelet...?"

"No, not now." The man shook his head. "We know it's in safe hands – you have as much to lose as we do. But he mustn't get it back – ever!"

"Who is he?"

"That doesn't matter now – it's over – at last." The South African walked across to his companion, they spoke briefly in Afrikaans to one another, turned to face Jason, smiled – and then disappeared.

Jason arrived back in the Round Room an hour after he'd left. He was too tired to go home, and with his father in Paris decided a night in Flamsteed Way was probably best.

It was business as usual for The Time Store the following day, as Sarah was out visiting a couple of clients and Dan was given no choice but to supervise the sales floor. They'd got some very select buyers over from Hong Kong to look at carriage clocks and Jason wanted to give them his undivided attention – after all, there were still bills to be paid.

After securing sales and locking The Time Store, Jason had wanted to discuss yesterday's events. First with

Sarah, and then with Dan – but neither appeared to be interested. Sarah was going out… again, and Dan… well, he was just being Dan.

Jason didn't want to go home – he wanted answers. South African time travellers? With bracelets. How? Why? Did they want the bracelet to be destroyed or not? *They know it's in safe hands now. I have as much to lose as they do. And why mustn't he get it back – ever?* He decided that a journey back in time to the following day, 31st July 1751, was needed.

Jason sat, ale-filled wooden tankard in hand, on the end of one of the benches next to the Feathers' roaring open fire. He listened intently to each and every conversation he could eavesdrop on. Scholars discussed the Calendar Act and the 282 day year. Dock workers talked about unloading ships from Holland, India and the Americas, then turned their attention to card games, fiddlers and food. Then in came the builders with their story of death and axe murder.

"It must have been bad then?" said Jason, waving over at the landlord. "Drinks for the table, Smithy – drinks for the table. Do they know who he was?"

"Sailor they reckon – got lost – someone took an axe to him. Chopped him good and proper – they reckon he could be the one who killed Annie Shilling."

"Annie Shilling?" asked Jason.

"Annie Fletcher – she'd do anything for a shilling."

"Prostitute?"

"Complete whore more like – Annie wasn't the cleanest woman on the…"

"Higgins!" shouted a burly man as he approached

the table. "That's enough talk – let the dead have their peace."

"Gaffer."

Jason had heard enough. Forty minutes later and with the name of Annie Shilling-Fletcher firmly embedded within his mind, Jason walked through the Greenwich foot tunnel towards the comfort of his own bed.

CHAPTER 12

Thieving Magpie

"And this Annie Fletcher... did you find out anything about her?" asked David, examining the milling on the bracelet's edge.

"Yes, quite a bit," replied Jason. "This is where the fun starts."

With the exhibition launch in Paris successfully underway, David and Jason were enjoying an after dinner Cognac. It was a delicate little number with subtle honey and vanilla characteristics recommended by David's close friend and recent Parisian guide, Jean Baptiste.

"Fun?"

"Well you'd expect to find reports of both her and our man somewhere. Given the gossip in the pub that is."

"And?" David was becoming more intrigued. Talk of South Africans, the mystery bracelet and now the Fletcher woman had pricked his ears and aroused his curiosity.

"I went back a few days ago and bought this." Jason

passed his father a newspaper. "It's a copy of the General Evening Post from 1751. Turn to page five."

David began reading. "BLOODY GREENWICH MURDERS..."

The body of seamstress Annie Fletcher had been discovered on the night of Monday 26th July 1751 off Fryers Road, Greenwich by parish constable William Firth. Annie, a well-known local nightwalker, was to have been arrested by Firth as part of the regular Monday night scoop which was run by the authorities in a bid to clean up the streets. Considered a hardened prostitute, Fletcher would have been taken before the mayor and probably ended up in Bridewell Prison or at best the local compter. As it was when Constable Firth found Annie Fletcher, yards away from the Ship Tavern, she'd been murdered... stabbed and slashed several times.

The second reported incident was that of an unnamed man found dead near the newly-built houses in what was now Flamsteed Way. The man, whose body was discovered on the morning of Saturday 31st July by workmen, was assumed to be a deck-hand from an offloading ship. He was said to have been fatally wounded as a result of a vicious axe attack. Constable Firth believed this to be a revenge attack for the recent murder of seamstress Annie Fletcher, as a pendant known to belong to Mrs Fletcher was found within the clothing of the deceased.

"Well it seems that's our mystery man then," commented David. "No reference to his missing hand though."

"I think that 'vicious axe attack' says it all. Don't you?" replied Jason. "Although I didn't think that I was really that vicious. I managed to speak with Constable Firth about it, about Annie – told him I was from the paper."

"What did you find out? Anything interesting?" said David as he folded the newspaper and handed it back to his son.

"It looks as though Annie Fletcher was a tad light-fingered with some of her clients… she was a bit of a jewellery magpie according to Firth."

"Do you think that's where the bracelet fits in?"

"Possibly… My guess is that she somehow stole it from the South Africans and our corpse stole it from Annie along with her pendant. She probably fought back – or at least tried to – and that cost Annie her life."

"Sounds reasonable. But it still doesn't answer the questions about the South Africans does it? Could there be a link between this Fletcher woman and South Africa? Husband or children perhaps?"

"Thought of that," replied Jason. "But not too sure if Mrs Fletcher was a Mrs Fletcher as I can't find any marriage records – and nothing about any children either. So not too sure where the South Africans fit into it all."

David let out a deep sigh. His options were to leave it be and wait for answers to come to him one way or another, irrespective of how long that wait was, or to head off into the future and dig around there for some resolution. There was nothing in The Time Store's historical records to indicate any bracelet thefts or involvement with South Africa – other than the occasional client trip – so whatever had happened in July 1751 had no impact on business.

"Appears we're at a dead-end with them then," said David, trying to not sound too defeated. It wasn't in his nature to leave things hanging, but he decided that as they didn't know from exactly where and when in time the South Africans had travelled, their investigations had finished.

They were happy that the corpse was in the wrong place at the wrong time – or more like the wrong port at the wrong time.

"What shall I do with the hand?" asked Jason.

"Where is it?"

"Downstairs. Still in the freezer."

"Incinerate it," replied David. "Along with this." He threw the platinum travel bracelet to Jason, and then poured more Cognac.

CHAPTER 13

Catching up Time

In late 2009, the next door adjoining property, No.3 Flamsteed Way, suddenly and unexpectedly came onto the market. The Bradbeers moved swiftly as they'd lost out a few years previously when No.9 came up for sale.

In February 2010 they finally completed on the purchase and this now gave them ownership of the middle three in the run of five substantial and elegant Georgian terraced houses. Space within The Time Store had been tight for a while and now with new pieces arriving almost on a daily basis due to the 23rd century South American war the problem was getting worse. In fact, had they managed to secure the property purchase a year or so earlier, then they may have been more hesitant over their participation in the World of Timepieces exhibition, although when it came to having the builders move in they were pleased that they had the extra room.

Also in February Jason and Sarah made time, between sorting and cataloguing the growing South American collection, to attend the funeral of Rob Gifford at Redditch Crematorium. It was a sombre occasion and although they'd never met, Sarah listened intently to the heavily expectant Tina recalling treasured memories of her brief, yet eventful few years married to Rob.

David, as head of the family and current custodian of The Time Store buildings and business, was proud of his achievements and of his three children. As time was progressing and he was ageing in true time, he had begun to feel that he needed some time and space for himself, something he'd reflected on last year whilst alone in Paris. David sorely wanted to have a relaxing time, without being hassled by the stresses of a complex working life. Consequently he had been mentoring Jason, as the eldest of the three siblings, to take over his custodial role. This wouldn't happen at the time of his death, which was not in any way imminent, but with his retirement from a full-time involvement.

He had always enjoyed fishing, and although in his earlier years, and in many different centuries, he had fished on the banks of some of the world's illustrious rivers, what he really wanted to do now was to nip a few miles down the motorway to a small river he knew, close to his parents' cottage, and spend the whole uninterrupted day there alone and in peace – wasting time, but his time. During recent months David had been pre-occupied with the raging war in South America and had less involvement with The Time Store's clients. "We could do with another pair of hands around here," he'd often say. This might be some way off though, plagued as he was with daily issues from the three kids, as he still thought of them. Plus with there being no immediate signs of young Bradbeer blood coming into the family – for Christ's sake none of them could hold down a relationship in true time for more than a couple of years – it seemed that at this rate he'd never retire.

However, he had found time to travel back one Sunday in spring and spend just over a year fighting in World War I, camel riding the windswept desert sands alongside T.E. Lawrence, known to most as Lawrence of Arabia, against the Ottoman Empire. David, for a few exciting moments, played a pivotal role in the capture of Aqaba and the fall of Damascus, although, in the Battle of Tafileh, he did receive a bullet flesh wound. "You're worse than Daniel sometimes, Dad. No wonder he does stupid things," scolded Sarah, as she patched up his arm.

David had, at one family meeting, intervened and flatly refused to give the thumbs up to a dangerous request made by one of Dan's clients. There was no way on earth he would sanction it. "Sheer lunacy itself," he'd called it. Then throwing in, "So many things could go wrong." No matter how many safeguards Dan said he had in place, the eruption of Krakatoa, or anywhere else in Indonesia during August 1883 was not a place anyone would be visiting.

Another big argument within the Bradbeer clan came when Jason tried to scheme his way onto the Apollo space program. David, surprisingly, had almost been seduced by it, he would have considered it a mighty accomplishment for one of his sons to have been on the Apollo 11 mission. Imagine, Jason could have had Buzz Aldrin's or Michael Collins' role, preferably Michael's as nobody remembered him. If David hadn't found out that Jason had bet Dan £100 that he could do it, then he could well have approved it. As it was, Dan was gloating over winning the money from his brother, and Jason felt rather cheated when Dan handed over half his winnings to Sarah.

With both of his siblings reluctant to go to New York, Jason had overseen the exhibition's move from Paris himself. He'd tried to convince Sarah to go, but she was too loved up with Roberto, her new boyfriend – the recipient of the countless texts and the reason behind so many new perfumes. She certainly didn't want to spend the best part of a month away from him. Dan said he just couldn't face being alone for so long in true time, away from his family and familiar surroundings. Truth be told though, he had plans in South Africa which involved a few football matches. Once the distraction of the World Cup had worn off, and still needing to keep himself occupied, he ventured north of the border to Edinburgh for the Fringe Festival.

Due to the renovation work on No.3 and the removal of certain adjoining walls, the Bradbeers were limiting their client numbers; this allowed them the chance to take extended true time holidays. Sarah relished this break as it gave her the opportunity to accompany Roberto to Rimini to meet his parents for the first time.

Since the event in the Round Room last year, Dan had been dreading the approach of October 2010. He hadn't been too keen on September either as he knew October was on the horizon. Finally though, Dan could not avoid the inevitable. At the beginning of October, as the anniversary loomed, he felt himself becoming increasingly agitated, unable to concentrate – although Sarah often criticised him throughout the year for his goldfish-like attention span – and worst of all somewhat annoyed, or in his own words, 'pissed off'. Annoyed because he knew that whatever was wrong, whatever had happened – there was absolutely nothing he could do about it. There was no evidence to prove he'd cocked-up at all, but he couldn't help but berate himself over it.

Dan confided in Sarah that he'd begun to have strange panic attacks, telling her that he thought that whatever had happened last year could happen again this year, and the next year, maybe forever. He explained to her that he thought, unwittingly, he'd released a strange quirk of time that was destined to haunt him for an eternity. Sarah struggled to keep a straight face, knowing that her brother was actually serious and genuinely worried about his fate, but she did feel that she had to nip it the bud. "Get a grip and stop being so far-fetched will you."

Although Sarah had made light of Dan's concerns, possibly in an attempt to prevent him from further worry, she decided to establish a careful, yet distant and secretive watch over Dan, just to check he was okay and to try to prevent anything like this from ever happening again.

The Time Store was thriving, and Sarah was kept busy, but she still tried to find time for a life outside work. This had led to her embarking on what, for her, was a long term relationship with Roberto Felluci, a man four years older than her. They'd spent a few months dating and it all seemed to be, in her opinion, going well, especially as when they returned from Rimini, Roberto asked her to move in with him. Sarah accepted eagerly because she was besotted. Although this initially didn't impact on the day-to-day running of The Time Store, David faced a new Bradbeer challenge – a Christmas without one of his children at the table.

The inclement weather that winter had delayed the

external renovations down Flamsteed Way. However, on a positive note the scaffolding had given Dan and Jason far more options than usual when it came to hanging their outdoor festive lights. A rather large inflatable snowman also made an appearance, much to the disgruntlement of those at No.9.

The spring of 2011 heralded, at last, the removal of the scaffolding, the structural work both inside and out was finally complete. Dan was thankful to be unexpectedly overseeing the World of Timepieces exhibition as it moved from New York to Tokyo. The last place he wanted to be was in The Time Store with a bunch of interior decorators.

This job, this leg of the exhibition, had originally been allocated to Sarah. But when she had revealed to Roberto that she'd be spending three, possibly four weeks away from home he was far from amused, in fact she was shocked at his vehemence. Not only did he ask her not to go, he also angrily suggested she change jobs, stop working for the family business and branch out into a career of her own so they could potentially 'spend more, not fucking less time together'. Also, as he put it – for once successfully using a quaint English expression – she wouldn't then be at the 'beck and call' of her family. Sarah hadn't expected this at all – she knew she would not, could not, ever leave The Time Store. However, just to keep the peace, she did agree not to go abroad.

March 2011 also saw the rush for Olympic tickets for the London games, although there was still another five-hundred days to go before the opening ceremony. Jason had decided to go mad and apply for loads of events. Sarah, electing to take the evening off from Roberto, stayed over for a few extra hours helping to complete Jason's applications. Once she'd headed off home Jason engraved himself a bracelet and sneaked forwards to June of that year to check out his credit card statement. He knew he was to be allocated a great deal, perhaps 40% of his requests. He resisted a trip to June 2012 though, he'd decided that he wanted to enjoy the sense of true time anticipation and surprise as to exactly how he fared in the event allocation process.

Dan returned from Tokyo with a new craving for sushi, and insisted on holding a dinner evening in his freshly decorated apartment. Roberto wasn't having any of it, 'raw fish indeed', although he was impressed with Dan's beef teriyaki. Dan pointed out that technically sushi was not raw fish, but Roberto was not to be moved on his decision and stuck to the beef. Sarah managed to wangle some time alone with her father whilst the boys played on Dan's newly acquired *PS5*, Jason convincing Roberto that the Japanese games market was much more advanced than anything to be found in Europe.

Sarah had wanted her father's permission to take Roberto on what would be his first time trip – to Pisa 1372 and the non-leaning tower. David refused quite adamantly, insisting that there was a two-year rule, which meant after two years – not during your second year. Sarah argued that if anything went wrong they could always 'clean-up', like they had done with Elisabeth, one of Jason's exes. David reminded her that it was due to the Elisabeth fiasco that he had introduced the two-year rule. Even in the face of this argument she still tried to remonstrate, pointing out that they take strangers on random trips at the drop of a hat, and occasionally have to do 'clean-ups' – so what's the difference? In the end Sarah begrudgingly accepted her father's decision and the matter was closed.

Summer passed without incident, business as usual as always for The Time Store. The low pressure hovering over the UK meant August was somewhat cooler than usual, this was ideal as it discouraged the sloth-like tourists from setting up camp for the day in Greenwich Park.

After her covert surveillance of her brother, Sarah was pleased with Dan's progress this year – he'd handled the move from New York to Tokyo professionally. He'd even started laughing at some of Jason's feeble and stilted jokes regarding singed body parts and amnesia. However, she began to notice, as October was approaching once more, that Dan was becoming more jittery and snappy. She suggested to her father that Dan should be given a bit of time off around his problematical day.

Dan appeared grateful for this suggestion, and returned from his break refreshed and back to his normal self. Sarah had also proposed a task for Dan – and so, throughout the month of November, he set about organising, tidying and updating their costume collection. Dan's somewhat anal ability to catalogue and sort into chronological order anything which crossed his path had not gone unnoticed in the Bradbeer family, although upon commencement of his task Dan had said, "You wouldn't say that if you could see all my gig stuff in the spare room, it's a right mess."

During one of Dan's clothes-collecting time trips that month, he met, and had a three month intense fling with Maggie, a lovely girl from 17th century London. She was an assistant to a baker, and, having survived the plague where many of her family and friends hadn't, she had adopted a surprisingly modern 'live for the moment' attitude which Dan had found refreshingly attractive. He was distraught when she was lost, presumed dead after the Great Fire – but he managed to get over it quite quickly, what with his mammoth Costume Room project; he was pragmatic enough to realise that it probably wouldn't have worked long-term anyway.

Sarah had her own problems as 2011 drew to a close. She was beginning to realise that her relationship with Roberto was far from the idyllic bliss she originally thought it was. Sarah was constantly irritated by his many faults – teeth grinding, eating with his mouth open, never tidying up – not to mention his mediocre penis and that he'd never ever bought her flowers. She'd overlooked these in the initial infatuation stages of their relationship or maybe she was just love-blind to them... either way they were starting to grate on her.

She knew it was her 'turn' to do an exhibition changeover, this one was from Tokyo to London. The British Museum was going to be hosting the World of Timepieces for pretty much the whole of 2012, the Olympic and Diamond Jubilee year. Sarah really wanted to go to Tokyo – Dan had enjoyed it so much. She wanted to, had to, contribute to the entire museum thing – the others said that it had added a whole new slant on The Time Store operation and business. However, she dreaded telling Roberto. After a few days of nervous tension and soul-searching analysis she eventually plucked up the courage to tell him she was definitely going. As expected, and in a similar vein to before, he hit the roof. She was prepared this time though, and when he gave her an ultimatum, she calmly said, "Okay, I choose my family. I choose Tokyo. I choose The Time Store. Goodbye."

She moved out of his suburban house and into one of the apartments above the newly-acquired addition to The Time Store buildings. She found time to go back in time to visit a particular period of interest to her – the Crimean War. She worked around the Black Sea for a few months as a nurse, and even got to meet Florence Nightingale herself. This demanding, intense and dangerous experience more than helped her get over the failed relationship with Roberto.

A happy bonus for David, after his daughter's split from that arrogant bastard, was that this Christmas he had all the kids back again. He closed The Time Store to clients for a whole month from mid-December, much to the surprise of Jason, Sarah and Dan, and they revelled in this extended true time alone as a family. With the exception of Jason, who had always insisted on retaining a smidge of independence, they all lived in apartments at the top of the enlarged Time Store, but Jason came over most days.

They were content in each other's company; reading books, playing board and card games, polishing and repairing clocks, listening to music, cooking delicious meals and even taking the odd family time trip to randomly selected periods. On Christmas Eve they were joined for a few days of festive celebrations by David's parents and Helen's mother – who, completely forgetting how old their grandchildren were, spoilt them rotten.

David was becoming very impressed with Jason, and was now more confident in his elder son's ability for the future role of new custodian of The Time Store. The knowledge, history, rites and guardianship of The Time Store had passed down from generation to generation – perhaps in the same way as it may have easily, but unfortunately undocumented, passed up from some distant far off future generation.

Jason had not only suggested the idea of their participation in the museum exhibition, but had played a large part in overseeing it, and verifying the locations, logistics and insurance. But Jason also had another project in mind, which he'd been mulling over ever since the incident with axe and hand.

He hated their dependency on multiple bracelets. Wouldn't it be much better if they each only needed one, which could be adjusted for wherever they needed to go? Plus why did they always have to leave from the Round Room? Much of Jason's spare time, which wasn't that much, was now spent trying to redesign the bracelets. He quite liked the idea of rotating digits, similar to a combination padlock; once set, lock into place and 'Hey Presto.'

For the first time in his life he wanted to fathom out how the bracelets actually worked. He'd tried to explain it once to Steve Barrett, one of his first ever clients and now a close friend.

"Steve. It's a bit like a remote control for a telly, you know what it does. You press buttons and it does what you want it to do. But do you know how it really works, as in the technology behind it?"

Steve had told him he didn't really care, as long as he could turn the bloody soaps off when they came on, then it worked.

In his primary school years Jason would often play with a bracelet. Fascinated by their amazing mysteries, he'd always known that when he didn't touch one it was dull, whenever he picked one up, whether engraved or not, it shimmered with its slight aura. If he took his ring off, the bracelet would still glow, yet he couldn't travel without the ring or without a destination on the bracelet. He knew he could repeatedly revisit a period in time using the same travel bracelet and never bump into himself. Eventually, he kept telling himself, one day he'd solve the bracelet problem – hopefully sooner rather than later.

For the summer of 2012 though, he focused on the London Olympics. As it happened, with the assistance of Sarah's additional on-line applications, he'd done well, very well. He was delighted when tickets arrived for seventeen events in all, including the prestigious men's 10,000m final, the men's long jump, and loads of swimming. He was planning to use his time travel abilities to attend two events which he was aware had a start time clash, but other than that Jason's Olympic experience would all be done in true time.

He'd done far better with his Olympic tickets than he had done with his women during the past few years. Of course he'd had a few flings, some of which he would boast about and the odd one which he tried to hide. However, he never liked any of them enough to commit long term. Jason was far from shy when it came to chatting up the ladies, most were quite taken by his confidence.

It was completely different when it came to Melissa at No.41, though. During the past month, since she'd moved into the apartments, Jason went from his usual unruffled self to an instant quivering wreck whenever he spotted her. However, he'd managed to find the nerve, encouraged by the imminent sporting feast, to ask her out. He had a date planned with her – she was so excited when he asked her if she'd accompany him to a forthcoming Olympic event, perhaps more so with the possibility of being caught by the television cameras than the particular event itself. Jason didn't care about her reasons for coming with him though, he just wanted to have the chance to spend some time with her.

CHAPTER 14

Death by Association

Breakfast time. Jason was sitting at the table enjoying a late leisurely start to his day. Pen in hand, he was poised to tackle 'The Extreme' Sudoku puzzle in his morning paper. Using his 'system' he'd already whizzed through both the easy and intermediate with little problem. A lazy day followed by an evening packed with Olympic swimming at the Aquatic Centre, for his first date with Melissa from No.41, were his plans for today. Jason felt quite calm given the circumstances but was sure that as the time for his date approached this wouldn't last. He put his coffee mug down, and was just about to bite into his second slice of toast when his phone rang. Grabbing it from the kitchen worktop, Jason raised his eyebrows and tutted as he noticed who was calling.

"Hi, Dan," sighed Jason, as he pressed the green answer button on his mobile phone. "You do know I'm not in today, I'm at the swimming."

"Have you seen the news?" Dan seemed agitated.

"No. Why?"

"Turn BBC News on... quickly. Dad's gonna be fuming if he sees it."

"Hang on." Jason quickly made his way over to his television and selected the channel on his remote control.

The banner on the screen read: 'LIVE – Museum Theft.' A newsreader was standing on the steps of the British Museum, umbrella in one hand, microphone in the other. A picture of a marine chronometer was inset to the main screen – not just any marine chronometer, this was theirs. Jason read the tickertape scrolling along the bottom of the screen. 'Breaking News: Priceless Harrison historical timepiece stolen.'

Yorkshire man, John Harrison, along with many other so-called lunatics and fools had spent his life 'finding the longitude', and through his endeavours he was credited with solving the Longitude Problem – it was not only through his marine chronometers, but also his dedication and inventiveness that he solved a navigational problem, a problem which had led to so many nautical tragedies. This particular chronometer, the Bradbeer loaned and now apparently stolen museum exhibit was somewhat special though.

When the Bradbeers released their chronometer to the museum exhibitions, it had caused a great stir – a new Harrison timepiece come to light. Apparently it had been in the Bradbeer family for years – a family heirloom.

At one time Harrison himself had been a client of The Time Store. Jeremiah Bradbeer, Jason's many times great-grandfather, had taken Harrison back to 1671 to meet Thomas Tompion, a man who would centuries later become known as the Father of English Clock making. The stolen chronometer had been a gift Harrison had given to Jeremiah for allowing him to meet Tompion.

"Fuck... I'm on my way."

By the time Jason was sprinting to The Time Store he'd learnt that the theft had occurred last night after the museum closed. It was only discovered when a Japanese tourist commented to a curator that the display item looked different from the one in the guide book. It had been switched. But how?

"They've been on the phone asking for you," said Sarah, unlocking the door for Jason. "Simon Ward... he asked if you could call him back. You have his number."

"Yes. Will do," replied Jason. "Sarah, you might need to re-arrange your morning clients to this afternoon. I don't want anyone in or around here until this is sorted... some little shit is gonna pay for this." Jason was fuming, his calm day in preparation for his evening date was now over almost before it had started. He was now angry and someone was going to suffer. By the end of the day whoever had stolen their chronometer was going to wish they'd never been born, and more than likely by the end of the day – they wouldn't have been.

As the three of them made their way to The Time Store's office Jason's thoughts were – inside job, it had to be. He and Sarah had been there, along with Simon, the exhibits' curator, they'd overseen and approved all the security measures. There was no way anyone could have taken the Harrison piece without having knowledge of the alarm system; bloody hell the gallery itself was patrolled 24/7. Pressure pads, cameras, light-sensitive cells and movement sensors galore protected the Bradbeer exhibits –

it had to be an inside job, there was no other explanation. Jason returned Simon's call.

"Jason. Thank you ever so much for getting back to me... I gather you've seen the news?" Simon, in an almost condescending tone, had promptly answered his phone.

"Yes, Simon. Yes I have... and what a bloody shambolic way to find out... from the BB – fucking - C."

"Yes. One has to apologise for that, it wasn't anything to do with my department unfortunately. If I'd..."

"Well, it's done now," interrupted Jason. Some of the venom in his tone had dissipated. "Any leads? What about the cameras? Anything there?"

"The police are still reviewing the CCTV logs along with our in-house security. Hopefully they'll be able to find some clues, perhaps shed some light on what may have occurred."

"Occurred... What's occurred? I'll tell you what's occurred. We've been fucked over... that's what's occurred." Jason's vitriol swiftly returned. "This is all I need today, ruin the bloody swimming why don't you!"

"Excuse me…"

"Mr Ward, this is utter bollocks." Jason threw his phone at Dan. "Here speak to him, for fuck's sake, I've had enough of this little shit."

"Jason, we need to sort this before Dad gets back," insisted Sarah.

"How long have we got, then?"

"Four hours… maximum. You know he's gone to the Peruvian Andes this morning trout fishing…"

"Rainbow trout. He has to be back for half three – he's got an appointment with the bank. So four hours tops."

"Thanks for that, Sarah." Jason calmed down again, or perhaps his inner conscience knew better not to rant at his sister. "We'd better get a move on then."

Sarah just nodded in agreement as she used her thumb to open the biometric door lock. Dan finished the call with Simon Ward and followed the other two into the office.

"Bracelets please. Grab a handful, we don't know how many we'll need." Jason turned the laptop on as he sat at the desk.

"Plan?" asked Dan passing over several glowing platinum bracelets which he'd taken from a shelved shoe box marked 'NEW'.

"Plan? Well – wing it as usual, of course. But I'd like to take whoever is responsible for this on a short trip aboard the Association."

"Very appropriate, Jase," remarked Dan, surmising his brother's intentions.

"Thought you'd agree with it," said Jason. "Did Ward have anything else to say?"

"Not really... But he did do a lot of fawning," replied Dan, handing back Jason's phone. "I asked him if he'd taken it though."

"And? What did he say?" Jason paused his screen-scrolling, somewhat impressed by his brother's directness.

"Flustered. I'd say his reply was flustered."

"In what way?" asked Sarah, before Jason had the chance.

"In an inane rambling sort of way, lots of stuttering and lots of gaps... I'd have expected a more direct 'No' as an answer, not a load of excuses."

"Fair point," said Jason, in response. "Here, take

this." He passed a newly-engraved bracelet to Dan. "Find out all you can, follow his every move over the past two weeks. But be mindful, two weeks means you'll be gone for over three hours and we are pressed for time – so run."

Without question Dan took the bracelet from Jason, clasped it around his left wrist, turned and made his way quickly to the Round Room.

"Did you check the safe room register?" asked Sarah.

"No... But too late now."

"No it isn't, check if it's in use. I'll phone him before he sets off if it is," insisted Sarah.

Since 1751 when the Bradbeers had moved to Flamsteed Way, the Time Store had kept a safe room – a room which any of the Bradbeers could use, irrespective of where in time they hailed from. This room was accessed from the rear of Flamsteed Way, no Bradbeer had ever set foot in it, at least not in their own true time. There was always a precise register kept of anyone who'd used the room, so as to avoid potential ancestral or generational clashes – Dan would certainly have need to use it as he investigated the preceding few weeks – or until he found out who had their chronometer.

It had taken Jason and Sarah just over two hours to assemble the clothes and accessories they'd need for Jason's Association plan, although in the main they had to guess at what they'd need.

"Shit... we need some TCP," said Jason. "I'll have to go and buy some."

"Stop panicking will you. I've got some upstairs... I'll go and get it."

"Okay. I'll sort the gravers out. Meet you here in five."

Dan had been gone a little shy of three hours when bag laden, Jason and Sarah entered the Round Room.

"Shouldn't Dan have been back by now?" asked Sarah, sitting in her father's armchair.

"He should be back soon. But we don't know the exact time he set out – so I can't calculate the time interval accurately," replied Jason, aware that his sister was starting to become agitated.

It was only a few minutes later when Dan arrived back.

"Finally!" said Sarah, her sarcastic tone disguising the panic she'd been feeling.

Dan was buzzing. "Bloody hell – you guys are really gonna like this. This is Russian mafia shit, big time."

"Come on, Dan. Explain. We haven't got time to piss about, who did it? Who took the Harrison?" Jason demanded.

Dan had only been away for thirteen days, firstly finding out who'd taken the chronometer, and then why. As Jason suspected, it had been an inside job, but nothing elaborate. The Harrison hadn't been stolen the night before, it had been moved eight days before the reported theft, whilst the museum was open – moved, but not immediately taken. Under the watchful eye of security officer Ilia Lemanski, Simon Ward concealed the timepiece within a hidden compartment in the display plinth and replaced it with an elaborate Victorian pocket watch – then removed the chronometer at his first opportunity, hiding it in a lunch box his daughter had given him. Once removed, Ward sat back and waited until someone had noticed the switch.

In true time, when questioned, he'd declared to the police that it had certainly been there the day before when he'd done his rounds and his guided tour with an American party from Seattle – he'd lied. Of course the CCTV log showed a timepiece in the display case, showed Ward's daily exhibit walk, and Ward giving his guided tour. There was no reason for the police to doubt him. But Dan now knew differently.

Once he'd arrived back in time Dan had made a beeline for the museum, where he saw the highly-polished Harrison chronometer on display. Several times a day Dan would go back to the exhibit room taking a sketch pad with him, he'd sit on a bench near one of the ancient clepsydrae and make rough drawings – all the time watching the Harrison. It was during one such visit, eight days before the reported theft, that he'd noticed the switch had taken place – not a bad likeness he thought, although a bit thin and less bulky. To his surprise 'No Photography' signs had now been put up in the room and security had asked to look through his sketch pad. Humph, cheeky buggers!!! What did they mean maybe I should consider pursuing a different hobby? Surely, Dan thought, my artwork isn't that bad?

Over the next couple of days he watched both Lemanski and Ward carefully. Dan figured that they were in cahoots with one another, but other than their daily exhibit walk he couldn't forge any link between them. Dan then resorted to following Ward from his Twickenham home to the museum and back every day – sleeping nights in a parked van, with Ward's residence well in sight. Simon, somewhat boringly, certainly was a man of routine, even working weekends.

During the night, whilst Ward was locked away in his home, Dan, between his fractured sleeps, scanned the internet, trawling for any snippet of information he could find which would link his two suspects in one way or another. He was also looking for any past misdemeanours which would give someone leverage over either of them. He found nothing.

Ilia Lemanski, a short stocky man with a nicotine odour which appeared to follow him around, originally hailed from a small forgotten slum, hidden in the centre of an otherwise modern urban area of the Russian city of Voronezh, not far from the Ukrainian border. Little more is known about him until his family moved to Kiev following the breakup of the Soviet Union. He'd been employed at the British Museum for little over a year, his application came with glowing references from the head of security at the Kiev Museum of Russian Art. Other than him living in Croydon and being a keen Fulham supporter, Dan couldn't find anything else about Mr. Lemanski – that was until his cocaine-riddled body was found floating down the Thames four days after the switch.

Dan had been sketching in the exhibit room when Simon Ward had given his tour to the Americans. He'd clearly heard him bullshit his way through a brief introduction into the life of John Harrison and the Longitude Prize, followed by a bastardised description of a cheap Victorian pocket watch dressed up to sound like a priceless marine chronometer. He desperately wanted to tear Ward to pieces, belittle him there and then, unmask him for the charlatan he was – but that would have to wait... for now.

That evening, Dan's micro-sleep was disturbed by

the arrival of two black Range Rovers outside Ward's home. Several thick-set men who wouldn't look amiss within London Zoo's gorilla enclosure alighted from the cars, two assuming guard position at either end of the parked vehicles. One man, slightly larger and older than the others, barked out instructions in some coarse Eastern-European language – Dan guessed Russian, he was right. Two of the men walked the street, checking inside nearby parked cars. One stopped abruptly on hearing a noise and drew out a gun from beneath his black leather jacket – Dan slumped down behind the van's seats until he'd passed.

Once the Russians had confirmed the area was secure, the man who'd been barking out the orders opened the rear passenger door of the second Range Rover. A tall well-built man got out of the car. He was brimming with an air of confidence and power. Dan immediately recognised him – Russian ex-KGB, possible links with the powerful Russian mafia faction – Solntsevskaya Brotherhood – and now international playboy, prominent football club chairman and owner of one of the world's largest private timepiece collections – Nikolay Ivankov.

After straightening his overcoat and checking his dark hair in the black-tinted door glass he beckoned one of the guards to open the rear door of the first car. A small crying child emerged – a girl, perhaps six or seven years' old, wearing slippers and a pale pink dressing gown. She seemed to be struggling with a school satchel and overnight bag, but no-one made any effort to help her.

Leaving the house Simon's wife, Mandy – tall and thin-faced – walked quickly down the short driveway, pushing her way past one of the steroid-enhanced henchmen as though he was a cardboard cut-out. Nikolay indicated to the child that she should go to her mother – both mother and child embraced each other with kisses and hugs. Mrs Ward exchanged some brief words with Ivankov, but Dan couldn't make out what was said. She grabbed the overnight bag from her daughter, Sophie, and swiftly ushered her towards the house... and out of the cool night air.

Once they were inside, Simon, still wearing his work suit and carrying a cartoon-emblazoned school lunch box, walked out of his home and towards the Range Rovers. He briefly paused several feet from where Ivankov was standing, and then approached the Russian with hand outstretched to greet him; the gesture wasn't returned.

Again, Dan wasn't close enough to hear any of the conversation between Ward and the Russian, but seeing Ivankov open the lunch box and take out the Harrison chronometer was enough for him. A grinning Nikolay nodded to Simon, closed the lunch box and returned with it to his car. The two Range Rovers left as quickly as they had arrived – in total they'd been there for less than five minutes.

Still sitting outside Ward's house, Dan searched the internet for details of Ivankov's luxury Park Lane home. Using the 22nd century software installed in his smartphone, it took him seconds to retrieve the exact GPS co-ordinates for every room in Nikolay's apartment. Jason may need these he thought, then he pondered his next step. Should he confront Simon Ward? What had he and his family been through – what psychological torment had that poor little girl of theirs endured at the hands of that Russian bastard? Was Ilia's death a warning to them? Perhaps a warning to keep quiet and they'd stay safe.

Dan chose to approach the Ward family. He wanted to reassure them that all would be okay – The Time Store would see to that. He paused in front of their door and tried to make out the conversation which could be heard coming through the lounge window – although, by the tone, the voices were strangely jubilant. He couldn't quite make out the gist of the talk. His right index finger pushed firmly at the door bell. There was no immediate answer, but he could detect a significant change in their voice tone, it was now more frantic – louder, yet still undecipherable.

Dan peered through the gaps in the horizontal window blind and into the Wards' lounge. Opened up in the middle of the floor was the school satchel, bundles of red fifty-pound notes scattered all around it. Mandy was desperately trying to force several bundles from the sofa back into the already bulging overnight bag. The entrance door opened. Dan was confronted by a gun-wielding Simon, who steered him through into the house.

An inquisitive, teddy bear clutching Sophie, who'd hurriedly been carried off to bed by her mother, came to the top of the stairs to see who had arrived. Simon insisted that she returned to her room, or she wouldn't be allowed to sleep over when Eva – Ivankov's daughter – was feeling better. Sophie obeyed her father without question.

Using his phone Ward took a picture of Dan and messaged it to Nikolay for advice. Mandy insisted their house guest had to be Ivankov's problem to deal with. They'd dealt, in their own way, with the greed of Ilia Lemanski – Ivankov could have Dan's blood on his hands, something he wasn't a stranger to. For Dan the jigsaw was now complete, he needed to return back to his own timeline, to his true time – but how? He couldn't just disappear in front of their eyes... or could he?

"Toilet. I need to use the toilet," said Dan fidgeting slightly.

"Just sit there and shut the fuck up," growled Mandy.

"Fine... Your carpet – your sofa," smirked Dan in reply.

"Don't even think about it." Using the back of her right hand Mandy slapped Dan sharply across the face.

"Here." Simon gave Mandy his gun, and pulled Dan to his feet. "Let him use the back one for Christ's sake."

At gunpoint Mandy and Simon directed Dan to the small toilet/utility room just off from their kitchen.

Closing the door behind him Dan flicked the light switch and looked at his face in the small mirror on the wall. His cheek, which was quite sore, had defined pink and white rash marks where Mandy had struck him.

"Bitch," he thought. Clenching ring to bracelet, he disappeared.

It had taken Dan several minutes to recount his past two weeks. Neither Jason nor Sarah could believe how devious Simon Ward had been, but then money, debt and greed can easily corrupt the weak. It came as no surprise at all when Dan mentioned Ivankov; he was ruthless in his approach to acquiring items for his collection. Death and destruction had followed him throughout his life – why should this be any different?

Whilst Dan had been bringing the two of them up to speed, Jason had been busy etching some bracelets using the various co-ordinates supplied by Dan, plus a few more he'd made notes of during his office laptop scrolling.

"Okay. We'll each bring one back, get them ready. Then to the Association," instructed Jason. "Questions?" Jason handed out two bracelets to Dan and four to Sarah.

"Four?" asked Sarah.

"Yes. The third is to sort the kid out. When we're all here, go back and call a relative, anyone who can look after her."

"For how long?"

Jason chose not to answer that. "The fourth is to get the Harrison back on its plinth before anyone notices it's missing."

"Thanks, Jason. Give me the easy bit why don't you," replied Sarah sarcastically.

Time, usually a surplus commodity to the Bradbeer family, was now running. They were balancing on a finite knife edge – they had forty-two minutes, short minutes, not to save the world from imminent cataclysmic doom, not to save one of their own family, be it past, present or future... they had forty-two minutes to save themselves from their father's scorn – they now had forty-one minutes and fifty-two seconds to save the British Museum from David Bradbeer's potential eruptional fury.

Clutching a bag of clothes and crouching down, directly on the Prime Meridian, Dan was the first to leave the Round Room.

He appeared, once again, this time crouched behind his van opposite the Wards' house. He watched briefly as Ivankov's Range Rovers turned the corner onto the main road, the second of the vehicles appeared to lose control and swerved slightly before disappearing.

"That'll be Jason then," he said.

Dan, mindful that he needed to allow his previous time travelled self to enter the Ward's house before *he* made a move, waited patiently behind the van. Seeing his original self being ushered into the house at gunpoint, he again chose to approach the Ward family home. This time he wanted to assure them that nothing at all would be okay – The Time Store would definitely be seeing to that. He paused at their front door, placed the bag of clothes he was carrying down on the doorstep, and using his right index finger pushed firmly at the bell.

"Who the fuck's that?" Mandy was startled, she'd not expected any callers.

"Probably Ivankov. Back for him," replied Simon pointing to the toilet door.

"What if it's not? What if it's someone with him?" Mandy was flapping, this certainly wasn't going to plan.

Simon grabbed a dining chair. "That should hold," he said wedging it under the toilet door handle. "Now calm down, and give me the gun."

Dan rang the doorbell for a second time. The entrance door opened. Dan confronted the gun-wielding Simon, and with one swift, forceful punch sent him flying off his feet and into his own hallway. At precisely the same time as Dan landed the punch, Mandy's head was sent crashing through the glass-panelled kitchen door. Dan recognised the glowing bracelet on the hand that had a tight grip on Mandy's hair.

"That'll be Sarah then," he said, pulling Ward up to his feet. "Slap her one for me please, sis!"

"My pleasure," replied Sarah as she dragged the kicking and screaming Mandy into the lounge.

Simon stared into the kitchen. The chair he'd forced tightly under the toilet door handle was still in place, and yet his captive was standing before him – how could that be?

"Daddy... Daddy. I can't get to sleep. It's too noisy!" Sophie, for a second time, teddy bear in hand, was at the top of the stairs shouting down.

"Tell her to go back to bed... Tell her again that if she does as she's told, when Eva is better – she can have a sleepover, maybe tomorrow." Using Ward's own revolver Dan applied direct force into Simon's rib cage, twisting the gun sideways. Ward complied – Sophie once again obeyed her father's wishes and returned to her room. Dan collected the bag of clothes he'd left by the entrance and then pushed Simon into his cash-strewn lounge.

"Where's Mandy?" demanded Simon. "What have you done with my wife?"

"Oh, don't worry. You'll see her soon. Very soon. Now get changed." Dan gave him a firm push and threw the bag of clothes at him.

Once Simon was changed he was dragged down to his knees and kicked sharply in the abdomen. Winded, Simon crumpled to the floor. Dan then took a hood from out of the bag, and placed it over Simon's head; Dan was now able to link arms with Simon without any resistance.

They disappeared.

Simon felt the grip release on his left arm as he was helped up to his feet. He'd been moved, he didn't know how, but he knew he was not in his lounge. The floor no longer had a warm, wool-rich carpet, this floor was cold and hard, not welcoming in the slightest. The whole room or area was cool. He could feel a chill on his legs, through the breeches and stockings he had been forced to wear, perhaps he was outside. There were no aromas – save for one, the hood made sure of that. All he could smell was antiseptic. He'd thought at first the odour was within the room, but his mind was telling him otherwise – however, now deprived of two senses, he was in a state of total disorientation. The man, whoever he was, certainly didn't want him to have any clues as to his whereabouts. Shit, where's Mandy? Was she here?

He heard a voice, a man's, immediately he knew it was Nikolay. He was ranting, death threat after death threat in his recognisable broken English. My, how the mighty have fallen, he thought, as he heard the Russian's threats turn to grovelling pleas for mercy – he was nothing more than a snivelling little coward without his thugs for company, Simon thought.

How he wished now that their paths had never crossed, how he wished now that he'd questioned his own stupidity in thinking the plan was – how had Nikolay put it to him? – 'simple' – but it was too late. Gambling debts, Sophie's public school tuition fees and now Ilia's murder on his hands. No... not on his hands, on their hands. After all, Mandy – she'd been the one who murdered Ilia, pumped his body full of drugs. Christ what tempest had he brought down on the ones he loved – down upon his family? His feelings of remorse were perhaps a little too late.

A hand grabbed at his doublet and pulled him sharply to the left, he could feel himself being jostled, herded, towards some others. After a few moments he could detect footsteps, someone was circling him... them. Then a man's voice, very calm – yet very assertive.

"I'll make this brief."

Simon had heard the voice before and started to sift through endless memories of names and places in an attempt to recall it.

"Over the past few weeks you've decided to steal something very valuable from me... from my family. You've betrayed the very trust we placed in you." He felt a finger jab at his forehead, not hard, but enough to tilt his head back slightly.

Simon had it now. He knew the voice, knew who it belonged to – Jason Bradbeer.

"You've killed. You've murdered Ilia Lemanski, a man who put his trust in you, albeit a thief – killed because of your greed, your own self-righteous greed."

Simon's right hand tentatively reached out from his side. First he touched material – a coarse, almost oiled, buff jerkin – and what felt like a silken blouse. He felt flesh, a hand – thank God, it was Mandy's hand, he'd know her cold touch anywhere – he clenched it tightly. His heart, at last – for now – thankfully slowed.

"And you, Nikolay. You've attained more from life than anyone, more than most men can dream about. What would some people give just to spend one day walking in your shoes? Living your extravagant ways?"

Simon detected something brush the side of his head, he sensed Ivankov had just had his forehead finger-jabbed.

"But Nikolay Ivankov, you're little more than a

power-crazed psychopath who happens to own a shit football team. You've corrupted, manipulated and twisted people throughout your entire life. God knows how many have died at your hands, or from your commands. But there'll be no more."

Again the Russian ranted a mix of threats, between pleading his soul away and offering Jason wealth beyond his wildest imagination – but Simon figured Nikolay had already lost – they all had. His thoughts now turned to Sophie; quietly beneath the hood, he cried.

He sensed another movement nearby.

"Ah good, all sorted?" Jason's tone was suddenly friendlier.

"Yes," replied Sarah, to Jason's question. "Hilary Kent from next door is with her now. Her aunt, Gemma, is on her way over – I've brought the cash back here, better that than countless questions."

Gemma, that's ok, thought Simon – she'll look after Sophie – far better than we have. By now, Simon had accepted his fate, whatever it might be.

"Do you know what a marine chronometer is, Mrs Ward? Let me tell you, I'm sure your two, er… partners here already know what one is, and the history surrounding the Longitude Prize."

Simon could still hear Jason's footsteps circling as he, ever so quickly, gave Mandy a lesson in maritime navigational history and the life of John Harrison.

There was no more talking. Once again Simon felt someone pull at him, almost positioning him on an exact spot. He felt his right hand being placed on his hip, and an instruction to leave it there – but not from Jason, it was from whoever had taken him, whoever had hit him.

He had a vivid picture in his mind. Behind him was a hole, a grave, which was to become – very shortly – *his* grave. Simon gritted his teeth and tightened his fists, waiting for either a bullet to strike him down, or perhaps a blade through his heart – if only he could see, if only he wasn't wearing this stupid hood. Someone clenched his arm.

"Friggin' hell... I never expected it this rough," shouted Dan as he clung to both Simon Ward and a davit which was swinging aimlessly on the quarter deck. "Hold on... I'll take the hood off you."

A few feet away, Nikolay was clinging tightly to the main mast for all his life's worth. Jason removed his hood and handed him a woollen Monmouth cap to wear. Spray from the mountainous waves lashed down on the decks of the second-rate ship of the line as it rode the Atlantic swells, in search of a safe route to Portsmouth.

Even seasoned mariners braced themselves in whatever way possible, riding out the massive roller-coaster high saltwater torrents. Finally, Sarah appeared with Mandy, as one of the stern lanterns from the poop deck broke free, the howling gale sending it crashing into the binnacle, and then over their heads – skimming along the deck, before smashing into the ship's belfry. Mandy froze to the spot, riveted by fear.

An almighty swell surged high, the wind growled with the energy of an enraged mountain bear, as the torrential rain lashed down at them. Nikolay's knuckles whitened as his grip tightened on the nearby lanyards.

Mandy was on her knees, crawling along the

quarter deck, helplessly seeking refuge from the cruel sea. A helping hand reached out, pulled her to her feet and pushed her through a doorway and into a dark, musty cabin. That was the last Simon ever saw of his wife.

"Welcome to H.M.S. Association – I'd hold tight if I were you," hollered Jason above the night wind.

"You bastards," screamed Simon. "You know where you've brought us. You know what happens."

But there was no reply. Jason Bradbeer had – along with the two others who'd brought them all there – disappeared.

Following a quick shower and change in The Time Store's safe room, Sarah arrived at the museum just before opening time, presented her credentials and then waited patiently for them to be verified.

She'd asked for Simon Ward, but was told that for some reason he'd not turned up that morning. Not an issue; she explained that she needed to gain brief access to one of the exhibits – a carriage clock.

A somewhat large group of Japanese tourists had descended upon the exhibition hall. Sarah had timed her arrival to perfection. On entering the gallery the curator she was with was approached by one of the tourists, who was trying to explain that the Harrison chronometer was nothing like the photograph in the exhibition guide. As soon as the curator opened the display Sarah was allowed to take over – a quick sleight of hand when turning her back, and the pocket watch and chronometer had once again swapped places.

"It must have been the light and the angle you

viewed from," she explained to the tourist, as the display was once again locked and alarmed.

With seconds to spare the three of them had managed to avert a major Bradbeer disaster, something their father never got wind of. Simon and Mandy Ward were reported as missing persons to the police, Nikolay Ivankov was believed to be cruising on his yacht somewhere off the coast of Zakynthos. Sarah decided that the money recouped from the Wards' lounge should be donated anonymously to her mother's favourite charity.

Sarah and Dan spent the next hour phoning clients and then, with their father's blessing closed the shop early. Too good an opportunity to waste, Dan headed for Aruba and a few hours of beach relaxation, whilst Sarah headed for 1960's Carnaby Street. In the end Jason's Olympic swim fest bore podium results for Team GB, in the Men's 200m breaststroke – what a perfect end to the day, especially as he shared it with Melissa from No.41.

The Scilly naval disaster occurred on the night of 22nd October 1707. A fleet of 21 ships, returning from Gibraltar, led by the Commander-in-Chief of the British Fleets, Sir Cloudesley Shovell was thought to be sailing safely west of Ushant, an island outpost off the coast of Brittany, France. Due to a combination of bad weather and the mariners' inability to accurately calculate their longitude, the fleet was unaware that it was off course and closing in on the Isles of Scilly instead. Before their mistake could be corrected, the fleet struck rocks and four ships were lost.

HMS *Association*, a 90-gun second-rate ship of the line struck the Outer Gilstone Rock off Scilly's Western

Rocks at 8pm and sank, drowning her entire crew of about 800 men and Admiral Shovell himself. The flagship went down in three to four minutes.

HMS *Eagle*, a 70-gun third-rate ship of the line also sank losing all hands. HMS *Romney*, a 50-gun fourth-rate ship of the line hit Bishop Rock and went down with all but one of her crew. The least unfortunate ship of the four – the fireship, HMS *Firebrand* – lost only 28 of her crew of 40.

The exact number of sailors who were killed in the sinking of the four ships is unknown. Statements vary between 1,400 and over 2,000, making it one of the greatest maritime disasters in British history.

The sole survivor from the three largest ships was a butcher, George Lawrence.

As for the deaths of three people who joined them, two of them would almost certainly have had Dan killed by the third, so in essence it was considered to be self-defence. Had they altered true time? Possibly, but then perhaps that's how true time was destined to be for the three of them.

CHAPTER 15

Time to Reflect

The World of Timepieces exhibition was originally planned as a four country tour. However, the subsequent interest and success of the exhibition saw the Bradbeers agreeing to grant the continued loan of their pieces as the tour was extended to include museums in Berlin, Moscow, Madrid and Amsterdam. This meant that once again each of them would, in turn, be spending time away from the family, though thankfully the relocation timings of the display meant that they'd all be together in March 2013.

March had arrived and the family were prepared for what they knew was going to be a very sombre month – one of memories, one of tears and certainly one to be together.

Twenty years ago David Bradbeer made the toughest decision of his life. It had been, and still was, the worst day of his life, the saddest day of his life – for that was the day Helen, his wife, passed away. Helen Bradbeer had been the most amazing, wonderful and loving person he'd ever known.

They'd met when they were teenagers. David, entranced by the way Helen smiled at him, would often carry her school bag for her as they walked home hand-in-hand from their respective Roan schools. Helen Lane, as she was then, was a student at Greenwich's Roan School for Girls, and was considered to be one of Mrs Barber's most outstanding pupils. David studied at the neighbouring Roan Grammar School for Boys, but would often be sent back in time by his parents to visit various academic scholars for extra tutorage to improve his grades.

For her eighteenth birthday, and with his father's permission, David had been allowed to take Helen to a 16th century Venetian Carnival. Helen had always known that she liked David, but it was on this day that she'd fallen in love with him. Three years later, during a true time walking holiday in Iceland, and on Helen's 21st birthday, David, romantic as ever, got down on one knee and proposed to her in their Reykjavik hotel.

"Yes! Yes! Yes!" Helen had screamed as she flung her arms around him, to the applause of the other diners in the hotel that evening.

David's parents readied an apartment above No.7 for the newlyweds to live in, and within two years they were proud to announce a future addition to the family.

"Don't you dare be going forwards to check what paint to buy, David Bradbeer," warned Helen.

David, mistakenly, read this as, "Don't waste money on guessing what colour we need... go and find out." And so the junk room was cleared, redecorated with a boyish pale blue theme and transformed into a nursery, in time for the arrival of baby Jason Matthew Bradbeer.

No sooner had Jason moved from the small nursery room into his own 'big room', the colour theme had to be changed to a pastel pink. Jason was three when his baby sister, Sarah Louise, arrived in the world. David and Helen's family was now complete, or so they thought, because a couple of years later, out came the blue paint once again, and along came Daniel Matthew.

Dan was only eight years old when, while on vacation with old school friends, Helen died during a freak, true time, Alpine skiing accident. The Swiss coroner's inquest confirmed that Helen, although a very competent skier, as a result of a bad fall, had suffered severe spinal damage and major internal bleeding. Cause of death – accidental.

Yes, they could have changed the course of events and prevented Helen from going on the piste that day. Even better, David could have had another holiday pre-planned to coincide with the skiing trip; that would have been easier. In fact, there were probably a million and one things the Bradbeers could have done to alter Helen's fate.

David's mother insisted – demanded – that they prevent the accident, if not for their love of Helen, then for their love of the children. Matthew, David's father, counselled his son on true time fate. Helen had died in true time. If they were to alter the past then they must be prepared to spend an eternity living out of sync with what should be. Matthew advised that this wouldn't be just for the Bradbeer generations of today, but also for those to come.

Consumed with grief, being torn apart by the decision which only he could make, David fled. He needed time to reflect, time to consider and time to mourn – for he knew deep down that his father was right. More importantly he knew that Helen would have said his father was right.

David went back in time and spent thirteen months in his favoured South America, living amongst the Uros people of Lake Titicaca on their floating island homes. He spent his days reaping the totora reeds, on which the lives of the Uros depended. Not only did they build their homes from the reeds, but also much of their diet and medicine involved the totora crop. He learnt to fish, a passion which never left him, he learnt to hunt for survival and he learnt the extent to which life depended on food and warmth. Finally he learnt to embrace life for the riches it held and the spirit it possessed.

He returned to true time cleansed of grief and sorrow, and with a renewed conviction and purpose; a man with one solitary ambition – to be the father Helen had wanted him to be. He would ensure that she'd always be proud of him... and that started with the simplest, but perhaps the most important things of all – hugs and lots of love for his children... their children.

His three children now raised their glasses and toasted the memory of their mother.

"To Mum. God bless you."

"To Mum."

"Miss you, Mum."

David lifted his glass from the table and the four crystal wine glasses rang out as they met smoothly over the centre of the table. "And I miss you too my love... every single day."

They'd just been enjoying a rather nice meal which David, along with more than a bit of input from Sarah, had spent the afternoon preparing and cooking. Portobello mushrooms stuffed with stilton and asparagus for starters, followed by Sarah's favourite dish, Beef Wellington, served with oodles of fresh organic vegetables. Several bottles of Dan's wine were well appreciated by all, especially a Catalonian red which he'd stumbled across via an article in the Guardian newspaper.

Dinner had been quite a muted family gathering. Out of respect for one another, each had wanted to be there, but the usual Bradbeer dry humour and sarcastic wit was somewhat missing and this further dampened the atmosphere.

It wasn't long after Sarah, the slowest eater, had put her cutlery down and declared herself as 'stuffed' that she along with her two brothers had each excused themselves from the table. "Bloody charming," muttered David. "Leave me here alone why don't you."

With Jason's help Sarah had cleared the table before she headed over to her apartment for what was, as she'd billed it, an amazing dessert. Jason loaded the dishwasher and then set about making some freshly ground coffee using the kit he'd bought his dad for Christmas, after finding it still unopened in the cupboard.

Dan had mentioned during dinner that he'd recently bought a rare French Massougnes 1805 Cognac, made during the Battle of Trafalgar, although it wasn't that rare when Dan had acquired it. With both David and Jason suggesting that Dan should have brought it to the dinner table, he was left with little choice but to go and fetch it. So with the three of them dashing off on errands David relaxed and finished off the remaining drop of red wine.

Idly flicking a stone with her left shoe, she once again turned her gaze towards her children who were happily playing with their friends. The woman, a very beautiful woman with striking auburn hair, was sitting on a park bench, on the edge of the children's playground in a corner of Greenwich Park.

Several children, three of which belonged to her, played noisily together on the roundabout and slides. The four swings, as ever, were all in use and had children queuing – some patiently, others not – for their turn to kick their legs outwards and rise in a strained attempt to get higher than their friends.

It was a pleasant summer's day, the sun was warm and bright, not too hot to warrant the use of sun protection, but warm enough to venture out without either a coat or cardigan. The park was in full bloom and a floral splendour awaited the tourists and locals as they entered to either visit the Royal Observatory, picnic, or just meander the day away amongst the park's numerous footpaths and trees.

A soft scoop ice-cream vendor was preparing to open up his shuttered kiosk, ready to face a busy day of consumer indecision. He'd not complain, far better to be busy than to have those book-reading intermittent drizzle days – they hadn't been the best spring months he could recall.

The woman's thoughts briefly drifted back to her first ever Venetian time trip and the taste of early ice cream. The memories of gondolas and gelato were abruptly interrupted by a voice from behind.

"Please don't turn around. I want to talk..."

The woman inched her head to the left – strained her peripheral vision – but noticed nothing. She moved a little to the right and through the extreme corner of her eye she could clearly see, resting on the back of the bench, a hand. She sensed by the calm tone within the voice that she had nothing to fear, but seeing the familiar ring on her visitor's hand filled her with an overwhelming desire to turn – though she didn't.

"How old are you now?" asked the woman, once again focusing on the children as they played. "No... Let me think. Around thirty I'm guessing – all grown-up now. So that would mean I've been dead for..." she paused.

"It's been twenty years. Today's the anniversary, your anniversary."

The woman could hear a slight catch behind these words, and although she couldn't – wouldn't – turn to give comfort, she could sense the upset and emotion in her child's voice.

"I just needed to see you, to hear you. I miss you."

The woman twisted her body slightly to her right, just enough so that she could touch her child's hand, enough to give it a firm, yet reassuring, loving squeeze.

Two small blue tits swooped down to take water from a drinking fountain, which was still running – they only had a brief moment to quench their thirst, in a few seconds the button would release and halt the water flow – the birds would then return to their oaken perch, and await the next needy human.

"Look at you over there waiting for the swings with Georgie Morrison. The two of you were inseparable. 'Best of friends forever', you'd say. Do you keep in touch?"

"No. The Morrisons moved area. Exeter I think." A pause. "I need to ask you something. Something's bothering me."

"What is it, child?" There was a shift in the woman's voice, concern. "What's bothering you?"

"There was an accident, a very bad one. Lots of tears and sorrow. Lots of regrets... many, many sleepless nights."

The woman didn't respond to this, she would want more information before commenting.

A young couple walked slowly past the bench, the man was proudly pushing a gleaming navy blue Silver Cross pram, his doting partner coochie-cooing at every opportunity.

"We argued. About going back in time and possibly fixing it. Making things not so bad, putting this family back together, perhaps."

"Family... those are always difficult decisions. Did you decide on what course to take?"

"Maybe. But I still don't agree with it, even if it's right. I don't agree with it – I don't have to, do I?"

"No... No you don't."

"I don't understand true time. I know I should, I know we cause blips every time we travel – some bigger than others – and I know that as we go through life the blips will naturally iron themselves out to restore time to how it should be."

"Then what is it you don't understand?"

"Why can't we just stop this accident from ever happening – surely it wouldn't be such a massive blip? Why must this family suffer? If we can't stop this... then what is our purpose?"

Suddenly there was a mass exodus of children running from the playground, scattering in several directions, returning to their parents or guardians, some aiming for the bench. Their peace had been shattered – and why? The ice-cream hut was finally open.

"Would you like an ice cream?" asked the woman. But there was no reply, her visitor had returned to their own time – in fear of the potential childhood inquisition which could have occurred.

Dan was the first to return to David's dining room carrying two different bottles of Cognac. As well as the 1805 he'd also brought along a bottle of Massougnes 1801 for comparison. David wondered if his son knew that he had over £250,000 worth of fine French alcohol in his hands. Perhaps not, he thought, judging by his haphazard handling.

Sarah, having changed into a more relaxing outfit of t-shirt and joggers was the next to arrive back in the dining room, bringing with her a homemade white chocolate and vanilla cheesecake.

"Just a taste for me, please. I'm not a brandy lover," she instructed, watching Dan pour out some of the amber liquid into four wide tulip-shaped glasses.

"That looks very nice," said David as Sarah placed the cheesecake on a table mat. "Is it the same one you made at Christmas?"

"Sort of – I've added some proper white Belgian chocolate this time, not that cheap stuff Dan bought."

Although there was a door between David's kitchen

and dining room, surprisingly it was the one leading from the hallway through which Jason entered, carrying a tray laden with the freshly made pot of coffee, together with cream jug, sugar bowl and coffee cups.

"I'll have to have a look at that door handle tomorrow," said Jason, nodding his head towards the door leading to the kitchen. "How long's it been sticking for?"

"I didn't know it was," replied David.

"Oh! Perhaps it's just me then. Who's for coffee?"

The remainder of the evening was spent eating cheesecake, drinking coffee and alcohol and passing the photo albums around. They shared in the warm, cherished memories that each had for Helen. David's children sat glued to his every word as once again he told them about how he'd planned the walking holiday to Iceland and his proposal to their mother. The matter of true time and changing things wasn't raised at all; the family had long accepted that they mustn't interfere in their own fate.

Dan, for the most, listened intently as his family laughed, joked and commented about events long past. He'd been too young to remember much about his mother, and what little he could recall he was unsure whether it was the memory of his own experiences or that which he'd heard recounted by others.

The one true memory he kept had unfortunately never been captured on celluloid, nor were his brother and sister watching at the time, as they were too busy eating their ice creams. But he remembered it as though it was yesterday. He could still feel the warm air brushing past his cheeks as he held onto the chains for dear life.

"Come on, Daniel. Lean back! Push those legs out!"

Those were the words he could always hear whenever he thought about his mother. He could hear them as clear as he could hear the voices around him in the room. It was as though his mother was behind him, giving a helpful push every now and then.

"Hello, Dan. Earth calling Dan."

"Oh! I'm sorry, I drifted for a minute," said Dan, realising that he must have zoned out for a few moments.

"Anywhere nice?" asked Sarah.

"Just the park," he replied casually.

CHAPTER 16

Radio Times

The day Dan had arrived back from God knows where, and collapsed in a frazzled heap on the floor of the Round Room, was now legendary, passing almost into family folklore. Dan's Anomaly, they all called it now – even Dan.

Of course, over the years, he had spent many a time trip searching for clues which could point to some explanation, but as time was so vast he had no reference point from which to start. He'd spent hours on the internet researching possible reasons for time travel on that date, but as clients could choose any period to which they wished to go, any research was in vain. He still berated himself over letting it happen at all, and hoped that he could eventually find something connected to the incident, no matter how tenuous that link might be.

It was now 2014. Five years had passed since the day of Dan's Anomaly. The Time Store had flourished, and succeeded in maintaining its primary objectives and goals.

Through the hard work and commitment of the Bradbeer family and with David at the helm, business was booming.

Dan had been given, and was more than happy to take, the last three days off work. It was now a regular occurrence for him, mid-October, to take a few days holiday on and around the time of his Round Room incident. Throughout the years he'd been subjected to a stream of friendly wind-ups, mainly from Jason, and for the most part was able to take these in his stride. However, even after five years, he still became tetchy around the 14th, finding jokes and jibes impossible to cope with. It was best for everyone that Dan should stay well away from The Time Store.

So Dan had spent the Monday chilling in his apartment on the fourth floor of The Time Store buildings, listening to very loud music – his favourite Dave Matthews Band of course followed by a bit of extra loud Foo Fighters. Sarah knocked on his door mid-evening and quite rudely and somewhat harshly, he thought, told him to turn his music down to a more friendly level. Not fair at all, he chuntered to himself, at least it was decent music, not like the soppy stuff she listened to. However, he dutifully turned it down, opened a bottle of wine, and had assorted cheese and posh biscuits before bed.

He thought he had it all under control, he'd only been a bit grouchy this time, but on the actual anniversary, the 14th, he'd woken up feeling furious with himself all over again, frustrated that he couldn't remember anything, still confused and bewildered. Why had his arm burnt? And where the bloody hell had he been? He was older now, supposedly wiser and less impetuous; more wary. What had he done back then, when he was more foolhardy? What dodgy time period had he gone back to... or forward to...

that had caused him to be deposited so cruelly in the Round Room that day?

Since then, he'd had more than a few urges to do something intrepid in time, but had mostly tried to resist, as he was worried about the consequences – scared that he would have another memory loss and frighten his family once more. He was aware that Sarah had been looking after him from a distance – she was becoming more like their mother every day – and although she probably didn't know it, he had noticed what she'd been up to over the years – letting him do his own thing, but caring and checking from afar. He liked that about her.

He spent a large proportion of the Tuesday trawling the internet afresh, trying to find anything vaguely relevant. He already knew about the 'legendary' Cliff Richard's birthday and the bleeding Battle of Hastings, neither of which required any further consideration. There was nothing of significance, except perhaps a Welsh mining disaster on that morning in 1913. There had been an explosion at Universal Colliery near Caerphilly, killing 439 miners and one rescuer. That could explain his burnt arm, his collapse and also his memory loss, but somehow it just didn't seem to fit. He was helpless. He couldn't very well scour the current internet for anything that might have happened in the future, could he...? So short of going forward in time to this date in a year, in two years, in three years... what could he do? And forward in time to where? So what was the point anyway? What he should be doing is somehow scanning the past – and possibly the future – from an all-seeing virtual vantage point for anything drastic that might have befallen him. Impossible.

Dispirited by his futile brooding, he felt too lethargic to venture out. He raided his freezer and retrieved a basic thin crust mozzarella pizza. He managed to track down two mushrooms and one slice of ham from the fridge, so he chopped these up, scattered them over the pizza, then finished off with a drizzle of olive oil. Twenty minutes later, having cut the cooked pizza into six, he sat in bed, eating with his fingers, the only way to eat pizza as far as he was concerned. He got up fleetingly to make a coffee, but fell asleep before drinking it all.

He woke up surprisingly late on his last free day. After a hasty breakfast of toast with butter and marmalade, and a cup of coffee, Dan decided that he needed a good therapeutic food shopping session to stock up on decent food. He also thought that a trip out would clear his head and prepare him mentally for his return to work. He decided to go to Borough Market – one of his favourite places in London – to buy some ingredients. He took a brisk thirty minute walk to North Greenwich tube station. There were closer stations to where he lived, but he always enjoyed this walk through the newly regenerated and still constantly changing Greenwich peninsular – plus it helped him avoid the main commuter rush period.

Once on the tube it was a few stops down the Jubilee Line to the station at London Bridge, and then a five minute walk to the market. Dan loved it here – even before getting into the market itself there was that wonderful mix of old and new buildings, and that incredible way the viaduct seemed to slice straight through them. He loved this area, it felt so personal to him. It was his city, where he'd grown up. He'd even travelled back a few times to different periods in the area's history, particularly enjoying his time in 1901 when the viaduct was widened, and of course he'd worked for a few weeks in the 1850's, helping in a small way to build the present day market.

He walked through into the main fruit and vegetable area and as always, marvelled at the many rich and vibrant colours and variety of what the world could offer. Vegetable stalls were filled with parsnips, sprouts, potatoes, carrots, onions, cabbage, peppers, turnips and aubergines. The assortment was vast and in the main all organic. Fruit stalls with pink-red pomegranates, lemons, conference pears, fresh green granny smiths, strawberries, raspberries and tayberries, along with every other berry you could possibly think of were there. Oranges, more lemons and limes mirrored in colour by the more exotic sharon fruit, star fruit and kiwis were available to taste – the latter sliced open to show their far more interesting, succulent interior. A mixed selection of tomatoes in surprising colours – as well as red – yellow, orange, green, and an almost black beef tomato were in abundance. Produce was displayed differently on each stall – some in basic wooden slatted boxes, some arranged on large tables to best show off colour and shape, and others in rustic baskets inviting the browsing customer to pick up and examine.

Dan definitely needed mushrooms – three different varieties to go with the venison he was intending to buy. He chose an eclectic mix of fresh shiitake, cèps and cremini, purchasing a few of each type. Fiery-coloured sweet capsicum and Argentinean red chillies were both ticked from his shopping list along with three purple deerfield garlic bulbs. Dan loved cooking with these, often describing the flavour as starting off mild but finishing with a fervour of spice. Still living life on the edge, he also bought one

Trinidad moruga scorpion pepper. He meandered happily around the market, taking in the hustle and bustle, along with myriad sounds and nose-tingling aromas.

A tall pock-marked youth sporting a green apron approached with a platter of fruit samples, and Dan tasted an extremely delicious strawberry, a slice of apple, and a grape.

"What's this one?" he asked, pointing at a strange slice of something he didn't think he'd tried before.

"That's tamarillo mate," replied the stall assistant. "It's from New Zealand – try it."

It looked to Dan like a strange cross between a tomato and a pomegranate. He took a slice, put it into his mouth, and chewed. It was lucky the vendor had moved on, to tempt other unsuspecting people, because Dan's face could then show exactly what he thought of the tamarillo fruit. He would not be buying any of that.

He wandered over to the meat counters, stopping off first at the exotic burger stall. He liked to check out if they'd added anything new to their range, which already included crocodile, zebra and kangaroo, along with buffalo burgers. He made his way to his favourite butcher's stall, and eventually after chatting with Harvey, the proprietor, he changed his plans. Instead of the venison, he decided to buy some Scottish wild boar, something he'd not tried before.

He bought a coffee and stood leaning against the side of a stall selling freshly baked bread. As he drank he indulged in a bit of people watching, a free pastime which he enjoyed; mums with screeching toddlers, old women who'd been shopping here since they were teenagers, young men trying to get free samples of food and beer, office workers weighed down by heavy bags and rushing in their lunch hour – they were all there.

Where others in this situation might make up characters and stories for each person, embellishing some with a hint of adventure, Dan liked to guess where they'd want to go if they time travelled. His favourite today was the gobby youth with a tattoo where his hair should be – he looked out of place in the market anyway. He'd benefit from a month's time travel back to the days of National Service, thought Dan, realising that he may be sounding a bit like his father.

He finished his coffee, and couldn't resist buying some bread. He then purchased some red Duke of York potatoes to make his special mini-roasties, finally he bought an assortment of tomatoes in various colours and shapes – red baby plums, yellow cherries and one of the black beef tomatoes he'd seen before.

As had happened with countless people before him, the food on display had brought on a stomach-rumbling hunger, so Dan aimed for the take-away food stalls. The warm aroma of this ready to eat hot food ensured that he made his choice quickly. He had a salt beef baguette with dill pickle and mustard which he troughed down at a remarkably quick pace, hooking his heavy carrier bags over the crook of his elbow as he ate.

Obviously the next step for Dan was a swift pint in The Market Porter, a pub near to the viaduct. He loved this pub, had loved it through the past century and a half, with its ever-changing decor, clientele, landlords and real ales, but still the same few photographs of Borough Market circa 1870 on the wall.

After his second pint he returned home.

He kept the music levels low that evening, and also, as he was tired and had already recently eaten, decided to save his newly-acquired ingredients for the following night, after his first day back at work.

On Thursday morning, he rose early, as was normal for a work day. Well, this year hadn't been too bad for the anniversary of that confusing day he acknowledged to himself, as he made his way downstairs to The Time Store's office. He had an easy first day back, Sarah had seen to that. The first hour was spent making coffee and listening to Jason recounting his latest Egyptian adventure. The detailed process of the ancient art of embalming and mummification was not really Dan's thing though – especially just after breakfast.

The remainder of the morning was spent with his client from the previous week, Adrian Masters, who had a bit of a thing about the Romans. Last week, when Dan had met him in the pub, Adrian had explained that his mother had wanted to call him Hadrian, but his father had put his foot down, and she'd been forced to compromise, hence Adrian. However, some sort of Roman influence had persisted throughout Adrian's life, and now, at the same age as his near namesake had been when he built his eponymous wall, Adrian felt an urge to investigate further.

He had arrived at The Time Store thinking it was a kind of museum – a place where every possible fact about Hadrian and his God-forsaken wall would be made known to him so he could take it all in, and then let it go, and move on with his life; maybe get a girlfriend or a career, like normal people did.

When, dressed for the part, he linked arms with Dan

221

in the Round Room, he thought he was going to get a kind of hi-tech son et lumière display showing the construction process of part of the wall. Instead, he found himself a few seconds later, stone in hand, ready to join a few hundred other legionnaires in contributing to the formation of a structure which would divide regions, last for centuries, become a minor tourist attraction and UNESCO World Heritage Site.

Adrian and Dan laboured for several hours, doing their bit for posterity, then Adrian announced that he was hungry, and was also actually quite desperate to use the toilet, at which point, to avoid the wrath of the nearest centurion, Dan linked arms with Adrian, touched his ring to his bracelet and hurriedly returned them to the Round Room.

"Wow," marvelled Adrian. "That certainly beats any museum. I don't know how you did that mate, but it was wonderful. Roman life isn't all it's cracked up to be though – don't think I'll bother with it any longer."

Dan grinned. "I know what you mean. But don't you want to visit that real Roman village we were talking about?"

"Nah, I've had enough. I need to get a life. Don't suppose you can fix me up with a girl...?"

Dan shook his head, laughing. "Sorry mate... there are some things even we can't do."

Dan grabbed a quick sandwich for lunch – he had a big dinner planned for when he got home that evening, so he didn't need to fill up too much in the daytime.

Sarah checked on him as he was finishing his food. "Everything okay?"

"Yes, all good," replied Dan. "I'm off to meet someone this afternoon, across in Stoke Newington."

"Well, enjoy," said Sarah. "I'll probably be gone by the time you get back. I've got a meeting in Oxford Street with someone after they finish work. So I'll see you tomorrow."

"Okay." Dan threw his sandwich wrapper in the bin and slurped the last of his coffee.

It took him nearly an hour and a half to get to The Three Crowns in Stoke Newington, and would probably take him longer to get back in the rush hour. He enjoyed his meeting though. He'd had a pint of Fullers with a young music student called Zak, who'd finished his college course that summer and was struggling to decide whether to continue with his studies at university or just launch his talents onto the world.

Zak told Dan that he really wished he could have taken his girlfriend to the Leeds Festival just over three years ago. They'd only been fifteen then, and at that age they couldn't afford to go, weren't allowed to go, and wouldn't have been permitted into the festival anyway. Crystal Castles and Bombay Bicycle Club had been on amongst others, and although Dan didn't include them as anywhere near the top of his list of favourite bands, he didn't mind a good festival or two. He didn't think there would be any problem convincing the rest of his family to agree to this particular time trip at the meeting tomorrow.

Once back at The Time Store, Dan researched the festival – there'd been a birth and a death there last year. He decided to check it all out more fully in the morning, and so, exhausted, but pleased with the day's events, he returned to his apartment.

"Now for the boar," he announced to his empty apartment as he walked through the entrance door. He showered and changed first and put on some music – loud, so that he'd be able to hear it above the cooking noises; sod Sarah for now he thought, cranking it up another notch.

The next forty-five minutes were spent with Dan singing at the top of his voice, setting the table for one, peeling potatoes and chopping them into cubes for his mini-roasties, griddling his boar, sautéing the mushrooms and slicing the tomatoes. He was planning to add a few chopped slices of his scorpion chilli for added flavour, but decided he wasn't that brave yet and settled for some Argentinean red chilli instead. He opened a fairly expensive bottle of Moroccan red wine – he'd bought it a few weeks ago from a local wine shop at one of their tasting evenings. When his food was ready, grudgingly mindful at last of Sarah, he reduced the volume level on the music, then sat down to enjoy his meal. Perfect evening he thought, good job I like my own company.

After finishing off the last mouthful of boar, he cleared the table, tidied up and loaded the dishwasher. Contentedly, if a little overfull, Dan then slumped on the settee, poured himself a third glass of wine and picked up the local paper. He turned to the classified ads section to double check The Time Store's cryptic advertisement. After a few moments pondering over it, he concluded that this version was getting a bit stale now. Maybe it could be discussed and reviewed at tomorrow's meeting. He flicked idly through the rest of the paper, but nothing held his interest. At about half-past nine he switched off the music and made a lame attempt to watch a comedy show on BBC2, but it was not really his thing so he ended up channel-hopping instead.

Dan felt restless. Bored by the TV, he turned it off, but he was too fidgety to go to bed early or read a book. The wine was going down well, very smooth. He might have to open the second bottle at this rate. He contemplated going down to The Time Store and doing a sneaky bit of time travelling, but he could imagine his father's disapproving look if he travelled anywhere whilst under the influence, so decided against it.

Nearly ten he realised, looking at his watch... time for some action. He stood up purposefully. He'd decided – finally – to once and for all sort and catalogue his rapidly growing collection of gig and music memorabilia – posters, programmes and ticket stubs. After all, everyone said he'd done a brilliant job of organising the Costume Room a few years ago – how hard could it be to sort a few bits of paper? He switched on the radio for a bit of background entertainment and headed off to his spare room. He hauled, one at a time, four large heavy Ikea bags and then a battered suitcase, all of which contained his collection. As he dragged the case into his lounge he caught the tail-end of tomorrow's weather. This was followed by a vaguely familiar jingle and the radio announcer's voice.

- Good evening and welcome to Late Night Live, with me your host Bradley Stokes. Later we'll be taking your calls on the legal aspects of returning goods. But first I'd like to introduce you to tonight's special guest. Late Night Live regular, newspaper columnist and adviser to the stars – she's your friend and mine – Psychic Tara. She'll be offering advice on anything from your horoscopes to mystical wellbeing so ring in now with your questions.

Dan rolled his eyes as the station played the phone and text jingle. "Load of bollocks," he muttered to himself, taking a sip of wine. He flicked through a pristine copy of Barclay James Harvest's *Turn of the Tide* tour programme. Two of the original musicians from BJH were now dead. Ah – maybe I should ring in – see if old Tara knows how Mel and Woolly are getting on up there. Dan smirked to himself and swigged the last of his drink.

- This is spiritual hour on Late Night Live with me your host Bradley Stokes and my guest, Psychic Tara. Call in now if you have any problems. Our first caller is Marie from Croydon. Marie? What would you like to ask Psychic Tara?

- Well, it's about my cat... she died last week... I need to know if she's gone to a better place.

- Tara, over to you.

- Hello, Marie, what was your cat's name?

- Squinge.

- O...kay... and Marie, what star sign are you?

- Pisces.

- That's fine, fine, Marie, your cat is happy, she had a long life and it was time for her to go. But it's all fine.

- Oh thank you, Tara. It's so good to know, we were so close... she lived to fifteen you know... we always used to sit together in the afternoon and...

- Yes, thank you, Marie! We have lots of callers to get through. Moving on to Timothy.

- Er... Hello... Timothy here...

- Hello, Timothy… this is Tara, what can I do for you?

- It's my mother, she died last Monday.

- Sorry to hear that Timothy.

- Thank you. She always said she'd leave a will, but I can't find it. I've looked after her for years, my brother and sisters live too far away, and she told me she'd leave the house to me in her will... they don't need it you see. But I can't find the will. Tara, can you help me? Can you contact her and find out where it is?

- This must be very upsetting for you, Timothy. I'll try to help. How old was your mother when she passed away, and do you know what star sign she was?

- She was eighty-eight, and she was a Capricorn. Can you get to her?

- Hold on, I'm getting something now. Timothy, I think she's saying something about an old box in the bottom of her wardrobe...

- Yes, there are a few boxes... I've already looked... one with clothes and the other two have photographs and papers.

- Well, Timothy. I think she's definitely trying to tell me the will is in one of those boxes, she can't remember which. You should go back and check again.

- Yes, Tara. Thank you very much for that... Timothy... maybe you can hang up now and check those boxes. Ring us back later and tell us when you find that will.

"Bloody hell, is this for real?" said Dan aloud to the radio. He had sorted his programmes into piles for different bands, and was about to sort each individual pile into chronological order. He needed more wine for this task, so he opened his second, and indeed last bottle of the gorgeous Moroccan red, filled his glass to the brim, and took a long drink. He would have to buy this one again, he thought tipsily.

In his head he could quite easily see the ordered,

catalogued version of the remaining disorganised mess on the floor. He knew where he had some flat-packed cardboard boxes, just the right size to store it all. He went out to his hall cupboard and sat on the floor of the hallway assembling twenty flat-packed cardboard storage boxes, with accompanying lids.

He could hear the radio, but not clearly – the jingles he could just about make out – music was easier to detect than words – the voices were muffled, and although he could hear the general tone, the words were unclear.

Dan, speedy as ever with practical tasks, even after a bottle and a bit of wine, finished his box building in just under half an hour. He picked up three boxes and carried them through to the living room, and set them on the floor next to the programmes, which he then realised he still hadn't sorted into chronological order. He sat down heavily on the settee and poured more wine.

- *Well, we're still waiting for Timothy to call back with news of his mother's will, but our time with Tara is coming to an end. In ten minutes we'll be joined by trading standards officer Cyril Richards, who's here to take calls on our second topic – returning goods – something with which we are all familiar. Now to our last caller on psychic related issues. Hello Emma.*
- *Hi Bradley, hi Tara – I've never phoned anything like this before, but it's twenty years since my parents died, and something really odd happened to me five years ago.*

"Join the club," slurred Dan, distractedly raising his glass in the general direction of the radio, and then abruptly plonking it down again on a small side table next to where he was sitting.

- *Five years ago you say? That's a long time.*
- *Yes, five years and two days to be precise. I have no clue what it could mean, but I think it must all be connected in some way. My sister's fed up with me talking about it. I thought you might be able to find a psychic link or something.*
- *Would you like to tell us what happened, dear?*

Dan again lifted his wine glass, this time also reaching down to the floor and grabbing a photograph, which showed himself standing with Jeff Coffin, taken in Pike Place Fish Market, Seattle. He smiled, reminiscing happily that he'd actually bumped into the sax player from DMB in genuine true time, no surreptitious time travel research trips involved at all.

- *I've got all week off work, always do this time of year. So five years ago I was going through some of my parents' possessions. I wanted to sort out some photos and things to show my sister. We'd planned to spend the evening together on the fifteenth anniversary, so I was getting the memories together a couple of days before. It's twenty years now since they died.*

"You said that already," Dan pointed out to his radio as he slurped more wine.

- *So I found a newspaper cutting – a report of the accident.*
- *Yes, and what did this newspaper cutting say?*
- *That's the thing, Tara. I've got it here now and the headline says COUPLE DIE IN ROAD TRAGEDY – and they did die, they're both dead. But it said something else back then – I know it did – a different headline – it just changed – right in front of my eyes.*

- Are you sure you hadn't had a few drinks, my dear?

- No of course not!

- A bad dream maybe?

- No, Tara. I was wide awake – it was the middle of the morning.

- Okay, so what do you think you saw? Before it changed?

- TRAGIC CRASH, WIFE DIES, HUSBAND SURVIVES.

- But they're both dead you say?

- Well, yes.

"Too much wine," said Dan. "Obvious."

- Can you tell me your star sign?

- What difference does that make? This is a freaky incident don't you think? I want you to tell me what it means.

- And when did this happen exactly?

- I told you already. Eleven o'clock in the morning, five years and two days ago, Wednesday the 14th of October 2009.

"Shit... what?"

- I think the mind plays tricks sometimes, my dear. It sees what it wants to see. I don't think that this is a spiritual or mystic matter at all.

"Yes it is! Come on, Tara!"

- Well thanks. I can see I'm not going to get any answers from you. I know what I saw, and you're just trying to belittle me.

- Thanks for that. Our final call. Thank you Tara for all your advice and help, we look forward to seeing you again next week.

Just to let you listeners know – Timothy has rung back to tell us he did find his mother's will, so thanks again to Psychic Tara! And now we move on. To the legal ramifications of returning goods...

"Hang on, wait! Hold on a minute – I need details," demanded Dan. He grabbed his phone. Then paused. He'd forgotten the number of the radio station, but it wasn't long before the annoying jingle repeated it again.

"Good evening, Late Night Live, how can I help you?"

"I need to speak to that last caller... is she still on the line?" Dan was agitated now, and failed to realise the possible benefit of toning down his panic.

"I'm sorry sir. We're taking calls on the legal aspects of returning..."

"No, I don't need that," persisted Dan. "I need to speak to that last caller you had. About the newspaper cutting."

"I'm sorry..."

"You know – the one whose parents died. The changing headline. I need her number."

"Again, sir, I'm sorry, we are unable to give out the personal information of our callers."

"But this is important – how else am I going to talk to her?"

"Sorry, sir. I'm going to terminate this call now."

"Oh God." Dan now concluded that he may have had a teensy bit too much wine and was not creating the correct professional impression. He poured himself another glass.

Any idea of gigs, boxes and collating had vanished. The only thoughts ravaging his mind were to do with the radio programme. Bloody Tara. Psychic my arse. That date – the time – the exact date and time. Dan's Anomaly. Surely that wasn't just an amazing coincidence. There must be a link.

He sat there alone, thinking, drinking, for another hour. When all the wine was gone, he stood up, put on his coat, and left his apartment.

CHAPTER 17

Wake up Time

"I'm coming, I'm coming," muttered Jason, as he slipper-shuffled along his magnolia-painted hallway towards the front door of his apartment.

A few seconds earlier he'd been fast asleep, in the land of nod, dreaming of adventures in time, dreaming the hero's life. His intrepid, storybook slumber had taken him from yomping across the Falkland Islands as a Royal Marine commando, preparing to liberate Port Stanley from her Argentinean invaders, to his exploits as a swashbuckling, scurvy sea-dog, fighting for Spanish gold in the heart of the Caribbean. But alas, the door-bell prevented him from attaining the elusive pieces of eight, and woke him from the arms of Morpheus.

Jason stopped at his beech-framed hallway mirror, knotted his dressing gown, then turned to look at himself. Regrettably there was no Jolly Roger emblazoned pirate's tricorn hat on his head, nor Python-esque dead Norwegian Blue parrot perched upon his shoulder. Surely that's not how he imagined himself in the dream, he thought, as the images of his epic travels faded from his memory. The bell rang again, followed quickly by an impatient, hard knuckle-rapping knock.

"I'M COMING," he shouted. "For fuck's sake... keep your shirt on will you. I'm coming." He smoothed down his tangled hair and straightened his robe – after all if it's Melissa from No.41 coming back for more of her man then I'd better look as good as I can, he thought, with more than a tad of wishful thinking.

Jason reached out and dropped the latch off the door, unlocking it, and then opened it up to greet his disturber. "Dan! Do you know what fucking time it is?"

"No. Who cares? I need to talk..." replied Dan, slightly inebriated. Pushing his way past his brother he strode off to the lounge. Jason slowly followed, pausing to look in the mirror once again, hoping for a glimpse of a cutlass, or at the very least a solitary eye patch.

Dan was helping himself to a glass of Jack Daniels; no ice, no mixer. As it vanished within seconds of hitting the crystal glass, he poured another. "Want one?"

"Might as well, if it saves you drinking it all I suppose."

Jason's lounge was also painted magnolia, an easy to maintain theme which ran through his entire apartment. Blockbuster movie posters in beech frames hung from three of the walls, his favourite being the James Bond *From Russia With Love* poster, signed by producer Harry Saltzman. Others included *The Shawshank Redemption* and *Grease* although the latter was a remnant from an old relationship, which, ironically, he never seemed to find the time to change, and now couldn't since he'd foolishly told Melissa that it featured among his favourite movies.

There was a nice thick, creamy white rug on the laminate floor, just under a stainless steel modern gas fire with imitation marble hearth. To the right was an entertainment stand housing quite an old, seldom watched television and also, in contrast, a state of the art Bang and Olufsen sound system, complete with turntable, always on stand-by, to play one of the hundreds of vinyl albums Jason possessed. Two non-matching sofas, one in a dark, almost burgundy red material, and the other, a slightly larger, somewhat battered black leather one, completed the furnishings. Jason sat himself down on the leather sofa and took the drink from Dan.

"This better be good," insisted Jason, still feeling a touch ruffled.

Dan, glass in one hand, bottle in the other, sat cross-legged on the red sofa, saying nothing. He slouched forward and stood the bottle on the floor, before balancing the glass precariously on the arm of the sofa. With one elbow on each knee he cupped his chin within the palms of his hands and then ran his fingers through to his unusually unkempt hair as he let his head drop. After a few seconds with his head in hands, Dan returned upright, unfolded his legs and took his glass in his hand, but didn't drink.

"There's someone who can help me – help us – find out what happened... I think."

"What the hell are you going on about? How much of that stuff have you had?" asked Jason, pointing to Dan's glass.

"Not enough," replied Dan, emptying the glass. He reached back down for the bottle, but Jason moved more swiftly, grabbing it before his brother got near.

"You can have another when you tell me what's going on," snapped Jason.

"I was listening to the radio, that Stokes guy... him who does the talk show... the phone-in show. He had a psychic on tonight," slurred Dan.

"What on earth are you trying to tell me?" Jason was starting to lose his patience with his younger brother. "Sit up and tell me what this is about."

"LCB... No wait, LBC... whatever. The one with Stokes on. Bradley Stokes, you know who I mean." Dan waited for a reply, but didn't get one. "He had a psychic on tonight, Psychic Tara, her off that lotto game show. Someone called in, a girl. Said that..."

Dan retold, as coherently as possible, everything he could remember from the conversation between Tara and the mystery female caller. Jason sat and calmly listened to his brother's rambling words, piecing together the story for himself, choosing not to jump in and either dismiss anything as irrelevant, or cast aside Dan's thoughts as drunken drivel.

"Well... what do you think?" asked Dan, when he'd finished.

"I think that you need to go to bed, and I need to keelhaul some conquistadores. We'll talk about it in the morning," answered Jason. "The spare room is made up, or you can sleep on the sofa – your choice."

Jason, still holding his bottle of Jack, headed off back to bed.

The alarm clock sounded off with an annoying repetitive buzzing noise. Jason's arm reached out from under his lilac duvet, yet another fragment of a past relationship, and struck the snooze button with pinpoint accuracy. It was the second of three he could permit himself before having to leap up and head for the shower. For the next ten minutes Jason lay in bed staring out at the near-empty bottle of Old No.7, debating with his inner self as to whether Dan's alcohol-fuelled gobbledegook had any credence or not.

His final ten minutes of eider-feathered warmth was abruptly cut short by the clashing and banging of doors and drawers in the kitchen – Dan's up then, he thought, as he heard the sound of some metallic kitchen utensil hitting the floor. Jason lifted himself up out of his bed, reached over to the alarm clock and reluctantly cancelled the snooze, then made his way into the shower.

Dan opened up the last of the kitchen cupboards and finally struck gold. He knew that there had to be a box somewhere in Jason's kitchen and so his search wasn't in vain when he pulled out a box of Frosties.

It was during Dan's second bowl that Jason, unusually wearing flared, faded jeans and a green and white tie-dyed shirt, entered the kitchen.

"What the hell are you wearing?" laughed Dan, munching away.

"Don't ask," replied Jason, taking a cereal bowl from the dishwasher. "I'm going to the 1970 Bath Festival of Blues with Jonesy."

"What… Neil Jones? I never had him down as having good taste in music… Christ the guy can only just dress himself." Dan looked Jason up and down again. "Seems you share his dress sense all of a sudden."

"Ha – very funny. He wants to try and meet Dave Gilmour."

"Ooh, look at you... name dropper," smirked Dan. "I suppose that's what these are about?" He pointed at a pile of albums with Pink Floyd's *Atom Heart Mother* on top.

"Well yes, but you can talk." Jason sat at the breakfast bar next to his brother and poured himself some Frosties – to his delight a plastic bag containing a small diving Tony toy launched itself from the box and into his bowl.

"Bloody hell, I didn't realise that you could still get toys in cereal boxes," remarked Dan in surprise, partly jealous that he hadn't landed the tiger toy.

"You do if you buy your groceries back in the eighties," laughed Jason. "Here – you can have it," he said, passing the toy to his brother. "Now tell me again about last night, but keep it short this time."

"I was sorting through my concert programmes, cataloguing them – year, bands and what have you." Dan stopped to shovel another mound of flakes into his mouth. "Can you get me one from the festival? I'll give you the money. That's if there are any." Dan fished into his pocket and pulled out several coins from which he selected a small, silver coin. "Here, that should cover it."

"A jolly, jolly sixpence," said Jason picking up the coin and examining it. "What the hell are you doing with one of these in your pocket? No, don't tell me. Let's get back to last night shall we?" He put down the coin and carried on eating his cereal.

"Okay. I didn't catch the first part of what was said. I knew that they'd been talking about wills and cats earlier. But it was when the caller, this woman, said that something really odd happened five years ago that my brain tuned in."

"Well that's a first," commented Jason sarcastically.

"Carry on."

Ignoring his brother's quip Dan continued. "She'd called in about the death of her parents, in a car accident. It had been the anniversary of the crash and she'd tried to tell this Tara, the psychic, that some newspaper headline had changed."

"What did Mystic Tara say? What was her explanation?"

"Psychic."

"What?"

"Tara. You said Mystic. She's Psychic."

"Does it fucking matter?"

"Does if you're Tara," replied Dan. "She implied that the woman was a piss-head."

"That show certainly knows how to attract them!" muttered Jason through his breakfast crunching.

"Then Tara really annoyed the caller by asking for her star sign."

"What difference does that make?" asked Jason.

"That's what she said. Anyway, Tara asked her exactly when it happened. And she replied, 'Eleven o'clock in the morning, five years and two days ago, Wednesday the 14th of October 2009'."

"Shit... what?" Jason dropped his spoon.

"That's exactly what I said. See, I told you it was important."

"You said something last night about calling the station to speak to her?"

"Yes. But I nearly lost it with them, so they hung up. Apparently they can't give callers' names out. It's that Data Protection Act shit. Then they told me they were terminating the call and hung up on me."

"They said what?" laughed Jason, pouring them both a coffee. "Do you blame them?"

"Well no... but... well, what the fuck. They could've at least listened to why I wanted to know who she was," crunched Dan, eating his last mouthful of now soggy breakfast.

"Oh yeah, and what were you gonna say? Hi... I'm Daniel Bradbeer... and I come from a family of time travellers... I think I might be able to help."

"Well, given their other callers... time travel seems quite lame."

"Alright. Okay, I'll call the radio station, and maybe e-mail them as well, see if we can find out who the mystery caller is, or at least where she's from. However, in the meantime I have some Pink Floyd to endure." Jason's face radiated the most amazing sarcastic smile it ever had, an almost 'beat that if you can' expression if ever there was one. "What are your plans? You don't have a client today, do you?"

"No... I've got a busy morning though. Very busy in fact," smiled Dan. "Dad's been on about us having an escape shaft leading off from the Round Room for quite a while now and I came up with this brilliant idea the other day."

"Which is?" Jason asked, putting his mug down.

"I'm going to convince Flamsteed to put a telescope down that well at the back of the observatory. He'll need to put a staircase all the way down."

"Ah, okay," replied Jason. "And how do you expect to convince him?"

"Oh, I'll play to his own self-importance. You know the sort of thing. Flamsteed, my dear man. In years to come people from all over the world will pay homage to your works and endeavours. Signposts will point the way to Flamsteed House, Flamsteed Way and so forth. Could you imagine how they'd feel if there was no Flamsteed Well?" Dan theatrically gave his great speech.

"Very good, very good. Let's hope he falls for it."

"He will if I offer some financial inducement, maybe a guinea or two."

"Right, I'm going, you walking with me?" Jason finished off his coffee, picked up a couple of Floyd albums and handed them to a nodding Dan. "Good, you can carry these for me."

Jason preferred to live away from The Time Store, as he attempted, but more often than not failed, to keep his work and social lives apart. It was far easier when going on dates to refer to work as 'The Watch Emporium', and consider it to be an exclusive jewellery shop, which wasn't too far from the truth.

He lived on the north of the river in a new apartment block just next to Island Gardens Park; he loved the view which his balcony offered. The River Thames, The Cutty Sark, The Old Royal Naval College, Greenwich Park and just a small part of the Royal Observatory were all in view. He'd once joked with Melissa that one day he'd take a chainsaw to a couple of old conker trees in the park, then he'd get a far better view of the observatory buildings. Jason smirked to himself a few days later, when she mentioned that the trees had disappeared, and when they walked the park pathway there were no signs of stumps anywhere – it was as if they'd just vanished into thin air.

The two brothers left Jason's apartment and took a brisk walk under the river through the 110 year-old Victorian Greenwich foot tunnel. The 1,200ft tunnel with its white tiled walls, although somewhat shorter, always reminded the brothers of their own passageway running under the park.

They emerged from the tunnel's glass domed south bank entry/exit building into the bright daylight. Jason gazed up in awe, as he did most mornings, at the masts of the now fully restored tea clipper The Cutty Sark. Was there any wonder that he often dreamt of an adventurer's life on the high seas, he thought. Dan was more inclined to look at the Gypsy Moth pub than the museum ship, although on one time trip he had sailed on the Ferreira, as The Cutty Sark was once called, at the turn of the last century, when it sailed under the Portuguese flag.

Upon seeing a large group of tourists with a flag-waving guide standing in front of the ornate black iron Water Gates, Jason and Dan opted against using their usual route to The Time Store. This would have led them through the well-tended grounds of Christopher Wren's impressive twin-domed masterpiece; a World Heritage Site, originally designed and built by Wren as the Greenwich Hospital in the latter part of the 17th century. It had been used throughout the 20th century as The Royal Naval College until its closure, and now the buildings were proving to be a popular tourist attraction, as well as some parts being leased to local universities and colleges.

During their walk to The Time Store both avoided talking about the previous night and the radio show. Dan was enthused with the Flamsteed Well idea, mainly because if it paid off, the tour guides up on the hill would be telling tourists of an idea he'd had when drunk one night; although the warm voice of last night's mystery caller continued to resonate in his mind as they walked. Jason, on the other hand, couldn't help gloating about his morning jaunt to the festival and the chance to meet with Dave. Of course he'd witnessed many of Floyd's live performances, but to actually watch one and then to have the possibility of meeting Mr Gilmour himself – now that was something completely different.

After crossing the Romney Road they cut through into the grounds of The National Maritime Museum. Outside the main doors to the museum stood two giant anchors, one each side of the entrance – a favoured tourist photo opportunity if ever there was one. Even the Bradbeers had taken many pictures over the years, using the anchors as a growth indicator for the three children.

The two brothers passed by a couple of early morning art students who were already encamped on the neatly trimmed lawns, engrossed in their pastel interpretations of the historical buildings. Dan stopped to take a brief look. The artist had beautifully captured the benched colonnade between the museum and The Queen's House, which was set in front of the rising park. However, the Royal Observatory and Flamsteed House in the background were still only faintly outlined in charcoal.

"Since when have you had an interest in art?" asked Jason when Dan had caught him up.

"About thirty seconds ago. Did you see how gorgeous she looked?" replied Dan.

It was Jason who stopped where the two footpaths crossed one another. "It's hard to imagine that a Royal palace once stood over there. I mean, King Henry VIII was born there. Anne Boleyn actually lived there – Mary, Elizabeth... We're standing where Kings and Queens of England once stood." They were looking at the Old Royal Naval College. The site's history went back further than the college and hospital, the Royal Palace of Placentia once stood there.

"Perhaps we should go back and take a selfie with them. Imagine the looks on their faces! Anyway I thought that you'd been back to when all this was just fields."

"I have. And I did take a selfie with Lizzie up by the oak," laughed Jason. "Come on. We need to get going, can't keep my client waiting."

The conversation turned back to Jason's passion for *The Dark Side of The Moon* and Dan's strained attempt to enthuse his brother in the world of underground telescopes. They passed a row of neatly parked cycles to their left, along with a security hut, at which they both raised a hand and gestured with a hello smile to Sandeep on duty, who in turn opened the barrier for them. A row of anchors were displayed by the exit gate, the closest a large iron one from a ship of the line, a constant reminder of their museum incident of 2012 and their brief trip to HMS Association.

They walked across Park Row and through to Feathers Place. Set back, concealed from the passing eye by a few large well-placed trees stood – looking somewhat out of place among the neighbouring Victorian and Edwardian houses – the almost regal looking Georgian buildings of Flamsteed Way.

"Morning, you two." They were greeted by a bright and cheerful Sarah as they opened the door into The Time Store.

"Morning, Sarah," replied Jason, giving his sister a

brotherly kiss on the cheek. "Is Jonesy here yet?" he asked excitedly.

"Shut him up will you please, Sarah. He's been going on and on and on about The Dark Side, you'd think he was going to be a bloody Jedi warrior not a frigging hippy."

"Unfortunately not," smiled Sarah, looking at Jason's attire with some amusement. "He's called though. Said he's been held up in traffic." She laughed, as Jason – records in hand – sulked his way through to the stairs.

Dan, as usual, walked along the meridian line, this time with arms outstretched for balance, his thoughts briefly leaving the world of Royal Astronomers, wells and telescopes, and entering the spectacular world of Charles Blondin.

"And the crowd cheer in sheer exaltation as The Great Blondin once again safely crosses The Niagara Falls. Blondin graciously accepts the rapturous applause from his adoring worshippers." Dan jumped from the meridian, turned to a sympathetically clapping Sarah, and bowed. "I thank you, I thank you... I thank you."

"You're a bit too perky today young, Daniel... What's got into you? Normally you're on..."

"On what, sis... on what?"

"Well, you know. Normally you're unapproachable this week – ready to snap at the slightest thing. But not today. Any reason?" Sarah, for once, didn't mince her words. She'd picked up immediately that this wasn't her brother's usual behaviour for mid-October. For the past five years, he'd been – as she chose to call him – a total grumpy arse.

"Well possibly," he grinned. "Come on, let's go get coffee... and I'll tell you."

"I can't, I need to greet my client from Manchester... But we could talk over a pub lunch if you want. My treat." Sarah knew that the offering of lunch would work; it always did with Dan, especially if the word pub came before lunch.

"Okay, see you in The Plume," replied Dan, disappearing through the archway.

"Yes, that's good, see you in there about half twelve."

The Plume of Feathers was less than two minutes away from The Time Store, and was a firm family favourite, though on the odd occasion when Dan and Jason had decided to race there, on a loser buys first pint basis, it had been reached in just under one. Both of them had at one time or another played for The Plume Rockets, the pub's football team, but as neither were really any good, three or four matches were all they'd played before being relegated to the subs bench.

David, a real ale enthusiast, had enjoyed many a beer there, and often boasted of having met every landlord of the pub since Jacob Bethell manned the pumps back in 1691 – usually only to his family – except on one occasion when he got really drunk and had a disagreement with one recent landlord. That was a day he'd rather forget.

Sarah pottered about doing little bits of nothing in particular as she waited patiently for Joanne Hewitt to arrive and take a trip of a lifetime to see U.S. President 'Honest Abe' Lincoln. Joanne's time trip would take her to the U.S. Congress and allow her to witness Abe push through the Thirteenth Amendment to the United States Constitution, the one which permanently outlawed slavery.

The Time Store's phone rang, just once, and then went dead.

A few moments later, and coincidently at the same time as a taxi pulled up outside, it rang again; Sarah managed to answer this time. "Good morning, how can I help you?" she asked. "Yes.... yes, that's right," Sarah replied to the caller's questions, as she opened the door for Joanne. "And do you have one?"

"Hi, Sarah," Joanne whispered as she entered the building.

"Morning," Sarah replied, covering the mouthpiece with her hand, "Won't keep you a moment, take a look around, I'll be with you shortly."

Joanne nodded in acknowledgement.

"Well, we may be able to assist you. I'd need to take some more details... Mmm yes, yes... I see..." There was a long pause whilst Sarah listened to the caller, her head swaying to and fro. Occasionally she'd mutter the odd, "Yes" or "I see" or "Could you repeat that please?" before finally, "Well, Mrs Fisher, if you could just leave me your number I'll call you back at a time when it would be more convenient if you wish... No, no... I don't mind."

Sarah picked up a pen from a small lectern by the side of a Comitti clock and wrote down Mrs Fisher's number on one of her business cards. "Yes, okay. Shall we say 11.45...? Lovely, I'll speak to you then... yes, you too. Thank you... I'm sure..." Sarah rolled her eyes, "Alright, will do," and with that Sarah cleared the call.

"Oh, I'm so sorry about that." She approached Joanne to greet her properly. "Did you have a good journey down from Manchester?"

"Any news on Jonesy?" Dan asked as he opened the office door.

"No, nothing. Not yet anyway." A despondent Jason moved away from the laptop and headed towards the door. "I'm going to get out of these clothes. Give my regards to Flamsteed will you?"

"I will... Oh! Sarah and I are having lunch in The Plume, fancy joining us? She's paying, we could have this afternoon's meeting there if you want."

"Possibly, it should be okay. I'll see if I can find time. I've sent an e-mail to the radio station by the way, told them I'm your psychiatrist – and God knows I feel like it at times." Jason closed the door behind him as he left the office.

Dan sat down at the laptop to verify that the co-ordinates of the well were suitable for the needs of The Time Store. Thankfully the map service they used could pinpoint locations using hundredths of seconds; this gave them total accuracy. Once happy with the co-ordinates, Dan selected a graver from the rack and set about preparing his travel bracelet.

"Just take a seat, we may have a slight delay. Can I get you a tea or coffee?" asked Sarah as she clicked down the switch on the restroom kettle.

"Tea please, if you don't mind," replied Joanne, sitting uneasily, not quite knowing what to expect from her visit to The Time Store.

Sarah placed a small milk jug and sugar bowl on the table, along with an unopened packet of digestive biscuits. "We shouldn't be too long. My brother Jason is still in the

Costume Room, getting ready for his client – we're next."

"Oh. It's some sort of theatrical re-enactment then? Are there going to be many performers?" Joanne asked, quite excitedly, thinking she'd finally worked out what her journey to The Time Store was all about.

"Isn't Congress full of actors and performers?" laughed Sarah as she placed two teacups on the table, followed by a freshly made pot of tea. She then returned to the kitchen unit and made a mug of coffee, with milk and one sugar, for Dan. "Back in a moment, just taking this to the office – feel free to pour away."

"We'll be getting changed next," said Sarah, placing the coffee she'd made for Dan on the desk.

"You might as well go in there now."

"Jase is still in there, isn't he?"

"Yeah, but he won't be long. I think his trip is going to be cancelled, he's not heard from Neil. So he's in there losing the hippy look."

"Oh. He won't be too happy then," said Sarah sympathetically. "You're becoming a dab hand at that, be careful you don't become too good, Jason will get you doing all of them – you know how much he hates it."

Dan replaced the engraving tool back into the stand and wiped the excess tallow from the slightly glowing platinum bracelet with a lint free cloth. "Thanks," he smiled. "But he'd never admit that mine were half as good as his, so there's no fear of that – thankfully."

"That's true. Is this mine?" Sarah asked, pointing to another travel bracelet – polished, yet lifeless – neatly laid out on a crimson velvet cloth.

"Yes."

Sarah took the bracelet, which upon her touch, immediately pulsed with the life aura. She then left the office to return to her awaiting client.

"How's the tea?" asked Sarah, returning to Joanne in the rest room.

"Good, thanks – I've poured one for you," replied Joanne, who was about to bite into her second biscuit. "That's pretty." She pointed to the radiant bracelet in Sarah's hand.

"Yes, would you like to have a look?" Sarah asked, handing it Joanne.

"Strange." Upon receiving the bracelet, Joanne couldn't fail to notice how quickly the charmed glow diminished. Within a couple of seconds it had returned to a normal, although still unique, piece of platinum jewellery. "How odd, is it battery powered?"

"No... It's something similar to solar powered – more lunar."

Joanne studied the engraving on the disc, and although she knew each of the different letters and the Roman numeral it represented she couldn't quite piece them together.

"Costume Room is all yours," said Jason, popping his head around the rest room door.

"Ok. Thanks, Jase. Sorry to hear about the festival," Sarah called back, as she retrieved the bracelet and fastened it on her left wrist. "Right, Joanne. Are you ready to get changed?"

"Ready as I'll ever be," she replied, standing.

After receiving a cancellation phone call from Neil Jones, Jason decided to go for a walk, feeling he needed some fresh air and some time to allow his built-up eagerness to subside. He briefly contemplated going back alone to watch the festival, and fingers crossed, meet Dave Gilmour, but feeling heavy of heart decided perhaps another day.

He walked left, out of Flamsteed Way and into Feathers Place, a narrow street with much-desired properties. Jason had almost bought one of the recently built – well recently compared to nearby properties – town houses with their unusually arched sash windows and doorways. Although he liked the neat little iron railings, composite doors and lavish interiors, he didn't care much for the views the houses offered.

Jason stopped outside the jumbled, mishmash of houses which made up The Vicarage, possibly the oldest buildings in Greenwich. He obligingly took a photograph for a couple of tourists who stood next to the Meridian plaque on the wall. Noisy children could be heard enjoying a morning's play, their screams and shouts echoed over The Vicarage from the park's playground beyond. Crossing the cobbled stones Jason entered Greenwich Park through the large iron Park Row Gate next to the National Maritime Museum.

He wasn't in a hurry – he'd got a couple of hours to kill before meeting up for lunch with Sarah and Dan in the Plume. Jason untangled his earphones and plugged them into his mobile, selected a bit of acoustic chill-out and headed towards the playground.

He loved the boating pond, or used to, it was where his dad would take him to sail their model boats whilst his mum would watch the other two on the swings and roundabouts. The pond was virtually bone dry and a couple of park workers were standing in the middle scratching their heads.

"Problem?" asked Jason, removing his earphones.

"Yeah, the pond seems to be losing water as quick as we fill it."

"It's been like that ever since they built that thing." Jason pointed towards the large Millennium sundial situated close by, which like the pond, stood on the Prime Meridian. "Disturbed the lining," he continued.

"Oh! Well the water must drain off somewhere."

"Yes, I could give you a few bucketfuls," mumbled Jason, putting his earphones back in and continuing on his walk.

He made his way through the playground, past the coloured swings, slides, climbing frames and roundabouts. Even over his music he could hear the children as they ran around after one another, under the watchful eyes of their adult minders. Nothing much had changed in the last thirty years, since his first play days here. Of course the floor was a bit spongier, and there was certainly more bright plastic than before, but other than that nothing much had changed.

There was a young couple seated on his favourite park bench enjoying a morning coffee. Jason waited for a few moments to see if they were about to leave, so that he could pass a minute or two on the bench; well, it was always his mother's favourite, and the one where she'd sit and watch them all play. The family had a memorial plaque dedicated to her on this bench – David had arranged for it on the second anniversary of Helen's death. Inscribed on the brass plate was:

"In Loving Memory of HELEN BRADBEER ~ Always Let the Children Play."

Speeding up his stride, Jason opted for faster music and switched from his acoustic selection to a mix of Queen and U2. He spent the next hour walking the many pathways of the park, stopping off at the refreshment van outside the observatory. He sat with his drink, marvelling at the view from beneath the statue of General Wolfe, the Conqueror of Canada. No matter how many times he'd been here, either for a walk or out running with Dan, he always appreciated the awesome view over historical Greenwich, with the Canary Wharf Tower on the new horizon. Of course he preferred it when all you could see were the tall mast ships with the wind in their sails, and the old hospital below, along with the dome of St Paul's Cathedral in the far off distance. But he understood progress meant change and so gone were the galleons and sloops and in came The Gherkin and The Shard.

Closer to hand he could see the two Royal Park workers still trying to patch up the pond below. If only they knew there was a tunnel beneath their beloved park leading straight under, to where he was sitting. He clocked the time on the twenty-four hour Shepherd by the gate and was just about to head off for an early pint of Pride when he remembered Dan's morning quest. Jason wandered around to the back of the observatory buildings, and sure enough there it was along with accompanying information sign, 'Flamsteed's well telescope... 1679'. Jason laughed out loud.

He took out his phone from his pocket and snapped a picture of the sign and noticed he'd received two e-mails. One was his monthly phone bill, which he ignored. The other he briefly scanned through. "Mmm! Dan's not gonna

like that." Jason put his phone away and headed off to The
Plume.

CHAPTER 18

Police Escort

The Plume of Feathers, situated on Park Vista, with its blend of olive and Lincoln green tiles, was as much a part of Bradbeer family life as The Time Store's bracelets and adventures. Many of their best plans, plots, schemes and hangovers started off in The Plume, and no doubt many more were still to come.

The Plume, or The Feathers as it was originally called back in 1691, was – as it always had been – a quaint, traditional English pub which served real ales and good food, unlike the modern contemporaries now down in the village. It had both embraced and endured many changes to the local area over its 300 year history. The pub shared the street with Hamilton House, the former home of Lady Hamilton, Admiral Nelson's mistress. The view from the front had always been of the twelve foot high wall erected by James I to keep the royal deer in the park, or perhaps to keep the local poachers out.

Of course the pub itself had undergone structural alterations throughout time with the current facade being added in the reign of George III, but thankfully long gone were the stables along with the cows and sheep kept by old Jacob Bethell.

Jason entered through the welcoming, open doors with the plume crest shield leaded into the upper panels. He immediately checked to his right, to the two non-matching round tables under the window to see if either Dan or Sarah had arrived first; they hadn't. He went up to the dark wood panelled bar with its line of beer pumps standing proudly to attention and waited for the barmaid, Kim, to serve him.

"Morning, Jase – the usual?"

"Please, Kim," replied Jason, fishing around in his pocket for some money but finding only an old sixpence. "Can you start a tab off? I've come without any money."

"No problem. You expecting Dan are you?" Kim asked, pulling Jason a pint of his favourite.

"Yes – and Sarah – working lunch."

"Working lunch? I've seen many a Bradbeer working lunch in here. More gossip than work," laughed Kim, putting Jason's pint on the bar. "There you go, love."

Taking his first sup Jason nodded a thank you to Kim, who'd moved on to a couple he didn't recognise. He took a newspaper from the bar and sat at the usual pew.

The walls of the pub served as an historical reminder, bearing paintings of naval ships long sunk or broken, feathered and epauletted ranks, The Plume Rockets and anything vaguely British. Commemorative plates depicting a variety of images from Royal Weddings to RAF bombers were displayed on a high shelf running around the pub walls. Usually when David came in he'd settle in the corner under the painting of Winston Churchill. Dan once asked him if by sitting there he considered himself to be a leader worthy of Churchill's stature. David had told his son to stop being stupid. "I sit here because it's less distance to walk to the toilet."

Jason, not being one for tabloid gossip, thumbed through the paper quite quickly, stopping briefly to read an article about the tension in the Ukraine, their debt and Russia's grip on Europe's gas supply. Perhaps The Time Store should intervene he thought, what with winter fast approaching, but he knew his father would just say it's a matter for the politicians to sort out.

Several people came into the pub, Jason's head turning towards the door as each entered, half-expecting his brother or sister to be the incoming patron, but other than Carl whatsisname from down Park Row and Joe Thompson the postie he didn't know any of them.

Jason was on his second pint and the back pages when his sister entered along with Joanne Hewitt.

"How was it then?" asked Jason politely, whilst Sarah was at the bar.

"Amazing, absolutely amazing." Joanne, on the instruction of Sarah, replied in a whisper. "I don't know, I can't tell if I'm excited about knowing that I've just been to America, and to Congress." Joanne lowered her whisper. "Or having just time travelled."

"Yes, it gets people like that," remarked Jason.

"God, do I need that drink. Look, I'm still shaking with excitement." She showed Jason her trembling hands.

"And here it is — gin and tonic. Kim's calling a taxi for you," said Sarah pulling up a stool.

"So how was Abe then? Where did Sarah take you?"

"His State of the Union speech," interrupted Sarah.

"December, eighteen sixty-four," Joanne whispered disbelievingly.

Jason listened attentively as Joanne recounted her trip back in time to experience Abraham Lincoln's speech.

Lincoln touched on the civil war in Mexico and insisted that America had to maintain its neutrality. He brought Congress up to date on diplomatic relations with other Central and South American neighbours and outlined how a war had been averted between Peru and Spain. He informed the assembled politicians that the Government of Chile had now settled claims arising from the seizure of cargo from the brig Macedonian in 1821.

It was unfortunate for Jason that Joanne already had an extensive knowledge on the speech and was able to recount it detail for detail. Thankfully, he was spared the entire story by the arrival of her taxi.

Sarah and Jason waved Joanne off as she headed back for the railway station and her return journey to Manchester, another satisfied client of The Time Store.

"What's wrong?"

"Oh, nothing," sighed Sarah in reply.

"Come on, Sarah. Don't give me that. You couldn't wait for her to go. So what's the matter with you?" Jason had sensed that his sister wasn't in the best frame of mind, and wondered if anything had gone amiss whilst back in time. "Something go wrong on the trip?"

"No, nothing. That was all good. I quite enjoyed it,

although it's weird going back there and not seeing the Rotunda Clock."

"So what is it?"

"It's the Congress Library clock." Sarah looked a tad puzzled.

"I know that," Jason tutted. "I meant what's the problem with you?"

"It was a phone call afterwards." Sarah picked up her wine and gulped down what remained in her glass. "Another?" she asked, standing up and pointing to Jason's glass.

"Please. Then I want you to tell me about this call."

When Sarah returned to the table with the drinks, she was accompanied by Dan, who'd joined her at the bar. "I'm going to order food. I'm guessing that you want the Police Escort?"

Jason nodded with approval as he accepted the drink from his sister. The Police Escort was an amazing, succulent beef burger, topped with a large flat mushroom and blue cheese sauce, served with a generous portion of hand cut chips – Jason's usual selection from The Plume's menu.

"I see the Flamsteed well idea worked then."

"Yes. I've just been up there to check everything is still in place." Dan beamed. "Just need to open up the last few feet and it's as good as new."

"Mmm… Have you got any clients to discuss?" asked Jason, wanting a subject change.

"Just the one," replied Dan. "Oh… and I want to talk about changing the newspaper ad as well."

"Why?"

"Just think that it looks rather dated."

"Yeah… It probably does. I'll talk to Dad about that. What's your client about?"

"Just some kid – wants to go to the Leeds music festival."

"That should be fine – just do it. I'm more concerned about Sarah. Any idea what's bothering her?" Jason asked.

"Dunno, she wouldn't tell me." Dan turned to look at his sister ordering food at the bar. "All I know is it had something to do with her returning a phone call."

"Yes. I know that... just wondered if you knew anything else."

When Sarah returned, an air of silence descended upon the table as the three of them sipped at their drinks. The two brothers waited patiently for Sarah to spill the beans on what was bothering her. Sarah sat there wondering if it all really made any difference.

"Not like you three to be this quiet. You been arguing?" asked Kim as she brought the cutlery and condiments to the table.

"We're fine," replied Sarah. "Been a busy morning all round I think."

"Oh well. Are you in for the afternoon?"

"Possibly," replied Dan. "We'll see."

Kim headed back to the bar to serve a couple who'd just entered. Jason picked up his drink and took a good mouthful, placed his glass down and then wiped his lips with the back of his hand. "Come on, then... out with it."

"Oh. It's the usual thing. You know, we've all heard them. The sob story." Sarah paused, waiting for a reaction, but none came. "We have all this amazing ability, don't we?

Yet we use it... for what? To give people like Joanne the trip of a lifetime." She stopped again, almost certain this time that one of them would jump in, but they didn't. "I mean for fuck's sake why do we do it? When we could be doing so much good. Why?"

Jason finally spoke. "You know why, Sarah. You know what happened in the past."

"Yes, but that was then. That was over a hundred years ago. And is the world any worse off or are we any better off? Face facts, Jase. We're not even sure what the hell happened."

The Time Store hadn't always operated as a bespoke travel agent with the obvious twist. Yes, one of their main goals was always to preserve timepieces, and to maintain what they knew as true time. However, prior to 1913 the custodians used their abilities to put right some wrongs. Not large scale, not the stopping of wars or major disasters, not accident prevention, more of a last resort service for people who the law couldn't help... or perhaps chose not to.

Oliver Bradbeer in the second decade of the last century had been the one who'd messed things up for everyone. No-one, either then or now, knew exactly what had happened to him, the general consensus being that he was buried somewhere in the tunnels that made up The London Underground system. The purpose of his travel trip and what effect it had on true time was never known. Several senior Bradbeers had considered theories over the years, ranging from Oliver's potential involvement with the Mexican revolution, to the disappearance of the steamship *Calvados* in the Marmara Sea. The jury was out as to whether he succeeded in completing what he'd set out to do.

Following the disappearance of Oliver Bradbeer, his father Edward had been forced to make a massive decision. He declared The Time Store was henceforth forbidden to use time travel for anything other than recreational activities. With the onset of the First World War, Oliver was soon forgotten.

"Your caller. What was it about?" asked Dan.

"It was my fault. I should have never have said we could help. But Joanne's taxi turned up at the same time and I must have missed something. I sort of switched off, thinking that I could get out of whatever it was when I called back." Tears started to trickle down Sarah's cheeks.

Jason reached out to comfort her and gave her a brotherly hug. "Hey, don't cry. It can't be that bad."

"Oh, it's probably just me," she continued, drying the tears away with the serviette Dan had taken from his cutlery. "You know it's not like me to get attached, but when I listened to this woman's story I couldn't help it. Jason, we need to help her... we must."

"Right. We have two Police Escorts and one Western with chicken." Kim had arrived with their lunches. She didn't need to ask who was having what, she knew the chicken was for Sarah – it always was. Whenever eating out Dan always had the same as Jason, not because he could never make up his own mind what to have, but having the same was the only way to stop Jason wanting to try some of his meal. Sarah didn't mind as she all too often couldn't manage the full plate.

"Looks like we have two things to discuss then," announced Jason.

"Two?" asked Dan, who was just about to take the first bite into his burger.

"Yes. But we'll talk about the second once we've decided what to do with whatever's upsetting Sarah."

Both brothers sat and listened as Sarah retold the conversation she'd had with Mrs Fisher less than an hour ago.

"I called Edith Fisher back. It was when Joanne was getting changed." Sarah put down her knife and fork and moved her plate to an empty table, and then took out a small notepad from her jacket pocket. "She lives in Middlesbrough, has done all her life. Originally from St Hilda's but moved to the Clifton Hill estate when she got married to Des back in the late fifties."

Dan piped up. "I've heard of that estate, think it was on the news a while back – more single mothers per head than anywhere else in Britain – or something like that."

"Possibly," replied Sarah. "Anyway, Des worked on the docks, had quite a good job apparently. They had two kids – Christopher and Dawn. By the time the seventies arrived Des had – and these are Edith's words – 'Pissed off wi' some slapper from up Noocastle'." Sarah took a sip of her wine and then flicked over the page on her notepad.

"Finished?"

"Yes thanks, Kim. Lovely as always," replied Jason as Kim came over and cleared the plates away.

"Anyway, like lots of places in the late seventies – early eighties – industry closed down and poverty crept in. Along with the poverty came the crime – and along with the crime came drugs, dealers, prostitution and pimps." Sarah stopped, composed herself, and then continued.

"Christopher committed suicide – left a note and hung himself from the loft hatch. She told me that she never went up the stairs for over five years, and then the council modernised her home – took out the outside toilet and put one in the bathroom. Upstairs. Edith had to beg them to board over the hatch, but she still sees Christopher's young, lifeless body hanging there – as if it was yesterday."

"Fuck, that's awful. Couldn't she move?"

"No, Dan. Too scared, too scared for her daughter, Dawn. I'll get to that."

Sarah, tearful all over again, stood up and went to the bar. After a couple of minutes she returned with a glass of iced water. Kim followed a few seconds later carrying two pints of beer, one each for Dan and Jason.

"Thanks, Kim," said Jason, as the barmaid put the drinks on the table. Dan just smiled and nodded.

"There was a note – a suicide note. A girl on the estate, one of Dawn's classmates – Stacy Clough – had died from taking bad drugs – supplied by Christopher."

"Bad drugs?"

"Dunno, Dan. That's all Edith told me – bad drugs. From what she found out, and from what the note said, Christopher was delivering drugs for one of the Tarelli family as part of his morning paper round."

"Paper round? How old was he? And who the hell are the Tarelli family?" asked Jason.

"Fourteen. From what Edith told me he'd collect the morning papers from the shop, along with some drug-filled envelopes which he'd deliver to Jimmy Tarelli's customers."

"Jimmy Tarelli? Should we know him?" asked Dan.

"I don't know... just let me finish, I'll tell you all I know. Apparently this Jimmy had threatened Christopher that if he didn't deliver the drugs he'd slash Dawn's pretty face with a knife – and to prove the point, Dawn came home from school with knife cuts in her school blazer, and so Christopher delivered the drugs. The day Stacy died, Dawn came home early from school, too distraught for lessons. The police got involved and then I suppose that's why Christopher killed himself. I'd hazard a guess at shame and guilt."

"The poor lad – what a waste!" Jason shook his head in disgust. "So what about the police? What happened?"

"That's the sad part. Nothing. They could only trace the drug chain back to Christopher, so he was the one they were after. Since he was dead – case closed."

"But the suicide note! Surely Mrs... Edith... took it to the police."

"No. She told me that Jimmy Tarelli and his father Tony turned up at her home that evening with a wreath and some hollow condolences. Edith was told that if she ever breathed so much as a word to the police then she'd have a daughter to bury as well."

"Fucking hell – what a pair of evil shits. So they never got caught? Nothing happened to them?" Dan asked.

"Apparently not."

"Why now? I mean why wait until... what is it? Over thirty-five years?"

"I get the impression she's dying. Dawn has moved away – Carlisle – with her husband and family. Edith has unsettled business and wants our help in settling it, before she pops her clogs." Sarah took a large mouthful of water, put down the glass and then picked up her wine. She finished it off in one swig, and then continued. "And just for the record, I told her we would help."

"I'll do some digging, see what I can find on the Tarellis," said Jason.

"Thanks, Jase. I just feel as though we should help. I think that's what we're supposed to do. Don't you?" Sarah felt relieved that Jason had listened. She was, although she didn't show it, very happy with him actually suggesting he'd look into it, as she'd anticipated a negative reaction.

"We'll see, Sarah – I'm not promising anything," he replied. "Right. Let's move on. Second on the agenda – Dan's issue." Jason swiftly changed the subject. "Dan, tell Sarah what you've told me. I'm off to the toilet."

Jason headed round the bar and was very surprised to see his dad sitting in his usual seat reading The Times. Both father and son exchanged brief nods and grunts as Jason passed by.

He's in here a bit early, Jason thought to himself as he looked at his watch. Wonder why?

"You're early. Surprised you didn't say hello when you came in," said Jason, coming out of the gents and pulling up a small red stool next to his father.

"I was going to. But Sarah was too engrossed in telling you something, so I just put a drink on her tab and sat here with the paper. What's new?"

Jason spent the next five minutes bringing his dad up to date with Dan and the radio show. He briefly mentioned the Flamsteed well, but decided not to mention anything about Sarah's caller. David seemed very interested in Dan's news and offered suggestions on what to do, yet advised Jason to be prepared for the worst and have a back-up plan.

Leaving his dad to the crossword, Jason headed

back to his brother and sister. Dan had already finished telling Sarah about the previous night's radio show and was now embellishing the details of his trip to see John Flamsteed.

"Oh... forgot to tell you about Flamsteed," said Dan as Jason sat down. "He nearly ended up with the diving Tony toy."

"How the hell...?"

"It was folded in with the plans for the well."

"You knob," laughed Jason. "Oh, by the way, Dan. I got an e-mail back from the radio station. Sorry, mate. They won't help."

"Fucking miserable wankers," chuntered Dan.

Over a few more drinks the three Bradbeers decided on Plan A. This basically involved Jason waiting outside the radio station and asking Tara to help. Of course they needed a fall-back in case Tara refused; this would be Plan B.

CHAPTER 19

Incensed

Sarah, on her way to Slough for the Mystic Moon Psychic Fair, had dropped Jason and her father off at King's Cross in time for them to catch the 7.15 to York. She didn't mind the early start as it gave her ample time to get lost and find herself again, if need be.

In the event, she had not got as lost as she'd anticipated and consequently she arrived early and parked her small hatchback in the pub car park. The side door leading to the upstairs function room was already open and as she entered, looking tentatively around for one of the organisers, she was almost collided into by a plump woman who had just clomped at speed down the threadbare carpeted stairs.

"Ooh... sorry," said Sarah, although it was not her fault.

"No worries, my darling, no worries. Are you here for the fair? Haven't seen you at any of the other ones I do." The woman had long blonde hair and was wearing a patterned flowery dirndl skirt and a t-shirt with an angel motif. She was obviously on her way back out to the car park.

"Oh, no, this is my first one," replied Sarah. "Just selling tarot cards and candles and stuff, you know. I'm looking for someone called Claudia?"

"Yes, Claudie's upstairs, fussing around as usual – you can't miss her – just go up and introduce yourself. She'll guide you through."

"Thanks." Sarah watched as the woman waddled out to her car, surprisingly light on her feet.

She made her way upstairs to the function room of the pub. It was as she'd expected, fairly large, with a bar at one end, now closed; carpeted all around the edges, with a laminated dance floor area in the middle. At fairly equal intervals on the carpeted sections of the room, tables had been placed, some of which were already showing assorted psychic and mystical paraphernalia.

Sarah had nipped back a few months in time to book her exhibitor's place, having found on the internet that it would be attended, as it was every year, by Psychic Tara. The original suggestion by her brothers was that she should be a spiritual medium, or a tarot card reader, but although she did have a method of accurately informing people of events in their past and future – it wasn't through the use of cards or crystal balls. She had managed to spend a few days learning basic tarot, practising on Kim in the Plume, but she couldn't be arsed to spend years back in time perfecting her art. So the Bradbeer family had come up with a revised plan, which entailed Sarah booking a slot at the Governor's Arms in Slough, as a seller of tarot cards, incense and votive candles.

She spotted Claudia supervising the setting up of the tea and coffee area to the left of the shuttered bar. Claudia was wearing black tailored trousers, high heels, and a pale blue silk blouse. Her dark hair was up in a chignon, her face was heavy with make-up, including deep red lipstick, and she was most definitely 'In Charge'.

Sarah began to make her way over, but Claudia spotted her in mid-approach and, leaving a parting instruction/order to her refreshment assistant, strode towards Sarah, hand outstretched.

"Good morning. I think you must be Sarah Bradbeer?"

"Yes, that's me." Sarah, impressed albeit reluctantly, nodded and shook Claudia's hand.

"Welcome to Mystic Moon. So pleased you could make it – it's always refreshing to have new exhibitors," enthused Claudia.

"Thank you," responded Sarah, looking around. "Do I have an allocated table, or can I set up anywhere?"

"Oh allocated my dear... allocated. You're over there, near the toilets. But on the plus side, you're three tables away from our most well-known participant. I assume you've heard of Psychic Tara?"

"Hasn't everybody?" Sarah replied through gritted teeth.

"Well – must get on," said Claudia, breezing away and leaving Sarah to it.

She looked across to her allotted stall, which was along the wall to the right side of the bar. The table nearest the toilets was already occupied and Sarah, newly inaugurated sole proprietor of Tassel Incense and Candles, made her way over to her table to survey her territory. Okay. One rectangular table. One chair. To her right as she sat in her chair, a pottery stall partially set up. To her immediate left an empty table. Three tables to her left Psychic Tara's domain. No sign of Tara as yet. The table in between was covered with a long flowing floral cloth. Sarah was not in the least surprised when the wearer of the flowery skirt she'd encountered at the bottom of the stairs plonked herself down on the fortunately sturdy chair a few moments later.

"Hello again," acknowledged Sarah.

"Oh hi, hello... mixed blessings for me – I'm next to Tara."

"Why mixed?"

"Well, there'll be a constant queue for her – I might get some overflow if they get fed up of waiting. Or I could just get completely ignored. Not being funny, but you're a newbie and then we've got flipping potty Janice next to the loos. Hardly a magnet for customers. And God knows who's in between us – Claudia won't say. Between you and me I think it's a cancellation. If there's no-one here soon I think we should shift the table out of the way."

"Really?" said Sarah, hoping someone would arrive to fill up the empty table, else she'd never have any peace.

She returned to her car to collect her merchandise. The car park was filling up now as more people were arriving, still well ahead of the ten o'clock opening time. She struggled upstairs with two large supermarket canvas bags, one packed full of candles, the other containing approximately twenty decks of assorted tarot cards, topped up with varied packs of incense in different fragrances. She'd also brought, as per the exhibitors' guidelines, the compulsory tablecloth, some printed pricelists, and a float of money.

Sarah spread her pale lilac cloth over her table, allowing the fabric to almost touch the floor at the front, sticking to the much appreciated online advice from Claudia, so as to hide the boxes and other detritus which would be under the table during public opening.

She'd brought a few popular fragrances of incense, in packs of twenty sticks – sandalwood, jasmine, vanilla and patchouli. She had ten packs of each, which she put in four cylindrical metal cutlery holders. She'd also brought a few unusual fragrances – anti-stress, arruda, cannabis, dragon blood, horus eye, and Archangel Miguel – whoever he was. She had twenty flat incense tray-style burners, where the incense stick could be slotted at an angle into a small hole at one end, thus ensuring that as it burned, the ash could always fall onto the thin tray. Who wouldn't want to buy this? Especially when they could also purchase a fragranced candle to further enhance the mystical ambience of their home.

She'd brought votive candles in black cherry, blueberry, freesia, lavender, lily of the valley, strawberry and wild cranberry. Considerate stall holder that she was, she also had on sale some basic clear glass votive candle holders, should her customers require them. She'd been unaware just how many varieties of candles and incense were available until she'd started this venture. Come to think of it, she could quite get into this. Tassel could become a viable business proposition.

In addition to her burnable delights, Sarah had tarot cards – which were part of the Bradbeer master plan. She was not overly familiar with the different designs of tarot so she'd selected a few purely based on the pictures and colours on the cards. Arranged strategically on her table, amidst the colourful candles and incense, were the Gilded Tarot set, Egyptian Tarot cards, and the Rider Waite deck which was apparently the first commercial deck produced in 1910. She really liked the artwork on the Crystal Tarot set, inspired by Gustav Klimt. She'd long been a fan of this artist, so she displayed a couple of these packs as well. Ideally, she would have preferred to be using these cards for her readings, but although beautiful in design, the pictures didn't aid her in deciphering the meanings of the cards. She'd been practising using the Hanson-Roberts deck, which was recommended for novices, and it now felt so familiar to her that she'd decided to stick with it and use it for her 'sting' as she thought of it.

Her display complete, Sarah lit a couple of candles and went to fetch a cup of tea from the refreshment area. The floral waddler was in a heated discussion with Claudia.

"It's bad enough you've positioned me over there as it is – now you're saying you're leaving me next to an empty table... it's just too barren... I can't focus properly. This lady here has said she'll help me move it." She pointed to Sarah.

"Well, not quite," corrected Sarah.

"Look, Angel. It's nine-fifteen now," said Claudia. "Let's wait until half past, then if no-one turns up, we'll move it. We're still waiting for Tara as well, but she always cuts it fine."

Sarah took a leisurely tour of the other stalls. She'd never heard of some of this stuff. There were about thirty or so tables offering a wide variety of holistic products, psychic readings and complementary therapy. She walked past exhibitors selling crystals, gemstone jewellery, Buddhas and angels, then paused at a stall specialising in small singing bowls. A young girl showed Sarah how to play the bowl with the padded mallet supplied; there were two ways – either to strike the bowl, or to run the mallet repeatedly around the rim. Apparently these bowls had a multitude of uses, such as meditation, yoga and music therapy. Sarah, after having concluded that even the largest was too small to be used as a fruit bowl, restrained herself from buying one.

In addition to the readings stalls – tarot, angel cards, rune stones, palmistry and psychic mediums, there were also therapy stalls, featuring amongst others reflexology, crystal healing and aromatherapy. Sarah stopped at this last stall, feeling an affinity with the aromas, which were similar to those of her candles and incense. She was persuaded to buy some rosemary essential oil and a diffuser – rosemary was supposed to be a memory enhancer, with the added benefit that it soothed migraines, which she sometimes suffered from.

When Sarah returned to her stall, she put her purchase in one of the bags under the table, and saw 'potty Janice' for the first time – a tall thin wisp of a woman whose facial expression was almost set in apology for her very existence. Come to think of it, her pots looked a little like that too. Sarah smiled in greeting but was then distracted by a flurry of excitement from the entrance door to the function room. Psychic Tara had arrived.

Claudia had been hovering near the entrance and she moved graciously to hug and exchange air kisses with the famous Tara. Sarah had seen recent pictures of Tara, and caught snippets of her guest appearances on certain television programmes, and had understood the attraction, but in the flesh, even from a distance, Tara looked far more captivating. Sarah had always assumed, and now from their recent research knew for sure, that Tara was older than her stated public age. She was dressed in a plain purple brocade knee-length skirt, black boots and a patterned black and white fitted cardi/jacket combo. She had a pale purple scarf draped, but not tied, around her neck and lots of chunky silver jewellery – earrings, beaded necklace, bangles, watch, and rings on most fingers.

Tara had attracted a small fawning crowd of admirers around her, and seemed to be enjoying the attention. Sarah could see Claudia pointing in her direction, and began to panic, until she realised that Claudia was indicating Tara's table. Tara, in turn, gesticulated to her young assistant, presumably ordering him to take her few items over and set up.

"Come on – this is our chance. Let's move that bloody table." Angel nudged Sarah, who rolled her eyes, but assisted with the relocation of the redundant table. They dumped it in the corner, on the other side of the door to the toilets. They quickly moved Angel's and Tara's tables closer to Sarah's, making the spacing more equal, having not dared to risk disturbing Sarah's intricately arranged display. Up to now, Angel's table consisted of the flowered tablecloth.

"So what is it you actually do?" asked Sarah.

"I read runes."

"Okay."

During the table-moving interlude, Sarah had been surreptitiously spying on Tara. She'd watched her conclude her brief chat with Claudia, savour the adoration of her fans, and then move on to a couple of stallholders she presumably already knew. Finally, Tara sat down at her table, in command of the situation, in her familiar territory, sure of herself and what she was required to do for the next few hours.

"Ha," said Sarah under her breath. "Don't get too comfortable."

At ten o'clock prompt, Claudia's stated opening time, the general public were allowed in – a few at first, but within half an hour the room was filling up – most of them, as expected, in the queue for Tara. Some people were perusing the other stalls, either not interested in the Tara phenomenon, or preferring to wait an hour or so until the queue had died down a bit.

Dan had better hurry up for this plan to work, thought Sarah – what we don't want is him not being able to get to her at all. Tara had been caught unawares the other night. Jason had engineered a bumping into her scenario as she arrived for her regular slot at the radio station. He'd politely asked if she could retrieve the contact details for a specific caller from a recent show – he then went on to describe the content of the call and had given her adequate chance to respond to the request. Tara had obviously remembered the event, she'd looked briefly guilty when Jason had recounted how she'd accused the caller of having a bit of a tipple and imagining the whole thing. No, not very professional at all, Tara. She'd refused outright to get any details for anyone, about anyone. Very 'more than my job's worth' kind of attitude, but Jason got the feeling that Tara would quite happily bend the rules if it ever suited her.

So yes, they'd done it the official way with the e-mail, and failed; the back door way with Tara, and failed. So now it was going to have to be done the Bradbeer way.

Sarah, to her great surprise and pleasure, was doing a roaring trade in incense and candles. By half eleven her table was already looking somewhat empty. In her head Tassel Enterprises had suddenly gone global.

She glanced across at Angel, who was in the middle of reading rune stones for a client. There was one more person waiting. Sarah believed that potty Janice had sold one or two pots, but this hardly constituted a retail success. She hoped Janice had an alternative income.

Just before midday, Dan strolled into the room, scanned around, spotted Sarah and sauntered over.

"Finally..." Sarah hissed.

"Sorry, sis. I did mention I had another appointment first – took longer than I thought," Dan replied, keeping his voice low.

"Just buy some incense and I'll do your reading."

This was stage one of the plan. Tara would probably not notice this interaction, but it had to be done just in case.

"Oh – I'll take a pack of cannabis and two packs of your Archangel Miguel – whoever he is," requested Dan. "Where did you get all this stuff?"

"Never you mind," said Sarah. "That will be four pounds fifty please sir. Would you like a bag?"

"Yes please – I see you've got tarot cards – do you do readings?"

"Yes, sometimes I do," replied Sarah. "I'm just learning – trying it out, you know. I don't think I'm any good yet, but I like to practise. Shall I do yours?"

As a reply, Dan looked across to Angel's table, where she was sitting, looking fed up. "Do you mind?" said

Dan, as he took the empty customer chair, placed it in front of Sarah's table and sat down.

Angel shrugged.

"Okay, let's get started," said Sarah. She cleared a space on her table – now she had sold over half her stock she was able to shunt her incense and candles over to one side. "I'll do a basic layout," she explained. "I need you to shuffle the cards. Stop when it feels right for you."

Dan took the Hanson-Roberts pack which Sarah handed to him and half-heartedly shuffled. He was not the best at shuffling, and although this deck, unlike some others, was the same size as regular playing cards, there were 78 cards in the tarot pack rather than 52. He dropped a card, which fell and landed face up on the lilac cloth. The Tower. The card depicted a burning castle-like tower.

"Oooh, ominous," said Sarah, picking up the card. "The Tower symbolises change, or the potential for change. You must embrace it. And it also means that in the past you might have singed your arm in mysterious circumstances."

"Oh. Ha ha. Don't you have to arrange the cards in an order or something?"

"Yes – you're having the Celtic Cross – it's the only one I know properly. Now, think of something you need to find out or ask."

"I don't know – can't you just deal some cards out and tell me what they mean?" said Dan impatiently.

"Whatever – let's just get this done," she growled. She took a breath, and then spoke calmly and firmly. "We're doing all this for you – based on a whim you have about *her* radio show – so try and act like you want a reading... have a question... and want a bloody solution will you."

"Okay... okay." Dan felt suitably chastised. "Ask the cards what happened to me."

"You can't ask that... maybe try... can you help me to find a way to come to terms with the mystery of what happened to me five years ago?"

"Yes... that then."

Sarah turned over one by one ten cards from the pack and laid them face up, as she had practised, in the Celtic Cross spread. She placed the first card in the centre of the space on her table and the second card horizontally over the first. The next four were positioned above, below, to the left and to the right of the first two cards, forming a kind of cross. Then there were four more to the right of this arrangement, one above the other, starting at the bottom and working upwards.

"Let's do it," said Sarah.

She studied the spread, trying to remember the meanings to the cards and their positions, and how they could relate to each other.

Dan drummed his fingers on the lilac cloth, and examined a candle.

"Oooh," said Sarah.

"Will you stop that – it's too creepy," said Dan.

"Have you had any odd dreams recently?"

"No, not really."

"Well, you should make note of any unusual dreams or intuitive feelings. Be alert for any subtle changes. You could be at the start or finish of an important situation – and it could be connected to water." Sarah pointed to the first two cards – The Moon and Knight of Wands.

Dan was unimpressed. But at least that bloody

tower hadn't appeared again. "What else?" he queried.

"We have King of Cups here – this could be a father figure – it's an older man. Actually you've got loads of cups here – it's to do with love and happiness." She took a breath. "Your love of wine probably..."

"Mmm," said Dan.

Sarah decided to be sensible for a while. "I was reading about an example spread the other day – it said Ace of Rods next to cups is telling you to look out for a letter, or a phone call – information of any kind."

Sarah was getting into it now, and was surprised to see that the cards seemed to have actually thrown up some stuff that was relevant to Dan. She didn't mention to him that Two of Cups meant romance – and it was in position five – meaning it could happen soonish. Oooh, she thought.

"You're good at this," Dan whispered. "You'll hook Tara in no problem."

"Six of Cups means it's possible to meet an old acquaintance, and – oh my God – I'm sure next to The Moon it means some concern from the past was never really understood."

"Well we know that," retorted Dan.

"Here we go – this one – it's Four of Pentacles. It means that you're a hard worker... this must have got in here by accident."

Dan ignored her. "What does this one mean?" He pointed to The Hermit.

"Oh... he looks a bit like Old Father Time, doesn't he? Your job must be connected with time in some way. Are you a clockmaker?"

"Are you taking the piss?"

"Sorry, couldn't resist. It means you have the ability to solve the situation... but take it steady. And this one, Nine of Cups, in this position means a positive definite yes."

"Yes to what?"

"The question, the situation, the issue... whatever."

"You've missed two cards out." Dan's OCD was kicking in.

Sarah was aware that she'd avoided mentioning Two of Cups, but she'd unwittingly forgotten about the other one. She pointed to it. "Oh this one – Eight of Rods – means there's news coming in, or there could be travel connected with business."

"Yeah, enlightening," said Dan. "And that one?"

Sarah had a brainwave. Dan didn't know the importance of the card's position. "Ah, that's just telling me you once had a relationship with a girl from a long time ago – you lost her – in a fire – but don't worry – it would have never have worked out. And that concludes your reading."

"Well thanks," said Dan. "Think I'll have a look around now."

"Okay, thank you for your time – I hope you find what you're looking for." Sarah was perspiring – that was hard – and it was only her brother. She hoped she wouldn't flunk it all in front of Tara, that is if the second part of the plan worked.

Dan returned the chair to Angel's table.

"Hey," said Angel. "Is that true about losing your girlfriend in a fire?"

"Yes, actually, it is."

"Wow."

Dan browsed the other stalls, in an almost carbon-copy journey to that of his sister earlier. He too had a singing bowl demonstration, but drew the line at buying anything, not even aromatherapy oils. He ended up in the queue for Tara.

It was nearly one o'clock, there were five people ahead of him, and the Mystic Moon Psychic Fair finished at three. He reckoned that each of Tara's clients would take about twenty to twenty-five minutes. He was hoping that he would then be the last, as closing time approached.

That fat flowery woman next to Sarah had no queue, and she was looking at him. Oh shit, surely she doesn't fancy me – that's all I need. Dan wished he was with Jason and his dad in Middlesbrough, but he knew that all this mystical claptrap could be the answer to his anomaly, so he obviously had to stick it out. As he stood in the queue, watching Tara dispense her psychic wisdom, he wondered what had made her recently stop reading tarot cards and morph into a spiritual medium. The look on her face, her lack of patience with people – she seemed bored, somehow fake, yet everyone loved her – why?

Dan didn't dwell on this though, and his thoughts soon turned to other subjects, firstly sport, especially this year's World Cup fiasco. And secondly this… er… psychic background music? It sounded like a strange mix of banjo, pan pipes and someone's central heating system that'd gone wrong. Dan smirked as he imagined going to their CD player, whipping out the so-called relaxation disc, and whacking on some Jethro Tull. After all – it had got a bit of flute in.

He also found himself unable to stop thinking about the mystery caller's voice – hopefully he would soon find out who she was.

Sarah was having a good day. Her sales were going well, she'd made a few business contacts, gained a sort of friend in Angel, plus Dan's reading had been a success. He was now nearly at the top of the queue for Tara, hopefully about to instigate the final stage of the plan.

Dan dragged his thoughts to the matter in hand, looked up and realised he was next in the queue for Tara. She appeared to have rushed her last two clients, and was just concluding her time with the woman in front of him. He looked at his watch – it had just gone two-forty. There was no-one behind him – probably people had checked the time and realised they had no chance with Tara today.

Dan moved towards her stall and sat down, clasping his hands and resting them on the table.

"Good afternoon – I see you've come for a spiritual session," said Tara, pleasantly. "You're lucky – this is the last one of the day. We've just got enough time... can you give me a personal item? Something that means a lot to you, to help me focus. Maybe a bit of jewellery – how about that ring? It looks quite unusual."

"Oh, sorry," said Dan. "I thought you did tarot cards. That's what I came for. I heard you were very good."

"I don't do the cards now," responded Tara somewhat brusquely. "I can give you an excellent reading without them. It's only fifty pounds."

"How much?!" spluttered Dan, genuinely shocked.

"It's my usual price," said Tara.

"Nah, I'll give it a miss," said Dan, standing up. "That lady over there did it for free." He pointed at Sarah. "Okay she's just a beginner – wants some more practice – but she's really good – spot-on with a few things actually."

"I'm sure." Tara sounded sceptical.

Angel, who'd had no customers for a while, had been eavesdropping and felt it was now time to interject. "Yes, Tara – she is good – very good. She hit the nail on the head about his girlfriend dying in a fire. Didn't she darlin'?"

"Well… yes she did," agreed Dan. He considered Angel's timely intervention at this point very advantageous and he was pleased now that she seemed to have taken a liking to him.

"You should try her," said Angel. She'd observed Sarah's reading for Dan, and had been quite impressed. She had actually sensed some sort of undercurrent between the two of them, but decided not to mention this, after all Psychic-bloody-Tara could do with being brought down a peg or two.

Tara stood up from the table and marched across to Sarah, who under the guise of very slowly packing away her few unsold items, had been sneakily watching the interaction. "I hear you're a bit of a whizz kid with the tarot cards," said Tara, raising an eyebrow. "How much are you charging?"

"Nothing," said Sarah, quivering inside. "I'm doing it for a few people – so I can practise and learn."

"Very altruistic, I'm sure."

Sarah was surprised that Tara seemed to have been lured over, not primarily because she was curious about any potential tarot reading abilities, but because she was a money-grabbing, fame-hungry, ex-tarot reader turned spiritual charlatan who couldn't believe that not everyone wanted to charge a fortune for their time.

"Here, have this chair," said Angel, sensing that this

could be entertaining.

Tara grabbed the chair and sat down. "Come on, then. Show me what you've got." She folded her arms and waited.

"Could you shuffle the cards please?" Sarah was feeling relief and dread in equal measure.

Tara, experienced but impatient, shuffled quickly and efficiently, then placed the cards back down on the table. Sarah had decided to do a layout she'd seen in one of her books – a kind of extended version of the Celtic Cross, but with four more cards at the bottom. She was not quite sure what these extra card positions signified, but she figured that the more cards she exposed, the more chance she had of blagging her way through.

The psychic fair had now closed and Claudia had ushered the last few stragglers out of the room. Most of the exhibitors were busy packing away, but there were four people who had spotted Tara at Sarah's table. Sensing something potentially gripping could be happening they swanned over to have a closer look.

Once the cards were laid out in the spread, Sarah concentrated – examining the pictures – trying to merge the card meanings with the positional meanings, trying to make them relevant to her plan. She was acutely aware that Tara would know these interpretations far better than her, and she also suddenly registered that she hadn't told her to ask a specific question. She glanced up at Tara, who had gone silent and still. Was that a good sign? Sarah tried to control her panicking pulse rate. She was a trainee card reader who'd miraculously come to the notice of one of the best in the industry. She needed to grab her attention.

She launched straight in. "You're always very

secretive about your past... shall we see if we can get the cards to tell us more?"

"Stop the dramatic introductions and just get on with it," said Tara. "And get these people away from me. Claudia?"

The crowd of four were curious, but more significantly, they were a tad in awe of Tara... and maybe more so of Claudia... and so all four of them walked swiftly away before the approaching Claudia had chance to instruct them. Angel, very reluctantly, decided to go with them. Dan, who had no intention of moving far, sat at Angel's table and fiddled absentmindedly with the edges of the floral cloth.

Sarah was conscious of the fact she had to ensure that Tara didn't have one of her famous strops and abruptly terminate the reading. She needed to get serious.

"Let's begin with the first two cards," Sarah said, starting confidently enough. "Queen of Swords and High Priestess. Both spiritual cards – they could both represent you, Tara. The basis of the problem is within yourself, and the immediate challenge is yourself. You're a very psychic person, we know that, but it seems that your spiritual depth has been caused by prolonged struggle."

"What are you talking about?" challenged Tara. "You're just rambling – get a move on – I've got somewhere I need to be."

Sarah was trying not to feel intimidated. The enormity of her task had hit home. She couldn't think straight. "This card – er – it's from the suit of pentacles. Meaning... work and money..."

"Seriously? You obviously should have practised more!"

Sarah tried not to let herself be browbeaten by Tara's antagonistic attitude. "Um... Eight of Pentacles. It shows that you studied hard at the start of your chosen profession... probably for not much initial monetary gain."

"Wonderful," sneered Tara. "That's the meaning of one card you've successfully learned. Keep going..."

Sarah hesitated, trying to decide which card to pick next – she didn't necessarily have to do it in the same order she'd laid them out. "Two of Rods – it shows you've achieved your goals in work. Your career was going how you wanted – you had more control."

"Money well spent on that book you bought," taunted Tara.

Sarah was rattled. Obviously she'd bought a book, quite a few actually. What else were you supposed to do when you started out? Maybe she should've had an educational time trip after all, one lasting a good few months, possibly a year or so. It was patently obvious she had no real clue about it at all. In true time calculations a year-long trip lasted no more than a few hours, but the trouble was it would actually take up a year of her brain time – her thinking and feeling time. She always felt out of sorts, remote and detached from reality when she returned from any long time trip. So this time she'd deliberately chosen not to do it.

"Ten of Rods... it seems you've been under pressure and experienced many changes in life. You may need to take another look at your original goal to see if you're still on course."

"Yes – but is that the best you can do? Churn out meanings all the time? You've got a good memory – but you're not interpreting at all. I think your pal over there just had a flukily lucky reading." Tara waved her hand in the general direction of Angel's table, where the fortunate recipient of the reading was still sitting.

Dan had been watching the interaction with a sense of impending doom, wishing he could do something to help. Instead, in his agitation, he'd succeeded in unpicking about a foot's worth of hem from the tablecloth and pulling out numerous threads, so some of the flowers now looked as though they'd been hit by a terrible insect attack.

"Come on, sis," he urged under his breath.

Sarah resumed. "Five of Rods – several problems all at once. This is happening now – look at the position of the card. Don't be afraid to give a little."

"You're twisting the meaning, darlin'," said Tara, obstinately. "And you've chosen the Hanson-Roberts deck – one of the few that calls the suit of wands by the name rods instead."

Sarah lost her rag. "Well if you're so good, which you obviously are... or were... why did you stop reading the cards? Why are you doing all that sham spiritual stuff?"

That stopped Tara in her tracks. "It's a private matter."

"Just curious," said Sarah, pointing to another card. "Seven of Swords – one thing after another not going right for you. This seems to be in the distant past. I think I can tell what happened."

"I doubt it."

"Six of Swords – travel by water – to get away..."

"I don't think so," said Tara, her bravado now diminishing.

"Look at this card, Tara. Ten of Swords. It says so

much." The card depicted a man on the ground with ten swords embedded in his back. "This is the worst it can get. It was the worst it got for you. Broken goals, deep distress, but now no more pain can come to you from this source."

"I do know what the card means, but it doesn't have any significance for me."

"This is your reading, Tara. Of course it does. You have quite a few cards from the suit of swords don't you? But we don't need to interpret this literally. It doesn't really mean there were ten swords, or seven or six. Just one knife or something. In the past? Before you travelled by water maybe? Does that mean anything to you?"

"What?!" Tara lurched forward in her seat.

Buoyed by Tara's reaction, Sarah was gaining in confidence. She looked at the Death card at the bottom of the spread. Lucky that came out. How fortuitous of me to have dealt those additional cards, she thought, giving herself a mental pat on the back.

"I can see your past. It shows you're older than you say. The cards depict you sailing across to England in a boat. From the positioning of this card I think it's far earlier than you say in your press releases – and not for adventure as you tell your adoring public, but to escape. That's what it says here – you ran away."

"Never! You can't see that in the cards!"

Sarah had an idea. Her confidence was boosted by Tara's burgeoning panic. "How about this then? Five of Cups and Two of Pentacles together. I know I'm still learning, but I'm beginning to think that Five of Cups is the only really negative card in the whole of the suit of cups. It's supposed to be the suit of love and happiness, isn't it?"

"Eh?" Tara was confused by this apparent swerve of emphasis.

"Yeah," Sarah continued. "I've always thought that Five of Cups might signify the bad side of physical relationships – prostitution maybe?"

Tara looked unnerved. "What are you trying to say?"

"Ah, nothing really." Sarah risked a snidey joke. "Maybe it would have been better next to a higher pentacles card though, eh? That prostitute could have earned a bit more money!"

"How can you possibly be getting this from the cards?"

"It's just a feeling I have – I'm linking the cards together – like you said to do."

"There are a few links you haven't spotted yet, you know."

"Maybe, maybe," said Sarah. "But I think I've done enough now, for a beginner. "Let's summarise shall we? You're a spiritual person who worked hard to change career and be successful. There's some stuff going on in your life now that you would do well to heed. But mainly what the cards are saying is that you had major trauma in your life a long time ago, potentially involving danger or threat or a knife. And then there's the prostitution. You escaped all this – ran away – by travelling across the sea in a boat and building the life you have today."

Tara fidgeted in her seat. "I don't know how you can say all this. You can't prove it – it's just a pathetic amateurish tarot reading."

"The evidence is here. I think I can prove that the

reading is accurate."

"Are you insane?! What are you going to do? Take a photograph of the spread to prove you're a good tarot reader? Have you bollocks got evidence. In fact, I'll have a photo of this dodgy spread myself, if you don't mind!" Tara whipped her phone out of her jacket pocket, and took several photographs of the fourteen cards.

Sarah calmly pointed to the Death card. "You know this card, Tara. Tarot readers always tell their clients not to be shocked. It's the end of a cycle of life. A new attitude or new circumstances may come, but the old way is dead and will never return in its original form. It means that you left the past behind and weren't afraid to start new projects. That's true obviously." She paused for dramatic effect. "But in your case this Death card looks as if a death did actually occur. A violent one."

"You have no proof, absolutely no proof." Tara's voice was trembling. Her defiance was gone.

"Oh, but I really do." Sarah reached under her table. She placed an envelope on the lilac cloth and pushed it dramatically around the tarot spread, past the remaining incense and candles, until it was directly in front of Tara.

"What the hell is this?" Tara picked it up.

"Open it."

Tara opened the envelope and pulled out a collection of about twenty photographs. She flicked through them, her face becoming steadily whiter. She was visibly shaken.

She looked at the spread of cards, back at the photos, then up at Sarah. "All right," she said, defeated. "What do you want from me?"

CHAPTER 20

Awayday Return

It had been over twenty years, perhaps more, since David had travelled any great distance by train, and that was when he was forced to journey from Stuttgart to Berlin because of a flight cancellation. Why he'd allowed himself to be talked into going to Middlesbrough of all places with Jason he didn't know... or perhaps he did... maybe he hankered for a little true time adventure. He'd been thankful of Sarah's offer of a lift to the station, trains were bad enough – but the tube was awful, especially with the early morning rush.

Jason had been wanting to discuss The Time Store's remit and future direction with his father for a couple of years, but for one reason or another had always put it off. More recent events – Dan's mystery radio caller and Edith Fisher's call to Sarah, both in very quick succession – had encouraged him to act. The three hour rail journey gave Jason a captive ear, hopefully enough time to get across his point of view to his father – without him having any excuse to leave the conversation.

They exchanged standard pleasantries for the first part of their journey; the weather mainly, then the punctuality and cleanliness of the train. The conversation, prompted by them hearing an Italian accent, then turned to how much David had loathed Roberto. This came as a surprise to Jason – he thought his dad actually liked him and that it was he and Dan who couldn't stand him.

"You know Sarah tried to do one of those bloody card readings for me last night?"

"No. She told me she was gonna get you though," said Jason. "What did she come up with for you?"

"I shuffled the cards and two fell on the floor," said David.

"What were they?" Jason was intrigued.

"Wheel of Fortune and a knight with a stick."

"Knight with a stick," laughed Jason. "Do you mean Knight of Rods?"

"Yes. Something like that – I think."

"So what did you think of her reading? Any good?"

"Oh a load of mumbo-jumbo. You know me... I'm a sceptical bugger when it comes to moons, runes and loons."

"Yeah. And you certainly don't believe in all that time travel bullshit – do you?"

David and Jason both laughed. Craftily David moved the conversation away from the two fallen cards onto his confidence in Sarah. They both acknowledged that Sarah had really taken to 'Operation Tara' with a great deal of enthusiasm, especially her time trips with Dan, collating the dossier photographs of Tara's past.

Once the train had pulled out of Peterborough,

Jason decided that now was the time to speak frankly with his father. "Can we change the subject?"

"Of course," replied David, who'd quite expected this.

"You know why we're heading up to Middlesbrough, don't you?"

"Well... yes, but only if what you and Sarah have told me is the truth. Is it?"

"Not really," replied Jason. "Well... some is."

Jason brought his father up to date on Sarah's return call to Mrs Fisher. He told the story of drugs, suicide and threats – of a mother's grief, anguish and fear. Jason didn't exaggerate; Mrs Fisher's life didn't need any padding out. It was – at best – grim.

The Tarelli family were out-and-out bastards, they always had been. It was a life they'd been born into, there wasn't anything pleasant about this family at all. Researching into Tony Tarelli and his little clan of thugs Jason discovered that they preyed relentlessly on the weak and vulnerable. Social decay, misery, violence and death were never too far away from their doorsteps.

Paul Tarelli was a product of Middlesbrough's Victorian workhouses and grew up as a pauper child living in the Broomlands Cottages. He later carved out a living as a petty thief and part-time pimp, often selling the services of his girlfriend, Angela, to the needy sailors visiting the Teesside port.

Although known as his wife, Jason couldn't find any actual record of Paul and Angela's marriage, even so, they'd started the 'family business' during the Second World War. Feigning illness, unlike others of his age, Paul managed to avoid the call-up to serve king and country. His black market dealings with visiting ships meant he'd always be found around the factory gates with an assortment of desirable goods for sale. For the right price Paul supplied everyday basics such as butter, eggs, meat, tea and chocolate for those who had bigger mouths than their ration books allowed. Of course for those who couldn't afford these luxuries there and then, there was always 'the tick'.

At the close of the war and following his demob from the army, Paul's workhouse blood brother Ron joined the business. Of course Paul needed a bit of muscle on his side to start collecting some of the debts that had built up during the war years. The family was complete when Paul's two teenage sons Tony and Marc returned from Barnard Castle where they'd lived out the war as evacuees. Redevelopment of bomb-blasted areas meant the family was re-housed by the local authority in Mendip Avenue, a small, quiet cul-de-sac on the newly built Clifton Hill estate.

Within five years of moving onto the estate, by bribing officials and through local intimidation, the Tarellis had control of all twelve houses in their street. By the mid-fifties their core businesses were financial and leisure services... or, in their world, money lending, prostitution and gambling.

Whilst Marc, always a mother's boy, never got married, Tony did. Within a couple of years he and his wife Maria had two boys of their own – Greg and Jimmy.

By the time the seventies had arrived the Tarellis had moved away from gambling and replaced the lost revenues with the introduction of drugs into their portfolio. As well as the Clifton Hill estate they'd expanded into the Pally Park estate along with the Netherfields tower blocks.

Business was booming for the Tarelli family.

"So what of the family now?" asked David.

"Paul and his brother Ron are both dead now. Angela lives in Sunny Bank care home, surprisingly owned by the Tarellis, across the river in Hartlepool," replied Jason.

"Mmm. She must be well in her nineties then. And what about the others?"

"From what I can gather, although he's retired, Tony still pulls all the strings. Prostitution died down with the demise of the port, but they still operate as loan sharks and drug pushers."

"Where do they get the drugs?"

"Newcastle, as far as I know. But I don't know how, yet. Coffee?"

"Yes I will have one please. How long before we arrive in York?" asked David.

Jason looked at his watch. "About twenty minutes. Then we have a fifteen minute wait before the train to Middlesbrough."

It was over coffee that Jason, as spokesperson for the three siblings, approached David with their feelings on how best they should be using their extraordinary abilities.

"I'm not saying that we should help every Tom, Dick and Harry with a sob story, that wouldn't be right. We know the world needs losers, poverty and greed. But the Mrs Fishers of the world... people like her... then we should be able to help them somehow."

"Where do you stop though? Just because we don't agree with something doesn't give us the right to play at being God, and we won't be interfering with the death of

Christopher Fisher if that's what you're scheming."

"No. It's not that at all. I spoke to Edith last night, she's well aware that we can't bring her son back to life." Jason was never going to tell her that they actually could go back and prevent him from dying. "All she wants is justice for her son. Sarah believes she deserves at least that, and so do I."

"Perhaps you're right," said David, musing over his son's words. "Let's listen to this Edith's full story, then decide how – or where – we go from there."

After a shorter journey – fifty-seven minutes in fact – their train from York pulled into Middlesbrough railway station. David was impressed by its Gothic style frontage dating back to around 1870. He'd done a bit of his own research prior to setting out – more on the local architecture rather than the local drug dealers.

The weather was warm for an October morning; a crisp, clear blue sky and hardly any breeze. Jason had pre-booked a local mini-cab to meet them at the station and spend an hour driving them around.

"Could you take us down Cargo Fleet Lane first please?" asked Jason as they sat in the back of the silver estate car, separated by Jason's briefcase.

"Ay nay problem. Any particular number?" replied the driver, in an accent very similar to Geordie, but without the pitches and swoops.

"No. We want to drive down there first, and then down Fulbeck Road please."

The taxi driver set off, and in the rear of the cab Jason tracked their movement using the GPS on his mobile phone.

"Yous from London are you?" asked the driver, in a strained attempt to make small talk.

Jason, following their route, gave his dad a nudge to answer.

"Yes. From London, just here for the day."

"That's a long ways to come fer a day. You ere for business?"

"Err," stuttered David.

"No. We're here to look at houses for my niece. She's coming up this way to study next year. Just want to get a feel for the area first before we visit the estate agents," interrupted Jason, helping out his dad.

Once past the car dealerships, builder's merchants and cash 'n' carry stores, Cargo Fleet Lane, one of Middlesbrough's main arterial roads, became more residential. An initial blend of post-war local authority housing, inter-mixed with shabby high-rise flats from the swinging sixties seemed the norm.

"What's this area like, any good?"

"Cack, loadsa doped up bag heads. They'll do you in to get enough for a bit of baccy or some cider."

"Gather it's not a great place then?" asked Jason, wondering if he was still in England.

"I don't see anything wrong," said David.

"They'll be at the Social, or still in thee manky pits," replied the cab driver, with a hint of contempt in his voice.

The taxi carried on, neither Jason nor David saw anything out of place. Yes, some of the stores had graffiti-scrawled metal shutters, but that was no different from anywhere these days. A few of the gardens were slightly unkempt, but as yet, there were no clapped-out cars supported by piles of house bricks in place of stolen alloys.

As the taxi passed by Pallister and Cranmore, there were still no outward signs of major poverty, crime or deprivation. The lane became more open, with wide well-kept grass verges, well-established trees and a never-ending procession of green steel railings.

Soon after, the railings ended, giving way to wider verges, larger trees and more housing – an assortment of privately owned and ex-local authority, with neat picket fences and sparkling cars on the driveways. A cemetery and then yet another tower block flashed past the windows as the taxi moved on.

"What did that mean?" asked Jason. "Tarelli Block."

"What?" asked the driver.

"It was sprayed on the wall of that tower we just passed. What's a Tarelli?" Jason had lied, there was nothing on the block at all. He was pushing the driver for information, to see what he'd say.

"Local mafia family. Least that's their reputation."

"Do they live there?"

"No way! That'll be there to stop gangs pushing their shit in there."

"Oh. And if they did?"

"They wouldn't dare, no-one around here is that much of a divvy. One way to end up at the bottom of the Tees."

After about another half a mile of much the same, except for some open land on the right, the taxi turned left down Fulbeck Road.

David looked at the sign embedded in the grass verge, and read aloud. "Welcome to Netherfields, please drive carefully."

Under Jason's instructions the driver went slowly through the estate, stopping at a row of shops. All were boarded up, save for a supermarket and bookmakers. A group of local teenage mothers, some wearing Milne character onesies, pushed prams towards several rowdy youths. They were leaning up against a trashed phone box, drinking Thunderbolt cider and smoking cigarettes, possibly rolled from duty free tobacco with an additional added extra. David shook his head in disgust at the tattoos down one lad's neck.

The car carried on winding its way through the estate. Several houses had green metal shutters clamped to their window and door frames. The driver casually informed his passengers that this was the council's attempt at stopping these properties becoming squats or crack houses. A couple of abandoned mattresses along with an old fridge had been dumped on a street corner, ironically under a sign declaring that fly-tippers would be prosecuted.

Although, all in all, the vast majority of the properties on Netherfields were clean and well-maintained it was clear to see that pockets of decay were also established.

"Could you take us to the Clifton Hill estate next please," requested Jason.

The taxi pulled away, leaving father and son standing on the corner of Malvern Road, the entrance to the Clifton Hill housing estate. Hastily built after the war on land acquired under the Acquisition of Land Act 1947, Clifton Hill had once been a very desirable area to live. Largish bay-windowed houses had been built in blocks of four, with the inner two houses gaining access to the rear down a shared arched passageway. They benefitted from good sized gardens and were near to open play spaces for both football and cricket.

Jason checked their route on his phone app and then tucked it away, out of sight. "Come on, this way."

There wasn't anything out of place, nothing which immediately pointed to a crime-ridden, drug-fuelled estate as they'd pictured in their minds. This wasn't thirties Chicago gangland for Christ's sake, this was North Yorkshire – Middlesbrough – of course no-one was going to come jumping out at them with a gun.

Net curtains twitched as nosy eyes watched the two strangers walking along. They didn't do themselves any favours though, stopping intermittently to discuss a shuttered property or a broken window succeeded only in drawing more attention.

"I'm sure that car has passed us once already," commented David as a black Volkswagon with tinted windows drove slowly by.

"Hadn't noticed," replied Jason, looking at the rear of the car as it manoeuvred between a couple of speed bumps.

They walked across the entrance to Mendip Avenue, home of the Tarelli families. On both corner houses multi-angled CCTV cameras kept a watchful eye on the comings and goings of visitors. Two men stood on one of Mendip's street corners, smoking and passing a can of lager to one another. Silent sentries thought David... although not so silent he re-thought when one of them belched.

After a few more houses they turned right into Pentland Avenue and immediately came across number four, Edith Fisher's house. It was second in a block and identical in style to every other house on the estate. The privet hedge was nice and neat, as were the lawn and flower beds, although the summer colour had long gone. Jason and David opened the small wooden gate, approached the front door and rang the bell. After a few seconds the door, restrained by a security chain, opened slightly.

"Ey up?" said an elderly lady as she peered over the chain.

"Mrs Fisher? Edith? I'm Jason Bradbeer, we spoke on the phone yesterday." Jason handed over a business card. "This is my father David."

"Hello, Mrs Fisher. Pleased to meet you," said David. "May we come in?"

"Ay. Suppose ya'd berra." Edith removed the chain from the door and showed her visitors into the front room. "Ave a seat. I'll stick tha kettle on and do us a brew."

Edith disappeared through into the kitchen and could be heard filling a kettle and pottering about making tea.

Her lounge was cosy, clean and warm. It certainly befitted a person of Edith's age and means. Along one wall stood an old polished sideboard, with an array of family pictures and a collection of honey pots arranged on top of some faded crocheted doilies. There was a matching bureau with a bottle of dark rum and a couple of tot glasses displayed in the middle. A television, a small dralon sofa and two armchairs, winged and not too different from David's, made up the furnishings. Jason noticed that one of the chairs had blocks under the legs, which raised it by a few inches – Edith's he thought – they'd make it easier for her to stand up.

Edith was still in the kitchen when there was a rapping knock on the front door, followed by persistent bell ringing. Jason looked towards the front door, then to the kitchen, then back to the front door; she hadn't heard the caller.

"Ey up Edie, are you in." The caller had opened the door and was shouting from the small hallway. "Now then." A large thickset beer-bellied man with greased back hair stood in the lounge doorway and greeted Jason and David.

"Hello," replied Jason standing up and holding out his hand.

"Haway Jimmy Tarelli." Edith scurried out of her kitchen flapping her hands towards Jimmy. "Yer neva welcome ere."

"Yer wha?" scowled Jimmy. "Just cum ta see who the sherts are, like?"

"What did he say?" asked David.

"Haven't got a clue," replied Jason.

"I said I've come to see who the fuck you two are." Jimmy's tone changed. Gone was his curt northern accent, replaced by a plain almost well-educated southern one. Jimmy moved away from the doorway and stood in the centre of the room. Two stocky well-toned younger men took his place by the doorway. "We look after our old folk round here, and don't want them conned out of their savings by a couple of suits. So I'll ask you again, who the hell are you? And what the fuck do you want with old Edie?"

Jason restrained himself from standing up and

knocking the living daylights out of Jimmy Tarelli. Instead he reached down to his briefcase and took out several brochures and some small samples of wood. He fanned out the brochures on the floor in front of him and placed the five wood samples by the side.

"We're funeral directors." Jason indicated to the coffins displayed on some of the pamphlet covers.

"What the ...?" said Jimmy.

"Mrs Fisher... Edith... has had a small policy, a funeral savings plan, running for a number of years. This has reached maturity and we're here to discuss her wishes. Do you have any plans for yours, Mr..."

"Tarelli. And no I fucking don't."

"Well you never know, death could be just around the corner. But let's take a moment to pray that it's not, shall we?"

"No we bloody won't. Is this true Edie?"

"Ay lad."

Jason had taken the precaution to discuss an alibi with Mrs Fisher when he'd called her yesterday. He'd sensed that their arrival on the estate may turn heads and he was right. Edith Fisher's three unexpected visitors departed, satisfied that her two callers were of no threat to her – and certainly, given their occupation, no threat to themselves.

After tea, served in the finest special occasion china cups, Edith took Jason and David upstairs. Jason half-expected Christopher's bedroom to be left untouched, a constant reminder or a shrine of some sorts, but it wasn't, not anymore. She explained that the family priest had convinced her that it wasn't healthy, that the memories of her son were in her heart, not in the four walls of a room. So after leaving it untouched for fifteen years she'd finally packed Christopher's clothes, books, comics, games, records and posters into two large cases, which were slid away under the single bed. Save for an old record player she'd won in the Social Club's annual raffle in 1972 – Christopher and Dawn's Christmas present that year – the room contained nothing more.

Leaving Jason and David upstairs to 'get to know Christopher' as Edith put it, she made her way back down.

Pulling one of the cases from under the bed Jason spoke quietly to his dad. "What do you think then?"

"Sad, very sad."

Jason pushed aside the fasteners on the clasps, opened the lid and took out a pile of American superhero comics. He flicked through them, smiling as he recognised some of the titles. "Collectors' items... some of these could be worth a pound or two."

He pulled out several vinyl singles with picture sleeves, a few football programmes and a couple of school exercise books. There was an old scrapbook full of Christopher's achievements and keepsakes including certificates, an unused Lindisfarne ticket, school mementos, and some folded newspaper cuttings showing reports, with pictures, of his Blue Peter badge award, a Sea Cadet parade and school rugby game.

After repacking the case and sliding it back in place they made their way back downstairs, pausing briefly to look up at where the loft hatch had once been – where Edith had discovered her son hanging thirty-six years ago.

"Canna giya this ta reed?" Edith handed over a large brown envelope to David. "It's wot ar Chrissie rote before he deed, like."

David took the envelope and removed a piece of lined paper which looked as though it had been ripped from the centre of a school exercise book. Written in blue biro were Christopher's words from all those years ago:

'Mam.

I'm very sorry for what have done I didn't wont any body to get hurt But when Dawn told me about her friend Stacy dying from drugs, Mam its my fault shes dead. I gave her the drugs I took them to her flat in my newspaper. Jimmy T made me. If I didn't deliver them he sed he would cut Dawns face all over.

Now Jimmy is saying I have to keep my mouth shut and go to prison as a murderer or him and Greg will kill you and Dawn badly... Mam i'm scared. The bobbies have been here. But I wouln't let them in.

Im so sorry Ive done this mam. Tell Dawn I love her and she can have my half of the record player. I love you too Mam.

Chrissie. X'

David put the note back into its envelope. "I'm sorry," he said, visibly shocked as he handed it back to Edith.

An hour later they were back on a train heading for York.

"Well... what did you think? Should we intervene?" asked Jason.

"Oh. I just don't know..." replied David, shaking his head. "If we do, we change so much. We cause a massive blip in the North East which could take decades to heal."

"Heal? Dad, come on. We couldn't possibly make that place any worse, could we?"

"No, I suppose not." David stared out of the carriage window at the undulating green fields, hills and copses, complemented by the cloudless afternoon sky. He knew what Jason wanted to do was no different from what countless Bradbeers had done for centuries before them. Perhaps this is what was always intended for the family – perhaps this was what The Time Store was all about. Was it time for a change?

He thought briefly about the two tarot cards he'd dropped whilst shuffling them. Sarah couldn't possibly have fixed it for those two to fall out – could she? The Wheel of Fortune and the Knight of Rods – maybe it really is time for a change as Sarah had said. Maybe that could be exactly what I need... what we need.

"The Time Store will be yours one day, Jason. When that time comes you'll be custodian. You'll make the rules, you'll be the one who has the potential to change the past and to control the future. It's a huge responsibility, one you've been born to take."

"I know," said Jason, acknowledging his father's words.

"If The Time Store is to change – if we're to change – then I want to steer that change. I want to guide the three of you."

"And Mrs Fisher? What about her and the Tarellis?" asked Jason.

"Do it. But be mindful. The Tarelli family should be brought to justice," replied David. "I want to know what you're going to do... and how. Oh, and no taking them to meet any dinosaurs."

After a late lunch in York, over which they discussed the city's magnificent wall, Jason's stuttering flirtation with Melissa and David's love for Leeds United, they boarded the train to King's Cross.

At some point during their return they'd each nodded off for forty winks or so, a micro-sleep as Dan would call it. Whilst watching his father sleeping, Jason pondered on how best to deal with Jimmy Tarelli and his family of thugs. But no matter how many different options he considered, they all came back to one – Pollard the butcher.

CHAPTER 21

Amelia

Tara hadn't had a good night. Her fitful sleep had been plagued by unsettling dreams, and her intervals of sweaty wakefulness were haunted by looming visions of yesterday's harrowing tarot reading... and of course her frightening life as a young adult back in America.

Realising it was futile to lie in bed any longer, she rose early, showered and dressed. She sat in her conservatory with a glass of freshly squeezed orange juice. Today would have been a normal relaxing day – she'd had nothing planned. But that was all changed now – altered beyond recognition. Her cushy life was under threat, and she had an appointment which would hopefully alleviate and bury that threat. Bury the memory back to where it had lain for years.

Except that wasn't true anymore, was it? No-one had known, no-one. Not even Claudia, who'd been her friend since she'd arrived traumatised and penniless in England all those years ago.

But now at least two more people were aware of her past secrets. Would they really not blab? That woman, Sarah – if that was her real name – had said that with the straightforward supply of one phone number then Tara's hidden past would remain undisclosed. Was it really that easy and basic? Why all that trouble for one number? It must be really important... but why? She simply did not get it.

Last night, as she had lain awake, she went over and over the scenario at the psychic fair. That man – the last one in her queue – he was obviously part of it all. And that woman Angel – what about her? She had pushed for her to have that tarot reading. She'd seen Angel a good few times at various fairs over the years – didn't think she'd have it in her to be part of a devastating plot.

And then, halfway through the night Tara had woken up from a feverish dream where the man from the psychic fair had merged with that other one who'd pestered her a few nights back as she was outside the radio station. She'd realised that the two requests must be connected and was surprised she'd not noticed before. Why had she been so obstinate and cantankerous? If she'd just supplied him with the damn number, maybe none of this other stuff would've happened. Easy with hindsight and bloody ironic for a so-called fortune teller.

She'd quizzed Claudia about Sarah, not revealing anything about the potential release of information, but saying that Sarah had asked a favour – specifically, the telephone number. Tara had asked Claudia's advice – should she give out a caller's number to a complete stranger? What did she want it for? Should she care? Maybe yes she thought, if Sarah had made a threat to Tara, she could be going to do something similar to that girl. Who was this Sarah anyway? Claudia didn't know – said that Sarah had booked the stall at the fair a few months back.

Hold on... what? Something was wrong here. That man had waylaid her on her way to the radio show a week after the one in question. The psychic fair was a few days after that. But Claudia had said yesterday that this Sarah had booked her place about three months ago. Bloody hell, Tara herself had not even 100% confirmed at that point. She was always going to be there of course – Claudia and Tara knew that – but no-one else would have definitely known. So what was going on? This just didn't make any sense.

Her meeting with Sarah was scheduled for two in the afternoon. Sarah had told her to bring the phone number and to be at the statue of King George II in the Old Royal Naval College square.

Yesterday afternoon when she'd left the fair, after a detour to the pub for a double brandy, Tara had made her way to the radio station. She'd gone in, asked Jasmine for the phone number, saying she'd had a thought about how she could help this particular caller. Jasmine had supplied this number, Tara had left and gone home. Job done – simple. Now all she had to do was give it to the mysterious Sarah and she could return to her life and pretend none of this had ever happened. Yeah, right.

For the remainder of the morning Tara tried to reply to her post and e-mails, but she couldn't concentrate. She tried to eat, but couldn't; tried to do some basic household jobs, but was unable to focus on the simplest tasks. She tried to sit and relax, but was too jittery.

At twelve-thirty she rang for a taxi. It was a good efficient taxi firm and the car turned up ten minutes later.

Tara wanted to be early. She put on her coat, picked up her bag and left the house.

"Greenwich, please."

She guessed the journey would take between forty-five minutes and an hour, depending on traffic. She fished her phone out of her bag, intending to put it on silent – she didn't want to be disturbed for the next couple of hours – but then recalled the photos she'd taken in her agitated rage-fuelled panic yesterday. She scrolled through them and enlarged the only one in focus.

Sarah had only a rudimentary knowledge of tarot, that was clear; she'd not been linking the cards together or using their positioning effectively. But as Tara examined the spread, she confirmed to herself what she'd seen at the fair, at Sarah's table. She'd seen the signs in the cards – all of them – the ones Sarah had missed. But Tara had fought against it – because Sarah was not a proper reader. She'd wanted to belittle her when instead she should have been helping her.

The cards were for her – they were definitely telling her something. They were suggesting that she'd had a traumatic past, which was true, but what Sarah had pretty much skimmed over was that the cards were also conveying a current problem – something that had been festering and brewing for a year or so, something which needed to be tackled. Tara had been ignoring this nagging in her head, and would now have to ignore it a while longer until the issue of the phone number was sorted.

However, one of the main things Tara had noticed was that there was a very obvious indicator of action. A minimum of three rods and Wheel of Fortune with Five of Cups, especially in position fourteen – she knew that meant a very definite sign to act immediately. But act immediately for what? The phone number? She was obviously going to do that anyway. Or her life?

The taxi was stuck in traffic in the centre of Barking. Tara looked out of the window at normal everyday life. A little girl in a pushchair dropped her ragdoll on the pavement as her mother stopped briefly to chat to someone. The girl started to cry, her mother was moving on, not realising what had happened. Tara wanted to shout out, but her taxi was advancing again, and it was too late.

She touched the screen of her phone and put it on silent, replaced the phone in her bag and drew out the envelope containing the incriminating photographic evidence of her earlier life. Fourteen photographs – she'd counted them last night, and again this morning. How the bloody hell...?

Sarah would probably never be a brilliant tarot reader, but she and her team were an ace bunch of private detectives. But still – how the hell had they managed all this? A snapshot summary of what had happened.

The first photograph showed a close-up of a much younger dishevelled Tara, lying on a crumpled bed. She was severely bruised, on her arms, wrists, legs, face, eyes – cuts above both eyes. Crying – sobbing. Stuck in this situation – stuck with the prospect of more abuse and pain. How could she escape from her vicious husband – from the poverty of the trailer park he'd brought her to? It was hopeless. She was helpless.

She wasn't called Tara back then. She was Amelia – twenty-four years of age, and married to a brute with absolutely no redeeming qualities whatsoever. It seemed to be accepted practice for the men to beat up their wives and girlfriends here. No use reporting it – even the local sheriff's wife had black eyes. Sarah hadn't supplied a photo of that had she? And then there was the certainty that she would get bashed even worse if she blabbed.

She had one friend – a seventeen year old girl – who lived with her alcoholic mother in the next door trailer. This girl had been living with her dad until about a year ago, when he'd suddenly died, and she'd been dumped here. She'd had a good life with her father – even going on holiday abroad.

The second photo showed Tara – Amelia – stealing the girl's passport. Tara put this picture behind the others as she had done with the first one. She flicked through the next four.

Close up of her hand; with a knife. Close up of knife plunging into comatose husband's chest. Pan out to show her panicked, shocked and elated face; with hand holding blood-stained knife. Another close up, slightly different angle, of knife plunging into chest.

Tara had stabbed him five times – just to make sure. She'd then picked up a small bag, which already contained a change of clothes, a few dollars and the stolen passport. She ran. And never looked back. She ran crying and laughing out into the night – ran for miles until she managed to hitch a lift to Nashville. She spent a day there, roaming around, trying to look like a tourist, and then hitched again – further this time – across a couple of states, in a freight wagon bound for Charleston.

Was it premeditated murder? She had taken that passport. She had definitely thought of running away. She was sure if she ran he would follow... find her... kill her...or maybe worse drag her back to continue the cycle of abuse.

So yes... maybe she did plan to kill. To seize a possible opportunity to stab him. She'd waited till he was drunk; maybe even encouraged him to drink more, so he'd passed out sooner than usual. She'd taken a life. Those photographs showed it in vivid colour.

The next photo showed her performing a sexual act on a dock worker. A sordid way to make money – but she was alone, running scared, and needed to survive. That was the best way she knew how – and it was better than the life she'd had before. She gave them what they wanted, they gave her money, and apart from the occasional smack around the face she got through the next few weeks unscathed.

The next picture was a shot of Charleston's docks – the sea and sky – a lovely morning – almost scenic if it wasn't for the large container ship which would soon set sail. Tara had been getting regular business at the docks, from the longshoremen, stevedores and seamen. She had enough to eat, pay for cheap lodgings, and save a little. But she knew she wasn't going to prostitute herself long-term, it was a means to an end. She was still scared that someone would catch up with her, recognise her and arrest her for the crime she had committed. She was intending to go across the water – hopefully to an English speaking country. By the time she'd accumulated just over a hundred dollars, which seemed a fortune to her, it was easy to find out which ships were going where. However, she was reluctant to ask for passage on a ship, for fear of being ridiculed, turned down and reported.

Her solution came a few days later. She'd been invited on board a ship by a group of raucous sailors who had been out celebrating their last night ashore before they sailed to England. Grabbing her bag from her lodgings she went aboard. She went with a couple of them up onto the bridge – this was the last time she sold herself. She wanted to offer them money to take her to England, but was still too scared to ask. They seemed to like her company though, so she joined the drinking party in the mess room.

She ended up in a cabin with a spare bunk belonging to a sailor who'd passed out in the galley. Unused to having so much drink, she'd slept late – and realised immediately on waking that things felt different. The ship was at sea. Panicking, she remained in the bunk a while longer, thinking they'd turn around, go back to the docks and kick her off. But when she finally emerged, they just laughed at her – said she was stuck with them for the duration of the journey – there and back. They would feed her in return for sexual favours. She figured that this was a fair deal, but for the majority of the journey she suffered from seasickness, so food, and also sex, was off the agenda.

The ship docked at Felixstowe and would be there for a couple of days. Her sickness subsided. She had no intention of making the return journey. She simply walked out of the port, hidden in plain view. She was intending to show her friend's passport, but didn't need to. But the next photo had captured the moment perfectly. Tara – pale, weak, scared, hopeful, happy – walking towards the centre of town with her small bag and a hundred dollars in cash.

She'd been unsure what to do – how to survive, where to live – but still, it all felt better than her previous life. She stayed a couple of nights in a local lodging house, fed herself up, lost her sickly pallor, and tried to make a plan. Then she met Claudia.

She smiled at this photo – her and Claudia at a cafe.

A young Claudia, before her heavy make-up days, when she took pity on a young stray waif of a girl, and bought her a coffee. Twenty-four year old Amelia, who'd always looked young for her age, suddenly became seventeen year old Tara. And she and Claudia had become friends for life.

The next photo was of happier times. The two friends together in Claudia's flat – bottle of wine, incense and candles. Claudia was a secretary for one of the shipping lines – she hated it, but she earned enough to pay the rent and bills on a small flat in Ipswich. For a number of years she'd had an interest in the occult, tarot and mysticism. She was teaching Tara the rudiments of the tarot. Tara took to it immediately, and over the next few months practised hard and long. She tried readings for Claudia many times, then the neighbours, even random people in the local cafe. She was good. She had an excellent memory for the meanings and she had a knack for reading people – a skill she'd developed in the trailer park and the docks. This enabled her to enhance the readings effectively. She was in demand, and people were willing to pay.

She was able to contribute fully to the cost of lodging with Claudia and for the following few years they had a brilliant time. Then Claudia met Martin – married him a year later. Tara took over the flat and the newlyweds bought a house nearer London. Claudia finally packed in her detested secretarial job and started selling incense, candles and tarot cards at psychic fairs. Tara also booked stalls at these fairs and started to make a name for herself. She was now living to all intents and purposes legitimately in the UK, albeit with a false name and age.

When there was a lull in the tarot, she took a part time job in a local cake shop to supplement her income, but she was usually able to survive on tarot alone. She wrote an instructional book – which although not a phenomenal success, had a small print run which led to her being interviewed a couple of times on the radio and once on local TV. Tara decided at this point in her life to buy a house in Chigwell.

Claudia meanwhile had set up Mystic Moon Psychic Fair, and it was an instant success, with one or two per month in the early years. Tara attended every single one. In the last few years, since Claudia's husband had died, she'd retired to a smaller house and only did one venue per year. Tara always attended.

The taxi braked suddenly. Tara had almost forgotten the purpose of her journey – she was so engrossed in her thoughts.

The later photos were not really incriminating – so why were they there? To show her full life history? To prove that Sarah could get into every avenue of her life? The next one showed Tara with Jack. Her only serious relationship. She loved him, felt totally relaxed in his company, Claudia liked him. Tara wanted to share everything with him – but couldn't. Even the reading she did for herself at that time had showed everything in a positive light. He wanted them to move in together, but she couldn't tell him the truth. And she was unable to continue the relationship knowing she was lying. So she ended it. Jack was devastated, Claudia was shocked and baffled, Tara was distraught. She'd not let anyone get close to her since then. She was a fifty-seven year old childless woman. Well, no – in reality she was a sixty-four year old pathetic childless harridan. Her real age was finally catching up with her.

The last two photos were fairly recent. A perfectly captured close up of Tara's fleetingly cynical expression as she performed one of her psychic readings. And the other – Tara raging at some admirer who had innocently requested an autograph.

I've become too jaded... and nasty... Tara realised. She'd stopped doing tarot just over a year ago. She'd read something absolutely devastating in someone's cards – much worse than she'd ever seen before – something she obviously couldn't tell them. She thought they'd read the shock on her face before she melded her expression into something more neutral, terminated the reading, and fled.

She couldn't face doing it after that, couldn't face seeing any more truth. So she'd moved easily into psychic readings, which she couldn't genuinely do... but she was able to quite easily convince everyone that she could. She figured that if she couldn't ever really do a proper psychic reading she would never again see anything bad. They were already on her side, ready to believe her – and ironically her fame had grown more over this last year. She'd become totally arrogant about the whole process, but hadn't properly acknowledged it until now. Were the cards trying to tell her something? Was Sarah trying to tell her something? Sarah was a novice in tarot, but experienced in... what? Detective work? Shock tactics? And all for a poxy telephone number. Why?

The taxi had arrived in Greenwich. Tara paid, included a generous tip, and got out. She'd been to Greenwich a couple of times, the first a good few years ago, to a private residence, to do tarot readings for the six guests at someone's birthday dinner, and the second more recently to visit The Royal Observatory – normal tourist stuff.

She found the pre-arranged meeting spot easily. She was twenty minutes early, so she sat down on a nearby bench and waited. Sarah arrived ten minutes later, spotted Tara and came to sit beside her on the bench.

"You made it," said Sarah.

"You gave me no choice," said Tara.

"So you've managed to get the number?"

"Of course." Tara handed over a piece of paper.

"Thank you," said Sarah.

"No problem." But it was a problem. "You're not going to release this stuff to the press are you?"

"No – if this number is genuine – no," said Sarah.

Tara believed her. "But how did you get all these photos? Forty years of my life... how...?"

"I'd really rather not say," said Sarah. "Look, I'm sorry we did this. Sometimes we go to extraordinary lengths to get the simplest things."

"But –"

"Thank you, Tara." Sarah stood up and smiled. "You've helped me. I'm hoping this number will lead to my brother being able to solve a mystery about himself that's been dragging on for the past five years."

"What...?"

"I have to go now." Sarah handed her a card. "I'm sorry to have caused you distress. If you need help or advice in the future – about anything – and I mean anything – please call us. We may be able to do more than you'd expect."

"Thank you." Tara clutched the card. "I hope your brother finds what he wants."

"I do too."

"Bye then." This was all very surreal.

Sarah took a few steps, then stopped and turned back. "Goodbye, Amelia."

CHAPTER 22

Bolt Gun

What the fuck, where am I? My hands... someone's tied my hands, tight. Jimmy Tarelli twisted his hands in an attempt to loosen the bindings on his wrists.

"Looks like another one's awake now. Hook him up and tape his mouth, Dan. Don't want him squealing – not just yet."

Not just yet? Squeal? Who the fuck is that? Jimmy opened his eyes. *Too bright,* he squinted and closed them again. *Southerner, he talked like a southerner.* "What the fuck is going on here? Do you know? Mmmrm." Too late, Jimmy's mouth was well and truly taped shut.

What's that noise? A cranking, someone's turning a handle, I can hear creaking. Whoa WHAT THE FUCK, what's happening to me? Something is dragging me up. Come on Jimmy, come on son... open your fucking eyes. The noise stopped.

Dad? Greg... Uncle Marc. What the fuck, what the hell is going on? Who the fuck has done that to them?

Jimmy surveyed his surroundings; *a barn.* His father was directly opposite him sitting on a bale of straw, gagged – hands tied, raised high above his head by a *meat hook,* wearing what looked like massive *Mickey Mouse gloves, fuck!* His brother, *Greg,* was to his right, exactly the same as his dad, *boiler suits, blue boiler suits,* he was wearing one as well. *Why the fucking suits? They're massive – why are we wearing these?*

"This one's coming round too."

A woman's voice, she's talking about Uncle Marc. I recognise her, that's the bitch from the party. She was next to me when we did the hokey fucking cokey. That's all I remember. Left leg in – left leg out – linking up, going into the middle – now I'm here. HOW? What was she doing at the party, how the hell did she get in there?

Two men. Look as if they can handle themselves. London gang, this has got to be about the drugs. Not seen them before. What was his name? Dan. He's gonna be the first to get it, fucking wanker.

"Are they ready?"

"Yes, Jase," the woman replied.

Jase, Jason. I don't know a fucking Jason.

"Gentlemen. I need to ask you some questions. However, before we start I have a little demonstration for you. Perhaps a taste of things to come... maybe."

What the..., he can't be serious. That's a fucking goat. Bollocks no way, they're gonna get us having sex with goats. Shit there's the camera – Dad – NO. He said questions, he had questions. Why doesn't he just fucking ask them?

"This is a good friend of mine. Gentlemen – I'd like to introduce you to Mr Pollard. Or as we like to call him –

Pollard the butcher."

Ask your fucking questions why don't you?

Pollard, standing at just shy of seven foot was a massive bloke, an ideal number eight in any union side. He was wearing a pair of blood-stained hob-nailed boots – minus the laces, Bermuda shorts, green t-shirt and a bright yellow rubber apron.

Pollard the butcher led the goat to the centre of the four bales where Jimmy and his family were sitting. He tethered it to a steel loop in the floor.

"Righto. I'm just gonna go and get my tools, back in a jiffy. Keep old Nellie here company, please boys."

They'd been left alone. The four of them looked at one another, exchanged nods, indicating they were okay. Greg and Marc tried to unhook themselves, but after a few moments of struggle, and several rope burns for their efforts, realised that it was futile.

They've left us to stew with a frigging goat. I can't believe this. What fucking gang has a pet goat?

It wasn't long before Pollard returned. "Okay. Sorry about that. Now then, Nellie here isn't very well, are you Nellie?"

No – and you won't be when we get out of here – fucking retard.

Pollard bent over and petted the goat, allowing Nellie to lick the side of his face. "Aw lookie. Nellie is giving me a kiss – daft thing."

Pass me a fucking bucket.

Pollard stood back up. "Nellie has a contagious disease..." He wiped Nellie's saliva from the side of his face with the back of his hand. "Johne's disease. Unfortunately it's too far gone now, and she's getting on a bit. So... anyway, I need to give her an injection first. Numb her senses so's to speak."

Pollard opened a small leather case and filled a syringe from a blue-labelled phial, then walked over to Jimmy. *What the fuck*, Jimmy struggled, tried to twist away from the approaching needle. *No way, no way – get the fuck away from me.* However, Pollard's strength was too much for him; he held Jimmy's head firm. "This won't hurt if you sit still, give it a few moments and you'll feel great." Pollard injected Jimmy, Greg, Tony and Marc in the neck.

"Oh... lookie here, seems there's not enough left for our Nellie." Pollard showed each of the Tarellis in turn the empty syringe. "Never mind – I have some more." He went back to his case and took out another phial – a red one this time. He refilled the syringe, took it over to Nellie and injected the full amount into her. "There. I don't think she'll mind sharing a needle with you fine gentlemen."

Why doesn't he just ask his questions, why this – WHY THIS?

"My dad was the slaughter man, as was Grandpa Lawrence before him – for half of East Yorkshire back in the day." Pollard stroked Nellie's back, as her legs gave way and she slumped down. "Dad used to travel the local farms – killing and cutting pigs, sheep and what have you. Course we'd always have good fresh meat on the table at home. They didn't have owt fancy though – for doin' animal in. Just one of these." Pollard pulled a large black iron bolt and what looked like a sawn-off shotgun out of a canvas bag.

What the shit is that for? Fuck, what's he gonna do. The goat, please let it be the goat.

"The bolt goes in here." The butcher slotted the bolt

into the end of the gun. "Of course I've already powdered the gun."

Of course you have.

"Then we say our goodbyes to old Nellie here, like this." Pollard placed the end of the gun to the centre of Nellie's head, just next to one of her small horns. He clenched the stock tightly as he squeezed at the trigger. There was a thunderous crack as the charge ignited, firing the bolt into Nellie's head, destroying her cerebrum. Placing his right boot onto Nellie's neck Pollard used a bolt cutter to remove the end of the bolt – Nellie's crimson blood dripped from it. "Now who'd like to lick it clean, whilst it's still warm?"

Gross, gross, gross... fucking gross.

Pollard removed another bolt from his canvas bag. "Right, who's next?"

"One moment, Mr Pollard." Jason walked back in. "We need to ask them some questions first. They might – just might – decide to answer."

"Now, now, Jason. That doesn't seem fair. You said I could do in at least one of them."

"We'll see... we'll see."

That's all Jimmy and his family saw or heard for a while, whatever Pollard had injected them with had worked, and they were sound asleep.

What's happening? Dad, Greg, Nellie, Uncle Marc? Shit wake up, Jimmy T. Sod the goat. My arms are fucking killing me – stretched. I can't see, something's on my head. Bucket, bowl or something.

"Sarah, you need to fetch Jason and the butcher.

They're all awake and swinging," said Dan.

Sarah, that's the fucking bitch's name from the party. Hokey cokey, yeah rite!! Wait 'til I get my hands on the skanky tart.

Sarah returned a few moments later with her brother and Mr Pollard.

"Okay. Cut one of them down and sit him here in front of the camera," said Jason, as he mounted a digital video camera onto a tripod.

Why me, why me... why choose me? Ow - fuck! Jimmy crumpled to the floor, and was pulled up to his feet.

"Let's see who we have here, take the helmet off him and tie him to the chair."

Dan and Sarah led Jimmy to an old wooden school desk and chair, securely tied him to it, and then removed a grey plastic full face knight's helmet. His mouth was still taped up and he stared directly into a camera. He'd never seen one as fancy as that before.

"Which one's this, Sarah?"

"Jimmy Tarelli, Jase. He's the youngest, I brought him here," replied Sarah. "We had a little dance together."

Yes you fucking whore – you better watch your fucking back – bitch.

"Okay... he's a bit skinnier than I'd imagined. Mr Pollard, you can pick another to play with."

Pollard looked at the three helmet-wearing, boiler-suited figures. He selected the one hanging nearest to him and dragged it away from the other two – this one was to be his new playmate.

Dad, Greg, Uncle Marc... Shit one of them is hanging next to the butcher bloke. No... which one? I can't tell, why the bloody helmets? Who did the bastard choose? Dad... please tell me it's not you, Dad.

"Right, Jimmy Tarelli. This is my barn and I make the rules. Do I make myself clear?" Jason waited for some form of indication that Jimmy understood. "Do you understand?"

Of course I fucking understand. He nodded.

"Good. We'll remove the tape and I'll ask you some questions. Co-operate and you can all go home safely. But please don't lie to me. One lie, just one... well, then you can sit and watch Mr Pollard at work again."

Who is this fucking hippy-haired sadist? Whatever happened to just shooting someone? Or kneecapping them?

"Tape please, Dan."

Aagh... Fuck that hurt, Dan ripped the tape from Jimmy's face, hairs and all.

"You fucking wait, you bastards. You fucking wait! You'll not sleep... never. We'll make sure you all burn in hell. Won't we Dad?"

"Mr Pollard, please," said Jason. "Unfortunately Mr Tarelli here needs to realise that we don't have time to play games. Could you?"

"My pleasure," said Pollard. He slowly raised the bolt gun, aimed and fired, impaling the bolt straight through the shoulder of his chosen captive. Blood oozed out onto the boiler suit as his victim writhed. Jimmy thought he heard muted screams through the tape.

Fuck! Jimmy hung his head in shame.

"I gather we're not having any more outbursts?"

"No," replied Jimmy, shaking his head from side to side. "What do you want to know?"

"Could you read from the cards please, Jimmy. Nice and slow, don't rush," instructed Sarah, holding up a large card with bold handwritten words.

"Testing – testing. One, two, three, four. This is my confession. My name is James Michael Tarelli. I live down Mendip Avenue, Clifton Hill, Middlesbrough, number eight. I'm twenty-nine years old." Jimmy paused.

"Problem, Mr Tarelli?" Jason asked.

"I'm thirty-five, not twenty-nine, the card said twenty-nine." *Fucked up there... fucking smart arse.*

"What do you do for a living, Mr Tarelli?" Jason ignored him.

"I work in the family business."

"Which is?"

"Finance, pharmaceutical supply, girls... you know the type of things."

"Mr Pollard... one in a leg please. Mr Tarelli here needs to know we require straight answers."

Pollard the butcher reached down to his canvas bag, powdered the gun then loaded another bolt and cocked back the trigger. "My pleasure, my pleasure. Left one okay?"

"No... No... We do drugs, prostitutes. We're money lenders... Please – NO!"

It was too late, Pollard had already placed his gun upon his target. The crack of the igniting charge resonated throughout the wooden barn – the bolt pierced through material, ripped apart flesh and muscle – and splintered bone as it exited. The leg flinched, twisted and flayed wildly as the bolt caused even more trauma, more pain... more blood.

"The next one will be the last. There will be no more playing, Mr Tarelli. Straight answers please. The drugs – I want to know where you get them, who makes the deliveries, when and how you distribute them... I want to know every precise detail," said Jason, calmly, but with authority.

"Hartlepool – we get them from Hartlepool, but they come down from Newcastle." *Shit, if I tell him who from and how, they'll kill us. How did we get into this fucking shit?* "We get them from a nursing home, an old people's home."

"Which one?"

"I can't remember – Greg gets them."

"Mr Pollard... if you don't mind."

"NO... Sunny Bank... SUNNY BANK... we get them from Sunny fucking Bank. Please don't!" Jimmy Tarelli wept, tears ran down his face as he pleaded desperately for the life of his kin.

Jason raised his hand, Pollard sat back down. "Not quite yet, Mr Pollard. Not quite yet. But put one straight through the head if Mr Tarelli here so much as stutters again." Jason turned to his sister. "Sarah, do you mind getting Mr Tarelli some water please."

Sarah, taking the top off, placed a bottle of mineral water in front of Jimmy, and walked back to join Dan. *And how exactly am I supposed to drink it with these fucking Mickey Mouse gloves on? Bitch.*

"Come now, Jimmy T. Answer these questions and you can all go home. You have my word that we won't touch you. Isn't that right, Dan?"

"Yep. Sure is – not a hair." Dan replied, playing with his bracelet.

Look at the smarmy bastard playing with his girlie fucking jewellery – twat! Just you fucking wait mate. You'd better kill all of us, cos if you don't you'll all be fucking dead.

"Carry on please, Mr Tarelli," instructed Jason.

"Sundays, we get the stash Sundays. Greg picks it up from Sunny Bank and takes it to Topper's shop. Gaz Topper, he has a couple of paper shops. We cut it there and get the kids to deliver it for us."

"Kids?"

"Yeah. You know? Newspaper rounds. We get the paper lads to post them for us. If anything goes wrong, then they take the shit."

"And has it? Has anything ever gone wrong?"

"No. No... never."

The sound was deafening. The charge ignited with a sharp ferocity. Pollard struggled to control the recoil as the projectile thundered from the bolt gun, cracking through the plastic helmet and into his target's skull.

"Shall I gut it open, Mr Bradbeer?"

"Unfortunately, Mr Tarelli has lied – so yes." Jason walked away. "I really hoped it wouldn't come to this."

Pollard took out from his canvas bag a large leather roll, untied the bow and then unrolled it on the top of a bale. The roll contained several knives and cleavers – all neatly arranged in size order. "Now let me see. Mmm – I think old Mr Wilson here will do nicely." Pollard unclipped an old, yet very sharp and well cared for blade, clearly stamped I.Wilson. His favourite. "Come on, Mr Wilson, we have work to do. Flesh... You do like a bit of flesh, don't you?"

What the fuck? No... No... Shit I'm gonna be sick. Jimmy

Tarelli had turned ashen, colour drained, he leaned forwards and retched.

Following the zip line of the blue boiler suit, Pollard thrust the knife inwards, as though punching into soft butter – he buried the knife to its hilt. Blood was oozing from the wound, running down Pollard's forearm and dripping to the barn floor from his elbow. He cut upwards with a deft sawing motion, the knife slicing through everything with ease.

Pollard stopped. "Oooh!! Lookie here, Mr Wilson. Looks like you've found the sternum – well done."

He placed the blood-drenched knife down on the bale, and took a huge rubber glove out of his canvas bag. He put the glove on his right hand, then returned to his new friend.

"This is the fun bit, I like this bit," said Pollard as he plunged his hand into the lifeless body and drew forth its intestines and stomach which he then held high. "There, Mr Tarelli. Would you like these – for dinner perhaps?"

But it was too late. Jimmy had already passed out with shock.

When Jimmy had been brought round, one of his remaining relatives had been placed next to Pollard. The body was still there too, hanging lifelessly, bolts through leg, shoulder, plastic helmet and skull; intestines hanging from the cut in the boiler suit.

Bastards... sick psychotic bastards.

"Right, Mr Tarelli. Shall we try that again? Has anything ever gone wrong?" Jason had returned to his questioning.

"Fisher... hung himself. Christopher Fisher. A girl

died on the estate when she found her brother's drugs. Chris blamed himself and we... well, I... let him. Told him if he grassed I'd kill his family."

"Where do you keep the loan books? I want the details. Every last detail." Jason looked around; Pollard, Dan – no Sarah. "Dan, where's Sarah gone?"

"Tescos. Dad asked her to get some garlic puree and basil. Think he's doing spag bol for us all later. You're invited, Mr Pollard," said Dan.

Tescos... she's gone shopping. Who are these people? Fuck, we're just fucking amateurs playing at being nasty.

"Thank you, young Daniel, would love to come," said Pollard.

"Gents do you mind? Business... can't you see Mr Tarelli here is in a hurry. Oh... Dan, call Sarah. Ask her to get me a box of Frosties will you?"

Frosties... I don't believe this. Death, intestines... and he wants fucking Frosties. SICK bastard.

"Sorry about that, Jimmy. Right – back to the loans. I want books, ledgers. Where do you keep them?"

"Dad's greenhouse. Behind the oil heater."

"Have they always been there?"

"No. The floor under the front door mat, it moves. Dad used to keep them there."

"And the prostitutes... I want a list of all your girls, clients, the lot."

"Same place... with the ledgers."

"Blackmail and extortion – especially in the police. I want names. Who and why."

There was no immediate answer from Jimmy Tarelli. He shook his head defiantly, this was information he'd take to the grave.

"Mr Pollard. Prepare three bolts... I'm tired of games, give them one each straight there." Jason lifted his right index finger and placed it on his own temple.

"INSPECTOR COLLINS. FUCK, DON'T SHOOT!" Jimmy was desperate. "Inspector Collins – he looks out for us, we have pictures – lots of pictures with him and some of our girls."

"Thank you, Mr Tarelli. I think that concludes my questions." Jason waved to Dan and Pollard, who packed their things; camera, knives and bolt gun. They then left the barn. Jason walked up to Jimmy and took a knife to his bindings. "You're free to go, Mr Tarelli. As promised, you're free to go."

Jason joined his brother out in the farmyard. Pollard was already driving off into the distance.

Jimmy Tarelli ripped off the Mickey Mouse gloves and ran over to where his family hung. He eased the first down and removed the plastic knight's helmet. "Greg... Thank God, thank God." Jimmy took off Greg's oversized white gloves then peeled off the tape which was binding his mouth. Greg in turn coughed and spluttered, gasping wildly for air. The brothers embraced.

They both eased their remaining relative down. *Shit... is it Dad? Uncle Marc? Dad, please... please God.*

Jimmy slowly eased the helmet off, "NO... Fuck NO... Dad... Dad."

Greg pulled the tape from their Uncle Marc's mouth and untied his bindings. Jimmy slumped to his knees, distraught, but full of vengeance as his eyes were drawn to the disembowelled body hanging before him. Grief and anger coursed through every cell in Jimmy's exhausted body and he let out a mighty scream. "DAAAAAAA-DD."

"Haway lad. What you fucking screaming at?"

Jimmy spun round in disbelief. There he was, walking through into the barn, his father, Tony Tarelli.

Jimmy looked at his brother and uncle, turned and looked at his dad. "Dad? B-But who's that?" Jimmy pointed at the hanging body.

"Drop it down, son," ordered Tony as he got closer. "Let's have a look shall we."

Jimmy and Greg dropped the body to the floor. Tony then ripped off the plastic helmet and the four Tarellis looked down with a sense of disbelief and bewilderment.

"Of course... Nellie the fucking goat," said Jimmy. *The bastards.*

"We need to get back home, fucking quick. Move the ledgers. Then we need to find who these fuckers are – and sort them." Marc led his brother and nephews from the barn.

"Does anyone know where we are, like?"

There was no reply. They hadn't got a clue.

"Well?"

"I can't thank you enough, Sarah. That was unbelievable. But what will happen now?"

Sarah and Edith stepped out from a shadow-filled corner of the barn. Edith had witnessed for herself Jimmy Tarelli's confession. She might now at last get justice for Christopher's death.

"We'll take all the information we have to a friend in West Yorkshire Police, a good man. He'll make sure

Inspector Collins has nothing to do with any investigation," replied Sarah.

"But won't they move everything?"

"They might... but today it's 1985."

Sarah told Edith that they'd take the evidence back to 1979. Give it a week or two, and the Tarellis would be banged up for a very long time. She explained that today would never happen in the lives of that family, none of this would actually happen.

"Will I remember it though?"

"Of course, of course you will – but prepare yourself for some changes when I get you back home. The Clifton Hill Estate and Middlesbrough could be a bit different now."

With that both ladies linked arms and disappeared back to 2014 and the Round Room.

CHAPTER 23

A & E

"Come on... come on, pick up will you?"

"Hi – you've reached the voicemail of Alice Brewer. Sorry I can't take your call right now. Please leave a message after the beep and I'll get back to you. Thank you."

"Alice... Alice. Come on where are you? Call me will you – it's important. Very important. Pleeeeeeeeeeease."

Together with several text messages that was the fourth voicemail Emma had left in an attempt to contact her sister since speaking briefly to Sarah Bradbeer.

Emma, a freelance PR account manager with City Tech Agency, had returned to her Hammersmith apartment after a hectic day at work. She poured herself a glass of Tanglefoot Creek, her favourite Australian Shiraz and ran herself a relaxing tea-tree and lemongrass infused bath.

With the water running Emma headed into the bedroom, kicked off her heels, removed her black leather biker style jacket, then unzipped, took off and hung up her black and white abstract-patterned shift dress.

Without heels she stood at five foot five and three quarter inches, although she preferred to tell people five-six, not only because it was more convenient to say – but by rounding it up she was the same height as her mother, Catherine, had been.

She took off her underwear, threw it all into the wash basket, clicked play on her answer machine, and then re-entered her en-suite bathroom.

You have five unplayed messages. First unplayed message. Today nine-twenty-seven. "Hello, this is Graham calling from Accident Claims Direct..."

Emma ignored this message as it rambled on about believing that someone at her address had suffered a recent accident. With the water now off Emma took a gulp of wine, replaced her glass on the side of the bath and then lay back until her neck and shoulder length black hair were in the water.

Second unplayed message. Today eleven-forty-one. There wasn't one. It was either one of those automated number diallers or the caller couldn't be bothered to leave a message.

Third unplayed message. Today twelve-twenty-three. "Hello. My name's Sarah Bradbeer. I wonder if you could give me a call back when you get this message on eight eight five eight... forty-one forty-one. It's a personal matter, reference a phone call you recently had with Psychic Tara on the radio... thanks. That's eight eight five eight... forty-one forty-one."

Emma, upon hearing Tara's name, sent a near-deluge of water crashing over the side of the bath onto the floor, as she tried to raise herself quickly upright. Once out of the bath she grabbed a large peach bath towel from the wall rail, wrapped it around herself, and rushed back into her bedroom, leaving a trail of wet footprints on the floor as she went.

Emma caught the end of the fourth message which was from her Auntie Claire; she could replay that later, but gathered that she had called to thank her for the birthday present she'd received.

Fifth unplayed message. Today fifteen-thirty-two. "Hi, Emms. I've got some tickets for the Augustines at The Roundhouse in December. You said you fancied it. Let me know will you? See-ya, see-ya – wouldn't wannabe-ya."

The last message was from Sue Hayden, a girl Emma used to flat-share with, possibly one of her closest friends and in the occasional absence of Alice, the friend who usually picked up the pieces when Emma fell out of love with someone.

She replayed Sarah's message three times, and allowed it to sink in word for word, flapped around for a few minutes in wonderment, then calmed down, drank her wine, refilled her glass and then replayed the message for a fourth time.

It was just before eight o'clock when Alice finally rang.

"Where have you been?" asked Emma, excitedly. "I've got news. I've got some news!"

"Oh, okay. No 'hello, Alice... how are you?'" replied Alice. "Must be something good then?"

"It is... it is. You know last week, when I told you I'd called that radio psychic?"

"Oh, Emma... not this again." There was a deep sigh on the phone. "Why do you insist on doing this? Can't you just let it drop – PLEASE?"

The conversation abruptly faltered, neither sister immediately continued. Emma, feeling as though the rug had been pulled from under her, began welling up. Ordinarily she was a tough-nut, not a tissue hugger by any means. However, in the past five years, on this subject, since she claimed to have seen the changing headline she'd searched out answers as if looking for the rainbow's gold. Countless times, far too many to calculate, Alice had to deal with the aftermath that the fading rainbow left behind.

"Oh... Look, I'm sorry, I'm sorry." Alice, fed up with looking at a pile of ironing that needed doing, broke the silence. "Go on then. I'm listening, what is it?"

"Someone called me. A woman – Sarah Bradbeer. She left a message on my answer machine about my call to the radio station..."

"And?" interrupted Alice.

"She left a number for me to call back on."

"Well, I'm guessing that you did. What did she want, this..."

"Sarah."

"Yes... this Sarah?"

"Well, I called the number back and got through to a place called The Time Store..."

"Did you Google it?"

"Obvs... Something to do with watches, clocks and what have you. It's been there – in Greenwich – for years. Anyway, Sarah asked me about the time and date of the crash. Wanted to know how it happened – then asked about the newspaper and the change I saw."

"Er... You think you saw."

Emma ignored this interjection from her sister. "She wanted to know more about the exact time of the change though – said it coincided with something that happened to her brother. Something they've been looking for an answer to, same as me."

"Okay... and...?"

"I'm meeting her to talk about it. But I want you to come with me – will you? Promise you will – pleeeeease."

"Of course I will, of course I will. When?"

"Harry's Bar – we need to be there before ten o'clock. Tonight."

"What the fuck... tonight?"

"Alice – I need answers. You know I need answers. Do you think I'd be able to sleep tonight if I knew there was a possible answer out there? Do you?"

"No. I suppose not... I'll come over."

Sarah had never been to Harry's Bar before, but had passed by on several occasions, it had just turned seven-thirty when she arrived there. Harry's was a nice little wine bar on Hammersmith's King Street, and was themed on the history of the nearby theatre. Thankfully the bar served tapas style snacks, as Sarah had missed dinner. For a Thursday evening she had expected it to be a little less busy, but there were plenty of office-types in there enjoying an after-work snifter or two, along with a few romantic couples who preferred to be tucked away in the secluded corners.

Sarah sat in a cosy armchair by the window. This allowed her to see everyone who entered the bar, plus it was the only available table which would seat three comfortably. She could see why Emma was eager for an immediate meet – Dan would be exactly the same – if he knew there was someone who could've given the slightest hint to what had happened five years ago he'd have dropped everything to see them. Good job she hadn't told him yet.

They'd arranged to meet any time after eight, Emma couldn't be any more precise on the time as she wanted her sister, Alice, to come along, but insisted that it would be no later than ten, so Sarah wasn't quite sure on how long she'd need to wait. She ordered a bottle of the house recommended red and a selection of tapas for one, which included some jamon, queso, steak tartar and fried squid.

During her wait, Sarah had been hit on by two different men and to her surprise a woman. Both men seemed to think she'd been stood up on a date and offered slurred condolences in the way of a drink. The woman was a bit more full-on than the men and got straight down to asking Sarah back to her place for some fun. Although she declined this offer, Sarah couldn't help but think the woman was very attractive and so found her approach quite flattering.

It was around nine-thirty when a couple of young women in their early thirties entered Harry's and appeared to be looking for someone. As Emma had already given a brief description of herself and what she'd be wearing, Sarah approached them.

"Hi. I'm Sarah. Are you Emma?" she asked, directing her greeting to the slightly taller girl wearing the leather biker jacket.

"Yes... Hi, erm – this is Alice – my sister."

"Pleased to meet you both." Sarah indicated to the table. "Shall we?"

They sat at Sarah's table and ordered another bottle of the recommended red, along with a bottle of Australian Verdelho. Sarah also ordered some more tapas, to share, this time without the squid.

"Thanks for agreeing to meet at short notice. Sorry we've kept you waiting... only I feel more comfortable with Alice here."

"No problem – let's hope we can all put an end to our mysteries, and move on."

"Mysteries..." Alice shook her head from side-to-side in disbelief, as she poured herself a glass of wine. "Chasing ghosts... chasing a past that never was."

"You'll have to forgive Alice. She's..."

"She's what?" Alice interrupted. "She's fed up of it all, that's what she is." Alice turned to look at Sarah. "You'll have to forgive me, forgive my ignorance on all this – but I've had enough of it. For five years now I've sat at bloody make-believe mediums, stupid psychics and tosspot tarot readers..."

"Have you tried rune stones?" Sarah commented, stopping Alice in her tracks. "I could suggest someone if you want – although I think you'll be wasting your money."

"You mentioned your brother on the phone? Dan...?" Emma was keen to get to the point.

"Yes – but before we go on can we just confirm the date and time again? Might save us a lot of trouble."

"Yeah sure. It was Wednesday the 14th of October 2009. Eleven o'clock," replied Emma. "In the morning."

"Are you sure of the time?"

"Yes, one-hundred percent. I had the radio on – the eleven o'clock news was on."

"Does this tie in with whatever happened to your brother?" Alice had started to pay more attention. Sarah had been the first person they'd met who hadn't discussed a fee of any description. "What happened to him?"

"A dream – a nightmare – morning-mare. I don't know, call it what you will. All we know is that he woke up screaming – he was soaked through, as though he'd been out in the rain all night. We thought it was sweat at first – but it wasn't – and the hairs on his left arm were missing, burnt off." Sarah had to tell the girls something extraordinary had happened to Dan – but she could hardly tell them that he belonged to a family of time travellers.

"Same date and time?" asked Emma.

"Yes. Same date and time – exactly." Sarah picked up her wine and took a sip. "We've been looking for something, anything which could in one way or another offer up some clues to what happened... no matter how vague or remote."

"Yes... but come on. You're in Greenwich, aren't you? We were in Oxford back then... there can't be any link. That would be unreal..." Alice had her sceptical head on again.

"I'm more interested in the car crash though – and the headline change. You did say it changed – that you saw it change?"

"Yes – definitely. Although there have been times when I've doubted it myself," replied Emma.

"The thing is..." interrupted Alice sharply, "I believe Emma – believe that what she thinks she saw is true. But that would mean that the past would've had to have been altered. I mean come on – let's get real for a minute – this isn't the movies."

"Well no, it's not – but then if you're willing to believe in psychics and mediums – then why not believe that the past could have changed?"

"That's the point – she doesn't believe in the spirit world. Neither do I really," said Emma.

"No. This is the only thing I believe in." Alice reached into her jacket pocket and pulled out a creased photograph of their parents. "Mum and Dad's grave."

"Alice – there's no need for that. Sarah's just trying to help me, that's what she's here for – can't you see that? I'm sorry, Sarah." Emma felt that she needed to apologise for her sister's actions.

"No, that's alright. I've seen it all before – we've been like that with Dan a few times. It *is* frustrating, I know. Look, why don't you two come to The Time Store and meet him?" suggested Sarah, holding out her card. "I'm hoping that if he sees or hears you, it might spark a memory or something."

"Okay. When?" asked Emma. "Tomorrow?"

"No, sorry. We have clients tomorrow and then I'm carving bloody pumpkins for Halloween." Sarah shrugged. "So… shall we say Saturday morning – ten o'clock?"

"Yes that's good," replied Emma triumphantly. "Alice?"

"Yes… I suppose so."

With that agreed the three ladies turned their attention to the wine and Emma ordered more tapas for them to snack on. They spent about half an hour or so chatting about psychics and mediums, especially Tara, although Sarah didn't let on that she'd actually met her. Then they turned their conversation to men. By the end of the evening Alice, Emma and Sarah were getting on as though they'd known one another for years.

Content that the meeting had gone as planned, if not better, Sarah made her excuses and left Harry's Bar just after eleven o'clock. Her journey home via the tube and light railway was a pretty uneventful one, but at least it gave her time to reflect on any new possibilities in time for tomorrow's family meeting.

Jason had kept his client presentations somewhat brief – for him extremely brief. He had the usual historical time trips featuring loads of high risk and adventure. Both Dan and Sarah – having more important things to discuss – rubber stamped these without question.

"My turn," said Dan, quickly handing out a sheet of paper to the others with a photograph paper-clipped to the rear. "Just the one from me – slightly mundane compared to recent events though. This is Joan Bullion, a writer from Seaford down in Sussex." They all unclipped the photograph to reveal a middle-aged woman with shoulder-length golden hair, radiant eyes and a smirky smile. "Joan's currently writing a book – her first – set in 15th Century Peru..."

"Peru – mundane – never," interrupted David, as he entered the rest room and proceeded to make himself a drink. "Nothing about South America could ever be called mundane."

"Dad... let Dan finish," laughed Sarah.

"Joan wants to research the Inca ruler Pachacuti

along with the sun-god Inti," continued Dan, ignoring his father's interruption. "Plus I thought it would be nice to see Machu Picchu being built, and then move onto The Land of the Four Quarters."

"You do know that's cult worshipping – all that Inti stuff?"

"Yes, Dad – that's what her book is about."

"Okay. When you thinking of?" asked Jason.

"Next Thursday, unless anyone else has anything planned for then."

The family nodded in agreement and approved Joan's time travel trip. Dan was inviting her to The Time Store so that she could get to see their collection of ancient sundials, then if all went well they'd venture back in time.

"Okay, okay... where are we? Are you all done?" David sat down with his coffee, and squared-up some newspapers which he'd placed in front of himself.

"Just Sarah's now," said Dan impatiently.

"That's good. But before you all move on I'd like to say well done on the past week's events, especially you, Sarah."

"Thank you," she smiled.

"By all accounts, not only was the tarot reading brilliant and well-executed, but the groundwork both you and Daniel put in for the dossier was excellent – well done the both of you on that one."

"Yes. Well done." Jason added his congratulations. "I also want to add that I was somewhat confused at the start of all this as to why you didn't just turn up and show her the photographs and get the number. But then I realised that doing it that way – we'd just have got the number..."

"Yes – but now we have the number and a potential future ally." Sarah finished off Jason's sentence for him.

David turned to his eldest son. "Jason – actually, all of you – thank you for opening up my eyes. I travelled back to Leeds Crown Court this morning for the Tarelli trial."

"Leeds?" asked Sarah.

"Yes. Just the sentencing actually. The Tarelli's had too much influence on Teesside, so their case was heard in Leeds," replied David. "You'll be pleased to know that they got fifteen to twenty years apiece." David handed each of them a copy of The Yorkshire Evening Post with its bold headlines – BORO' DRUGS FAMILY JAILED.

"But doesn't that mean that they're out now?"

"Yes, Dan. I didn't look to see what the others are doing – if they're still alive that is – but Jimmy Tarelli works in a garden centre near Merthyr Tydfil now." David pointed over to a small potted plant and a couple of pumpkins he'd placed near the kettle. "The pumpkins are for you, Sarah. The plant is for Edith. I think she'll like it, don't you?"

Sarah turned towards the plant. "Yes, I think it's lovely – she'll love it. And the pumpkins are just right. Thanks, Dad."

"Right, Sarah. Your turn now," said Jason.

"Finally," mumbled Dan.

"Perhaps we should break for lunch first? What do you think, Dan?" smiled Sarah.

"Er. Perhaps not!"

Everyone laughed – including Dan.

"Right. As you're all aware by now, the number Tara gave us belongs to a Miss Emma Brewer."

"I wasn't aware of that," snapped Dan, looking

miffed. "No-one's told me her name."

"Sorry – you must have been with a client. I thought you knew," lied Sarah. "Anyway I called Emma yesterday afternoon to arrange a meet..."

"When? When are you meeting her? I want to come." Dan excitedly butted in.

"Dan – let your sister finish please," insisted David.

"I met her last night."

"What the fuck! Why wasn't I told any of this?" Dan stood up, enraged. "You guys have no right to keep me out of this. I had just as much right to be there – if not more."

"DANIEL – sit down, or get out."

Dan, obeying his father's words, gave his sister a look of contempt, shook his head in disgust and bit his lip.

"I'm sorry, Dan – I had to make sure she was genuine. I wanted to know for myself whether she could possibly help us – help you. I didn't want you to be let down."

Dan acknowledged his sister's words with the slightest of nods and the thinnest of smiles, then sat tight-lipped as he allowed Sarah to recount both her telephone conversation and her meeting in Harry's Bar with Emma and Alice.

"So you think it could have something to do with this car crash then?" asked Jason.

"Possibly," replied Sarah. "As good a place to start as any."

"Does a car crash or the name Brewer mean anything to you, Daniel?"

"No, Dad," he replied, shaking his head. "Not a thing."

"The girls are coming here tomorrow morning. I want Emma to meet Dan – let them spend some time together, see if it jogs anything at all."

"And are you planning on going back to this crash?" asked David.

"Yes of course – but I think we should take them somewhere else first. Last thing we need is for them to freak out in the past. It's not going to be nice watching a crash that kills your parents – is it?"

"No – no it isn't," David acknowledged. "Right, lunchtime. The Plume anyone?"

David, Dan and Jason went on ahead to order food and drinks whilst Sarah tidied up the rest room. She washed, dried and put away the four coffee mugs, straightened the chairs and gathered in the newspapers.

Funny – I thought it was later than that. Sarah was looking at the print date on the Yorkshire Evening Post. *May seventeenth, nineteen seventy-eight.*

Thinking nothing further of it she dropped the papers into the recycling box, and then joined her family in The Plume of Feathers.

CHAPTER 24

Bradbeers & Brewers

For over thirty minutes Dan paced up and down the store, almost in danger of wearing away the floor between a couple of clock display plinths. He'd been to the window three, perhaps four times, to have a peer through, and went into a state of near panic when a taxi wrongly reversed down the quiet cul-de-sac.

"Calm down will you. You're worse than a bloody child," said Sarah, tutting. "I've told you it's not them. I'm sure they'll be here soon."

Dan hadn't got a wink of sleep in bed the night before. Of course he'd tried several times to get to sleep, but couldn't. In the end he gave up at about three, put on some Zucchero to listen to and settled for a relaxing bath along with a whisky on the rocks. His mind flitted between car crash – the name Brewer – Sarah's description of Emma – and his recollection of events five years ago. As far as he could see there was absolutely no link, which to his logic was as good as any link – if not better.

"I think this is them," said Sarah. "Yep... they're outside now."

Dan flapped into panic mode again, making stupid bunny hops along the prime meridian line.

"Get a grip will you. I'll go and get them… Go next door for a minute and pull yourself together," ordered Sarah, giving Dan a little push.

Outside The Time Store, Alice and Emma Brewer had finally agreed that they'd found the right place. They walked up the slightly worn steps, through the open front door, and towards the ornate glass-panelled wooden door of The Time Store's vestibule. Emma, who'd also had difficulty in sleeping, took in deep breaths as she walked, in order to calm herself down.

"Morning. You found us then," said Sarah, opening up the door for the Brewer sisters.

"Yes," replied Alice. "Quite easy really."

"Come on in. Dan's dying to meet you," said Sarah, as she welcomed the girls into The Time Store.

"Wow, this place is amazing," Alice said, as she entered the clock display room. "I've always had this thing for clocks – I find the ticking of a clock so soothing."

"Yes, it can be," said Sarah. "As well as annoying at times – especially when you're in a room full of the damn things."

"I like that painting," said Emma, staring at a large canvas on one of the walls. The picture was of a brown and beige helix effect with Roman clock numerals spiralling away into infinity, inter-mixed with time-related quotes.

"Yes. The artwork is quite a recent addition to our walls. Sort of brightens the place up a bit, don't you think?"

"Very much so," replied Emma, smiling.

"Ah, this is Dan," said Sarah, as he came in through the door which led from number three. "Dan. This is Alice."

"Hello." Dan offered out his hand and firmly, but not forcefully, shook Alice's. "Pleased to meet you."

Alice just smiled. "This is my sister Emma."

"Hi, Emma." Dan beamed. "Pleased to meet you, finally. I couldn't stop thinking about you in bed last night."

"Pardon!?" replied Emma, befuddled.

"Oh no – no, sorry," blushed Dan. "Not like that – sorry – I meant you kept me awake all night."

"Dan," laughed Sarah.

"Oh, come on – you know what I mean," said Dan, reddening.

Although the three ladies laughed out loudly together at Dan's expense, Sarah couldn't help but notice a slight glint in Emma's eyes when she looked at him. Cute, think I deserve a pat on the back, she thought, as she reminded herself of the tarot reading she'd done for Dan.

"Shall we go to the rest room?" suggested Dan.

"I think we can do better than that," said Sarah. "This way ladies – I've got a pot of fresh coffee brewing upstairs in my apartment. And some nice cakes."

"How did you get on with the pumpkin carving?" asked Alice, taking a seat on Sarah's red leather corner sofa.

"Not too bad. Didn't win any of the prizes though," said Sarah, trying not to look too disappointed.

"Have you lived here long?" asked Emma.

"All our lives," replied Dan. "Jason moved out a few years back, but he still lives close."

"Jason?" asked Alice.

"Jase is our older brother," answered Sarah. "We have three apartments here. Dan's, Dad's and mine. Dan, can you help me bring the coffee through?"

Once Sarah and Dan had left the room, Alice leant forward. "Did you see the way he looked at you? He fancies you," she whispered.

"Don't be silly, Alice." Emma blushed. "You say that about every man I meet."

"It's true, they all fall for you. It's that innocent look you give them."

"Erm... so you keep telling me. Not done me any bloody good though," replied Emma. "So... what do you think of them now? Now that we're here?"

"Dunno. All seems, dare I say it – normal. Let's see what they come up with," replied Alice. "My money's still on hypnosis though – you wait and see, they'll get a bleedin' watch out and send you to sleep."

Sarah reached down four patterned mugs from one of her kitchen cupboards. "She likes you. Did you see how...?"

"Sarah, this isn't Blind-fucking-Date you know." Dan laughed off his sister's comment. "Anyway, why can't we just go back to this car crash ourselves and see what happens?"

"We could – but that would be selfish, wouldn't it? Especially when we know that there's someone else we could help at the same time. Grab the coffee and that box of cakes – I'll take the tray through."

Sarah poured them all a coffee and for several minutes they talked about The Time Store. Alice, as ever, had done her homework. She'd followed the history of the Bradbeer family as far as the internet would permit, although that was only what David saw fit to have out in the public domain. Anything contentious written about any of them was soon removed using twenty-second century software.

As far as Alice knew The Time Store was a place where the rich and famous came to buy exclusive watches, and it was a place where museums of the world would come for advice on the restoration and maintenance of historical chronometers. She also knew that they donated quite a bit of time and money to individuals, as opposed to charities – plus she learnt about the World of Timepieces exhibition and the more recent Longitude Punk'd celebrations at the observatory, for which the Bradbeers had loaned their Harrison timepiece. Other than that – as far as Alice could see, the Bradbeers hadn't so much as received a parking fine.

"So… does having Emma here remind you of anything?" asked Alice, somewhat cheekily.

"Alice! Sorry, I think my sister means…"

"No, that's okay… I know what she means," Dan laughed. "To tell you the truth… no, not a sausa…" Dan stopped mid-sentence and chose his word more carefully. "Not a thing."

Again the three girls laughed in bemusement at Dan, who'd now declared to himself that they weren't going to trip him up again.

"So a wasted journey then really." Alice looked at Sarah, and then backtracked. "I mean, wasted insomuch as we're not any closer to solving our mysteries."

"Oh, I wouldn't say that," replied Sarah, more

seriously. Leaning towards the coffee table she placed her empty cup on the tray. "You said that you'd tried psychics and what have you?"

"Oh... here we go again," frowned Alice.

"Yes, we have," replied Emma, a bit more courteously.

"Okay – so you have an open mind then. I mean if you're willing to listen to soothsayers and whatever – then you must have an open mind."

"Well yes... I suppose you could say that."

"And you?" Sarah directed this towards Alice. "Do you have an open mind... or do you just doubt anything that you have no personal belief in?"

"Well, I think it's a bit like religion – I personally don't believe in God, but there are plenty who do. Perhaps I'm right – or maybe they are – who knows," replied Alice, defensively. "Same with the psychic stuff – only this time I've seen Emma spend a shitload of money, with fuck-all to show for it."

"Mmm – perhaps I can see why you feel that way. But what would you say if I told you that we were able to offer you something you've not tried?" said Sarah. "Totally, one-hundred percent free, of course. You have nothing to lose – but perhaps answers to gain."

There was a light knock on Sarah's living room door. "Morning," said Jason as he entered. "Hope I'm not disturbing anything... just thought I'd pop through and say hello."

"No – not at all," replied Sarah. "Emma, Alice. This is our brother Jason."

"Pleased to meet you both. I hope Sarah and Dan

are looking after you."

"Yes, very much so," replied Emma, standing up to greet Jason. "Sarah was just about to explain to us how she, sorry – you – may be able to help us."

"Well yes, hopefully taking you back may provide us all with answers," replied Jason.

"Back? Taking us back? So it is some form of hypnosis then?" asked Alice, secretly revelling in the fact that her assumption appeared to be right.

Sarah laughed. "No, Alice. Nothing like that at all, nothing like it."

"Shall we get going?" asked Dan, as he gathered up the empty cups.

"Here, let me help you with those," said Emma, standing up and following Dan into Sarah's kitchen with the coffee pot and sugar bowl.

"Just put them there," said Dan, pointing to an empty space on the kitchen worktop. He then turned to Emma and held her gently by the hand. "Can I ask you something?"

"Yeah. Sure," she replied, allowing him to hold her hand more freely.

"Do you remember much about your parents? I mean, can you remember what they were like? Their smiles and laughs and..."

"A little, yes. Birthday parties, Christmas, holidays – those sorts of things."

"Only I... I mean we... lost our mum when we were kids. I don't remember much about her at all. Of course I can still feel her touch if I want... and talk to her."

"Talk to her?"

"Yes. Well, you know what I mean." Dan released Emma's hand.

"In your prayers?"

"Sort of... I guess," he replied, turning away.

Dan started to walk back into Sarah's living room; Emma held him back by his arm. "I remember our last weekend together – the last time we were a family. Mum and Dad took us on a picnic to Ironbridge. It was wonderful – we loved picnics. Still do when I get chance." Emma released Dan's arm.

"Go on – tell me more. Please," said Dan.

"Collecting flowers to press. I used to love doing that – Mum said it reminded her of when she was a girl. I still have some of them – perhaps one day I'll show you them." Emma laughed and shook her head. "Look at me – ready to pour out my heart and soul to a man I've just met. What am I like?"

Dan held Emma by the hand again. "Don't laugh. I think it's nice. I wish I had memories like that – maybe not flowers though, but the memories. Do you ever go back to Ironbridge at all?"

"No, I don't. Never have since then. I keep meaning to." She looked down at the floor. "But I never have. Perhaps one day. Alice has though – she mastered in History. I think she knows pretty much all there is to know about the Industrial Revolution."

"Are you ready?" asked Sarah as she entered her kitchen, and caught Dan releasing Emma's hand. "We're about to go downstairs, just waiting for you two."

"Sorry, sis. We were talking about Ironbridge – Emma said she'd love to go back there one day."

"Ironbridge. Nice," said Sarah, smiling and tipping a wink at her brother. "Come on. Let's get going."

With Jason going on ahead to make preparations, Sarah and Dan gave Alice and Emma a guided tour of The Time Store. Alice was well enthused on the watch and clock sales floor and recognised most of the prestigious brand names on offer, even stopping at the odd watch or two to play guess the price with her sister – though neither were anywhere close with their appraisals.

They had a quick peek into David's workshop before heading on to the Globe Room. The Brewer sisters were suitably impressed by the collection and they, like countless others before them, marvelled at the clepsydrae on display.

"Almost hypnotic, don't you think?" said Sarah, smiling at Alice.

"Yes it is rather," she replied, briefly forgetting that she'd had the Bradbeers down for a family of hypnotists.

"Where is it we're going?" Emma asked.

"Oh, you'll see," said Dan. "We have a special room downstairs. Bit of a..."

"Surprise room, Dan. I'd say it's best described as," said Sarah, butting in.

"Sounds like we're in for a surprise then," said Emma.

"Oh yes, definitely," replied Sarah.

CHAPTER 25

The Iron Bridge

"Some surprise this is," muttered Alice to her sister as they walked a couple of paces behind Dan and Sarah. "A dingy tunnel."

Emma, although she liked, and thought she trusted the Bradbeers, was also beginning to wonder what was going on. Her introduction to the Costume Room was incredible – where had all that stuff come from? She'd been amazed by the entrance door to the passageway with all the different moons, and now she was impressed by the lighting system, obviously operated by sensors, she realised. But where was this leading... and to what?

"Nearly here," announced Dan.

Alice and Emma followed Sarah and Dan, past an old winged armchair, and into the Round Room.

"Yes, okay. It's a very nice ornate underground cellar," said Alice, looking around, and then up at the star patterned ceiling. "But I still don't see – "

"Stand just here... in the middle," instructed Sarah,

positioning Alice to the left of the meridian. "Link arms with me."

"What?"

"Come on, Emma. We need to link too," said Dan.

Emma, although bemused, couldn't find even one small reason not to link with Dan.

At a signal from Sarah, Dan touched his ring to his bracelet, knowing his sister would do the same.

Two seconds later the Round Room was gone; they were all standing together in some sort of woodland glade.

"What the fuck? What have you done with us?" Alice demanded.

"Please – just give it a chance." Sarah hoped that she could reassure Alice. "Let's walk."

It was a gorgeous summer's afternoon, and as they walked to the edge of the trees they could see the glinting of the sun on the river, and in the distance, an immense iron structure spanning the water.

"What is all this?" Emma was astounded. "It looks familiar. But it's not quite the same... it looks kind of... unfinished."

"Yeah," said Dan. "Looks like they've done all the arches, but they've still got the top bit to do."

They walked steadily along the river bank, and as they drew closer to the construction site, they could hear cursory shouts, and see workmen balancing precariously high above the river.

"It's the bloody Iron Bridge," said Alice, suddenly getting it – understanding why they'd had to wear these freaky clothes.

Beyond the bridge they could detect signs of further

activity – clouds of smoke were rising up, and there was a distinct smell of something similar to an old steam train.

"Welcome to the latter stages of construction of the first ever iron bridge. Summer 1779." Sarah smiled.

Emma still didn't understand. She thought she did, but then thought she must have got it wrong. She felt dizzy, and grabbed Dan's hand for balance.

Dan was happy to help. "Let's go a bit closer, shall we?"

As the two of them walked on ahead together, they talked. Dan confirmed that they were indeed over 200 years in the past. Emma's shock subsided a little, and she began to accept that they were back in time, in the year 1779. All the evidence was there, and she now realised why Dan and Sarah had wanted to come on a 'little jaunt' as Dan had put it.

They were standing not far from a small throng of people – a few women, but mainly men, who were also watching the action on the bridge. Not time travellers; Emma's heart thudded as she came to terms with it all.

Sarah and Alice, having deliberately lingered behind, now caught up with Dan and Emma.

"That's the odd thing," Sarah was saying. "It's the first bridge to be built from iron, but there are no real written accounts of the construction process, and only one painting. Plenty of artwork showing the finished article of course."

Dan, in his element, took up the explanation. "They used local sandstone to build the footings, and topped them with iron base plates. Then they used derrick poles in the river bed – as cranes. They made the large castings at

Bedlam Furnaces down the road. They've been working on the arches for the last few weeks – each one's been put up separately, and bolted together."

"Complicated," said Alice, marvelling at Dan's intricate knowledge. "And dangerous, I'd guess?"

"Yes, no-one was injured though," said Dan. "They're doing the deck bearers now. Making these smaller castings on site."

"Is that what all that smoke is – over there?" Emma pointed.

"Yes, it's the Square – a temporary furnace. Just for the bridge. You'll probably see them levering something into place soon."

"Amazing," said Alice.

"After the deck bearers, they'll do the deck plates, then top it all with a road surface made of clay, and slag from the blast furnace... Oi!" Someone had given Dan a hearty slap on the back.

"Excellent knowledge, sir, excellent. Abraham Darby at your service." A young, but imposing well-dressed man moved to stand beside Dan. "You should be working for me, my good man."

Dan recovered his composure. After all, he was a seasoned time traveller. "I'm employed elsewhere, Mr. Darby – just visiting this area for the day – to see your bridge. A wonderful construction, if I may say. I imagine in years to come it will attract thousands."

"Thank you, sir. I intend to commission a painting upon its completion."

"So you should, sir."

"If you'll forgive me, I must supervise the men."

"Yes, of course. Thank you for taking some time to talk."

"My pleasure," He walked towards his iron bridge.

"Abraham Darby! Oh my fucking God!" said Alice.

"Abraham Darby the third," Sarah clarified.

"Bloody hell, we'll be bumping into John Wilkinson next." Alice was fizzing. "Iron Mad Wilkinson, I bloody love him!"

"Calm down, will you," Emma laughed. "For a sceptic you certainly seem to be getting into the swing of things."

"Yeah, yeah. I'm only a disbeliever when there's no proof," responded Alice.

"And we've certainly given you proof," said Sarah.

"Yeah, she's mad on the Industrial Revolution – has been since school."

"Well, let's enjoy our day then," said Sarah.

So they spent the rest of the afternoon and early evening in 1779, in what would eventually be the village of Ironbridge, sitting on the river bank, watching the castings being brought from the furnace, and watching the workmen on the bridge. They chatted idly about a mixture of topics – Emma's job, Alice's job, The Time Store, Jason's amusing and clumsy beginnings in his attempt at a relationship with Melissa, the Iron Bridge, and the Industrial Revolution.

Sarah even managed to get them a loaf of bread to snack on. A woman, one of the onlookers, had cautiously approached them, trying to find out who they were and where they were from. Sarah gave out no information, but did manage to acquire the freshly baked bread in exchange for her hat, which the woman had greatly admired.

"Got plenty more of those back home in the Costume Room. That woman's gonna be ahead of her time – I think that hat was made in 1789!" laughed Sarah, ripping the bread apart and sharing it out.

"You got your picnic, Emma," said Dan.

At the onset of dusk, the four of them walked to a vantage point about a hundred yards away from the nearly completed bridge. The River Severn was calm, a thin mist hung above the water, and the arch of the bridge was reflected, almost looking like a full circle of iron.

"Come on, time to go home," said Sarah, walking to a gap within the trees. Alice followed.

Emma and Dan looked at one another.

"What a perfect day," sighed Emma, feeling her eyes tingle with the tears of happiness.

"Time travel can be like that," said Dan.

CHAPTER 26

Talking Time

"That was bloody brilliant. I know I'm going on about it, but I still can't believe it." Alice hadn't stopped talking about the trip to the Iron Bridge since they'd returned to the Round Room. She'd already fired question after question at Sarah as they'd walked back down the tunnel. Is it this? Is it that? How long? How much? How far? All of which Sarah answered with as much detail as she was allowed to.

Dan and Emma had purposely held back a bit in the passageway, allowing their respective sisters to walk on ahead.

"So, how long have you been able to time travel then?" asked Emma.

"All my life – ever since I can remember."

"Awesome – it must be amazing. Can you go anywhere – anywhere at all?"

"Yes… but we don't."

"Don't? Oh, I would." Emma stopped walking and

turned towards Dan, beaming. "I mean could you imagine what it must be like to be able to go anywhere, to see anything – building the pyramids maybe? Or anyone – Archimedes in his bath?"

"Well yes," laughed Dan. "But trust me, it's not all Eureka – it does become boring at times."

As the closest motion sensor could no longer detect any movement it turned off the light above Dan and Emma. Sarah and Alice were at least two sensors in front of them now and so they continued to follow at a brisker pace, which in turn immediately woke the sensor again.

"In the kitchen earlier – when you asked about my parents and then about Ironbridge…"

"Yes."

"Were you really interested? I mean, interested in me? Or were you just deciding where to take us back to?"

"You, of course."

Emma reached across and held Dan's hand in hers. "Good," she said, giving his hand a squeeze, and although Emma didn't notice, Dan blushed.

After they'd all changed clothes, the four of them, now also joined by Jason, sat around the table in the rest room. Over coffee, Emma briefly joined in with Alice's excitement, as they recounted to Jason their meeting with Abraham Darby and described his bridge almost down to the last detail.

"Right," said Jason, once the enthusiasm had calmed down. "We need to discuss some possibilities about why we're all here."

The mood in the room altered. The cheerful chat was now replaced by a reflective silence – only to be broken by the message alert of Sarah's phone.

"It's Dad. He wants to see me. Apparently he's got some sort of job for me," she said, relaying the contents of the message. "I'll catch up with you guys later – perhaps in the Plume?"

Dan and Jason both smiled and nodded as Sarah, saying her goodbyes to Alice and Emma, left the room.

"Any idea what that's about?" asked Jason.

"No – thought Dad knew she was with us all day," Dan replied, shrugging his shoulders.

"Anyway. Let's get back to why we're here... I have a theory about what might have happened," said Jason, immediately recapturing everyone's attention. "On October 14th 2009 a member of the Bradbeer family – probably you Dan – went back in time to the night of the car crash." Jason turned to the girls. "The crash which killed your parents."

"So what are you trying to say? Dan killed them?" blurted Emma, horrified.

"No, of course not," reassured Jason. "Dan would have gone back there for a reason – with someone. But it certainly wouldn't have been to kill anyone."

"But surely I'd have remembered it all? You, Sarah, Dad – you'd have remembered – there'd be a record?"

"Not if you never went back – not if there was no reason for you to go back."

"So what are you trying to say, Jase?" asked Dan.

"I'm trying to say something serious must have happened that caused you to have no memory," said Jason.

"I'm lost," muttered Alice.

"Hang on, Jase. We've all gone back and done stuff that changes things – yet we always remember both timelines."

"What do you mean?" asked Emma. Dan and Jason were discussing things that she knew very little about. Other than what sci-fi had taught her about time travel, she knew nothing.

"If I go to the pictures and there are two movies that I want to watch, both on at the same time... I can watch one, then go back in time and see the other. When I'm back in my true time I can remember what's happened in both." Jason tried to clarify the situation.

"Okay – so what did you mean when you said Dan went back – and then said that he didn't go back – because there was no reason to?" asked Alice.

"Right... let's say that your father *didn't* die in the crash. In 2009 he comes here, to The Time Store and Dan takes him on a time trip to see the crash and something goes wrong."

"Yes. But that wouldn't account for my memory. You know I don't remember any of that." Dan looked puzzled.

"Hold on a minute. What goes wrong?" interrupted Emma.

"Okay," resumed Jason. "When Dan and your father go back, there are two John Brewers in 1994. An old one just visiting and a younger one in his own time. If old John shoots young John and kills him – old John would not exist in his own time, 2009."

"Not exist – do you mean he'd just fade away?"

"Possibly, I don't know. I'm guessing that if, as Dan was trying to bring him back to their time, then old John would have ceased to exist – spontaneously combusted or something – the moment he attempted to travel, because young John had died. In which case if he then doesn't exist in 2009, he would never have visited The Time Store in the first place to have gone back."

"So that would account for the burning and me not remembering anything?"

"Yes, because there'd have been nothing to remember."

"And my headlines – the newspaper?"

"That would have changed at the exact time Dan fell to the floor in the Round Room."

"So what happens now? Do we have to stop Dad from shooting himself?" asked Alice.

"Yes. Or whatever he – or Dan – did to interfere with the past."

"When? Today? Are we doing it today?" asked Emma.

Dan was about to say something, but instead looked towards Jason for some kind of approval; none was forthcoming. Emma was also looking at Jason – searching in his eyes for a 'yes', yet he remained silent.

Alice didn't know what to think or do – had her sister been right all along? Had the past twenty years of their lives been a total sham? Not that they could have done anything about it. What was supposed to happen next? Did she actually want her life to change? Would she actually know about it if it did? She needed to be sure that going back was the right thing to do. But of course it was, her parents, their parents – who wouldn't want to have that togetherness. She spoke. "Yes, when? When can we go back?"

"Now. We can go back now," replied Jason, happy that he'd got approval from Alice, the most sceptical of them all. He stood up. "Give me a minute, I'll do the bracelets."

Thirty minutes later, and dressed for the nineties, they were back in the Round Room. Both Dan and Jason were wearing new travel bracelets, with their all too familiar ethereal glow. Dan, facing the North Pole, stood Emma to his left, to the west of the Prime Meridian – Jason and Alice stood behind them.

"Ready?" asked Jason.

"I've been ready for this one for the last five years," replied Dan.

"Let's do it then."

"Okay." Dan linked arms with Emma, and they both disappeared.

"What the fuck? Where are they?" screamed Alice, pulling away from Jason as she realised that she was still in the Round Room.

"They've gone back," replied Jason. "Back to the crash. Sorry…"

"Back? We were all supposed to go. Why the fuck aren't we? Come here." Alice looped her arm. "Take me there. Now. I want to be with Emma – she needs me."

"I can't."

"Can't… can't? Of course you fucking can." Alice pointed towards Jason's bracelet. "You've got that fucking thing on. Who said you can't?"

"I did young lady," said David, walking into the Round Room. "This is Daniel's and Emma's problem to sort out, not ours – and certainly not yours. They're the ones who've lived with this for the past five years. They're the ones who need to restore true time. Now shut up."

CHAPTER 27

Restoration of Time

Emma let go of Dan's arm as she felt the sudden raindrops hit her face. "Where the heck are we?"

"Dunno, it's too dark. Somewhere behind the pub I think," replied Dan, unfolding a telescopic umbrella he'd brought along. "Come on, we need to find a dry spot."

"Where's Alice? Why isn't she here?" Emma turned to Dan and started to panic. "Where are they?"

"I don't know, but we need to get out of this rain or we'll be soaked through in no time. Let's get to the pub." Dan grabbed Emma's hand in an attempt to lead her towards the welcoming lights of the pub, but she was having none of it.

"We have to find Alice first," insisted Emma, refusing Dan's hand.

Dan was just about to try and reason with Emma, offer up some explanation as to why Jason and Alice weren't there, when they heard alarming rustling noises in the bushes. Something seemed to be approaching them.

"Shh! What's that noise?" whispered Emma, grabbing at Dan's arm.

"Sounds like birds."

"What?"

"Chickens, I think."

"Chickens? Are you sure?" questioned Emma.

"Yes. Unless the rats around here have learnt to grow wings. Look." He pointed at a chicken sheltering from the downpour under a nearby bush.

Dan held the umbrella over Emma's head, but it offered very little protection from the rain as the wind forced it sideways onto them. As they headed towards the pub they passed several startled chickens flapping in every direction. Dan, now holding Emma's arm, guided her past an empty chicken coup, the door of which he assumed had blown open because of the torrential weather.

There were several people in The Raven's car park, dancing around the puddles, making a dash for a waiting taxi. Rather than run around the taxi and risk a seriously large puddle, Dan and Emma stopped off at a dimly-lit bike shelter to wait until the cab had left.

"Looks like some poor sod's gonna have a wet ride home tonight," said Dan, looking at the lone bike locked in the shelter.

"Probably Nathan Cross's. He was first one at the crash scene – riding home from the pub. He called the ambulance," said Emma, as she recalled the newspaper report.

"Won't be needing this." Dan folded up and discarded the useless umbrella.

"Looks like someone else had the same idea," said

Emma, pointing into the bin.

"Yeah, probably me," replied Dan, watching the taxi pull away. "Shall we go inside now?"

There was a group of people in the pub foyer, some waiting for their own taxi to arrive and others plotting their best route across the puddle-filled car park.

"Try to avoid that big puddle... just to the left," suggested Dan as they walked past the group. "Seems to be a lot busier than we expected in here tonight."

"Yeah, okay. Thanks, mate," replied one of the men. "Didn't you just say that a few minutes ago?"

"No – not me. Never been in here before. Where's the gents?"

"Straight through – on the left just after the fruit machine." The man, feeling an overwhelming and uneasy sense of déjà vu, turned and pointed to the exact position of the toilet door.

Emma pulled open the door to the bar. The first thing to hit her full in the face was the cigarette smoke which caused her to cough as she inhaled the nicotine-filled air. Of course, thought Dan, the smoking ban isn't in yet. The room was warm and, partly due to the weather outside, very busy. It looked as though about thirty or so people were in. Some, if not most, were obviously there for a local darts league match and sat around in their teams. A few were there more out of social habit. Keeping between Emma and the door, so as not to be on full view, Dan scanned the bar looking for himself.

"Shall I get some drinks in? I think we've time for a quick one," said Dan as he walked to the bar, happy that he wasn't already in there. "What would you like?"

"Oh, just half a lager please," replied Emma, following Dan further into the bar.

Whilst waiting to be served, they surveyed their immediate surroundings. There were two men at the dartboard taking it in turns to throw arrows. Although Dan hated darts he still double-checked in case he was one of the players. A rotund woman, whose shape reminded him of Angel the rune reader, was calling out the scores.

Emma casually pointed to a man sitting in the corner with a couple of friends, just finishing off what looked like a pint of cider. "That's Nathan Cross."

"How can you tell?"

"I met him a couple of years ago. Just to see if there was anything he could remember about the crash – perhaps something which might have come back to him," replied Emma.

"So you stalked him?"

"Yeah, kind of," laughed Emma, feeling somewhat embarrassed she'd divulged that piece of information to Dan.

"Finished that one quick. What can I get you? Same again?" asked the barman as he approached Dan.

"Erm… yes please," replied Dan, searching in his pockets for some money. "Oh… hang on, mate. I thought I'd got at least a fiver on me – must've dropped it somewhere."

"I left it here for you," said the barman, reaching for a small plate on the shelf next to an ice bucket. "£6.60 – the change from your first drink. Thought it was too much to be a tip."

"How fortuitous," commented Emma, accepting a

pint of lager instead of the requested half.

"Forward planning, my dear lady – five years of forward planning," said Dan, mentally adding one to his brownie point tally.

"Yeah, right."

"Drink up, we need to get going," said Dan, replacing his half empty glass on the bar. "I'm going to the toilet. You check out the lounge – see if you recognise anyone."

As Dan entered the toilets there was a man standing under a window. It was open, allowing the rain to blow straight through and cover the floor.

"Cheers, mate." Dan heard someone shout from the car park and then the window was pushed shut.

"You're welcome," replied the man under the now closed window.

"What's that all about?" asked Dan.

"Oh, some guy on a blind date wanting a quick getaway," laughed the man as he finished his business, zipped up, quickly ran his hands under the tap and left.

He walked virtually straight into Emma as he entered the lounge. "Oops. Sorry, love," he apologised.

"That's okay. Did you see a man in there – I mean is there anyone else in there?" asked Emma.

"Yes, there were two – what's he look like?"

"Him sitting over there." Emma pointed over to a table where a slightly younger Dan was sitting.

"Yes, he's in there," said the man as he looked over to Dan, who appeared to be in mid-conversation with an attractive blonde woman looking at her watch.

"Thanks," said Emma.

"How the fuck did he get out here before me?"

Emma had already left the lounge and was heading over to the door leading from the toilets back into the bar when she saw Dan.

"Come on. We need to get going," urged Dan, heading towards the lounge.

"Not that way." Emma grabbed his sleeve. "You're in there."

"Alone?"

"No! With a blonde – but we'll talk about that later."

Nathan Cross was just about to raise his left foot off the floor and attempt to squeeze into his bright yellow waterproofs when Dan and Emma rushed for the exit door and knocked him over. "Sorry, Nathan," said Emma, stopping to help him up.

"How do you know my…?"

"Get a move on, will you. We haven't got time for pleasantries," shouted Dan, as he ran past the same group of people in the foyer.

"Watch out for that puddle!" screamed the man who'd had a double-dose of advice from Dan. "On the left. Ah… too late."

"Fuck!" shouted Dan, as he stood up to his ankles in water. The group of people from the foyer hurried past him towards their waiting taxi, coats raised over their heads for protection.

"Get a move on, will you. Stop splashing about. We haven't got time," shouted Emma as she ran past, keeping to the left of the big puddle.

She stopped at the bike shelter and waited for Dan to catch up. It was now raining much harder than earlier, and the rain rattled like hail as it hit the shelter's corrugated roof.

"Look at that," said Dan, pointing to the mountain bike's rear wheel. "Someone's given that a good kicking."

"Who?"

"Could be your dad. I'm still in the pub remember?"

"But why? Why would he do that?"

"Probably to slow Nathan down. Didn't you say that he was the first on the scene?"

"Yes. But… are you saying that a kicked in wheel is what killed them?"

"Possibly – I don't know. We need to hurry, we haven't much time."

The rain continued to fall without any sign of abating as they crossed the narrow country road and headed for the T-junction. The headlights of a truck flashed across the main road ahead and they could see, stumbling away from them, a lone figure in the distance. They assumed that it was Emma's father – John – heading for where, in a few minutes time, the crash would occur. They avoided a fast-flowing build-up of water streaming along the roadside as they ran. Knowing that they were catching up with John, Dan hastened their pursuit.

"You'll have to go on ahead," gasped Emma, who was now struggling to keep up. "It's these bloody shoes – too clunky."

Dan's response was to increase his speed. Although usually dressed in more suitable clothing, he'd raced Jason around Greenwich Park in much worse weather than this. Now, without Emma slowing him down he could easily close the gap in front. As he turned left, out on to the main road, Dan noticed a much smoother footpath. Distant headlights lit up his destination, a small concrete bus shelter beneath a massive horse chestnut tree. It has to be them, he thought, as he got even closer.

A sharp gust of wind nearly forced Dan into the roadside trees; they seemed to cry in pain as their branches creaked under the pressure, yet they stood firm. Dan noticed that the effects of the wind caused the approaching car to veer off slightly to the right, but then the driver regained control.

Dan, now crouching inside the bus shelter, watched as the car came closer. He knew someone, probably John, was only a few inches away from him on the other side of the thin concrete wall. His mind was drawn to a strange, yet familiar sound faintly echoing in the wet night air. Singing – Dan smiled as he realised John, outside in the pouring rain, seconds away from a fierce tragedy, was singing. And then it stopped, leaving the wind once again to take over.

Dan could now see the spray coming from the wheels of the car as it displaced the surface water. Then he heard it. It was as though a shotgun had been fired off nearby, both barrels at once. But Dan knew it wasn't that at all. The car, moving at speed, had hit a pothole, hidden by water – the impact causing the tyre to burst under the pressure. The car was out of control.

"Brake... Brake!" Dan heard John shout at the approaching car. Seconds later came the piercing sound of the tyres as they screeched out against the wind-filled night. The car was spinning. Round... round. Dan saw the wall of water which surged up around the car as the screaming tyres sent it spraying high off the tarmac surface of the road. Round... round. The car spun.

The tree held firm. Dan, only feet away, watched helplessly as the car smashed into its trunk. He could see from the twisted metal that Catherine had stood no chance of survival. The front of the car had folded with frightening ease as it hit the mighty conker, but had scarcely scratched at the tree's bark. Steam spewed out from the engine's fractured cooling system, and Dan noticed the wiper blades shudder to a stop across the shattered screen, leaving the rain to tap dance its own way to the ground.

Dan could see that John, standing rigid with carnage all around, was in shock, rooted to the spot. If John had the will to turn he would have seen Dan just inches behind, but he didn't. Somehow John mustered the strength and moved closer. Dan watched as John wiped the beads of water away from the side window, and then from his own face.

"No! Get away!" John, suddenly noticing Dan's reflection in the glass, twisted round and lurched for him. "I need to hold her – touch her again."

"But you can't interfere, John – I can't let you."

"Oh, bollocks – why didn't you just stay in the pub? Leave me be. Let me hold her."

"I *am* in the pub." Dan grabbed John and pulled him away from the car. "You don't understand – I'm from the future, from your future – I'm not the Dan you left behind in the pub. Whatever you're about to do will kill the both of you – don't you understand? I can't let you tamper with time – you shouldn't die!"

"I don't give a shit who you are, son – that's my wife in there." John pulled back his right hand and with clenched fist swung for Dan. "And I'm gonna say my goodbyes fucking properly."

Although the punch didn't hit Dan, it was enough

to throw him off balance. Losing his footing he slid down the muddy embankment.

With Dan out of the way, John reached for the passenger door handle and pulled open the door. He looked straight at his wife Catherine; there was blood trickling down from an open cut above her right eyebrow, where her head had struck the side window.

He wanted to hold her in his arms for one last time, but he didn't have time. Having to kneel on his own left leg he leaned over as far as he could. John gently kissed Catherine's soft, tender lips. "Sleep well. I love you to the end of the stars... and back."

He pulled himself away, pressed the latch on the inner door handle and took one last look at Catherine and then...

"Is that Mum? She's far more beautiful than I remember."

...he stopped. John could feel an arm wrap tentatively around him.

"Of course, I was only little then and I don't recall that much really." Emma lowered her arm and took her dad's hand. "I remember though, when Auntie Claire told me and Alice what had happened. The crash and both of you dying."

"Both of us...?"

"Yes. Is it really you, Dad? Both of you died. We cried ourselves to sleep for weeks. Sometimes I still do – and I know Alice does, but she never admits it." Emma could feel her father's cold hand gripping at hers, holding it so tight, as if he could never let go, and yet so gentle, as though he was still holding his little girl's hand.

"Emma." John turned and fell to his knees sobbing, distraught and yet happy. "What have I done? What have I done?" he cried.

In the distance, slightly delayed by being knocked over in the pub, Nathan Cross was running, together with a passing motorist he'd flagged down. Within seconds they'd be there, at the car, rescuing John.

"We need to leave now. Unlatch the door and let's go – let them save you. For me – please."

"Hurry," shouted Dan, from the bottom of the embankment. "Before they get here."

Within seconds, Emma and John had slid down to join Dan, who helped them both to their feet and then hugged Emma. It took less than a couple of minutes for Dan, as he led them away, to give John a quick but intense recap.

"So what will happen now? When we return – how will I find you?" John asked.

"You won't. Not straight away. You'll have to wait five years," answered Dan.

"Five years?" said John, stricken.

"Look on the bright side – for us, that is – we'll get to see you again later today."

With John hobbling, they walked slowly back towards The Raven. Dan held back, allowing father and daughter to capture some lost time. Over the sounds of the howling wind and driving rain they could clearly hear the sirens of the emergency services as they headed to the crash scene. Nathan Cross had played his part in the proceedings and now true time was being repaired.

"We have to leave you now," said Dan, as the pub

came into view. "Be careful what you tell me – I'm not to know about this – the young me, that is!"

John nodded in bewilderment, and shook Dan by the hand. "See you in five years then…"

Father and daughter didn't say any goodbyes to each other, just hugged and then hugged again. Emma removed her necklace; a small pendant which contained two photographs, one of John and Catherine and one of Alice and herself. "Keep this, give it back to me when we meet again."

John smiled, held back his tears and walked towards the pub.

"Oh… thank God. There you are!" John was confronted in the pub car park by a rain-soaked younger Dan. "Where the hell have you been? I've been looking everywhere for you." Dan was relieved to have finally found John.

"I was worried about the time. I thought you were behind me, following," replied John, still quite emotional from having seen Emma.

"Come on. Tell me what happened." Dan placed a comforting arm around John's shoulder, and gave it a firm, reassuring squeeze. "You can tell me."

"I really didn't know what I wanted…" he sobbed. "I didn't know whether I just wanted to watch – to see what happened – to understand what happened to us both, to Cath."

"And?"

"I took your advice. I did what you'd have wanted. I watched from the other side of the road. There wasn't anything I could've done to save her. Nothing at all."

Dan didn't ask any more from John, he'd heard enough to know that true time hadn't been altered. Hopefully, Dan thought, what John had seen would be enough to enable him to rise from the life he had, and become the man he should be.

"It's done now." He turned his signet ring around once again so the motif was palm side, and linked his left arm with John's right. He then checked that they were well out of sight, away from anyone leaving the pub. Dan placed his right hand over his bracelet. "Time to go home."

"Will he be alright?" asked Emma as she watched her father walk into the distance. "Five years is a long time."

"He'll be fine. He'll have to be. Anyway, we'll find out when we return," said Dan, twisting his ring.

Emma looped her arm expecting Dan to link with her, but instead he put both arms around her and then touched his bracelet.

For the first time since David Bradbeer had taken Helen to Venice, a young romantic couple returned to the Round Room, kissing.

CHAPTER 28

Reunited

"Hey! You can put her down now, Daniel. We haven't got all day, you know!" said David, pot plant in hand.

Jason and Alice laughed as Dan and Emma, both soaked to the skin, released each other. Emma reddened as she realised they'd returned to a small audience.

Dan looked upwards at the celestial ceiling. It was shining far brighter than usual – this made him smile. "Emma, this is my dad. Dad... Emma."

"Emma," said David nodding. "Pleased to meet you. Dan? Is it all sorted?"

"Yes, Dad. It's all sorted."

"Good. That's what I like to hear. Now if you'll all excuse me I'd better get this plant to Middlesbrough before it dies. You can fill me in with the details later." David walked to the centre of the Round Room, crossed the Prime Meridian and twisted his ring. "You two get out of those wet clothes else you'll catch your death. I'll be back in an hour or so. Meet you all in the Plume," he said, then disappeared.

"You went without me," said Alice, pushing Dan aside and hugging her sister. She was calmer now, having pretty much accepted David's rebuke and subsequent explanation of why Dan and Emma had been to the crash scene without her. "Tell me everything. Did you see Dad?"

"Yes. Yes..." replied Emma, still very much on a high from her time trip. She recounted every last detail to her sister, as Jason and Dan led them back along the passageway to the rest room.

"What about Sarah? Did Dad say where she was?" asked Dan.

"Not really. I did ask... he just said she was doing a little job for him, and that she'd be back soon," replied Jason.

"Don't you just hate it when she does all this cloak and dagger stuff for him?"

"Yes... and then comes back with a fresh friggin' cheesecake."

The two brothers found this hilarious. The sound of their laughter echoed from the walls of the passageway, for a while drowning out the squelching from Dan's wet boots.

It was just after five o'clock by the time Emma had showered and changed. She re-joined Jason and Alice for coffee in Sarah's apartment.

"Where's Dan?"

"He's in the hallway calling the pub. Sorting out a big table... I think."

"That suits you," commented Alice, referring to Emma wearing one of Dan's navy pullovers.

"Thanks." Emma looked up at Dan as he entered the living room and walked over to her. She gave him a quick kiss. "I might just keep this top of yours. If you don't mind that is?"

"What did I tell you?" Alice laughed as she looked at a speechless Dan. "It's that innocent look all over again."

"So how do you feel?" asked Jason, handing a freshly poured cup of coffee to Emma.

"Well it's kinda strange," replied Emma, curling up in an armchair with her steaming hot drink. "I mean... I know I've been back in time... twice... and I know why... stopping Dad and everything. But my memories are all over the place. For years I accepted without question that he died, and I still have that feeling – but now I know he survived."

"And do you remember calling the radio show?" asked Dan.

"I do... yes definitely." Emma paused. "But... I can't quite remember what I said."

"Do you remember the newspaper changing?" asked Jason.

"No." She paused. "What newspaper?"

"Your mind is sifting through thoughts and memories, trying to allocate an order to things." Jason tried to give an explanation. "Basically it can't undo true time. So everything before 2009, before your dad went back, is how it happened – accident, mum's death, newspaper report and so on, even Dan's memories should be restored."

Dan nodded. "Yeah... everything slotted pretty much into place as soon as I got back – meeting John in the coffee shop – the 2009 trip – coming back."

Jason continued. "Everything from today is how things *will* happen – so you'll always remember this conversation."

"Yes, but what about the five years in between?" asked Alice.

"That's where you'll have conflict of thoughts – or two memories."

"A bit like when you could go and see the two films with the same start time?" Emma thought she was beginning to understand.

"Yes. Exactly that, Emma. Like the two movies." Jason replaced his near-empty cup on the table. "Shall we go and eat? I'll call Melissa. She can meet us at the Plume. Looks like we've got some gossip for her eh, Dan?"

Dan winked at Emma, and then looked at his watch. Not quite time to go yet, he thought. "Give us a few more minutes… another coffee first?" He filled his mug from the coffee pot. "Anyone else?"

"Not like you… coffee before a beer. Looks like Emma's changing you already."

Dan didn't mind Jason's jibe at him – this time. "Kim's sorting out a table for us. I told her after six."

"Oh," said Jason. "Well, we could still go and have a drink, couldn't we?"

Dan didn't reply. He just sipped at his coffee and kept a watchful eye on the time as he listened to the girls talking about time travel, where they would want to go, who they would want to meet. Thankfully the time to leave coincided with Alice's quip that one day Emma could become the next *Time Traveller's Wife*.

They descended the staircases of number five and

left through the front door. They could hear the clocks inside The Time Store chime six with an almost regimented precision as Jason, the last one out, pulled the door shut.

It was a bit nippy outside and the leaves on the trees were all but gone, but given that it was the start of November it was only to be expected. Last weekend the country's clocks had been put back an hour, back to Greenwich Mean Time, and the swan-necked street lights had already turned themselves on. Other than a black cab with its diesel engine idly chugging away outside No.1, Flamsteed Way was, as usual, quiet.

They walked the short distance to the Plume, Emma and Dan holding hands all the way, Jason texting Melissa, and Alice rolling her eyes at all three of them.

Although the pub was quite busy, their usual corner tables were free. With requests for two large pinots, Dan stood at the bar.

"Dan?"

"Two large whites please, Kim. One with soda and ice."

"Chardonnay?"

"No pinot... and two pints of... erm..." Dan looked at the cask ale pumps. "What's that one like – Blue Moon? Not seen that before."

"It only came in yesterday – American – want to try some?" Kim didn't wait for an answer, she just went ahead and pulled a half pint for Dan to try.

"Not bad," he said, gulping it down. "Two pints of Blue Moon as well please. And can we have a large table in the back?"

"Yeah, sure... I'll call you when it's ready."

Dan took Alice's and Emma's drinks to the table and then, after a trip back to the bar, returned with two pints of Blue Moon, both of which had a slice of orange over the rim of the glass.

"Cosmopolitan all of a sudden," smirked Jason, accepting his pint.

"Seems that way." Dan also hadn't expected the orange. "Kim said she'd call us when the table's free."

"Oh, God," said Jason looking at his phone.

"What? The table's gonna be free soon," said Dan.

"No – it's Melissa – she can't come after all."

Dan, not in the least surprised by this, put on his sympathetic face.

Ten minutes later David arrived, this coincided with Kim's announcement that their table was ready, and the party of five followed her through to the rear dining area.

"I've laid a table for ten. If you need any more, let me know."

"That's fine," said David. "Could you bring us a couple of bottles of wine and three pints of whatever they're drinking, please."

"What've you done with Sarah?" asked Dan.

"She's gone to have a look at something for me – she should be here soon."

"And how was Edith?"

"She's fine – she loved the plant." He passed Jason a small carrier bag. "She gave me these. Said they were for you. As a thank you for everything."

Jason opened the bag and took out the contents. "Wow… look at these, Dan!"

"Comics! Good old Edith. Pass one over."

"Boys," laughed Emma.

"Not just boys – here let me have a look," said Alice.

"Alice – I think I should apologise for coming across so harsh earlier – I hope you understand why I couldn't let you go back," said David.

"Yes, it's okay, I understand," replied Alice. David seemed a bit mellower now – anyway she'd have to get used to him if he was ever going to be her sister's father-in-law.

"Flowers for the lovely ladies, sir? Flowers for the ladies?" A man wearing a blue Berghaus jacket approached the table.

"No – we're good, thank you," said Jason.

"I insist," said the man, pulling down his hood and handing Emma and Alice a small posy of flowers each. "After all, it's not every day I get to give flowers to my daughters, and these were their mother's favourites."

"Dad! Oh God!" Alice jumped from her chair and wrapped her arms around John Brewer. Emma held back to let Alice have her moment with their father; she'd had several large hugs already today – even if they had been five years ago. Then John embraced his girls together – and wept with tears of joy.

"But how did you know we'd be here?" asked Emma.

"It was Dan. He called the hostel earlier. They rang and told me you'd be here."

"Thank you, Daniel Bradbeer." Emma placed her arms around Dan and kissed him. "Thank you for everything."

Dan introduced John to Jason and his father. John

thanked the Bradbeers for giving him his life back.

"I've brought along a friend. I hope you don't mind." John waved through to the front bar. "Only, I owe this friend as much as I owe you guys... maybe more in some ways."

Jason was the first to stand up and greet their new guest. "Mrs Holroyd – Winnie – it's nice to see you again."

"You too, Jason," replied Winnie, impressed that he'd remembered her.

"Here, come and sit next to us." Jason pulled out a chair for Winnie, and introduced everyone.

Winnie was delighted to meet Alice and Emma at last, after all since she'd known their father she'd heard so much about them – and they were just as beautiful as John had described.

She'd been there at the hostel when Pete had been talking to John on the phone. She'd heard Pete saying the names 'Dan', 'Emma and Alice', followed by 'urgent'. Then Pete had passed the phone to her, John having asked if she was there. John wanted her to come to Greenwich with him, to The Plume; the taxi would pick her up on the way.

During dinner John told how, after he'd returned from the time trip, he'd attended Paddy's funeral – how long ago that seemed now – then he'd set about life with such renewed hope for the future. The nightmares – along with his need for alcohol – had vanished. He was happy to report that he'd had complete peace of mind since his visit to 1994 with Dan.

Over the past five years, with help from Winnie, the hostel and all at St. Michael's Church, John had begun renting a place of his own – a place he could finally call home. Although not employed yet, he helped the local church diocese with maintaining the grounds of several parishes, and during his spare time he volunteered at the hostel, helping the homeless and vulnerable get through life one day at a time.

They all acknowledged his achievements and although in the grand scheme of things they were small, for John Brewer they were life-changing. Feeling relaxed and with the conversation flowing, Jason decided to make the most of Dan's tab and ordered a few more drinks for the table.

"Just a thought, Dad," said Jason. "You've always said that we could do with an extra pair of hands. Perhaps if we had, you could spend a bit more time down by the river."

"You make a fair point, son… is there anyone in particular you're thinking of?" David glanced over at John.

Over dinner, Winnie told Emma and Alice about her trip to Chicago with Sarah to see Elvis, and showed them her photos. The one of the peacock doors had come out beautifully. The Chicago stadium picture was not so clear, but Winnie didn't mind. She pulled out the Elvis mirror from her bag.

"I know it's a bit tacky," she told Emma. "But I love it anyway."

"I went to the British Museum, you know," John said, directing his comments to David, Jason and Dan – anyone who was listening really. "Saw your World of Timepieces with Winnie. Where's it gone now?"

"Oh, it's over in Madrid," said Jason, briefly recalling the Association drama and the scheming Simon Ward once again. "Hope you enjoyed it."

"Yes, thank you."

John had been flabbergasted originally, with the prospect of him unintentionally/unwittingly bringing about his own demise – seeing two Dans – the drama of the crash – if it wasn't for the fact that he felt so serene and peaceful he might have gone mad. He knew back then that he would eventually see his daughters. But five years was a long time. The few photos he had of them had kept him going. John, with the knowledge he had, was often tempted to visit The Time Store… to see Dan… to… but he was not actually sure what he would do. So he'd got himself straight, and waited for someone to contact him. He'd been to see the Bradbeers' exhibition three more times, without Winnie; the comforting sound of the clepsydrae gave him some small connection with The Time Store.

During pudding, John suddenly sat up straight and dropped his spoon into his bowl. "Emma… I've just remembered! I've got something for you." He reached into the pocket of his jacket, which was hanging over the back of his chair, and handed Emma a small box. It contained her pendant – the one he'd been given five years ago.

Both Jason and David, although enjoying the evening, were mindful that Sarah hadn't arrived as yet. They'd tried her phone several times, but each time they did, it went straight to voicemail. At eight o'clock David made his excuses to the others and set off home in search of his daughter.

CHAPTER 29

A Watchful Eye

Thankfully, the wind was blowing the relentless rain in the opposite direction and although cold, her vantage point, a small concrete bus shelter, was probably the driest spot around. A truck thundered by, far too fast given the conditions Sarah thought, but it had lit up the shelter across the road perfectly. As yet nothing had happened.

About another minute had passed when she saw a shadowy figure, *John*, reach the opposite shelter. He slouched down against the outside wall. She thought she heard singing, but decided the wind was playing surreal tricks with her head. Then another man arrived at the bus shelter. Sarah smiled, *Dan*.

She saw the car approaching, saw the slight swerve and then heard the thunderous bang made by the bursting tyre as it skewed over the pothole. The wall of water, the screeching tyres, the spinning car. The impact.

Sarah saw Dan standing behind John. Then came the twist, the swing, the punch – Dan disappeared. Sarah knew she wasn't allowed to interfere, but should she? Should she intervene? No – not yet – she decided. She saw John reach for the car door, saw him lean into the car, and again she smiled as she saw a third figure approach, *Emma*.

To her left, two people were running towards the car, they were still about a minute, perhaps less, away. Emma was holding John's hand. Sarah longed to hear what was being said; father and daughter meeting for the first time in twenty years. Sarah saw John sink to his knees. She turned once more to look at the approaching figures, then back to John and Emma – they'd disappeared.

She watched as two men, one dressed in a bright yellow reflective suit, reached the scene. Fighting against the wind and rain, they pulled the injured John from the vehicle. One commenced CPR, the other called for help. Within ten minutes the emergency teams had arrived at the crash, their flashing lights covering the scene with an almost pulsating blue cloud. Sarah felt a huge relief as a stretchered John was loaded into an ambulance. And then wept silently as she watched the cutting apparatus being brought out to remove Catherine's body. She stayed to the bitter end, watching as all the debris was cleared and the mangled wreckage was towed away.

It had only taken one brief moment in time to cause so much devastation, to rip out the heart and soul from a loving family. Sarah sighed; how she wished things could be different, but she was now content she'd fulfilled the task that her father had set for her. She'd observed and checked – and she was happy, as David would be, that true time had now been restored.

Sarah turned her ring, touched it to her bracelet and returned to the Round Room.

"Good day to you. You must be Sarah."

There was a well-dressed young man leaning against the wall of the Round Room, arms behind his back.

"Who the hell are you?" Sarah was on full alert, ready to run, or fight, or use her bracelet again.

The man took a step towards her. "Don't you know? I think you must recognise me."

"Stop playing games," said Sarah, beginning to think that the man looked vaguely familiar. "I'll ask you again – who are you?"

"I'm Oliver Bradbeer," he announced, with a slight inclination of the head. "And I've come to collect my hand."

END

For news and updates about the forthcoming adventures of the Bradbeer family, follow The Time Store on Facebook.

https://www.facebook.com/The.Time.Store